"*The Healing of Natalie Curtis* [...] bringing to life a real woman fro[...] with issues that are startlingly [...] and cultural appropriation. You will find yourself drawn in by the story of Natalie Curtis, an early twentieth-century musical prodigy nearly broken by the rigid conventions of her era, who leaves her loving but somewhat smothering New York family to travel with her brother through the wild expanses of the American Southwest. Curtis finds her health, her voice, and her calling in recording the music of the Southwest's Native cultures, and determinedly fighting for their rights. Fair warning: once you begin this compelling tale, you won't be able to put it down."

Susan J. Tweit, author of *Bless the Birds: Living with Love in a Time of Dying*

"Natalie Curtis was a force to be reckoned with in the early years of the twentieth century. Her life as a musician, an ethnomusicologist, an advocate of social justice for Native Americans, and as a single woman breaking gender and culture barriers to find a life of her own in the American Southwest is a story worth telling and retelling. Kirkpatrick's novel *The Healing of Natalie Curtis* is a welcome addition to the body of literature celebrating Curtis's life."

Lesley Poling-Kempes, author of *Ladies of the Canyons: A League of Extraordinary Women and Their Adventures in the American Southwest*

"'It's less time that heals than having a . . . creative purpose.' Encapsulating the heart of *The Healing of Natalie Curtis*, these words landed on my soul with the resonance they must have carried a century ago, when one woman's quest for physical, emotional, and creative healing led her on a journey that would broaden her vision to see her struggles mirrored in the losses of an Indigenous culture vanishing with alarming brutality—and to take extraordinary action to preserve that heritage. Jane Kirkpatrick presents us with talented musician Natalie Curtis, a woman broken by the very thing she loved, in search of hope and healing yet extending both to those Native singers her path inevitably crosses. Natalie grows across these pages to be a heroine worth rooting for—all the more because this story is true."

Lori Benton, award-winning author of *Burning Sky*,
Mountain Laurel, and *Shiloh*

Praise for *Something Worth Doing*

"I have long admired Jane Kirkpatrick's rich historical fiction, and *Something Worth Doing* is well worth reading! Oregonian Abigail Duniway is a vibrant, fiercely passionate, and determined activist who fought for women's suffrage. Women of today have cause to respect and admire her—as well as the loving, patient, and supportive husband who encouraged her to continue 'the silent hunt.'"

Francine Rivers, author of *Redeeming Love*

"On the trail to Oregon, young Jenny Scott lost her beloved mother and little brother and learned that no matter what, she must persist until she reaches her goal. Remembering her mother's words—"a woman's life is so hard"—the young woman who became Abigail Scott Duniway came to understand through observation and experience that law and custom favored men. The author brings alive Abigail's struggles as frontier wife and mother turned newspaper publisher, prolific writer, and activist in her lifelong battle to win the vote and other rights for women in Oregon and beyond. Jane Kirkpatrick's story of this persistent, passionate, and bold Oregon icon is indeed *Something Worth Doing*!"

Susan G. Butruille, author of *Women's Voices from the Oregon Trail*, now in the 25th anniversary edition

The
Healing of
Natalie Curtis

Also by Jane Kirkpatrick

Something Worth Doing

One More River to Cross

Everything She Didn't Say

All She Left Behind

This Road We Traveled

The Memory Weaver

A Light in the Wilderness

One Glorious Ambition

The Daughter's Walk

Where Lilacs Still Bloom

A Mending at the Edge

A Tendering in the Storm

A Clearing in the Wild

Barcelona Calling

An Absence So Great

A Flickering Light

A Land of Sheltered Promise

Hold Tight the Thread

Every Fixed Star

A Name of Her Own

What Once We Loved

No Eye Can See

All Together in One Place

Mystic Sweet Communion

A Gathering of Finches

Love to Water My Soul

A Sweetness to the Soul

NOVELLAS

Sincerely Yours

A Log Cabin Christmas
Collection

The American Dream Romance
Collection

NONFICTION

Promises of Hope for Difficult
Times

Aurora, An American
Experience in Quilt,
Community and Craft

A Simple Gift of Comfort

A Burden Shared

Homestead

The Healing of Natalie Curtis

JANE KIRKPATRICK

Revell

a division of Baker Publishing Group
Grand Rapids, Michigan

© 2021 by Jane Kirkpatrick

Published by Revell
a division of Baker Publishing Group
PO Box 6287, Grand Rapids, MI 49516-6287
www.revellbooks.com

Printed in the United States of America

Library of Congress Cataloging-in-Publication Data
Names: Kirkpatrick, Jane, 1946– author.
Title: The healing of Natalie Curtis / Jane Kirkpatrick.
Description: Grand Rapids, Michigan : Revell, a division of Baker Publishing Group, [2021] | Includes bibliographical references.
Identifiers: LCCN 2021004752 | ISBN 9780800736132 (paperback) | ISBN 9780800740535 (casebound) | ISBN 9781493431786 (ebook)
Subjects: LCSH: Burlin, Natalie Curtis, 1875–1921—Fiction. | GSAFD: Biographical fiction.
Classification: LCC PS3561.I712 H43 2021 | DDC 813/.54—dc23
LC record available at https://lccn.loc.gov/2021004752

Scripture quotations are from the King James Version of the Bible.

This book is a work of historical fiction based closely on real people and events. Details that cannot be historically verified are purely products of the author's imagination.

This is a work of historical reconstruction; the appearances of certain historical figures are therefore inevitable. All other characters, however, are products of the author's imagination, and any resemblance to actual persons, living or dead, is coincidental.

Published in association with Joyce Hart of the Hartline Literary Agency, LLC.

21 22 23 24 25 26 27   7 6 5 4 3 2 1

He, our Father,
He hath shown His mercy unto me.
In peace I walk the straight road.

From "Morning Song" as sung and told by Cheyenne Chief
Honíhi-Wotoma (Wolf-Robe) in *The Indians' Book*,
recorded and edited by Natalie Curtis

The song of the southwestern Indian is the voice of the American
desert. It is outlined on the vast silence as the clear-cut mountain
line is traced upon the rainless sky.

Natalie Curtis in *Songs of Ancient America*

Dedicated to Jerry,
who is the song in my heart.

Cast of Characters

Natalie Curtis—Classically trained singer and pianist

George Curtis—Brother to Natalie; former librarian; ranch
  hand

Mimsey and Bogey—Natalie's parents

Bridgham, Constance, Mariam—Natalie's other siblings

Charles and Eva Lummis—Builder of El Alisal, journalist,
  and historical preservationist; and his wife

Alice Klauber—Artist and friend of Natalie's

Chiparopai—English/Spanish/Yuman–speaking Yuma
  woman

Texan—Friend in Yuma

Frank Mead—Indian activist and architect

*Mary Jo Brigand—Co-owner Bar X Ranch

Lololomai —Tribal leader of Old Oraibi, Hopi village

Charles Burton—Indian agent/superintendent at Oraibi

*Mina—Hopi girl at Oraibi

Tawakwaptiwa—Hopi chief, nephew of Lololomai, at Old
  Oraibi

Pelia —Yavapai man bringing a gift to Roosevelt

Nampeyo—Hopi potter, Hano village

Hiamovi—Cheyenne and Dakota high chief, interpreter, and policeman

Theodore Roosevelt—President of the United States

*Bonita—Natalie's burro

*Fully fictionalized characters

Prelude

NEW MEXICO, 1905

*S*he followed the blind boy up through the crevice, up through the warm rocks the colors of weeping rainbows, up to a life beyond any she had known. Natalie Curtis watched where the child put his moccasin-covered feet into the ancient footholds and finger ledges, copying his movements, though not as deftly. Her breath labored as she tucked her small boots into the toeholds he'd just left, toeholds made by ancient ones moving from the desert floor to the mesa above.

The boy was no taller than her, his cotton pants wide against his thin legs. Chopped black hair stuck to his neck. His calico shirt fluttered as he reached, ever climbing. Natalie pushed ahead in her khaki riding skirt, white linen blouse, and a flat, wide-brimmed hat she'd bought at the trading post weeks before. It was held with a cord she felt against her neck, having pushed it from her head so she could bring her face closer to the rock. Up they climbed. Her muscles strained. She was a blonde, blue-eyed Anglo following an Indian boy. An interpreter and her brother came behind them both. Resting for a moment, she tipped her head back to see the lake-blue sky, a patch framed by the towering rock crevice. She could see it widened. They'd soon be at the top. In the distance she heard the singing.

"What's that, then?" she asked, her voice spoken in that New York hurried way.

"Corn Planting song," the interpreter called up to her, his soft voice carried by the wind. "It is the time for planting. Those songs, you'll hear now."

Corn Planting song.

"Lovely."

A smile crossed her face. She inhaled the desert scents, reached for the next stone step, and continued climbing in a foreign land. Then, there she was, at the top of the mesa, wispy clouds sailing across the vast sky and reflected in the water of the stone reservoir. A whole new world lay before her—so far from where she'd been, so much closer to where she hoped to be.

1

From Broken Things

AUTUMN—1902, THREE YEARS EARLIER

Though she had not seen the desert-bronzed face of her brother for two years, Natalie Curtis recognized in the sparkle of his eyes what was different. "You've found yourself," she said.

"And you haven't."

George Curtis dropped his leather travel pack in the vestibule of the New York family home, shaking the umbrellas in the brass stand. He held Natalie's shoulders, and she looked into blue eyes that matched her own. They shared the same wispy blond hair. George pulled her to his chest. "Come here. Let me hug my little sister."

Natalie leaned into the scent of leather as her shoulders relaxed for the first time in months. She hadn't realized how much she'd missed him. George was like an apparition arriving from the exotic West.

Natalie backed away first, looked her brother up and down. "You're brown as a walnut. You look . . . rested."

17

"I am, but for the train ride." He flipped his hat to the hat rack, then ran his hands through his hair. "It's so good to see you. So good." His voice carried warmth and wistfulness, but his eyes said *pitiful*. And she was.

The chambermaid appeared from nowhere to take his long coat. "Shall I place your bag in your room, Master George?"

"No, leave it here. I'll take it up later, Bella. Thank you."

"Very good, sir." She curtsied and disappeared.

"Your years away have fortified you." Natalie watched his easy smile expand to his warm eyes.

"Asthma, gone." He paused. "Wish I could say the same for you."

She'd put on weight in her malaise and she knew her skin was pale as a piano key. Simply getting out of bed exhausted her. Fortunately, she'd had the day to get ready for her brother's return.

"Are you feeling any . . . stronger?" George asked.

"I'm not sure it's about strength so much as overcoming the doubt."

"About never playing again?"

She forced her voice higher. "Come on." She slipped her arm through his. "They're all waiting, but I begged them to let me see you first, before you put on any western airs."

He laughed, didn't move. "No airs. But I do feel the confinement here between the brownstones, all the cabs, the hawkers on the streets." He shook himself like a dog of rain. "The desert, Natalie." His eyes grew distant. "It's astonishingly magnificent."

"Astonishingly." She smiled. "Do your cowboy friends mind the way you talk?"

"They tolerate my vocabulary, now that I'm a good hand. That's all that matters on a ranch. Whether you can stay on a horse while moving cattle through greasewood and sage, up and out of arroyos. That's how you're graded. I call the cows 'bovines of a recalcitrant nature.' My cowboy colleagues wondered if those words were a form of foreign profanity." He smiled. "A few have picked up on calling them recalcitrant."

"Oh, you." She punched his shoulder. *Solid muscle.*

"It's been the best thing I ever did, Nat. Leave here. Head west. The postcards I've sent don't say the half of it."

"But why did you have to go in the first place?" Natalie had a little girl's voice rather than a whine.

He lifted her chin. He was nearly a foot taller than her. "You should come back with me."

She stepped away. "I couldn't. Mimsey would never permit it nor Bogey either. And I'm not strong. I'm so very tired almost all of the time. I cough. There are other things . . ."

"You're twenty-six years old. Old enough to be an independent woman, I'd say."

"There's no such thing as an independent woman in this era. At my age. I'm a woman with nothing to consume her life. The doctor says I . . . still have healing to do to rid myself of the . . ." She squeezed his arm. "I'm struggling a little, that's all. Bogey says it'll get better."

"It's been nearly five years, Nat." The kindness in his voice, not pitying but sympathizing, caused her to blink back tears.

"I know, I know."

He patted her fingers as he pulled them through his bent elbow. "Promise me we'll talk about it later."

She nodded assent.

They were the closest of the Curtis children. Though George was four years older than Natalie, he understood her. He lived in an inner world of words as she lived in an inner sphere of music. But then he'd headed to the West and he had changed.

As had she five years before.

"They're waiting for you," she said.

Arm in arm they sauntered into the dining room where siblings and parents greeted George with joyous shouts. Mimsey, as the Curtis children called their mother, usually so organized and proper, fluttered with tears in her eyes as she clung to George, welcoming home her wayward son. "Come, come. Tell us all about

19

your latest adventures. How was the train ride?" Mimsey took his hands in hers. "You're chilled." Then, releasing them, "Are you home for good, one can only hope?"

"I'm used to desert heat." George rubbed his palms, as though before a fire.

"My friends are all atwitter wanting a luncheon with you to hear your stories. We'll get that on the schedule." She pronounced it *shed-ule*. Natalie remembered she'd picked that up on that last trip to Europe. The *healing tour* that didn't heal.

"In due course, Mimsey." Her father intervened. "Let's let the lad have a bite to eat. Cook's prepared something healthy for you." Their father—called Bogey by his children and friends—stood with hands clasped behind his back, warming himself at the fireplace in the living room. "A little food will warm you up. Just what the doctor ordered."

Their father was a prominent physician, currently an emeritus professor. As a major in the army, he had attended President Lincoln's bedside during his final hours and helped with the autopsy. He'd known sorrow, and Natalie knew he grieved for her current emotional state that he seemed powerless to change. She couldn't change it either. Or hadn't.

Bogey herded his family into the dining room. Natalie held back as the siblings crowded around George at the table, passing him the silver saltshaker, the platters with cheeses and cold chicken and ham that the cook brought in. Pickles and coarse brown bread were next. George told his stories with wide swathes of his arms. He was more animated than Natalie remembered him being. He'd always been the shy one, along with her. She'd been bold only in her music, excelling at everything she tried, especially the piano. Until that day.

Laughter. Oohs and ahhs and exclamations. She scanned the room of her brothers and sisters. Except for George, they all lived together, still. Constance was nearly forty. Natalie supposed they were considered "old maids," or "at home" as the latest census described single women. She as well. She had hoped for a life beyond, maybe one day marrying and managing a household staff—after her career. She'd been on the road toward that when her life—like shattered silk—ripped apart.

She shook her head of the painful memory. She focused instead on the light in George's eyes, noted the tiny crow's-feet, the tanned face with laugh lines. He was thirty-one and wore the look of an explorer, someone who had gone beyond expectations, even his own.

"Don't you think so, Nat?" George spoke.

She hadn't heard what he'd said.

"About what?"

"About coming to Arizona with me. And California. And New Mexico. Some people seem to think New Mexico is still a part of Mexico."

"Isn't it?" This from Marian, the youngest Curtis at twenty-two.

Her siblings teased Marian for not knowing such a fact of geography, and Natalie was grateful the subject had changed as she watched them chatter. George had a broken canine tooth. There was probably a story about what happened to cause that. She'd have to ask.

"You haven't answered my question." George returned to her.

"She couldn't possibly make such a trip," Mimsey said. "She's not strong enough."

"And what would she do there?" Miriam asked. "Sign on as a ranch—what did you call yourself—a ranch hand?"

"Let her breathe in the air. That alone will heal her. Look what it did for my asthma."

"You do look healthy," their father-doctor said. "Good to see that, son. Good to see." He appeared to consider George's offer. "It might benefit Natalie."

"No." Mimsey's word was dressed in finality. Her husband frowned and she added, "She's simply not strong enough."

"The West could heal her. Why, I've—"

"I am here." Natalie spoke more forcefully than she'd intended. "In front of you all. Please, don't talk about me as though I'm not present."

Silence like an early morning fog filled the formerly boisterous room. Her siblings looked away, caught each other's eyes. *Pity. They pity me.*

George cleared his throat. "I nearly forgot. I brought gifts for you." He wiped his mouth with the linen napkin. "Let me get my pack."

"Bella can fetch it for you." Her father motioned to the maid who'd been standing by the sideboard. She curtsied, then moved into the hall and returned with the leather knapsack while the cook entered and cleared away George's dishes. George thanked her for the meal and the maid for his bag and set it on the dining room table, plopping it with a sturdy *thump!*

He unlatched the buckles, reached inside, and pulled out treasures. Colorfully woven lengths of cloth that could be table runners or a dresser scarf. "Navajo," George said. A red sash he described as part of a Katsina regalia. "Katsina dolls are Hopi. And dancers represent Katsina spirits which are powerful helpers in everyday life and who carry their prayers. The red sash represents the earth in blossom after rain clouds have made their way to the desert." He pulled out a rattle made from a gourd, something he described as a musical instrument. A selection of turquoise stones. A silver bracelet. A coral necklace.

"So beautiful. Such smooth stones." His siblings passed the items to each other.

"It's like Christmas in October," Miriam said.

Then he unwrapped from sheepskin a piece of smooth pottery that he set at the end of the woven runner displaying his gifts. The pot could be held in the palm of a woman's hand. It was bowl-shaped with a small nozzle-like protuberance at the top. George pointed to that feature. "It's a seed pot. For corn, mostly."

"They're all precious." Natalie reached out as though to touch the pottery, then pulled back.

"Go ahead and pick something, each of you. Mimsey too."

"You pick ours then, Bogey. Or we can take what's left. Yes, go ahead, children. Natalie, you first, dear."

Miriam pouted. "She always goes first."

"Shush." Mimsey motioned Natalie to proceed.

Natalie chose the pottery bowl. She held it in both hands. The clay felt warm almost, though she knew that must be just a feature of its artistry as it was October and the outside air cool. "The design. It's so delicate. And such lovely colors."

"It's Acoma, from a pueblo in New Mexico. They work with an aloe tip dipped in the paint they make themselves from insects and seeds. Then they draw the designs using the plant rather than a brush."

"With a very steady hand," Constance said. "Not a wavy line in sight." She donned the coral necklace, turned to look at herself in the mirror above the sideboard.

"An aloe plant," Natalie said. "Like the one Cook has in the kitchen? The one we break open to heal burns?"

"The same," George said.

"And you say they were done by aboriginal people?" This from Bridgham, the only other Curtis son.

"They're natives to that land. American Indians."

"And you brought this all the way from the West. And it didn't break." Natalie examined the pottery piece with red and green designs artfully arranged, crossing each other in a delicate pattern around the entire pot, including the throat, as she thought of the protuberance. "Such thin clay walls."

"About that," George said. "They use pots for everything, the way some tribes use baskets for storage or how we use glass containers to hold salts or buttons. What I learned about the Acoma pot is that long ago, when they made them from the local clay, the pots would be quite beautiful after painting and firing, but they were fragile, easily broken. They tossed the broken shards out onto the desert and made more." Storytelling and enthusiasm brightened his eyes. *Telling stories is what he did at the library before he moved west.* "The tale goes, that some ancient grandmothers were out on the desert and began picking up the broken pieces and pounding them back into powder. One ingenious potter added the old clay to the new clay, and those pots when fired became strong." He clicked his fingernail on the side of the piece Natalie had chosen. "Very strong. And beautiful. Both."

"And the broken pieces mixed in the new clay, that's what brought the resiliency?" Natalie asked.

"That's what they say."

Natalie turned her pot around in her small hands. "And these are used for storing seeds, and then the throat allows but one seed out at a time during planting?"

"Supposedly. They walk across the fields and drop them in, singing as they go."

"Singing."

"So the traders tell me. I've never been there," George said.

"Could be a good sales pitch for gullible outsiders," Bridgham said. "Everyone likes a story to go with their purchases."

"I love that story." Natalie felt tears she blinked away. "That out of broken things, already gone through fire, when mixed with new clay, something totally different is created. Something stronger."

The family chatter over their gifts and George's stories faded as Natalie held the art piece: practical yet a metaphor too. New purpose could come out of what was broken. Natalie imagined herself as a cracked and damaged piece of clay. What was the "new" she could blend it with to grow stronger?

"Are there other Indian artists like the one who made this?" Natalie asked.

"Dozens of tribes, so I'd suspect so," George said. "They're not all in New Mexico. They're scattered around California and Arizona and have names like Zuni and Taos. Apache, Navajo. Many others. It's like stepping into another world there, Nat. Anthropologists, even some women, descend on certain ruins during the cooler season because the artifacts there are so old. It's our nation's history written in clay and stone."

"Women?" Mimsey said. "Oh yes, I think I did read about a Mr. and Mrs. Stevenson spending six months among the Pueblo people, she called them, some twenty years ago. They were looking for patrons—remember, Bogey?"

Natalie's father nodded agreement.

Natalie said, "It must have been very interesting work."

"Surely not for a single woman though. Unchaperoned? Egads," Constance said. She stood, holding the ceramic piece Natalie had handed to her. "Whatever will you do with this? We've no garden to plant."

"It's art," Natalie said. "Beautiful in its own right. And it's . . . history." She looked at all the items George had brought back. Each was singularly precious. Handcrafted.

"My bedtime is long overdue," Miriam said, standing. "And I imagine you're exhausted, George. You'll be here for a while, won't you, dear Brother? To regale us with more adventures?"

"A week or so." He hesitated, then added, "Long enough to talk Natalie into going back with me."

"It'll take longer than a week for a negotiation that's going nowhere." Mimsey put her arms around Natalie's shoulders. She felt her mother's warmth but also the containment. "I have all my chicks at home for the first time in two years, and I'm not going to let you spend one moment trying to break up the flock, George."

Natalie's heart beat a little faster. She caught her breath and stepped away from her mother's arms, the cloying of family suddenly suffocating in a way she hadn't known before. "I could go at least for a visit, couldn't I?" She answered her own question. "Yes. I will go, for a visit."

"Good for you, Nat!" George said.

"We'll see," Mimsey said.

"I have to go back to Arizona in a week, but I'll come back

25

for Christmas and we'll head west for the New Year, you and me, Nat."

Natalie rubbed the pottery as if a genie might pop out and grant her three wishes. "I want to meet the person who made this."

"It'll be our goal."

"Bogey, say something?" Mimsey pleaded. "She's not up to this."

"I see a little spark in Natalie's eyes I haven't seen for years. I won't put that out."

Natalie let them discuss her. She had something more important to engage her heart. A glorious work of art crafted from the clay of broken things had found its way into her hands. George had found himself in the West. *Maybe there's hope for me.*

2

A Grace Rest

*F*atigue like a heavy quilt lay on her. It was the same heaviness she awoke to, the weight that had held her for five years. Tossing it off to even get up took so much will. Her life had paused, a *fermata* in musical terms. "A note can be carried into the pause, but it is not a rest where silence reigns," her instructor, Walter Damrosch, had told her. Such a pause was intended to shorten the duration of the preceding note but not the tempo. "It's a 'grace rest,'" Damrosch said. The composer's pause-mark for the singer was a sign to take a breath. She'd been taking a breath for five years, but nothing had changed. This was but another morning like all the others.

Then she spied the Acoma pot. This would be a different day.

Natalie eased herself from beneath the coverlet. Just that much effort caused her to grimace. But she stood, opened the drapes herself, not waiting for Bella to bring her cheery "Good morning, Miss Natalie."

A pale sunrise surprised her. *It's early. I haven't slept the day away.* This morning, Natalie changed her routine. She completed her toilet, then eased down the stairs, her fingers gripped to the handrail to steady herself. She entered the dining room, where she thought George would already be. Ranch hands, he'd told her, rise early. They'd spoken well into the morning, the two middle children, heading to bed after midnight. She'd slept the best she had for months, even though she woke to the same heaviness of heart—until she saw the seed pot.

It had been a long time since she'd felt excitement. She wasn't sure if it was the idea of a change of scenery that gave her an added boost this morning, or if it was that she had actually made a decision more important than should she dress or simply remain in nightclothes, or what vegetable to eat first. Yes, that was it. After years of drifting, she had acted. Telling George that she would join him for a visit helped her feel a trajectory of confidence replacing the years of wariness. *But will it last? And will I have the stamina to make such a trip?*

She poured coffee from the silver urn, warmed her hands as she sat alone in the mahogany-paneled dining room, the scent of linseed oil fresh in the air.

She hadn't always been so indecisive, had she? No. She remembered a time when she and Mimsey were in Germany, where she hoped to study at a Wagnerian school in Bayreuth, and she had pushed her way into a rehearsal, overwhelmed people by gushing her enthusiasm for music as she often did. But she could also be disciplined, steady, and became one of only five students accepted into that rigorous program with its structure of lessons and scales and practice for eight to ten hours a day, attendance at concerts at night, always under the tutelage of Wagner's widowed wife. Natalie reveled in the work, the demand, and in the performances of Wagner's operas during the festival held each year in the little German town. She'd been filled to the brim and returned to New York ready to take on the classical music world.

But the musical world that had fueled her, the life that had driven her as a child prodigy, had gone cold, much as the coffee in her porcelain cup on the table before her.

"Finished, miss?"

"Oh, yes, thank you, Bella. I'll have my eggs now, if you please."

"Yes, miss."

The maid retreated as George entered. Natalie had gotten up earlier than him. He poured his own coffee, then stood by the sideboard.

"Sleepyhead. Have some eggs."

"You'll be fixing your own eggs where we're headed." George brushed his longish hair back behind his ears. Natalie could see where the sun had been kept from his head by his hat. Without the Stetson, as he called the wide-brimmed western cut, he revealed a receding hairline, rimmed by untanned skin. "Out under the morning stars."

"Didn't you send a postcard writing of a cook's chuck wagon of some sort? I don't think it's quite so rugged as you say if you have a cook out there for all you cowboys."

"Only during roundups. When we're off making or mending fences, we're sleeping under the stars on the hard ground. Bracing." He poured a glass of fresh-squeezed orange juice. "And the bacon tastes ten times better than what sizzles in Cook's pan."

"Don't let her hear you say that."

Mimsey swished her way into the room then, lithe and gracious. "My renegades." She kissed each on the cheek. "I hope you slept well." She allowed Bella to lay the linen napkin on her lap and pour her coffee. "I've had second thoughts. George, you know better than to entice Natalie the way you did." She shook a scolding finger at him. "I know the two of you traveled well together in Paris and the halls of European grandeur. But it's hardly the situation for our little girl venturing into the Wild West. And it is still wild with Indians, and Natalie is, well, frail."

"I was ill in Paris, too, you remember," Natalie said. *And much thinner than I am now.*

"A different kind of feebleness, Natalie, caused by a medical emergency. The past five years—"

So Mother has been counting too.

"—you're much better, we can all see that. But truly, George—"

"Mama. Please. This morning is the first time in forever that I've felt like getting up. I don't even understand it. It doesn't mean I'm moving west the way George has." Natalie leaned back to let Bella serve her eggs. "It means . . . I'm making a conscious choice to take a pause from the recent past."

"Your stamina, Natalie." Mimsey shook her head. "Aren't you frightened?" Her mother surely was. For her.

Natalie lowered her voice, teasing. "Of snakes and wild wolves and—"

"Indians." Mimsey interrupted her daughter. "The reports, I mean, there are still killings and uprisings."

"As there are on the streets of New York, Mimsey," George said.

Natalie took in a deep breath. "People who make such delicate pottery surely can't be as fearsome as the newspapers report. Besides, there are archaeologists out there working with . . . what did you tell me, George? The Navajo? And others."

"Our president has taken an interest in the Indians," Bogey said. He'd taken his place at the head of the table, and though no longer operating his medical practice, he dressed in his suit—coat and vest and tie perfectly set.

"People like Teddy's books," George said. The Curtis family had a mild acquaintance with President Roosevelt, as Bogey and a deceased brother had been Harvard classmates. "Archaeologists refer to them, I'm told. The West is highly regarded as a place for exploration, advancing human thought and understanding."

"But Natalie's hardly an archaeologist. Or anthropologist." Mimsey set her teacup down in a clatter, as though it was the final word.

"She doesn't need to be, in order to explore," George said.

Once again, the family pattern of conversation cut Natalie out. She inserted herself back in. "George says there's a fine publication from 1895 made by a one-armed military man, Major Powell, that I can read. There's a copy at the library," she said. "It'll tell me all kinds of important things about the West, right, George?"

"*Canyons of the Colorado*." George moved to kiss his mother on the forehead before he lifted his leg over the back of the Regency dining room chair to sit.

"George! Manners." Mimsey sounded shocked, but she brushed her son's hair as she might have when he was a boy. "Goodness."

"There's more than one way to seat a chair, Mimsey. Just like there's more than one way to seat a horse."

Natalie laughed.

"You, young lady, don't even know how to ride." George pointed his toast at Natalie. "You'd better get some lessons."

"While her siblings were enjoying the stables," Mimsey defended, "your little sister was diligently at the piano, taking lessons, years spent practicing." She sounded wistful then and spoke to Natalie. "You'll be riding for hours out there in George's West. I'm not sure you can tolerate that. It's work, wouldn't you say, George?"

Before George could answer, Natalie said, "Then it's time I caught up on things I've missed. I may as well get a leg up, as they say, on my mode of transportation once we arrive in . . . where is it?"

"We'll head to Pasadena first, in California," George said. "From there we'll leave civilization and turn east toward Arizona. Take the train, do some riding. I'll introduce you to the traders I've met."

"A couple of months, then, correct?" Mimsey asked.

Natalie heard the worry in her mother's voice but also her beginning to set aside objections. "I'll be alright. You know George will take good care of me."

"I know." Mimsey sighed. "It's that . . . the last time the two of you headed off together for a few months in Europe, you ended up with appendicitis, so sick you nearly died, and I arrived to take you to Switzerland for weeks of medical care. There won't be such fine medical facilities in those far-off places of California or Arizona, should something go wrong."

"Nothing is going to go wrong." She wanted to sound convincing. "We'll be cautious, won't we, George?" Natalie coughed, caught her breath.

"Like tentative little Curtis lambs, we'll step out into the meadows." George bowed his head toward his mother. "First, we'll visit Charles Lummis's home."

"That scamp," Mimsey said. She crunched her toast.

"He was a friend of Uncle's," George reminded his mother. "He's a highly regarded editor, and he started the Sequoya League, in support of Indian rights, in fact."

"Yes, and a flamboyant man with an eye for the ladies," Natalie's father said. "You keep tabs on Natalie, George. The man is, well, he has a reputation."

"But he has quite a collection of artifacts himself, I've heard. He wrote a book. *The Land of Poco Tiempo*. The Land of Pretty Soon. It'll be a good introduction for Natalie."

"Did you get the pottery from him?" Natalie asked. Somehow the bowl she cherished arriving via an eccentric, flashy man rather than from the potter herself tempered the romance she'd begun to spin around the unknown artist.

"I got it from an Indian trader, but he knows the potter. She's made a mark on the bottom. A small one that's only hers. Trust me, we'll find the maker and you can thank her in person. Or him. Men make pottery too."

"And once you do, you'll come home. Straightaway, right, Natalie?" Mimsey's eyes pleaded for reassurance.

Natalie said, "I'll write a postcard a week, maybe even more, and keep you aware of our plans. My plans. Once George returns to his ranch work, I'll have other decisions to make. But I'll let you know them."

Her mother reached out to touch her hand. "Natalie, Natalie. Don't even think about staying on somewhere without your brother. You won't let her, will you, George?"

"Mama. I'm old enough."

"Yes, but not experienced enough. You're a woman of this new century, I'll grant you. But women of your age come home to their parents after they travel. Unless they have a husband to return to."

And therein lies the heart of my malaise. What life does an unmarried woman have to look forward to in this new century? Even a trained musician who once dreamed of a future wrapped inside the notes has no future in performing. I'm relegated to giving lessons, living at home until I die. There has to be something more. George has found something.

If she was ever to move from the malaise, she must make a commitment. She was telling her parents what she was going to do, even though she didn't know herself. Most important, she wasn't seeking permission. She was intentionally stepping into the grace pause, bringing the past with her, and for the first time in so long, the tempo of her life had picked up.

3

Planting Seeds

"Will you play for me?" George asked, nodding toward the piano. "A goodbye song?"

"Don't, George. I'm . . . I'm not ready for that. I . . . I'm sorry."

He nodded, kissed her on the top of her head. "That'll be a goal too," he said. "It would be a shame for something you loved so much to hold you hostage now."

"I have almost two months to prepare myself. You best get ready for your little sister to take over your life." She laughed.

The family sent him off with greater peace, knowing he'd return in less than two months.

Immersion was how she took on new things and heading west was no exception. It was how she'd always learned, through absorption, taking on new challenges deep within her soul. She built relationships through books, stories, and music. She was less successful with people.

Up early for breakfast with family, then off to the New York Public Library reading room. Natalie looked for reports on the

34

Navajo Reservation to learn the prehistory of "The People," as George said they referred to themselves. A Norwegian summary had to be translated into English, and she silenced the voice that said she ought to learn Norwegian so she could be certain of the text. She knew German. *I could learn.* She stopped herself. This was where her intensity and perfectionism led her down a terrible trail. She already knew what lay at the end of that.

She found the report by Major Powell, who made mention of various celebrations that must have had music. One could hardly commemorate anything of importance without sound. Powell's only word to describe the Indian music was *mesmerizing*, which told her little about the rhythm or tones.

After finishing the archaeological excavation reports, Natalie looked for a book George had recommended. *The Land of Poco Tiempo* by Charles Lummis, the friend of her favorite uncle. He explored various tribes and their customs and the more warring nature of some. There was little mention of women, she noted, but Lummis's book provided descriptions of the landscape and glimpses of individual pueblos like Zuni and Acoma. *Acoma!* He wrote that one should see the Acoma stone reservoir "at sunrise" to be enchanted by the shadows and light reflecting from the water. Natalie sat back in her chair as she read that. Something new, now, she wanted to do besides meet the potter was to see the reservoir at sunrise. *It must be healthy that I am imagining good things in the future.*

∞

She found an entire chapter in the Lummis book about Indian music. Lummis had been trying to capture what he called folk music before the "airs" and "ditties," as he called them, disappeared from memory as they were being silenced by new anticultural laws. Who could be opposed to culture? Lummis said the Pueblo singers sang with clarity, while others were worn down by, he supposed, the wind and desert sands to a thicker, more guttural sound. She could be sure there were no pianos among the Acoma but was curious about what instruments might have been used. George said the pueblo was atop a mesa not easily accessed, though the people brought their sheep and burros up and around and through the lands of sand, sage, and wind.

Later over breakfast one morning, she mentioned to her father Lummis's interest in anticultural laws.

"Yes. Adapted in 1883, I believe," her father said. She poured his coffee. "Thank you, Natalie." He took a sip. "The Code of Indian Offenses, it's called. Set up courts and Indian police, I believe—tribal people but responsible to the federal superintendents. Not without controversy." Natalie moved to join him at the table and watched absentmindedly as he buttered his toast, then slathered it with peach marmalade Cook had made earlier that summer.

Her father continued. "The penalties for various offenses such as using face paint—it causes blindness, you know—dancing, the healing by medicine men, and men refusing to cut their hair."

"They're forced to cut their hair? That isn't still going on, surely?" Natalie said.

"Oh, I suspect things are more civilized now. You don't hear much about the status. They've boarding schools, I believe, as the British have. There's one in Pennsylvania where Indian students love to attend, from what I'm told. Parents are happy to send them."

Could that be true, that parents are happy with their children far away?

She would find the Code of Indian Offenses and see what besides singing was considered worthy of punishment. Were they making pottery in opposition to the Code? When Lummis described their dances and music, was he reporting on clandestine, even illegal, activities?

Mimsey narrowed the guest list for Thanksgiving to one couple: wealthy friends of Mimsey and Bogey, the Masons, who supported many of Mimsey's causes, suffrage and immigrant and refugee services just two. "Perhaps you'll sing for us," Mimsey suggested. "Charlotte would like that."

"I . . . my throat is sore, Mimsey."

"Well, it will be a joy when you can sing again. It brings such pleasure to others and you always seemed happy when you sang."

"Maybe . . . we'll see." She'd had a mountain of voice lessons through the years at her parents' expense. "If I feel better."

Mimsey nodded.

I'm a bad daughter.

Even during dinner, the conversation of Natalie's siblings and parents and their friends became a background noise to Natalie's mental seeking. Music had once been her place of refuge, the notes drowning out the chatter of others, giving rise to imaginary scores on which she composed whole and quarter notes. Today, her body was in the Regency chair, but her obsession—no, intense interest—was in the concerns of these native people whose songs and dances violated a government code.

Mimsey broke into Natalie's reverie. "Natalie?"

Will she ask me to sing?

"Natalie, why don't you tell Charlotte and Rufus of your interest in the natives of the West." To the Masons she added, "She's going to join George for a visit. I suspect she could school the government on their conditions when she returns. She's such a good observer."

Dr. Rufus Osgood Mason, like her father, was a surgeon, theologically trained. And he was her parents' friend, he and his second wife, Charlotte. "Indian entertainment," Mason said. "I hope you enjoy yourself," he added, as though indulging a small child at her birthday party. She was used to it.

Mere entertainment, that's how he sees my interests. I am short, round as a butterball, look like a twelve-year-old. I am easily dismissible. And he would know of her failed debut. Everyone knew of that. But they weren't aware of the rest.

This dismissiveness had happened before, mostly with professional men who saw any independent unmarried woman as lacking brains and capable of nothing more than sitting at Daddy's table and taking nourishment from others. She felt her stomach clench and her jaw clamp shut, as though her body knew she wanted to say something, but her head told her to stay quiet, be the proper daughter. That tug of speech and silence had been a feature of these past five years. She let silence win, a choice rewarded when Charlotte said, "You ought to talk with Roosevelt for her, Rufus. The president used to be head of Indian Affairs," she explained to Natalie. "He had to read all the agent reports. Indirectly, such missives between agents and superintendents, and the Indian Affairs commissioner ended up documenting some of the aboriginals' customs and what the agents most feared. Or so I hear." Charlotte played with a necklace of pearls. "They had to codify the offenses in order to outlaw them and form the punishments."

"Charlotte has taken quite an interest in the Indians," her husband praised her. He was considerably older than his wife, who was tall and slender and wore thick glasses that defied her socialite life but suggested her interest in intellectual pursuits that matched her husband's.

"You'd have to go to Washington, of course," Charlotte said. "But the president could grant you access."

"I don't think that's necessary," Dr. Mason told his wife. "Anyone can get into the archives with patience and persistence."

Natalie spoke up. "That would be me."

"I'll go with you to the archives," Charlotte said.

"Oh, I couldn't ask for such generosity of your time." Natalie found herself meaning those words and at the same time being quite sure she did not want company where she'd have to adjust to another person's *shed-ule.* She might want to forgo a lunch if she found the material consuming, stay overnight if she got exceptionally tired. She disliked having to negotiate her time with others, except for George, who understood her wish to be absorbed. "But thank you. I need to do more things on my own."

"Natalie," Mimsey cautioned. "You haven't gone to Washington by yourself since . . ."

"I'm perfectly capable." To Charlotte, Natalie said, "Mamas do worry, but we women have to practice independence, don't you think, Mrs. Mason?"

"That I do."

"I shall attend you, then," Mimsey said. "Or Marian, you could go with her."

"She takes too long," her youngest sister said. She passed a piece of English plum pudding to her father.

"Please. Each of you," Natalie said. "You remember how I get lost in time. Indulge me, Mama. It'll ease us both into being apart."

Her mother sighed. "I suppose so. I'm hoping to hold on to you for as long as I can."

She leaned her head to touch her mother's as they sat beside each other. "I'll be fine. You've given me all I need to survive that government city." She made her voice light. "If I'm going to make it in the wilds of the West, I can get my feet wet on the streets of the capital."

She set aside the niggling worry that began when she did anything new. The possibility of things going wrong was endless. She excused herself from the gathering as she felt her breath grow short—and before she was asked to sing.

∽

Natalie took the train to Washington, DC, alone. She made no eye contact with other passengers, kept her nose in a book, glancing up to be sure she didn't miss her station. She even went through a scenario of what she'd do if she *did* miss her station. *Get off. Buy another ticket. Get back on.* No one was there to click their tongues and say, "Oh, Natalie, you can't take care of yourself. It's a good thing you didn't try to go alone."

But she found the correct stop the first time. Snowflakes covered the black soot the locomotive puffed out, dropped wet dots on her eyelashes as she left the station and hailed a cab to take her to the government building. She'd need the librarian's help to find the superintendent's individual reports and letters from agents who lived on the reservations, who knew things firsthand and made their concerns known.

Help having been provided, she removed her muff, pulled off her gloves, and began taking notes as she turned the pages to find the Code that began in 1883. It had been in effect for twenty years? She was stunned that she'd never heard of it while it had been affecting people's lives. Of even greater concern was her ignorance of what was considered offensive in the Code. "Feasts or dances such as the Sun Dance, Snake Dance . . ." Each tribe had their own festival or ceremonial customs and these were outlawed. Medicine men were considered devious and perilous to the managing of the people and were urged to be squelched. "Marriage relations" required intervention too, according to one official, so that only one wife be allowed, there being no need for a man to care for a deceased relative's wife "since the government now supports all of them." Cutting of long hair; forcing western clothes so the "savages could be assimilated to meet Indian policy"; changing how property was defined (which affected burial customs). A description of the courts was included, and the ultimate role of the agent who could decide if the judgments were proper and who had the power to use whatever means might be needed to enforce the verdicts.

And there it was, in black and white: the silencing of song.

Daylight disappeared before Natalie realized it. She was caught up in the dictatorial nature of these agents. Surely these things were not still happening? From blocking dances and describing so many everyday things as illegal, then forcing people to move from their homes or imprisoning them as punishment if they disobeyed. Why, if that continued, there'd be nothing left of these people or their traditions.

She bustled about, picked up her muff, grabbed her notes. Would she miss the train? Mimsey would be livid. She hailed a cab, the *clop-clop* of the horse a steady rhythm on the cobbled streets. *If I miss the train, I will get a hotel room. I will call home. I will be fine. I'll be fine.*

She was having trouble breathing. The doctors had told her to think happy thoughts when these episodes threatened to engulf her. She thought of her family stories, customs, and that even the Curtis name had a history meaning "courteous, polite, well-mannered, well-bred." English to its core. She wouldn't want some government telling her family what traditions they could and couldn't commemorate, talk about, cherish. George had said nothing of these things, had he? Maybe that was the Code twenty years ago, but in this new century, there'd been improvements, surely.

"We thought you were taking the earlier train," Mimsey told her upon her late arrival home.

"I got lost in time. The reports, Mimsey, they were so . . . tragic." She told her mother some of what she'd read while she pulled her gloves from her fingers.

"You aren't going to those places, Natalie. You'll visit George's friends, enjoy the ranch, and visit that one village where your pot came from." She helped Natalie from the carriage. "You're a tourist, dipping in here and there. Don't get involved beyond that. Two months. That's your time frame."

Back in her room, the gaslight bright enough for her to write by, Natalie penned questions she wanted answered. She lifted her Acoma seed pot. Had this piece of art been formed out of resistance, at great personal risk? Were dances held out of sight of any Anglos, the Katsina dancers' feet risking jail but still happening as that thread to a people's past, even their religion? Maybe George's friend Charles Lummis was right in trying to save the dances and the music. But whoever would have thought her own government would be behind such desecration? She felt the warmth of the pot, set it carefully down, crawled into bed. Seeds of concern had been planted in her newly plowed field. Was she strong enough for the harvest?

4

The Shards of Broken Songs

*Y*ou're not going alone."

"I did fine on my own in Washington, Mimsey. The stable is a perfectly reputable business."

"But not the place where your sisters and brothers frequented." Her mother fussed with the hatpin nearly as long as her forearm. Mimsey wore a long coat over her skirt, boots lined with lambskin. Snow had fallen and still dotted the walks, fluffed the shrubs beside the door, looking like cotton waiting to be harvested.

Natalie had donned the new reform dress that active women used for bicycling: split skirt whose length revealed her leather-clad shoes and more ankle than proper ladies usually allowed.

"No corset?" Mimsey frowned.

Natalie ignored her mother's last question, responded to her previous one. "Your other children mastered English riding, Mama. George said I should accustom myself to western paraphernalia. Riding astride."

Natalie had arranged for a visit to the stable on her own. *Another positive decision.* She'd have to notch those choices like

George said sharpshooters noted their successes on their rifle stocks. She'd make notes in her diary.

But this morning, Mimsey had insisted on coming with her, and knowing that her mother struggled with her planned departure, Natalie had relented. Besides, the two of them had traveled together so often through the years, it was appropriate that she would join Natalie once again. They'd taken a carriage a few miles from the city to a country stable. Mimsey knew how to ride English and had seen western riding events that had sprung up after the Wild West shows of the late 1880s in Madison Square Garden. Natalie had attended these events as well and watched women stand on a horse's back and wave their hats at the cheering crowd. She planned for a less vigorous experience.

She'd also seen Indians there. The closest she'd ever come. George said they weren't like that in the West.

The stable was a large barn surrounded by winter-dressed trees. Human introductions were made, followed by a chestnut mare being led out to stand before Natalie in the middle of the barn's arena. Mimsey agreed to remain behind the split-rail corral, lounging in a comfortable chair, where tea was served her, a colorful quilt laid across her knees. It was a glorious December day. Natalie smiled to herself at the luxury her mother posed. According to George, there'd be little tea service where they were headed. The air was brisk with a warming sun.

"This here is Daisy. Fourteen hands, that's her height." The instructor held the reins while Natalie fingered the horse's mane, recently combed. Smooth yet firm. An earthy scent greeted her nose, distinctively equine, she decided. The horse was huge beside her. One stomp on her small foot and she'd be back using a crutch.

Natalie stepped back and remembered why she hadn't felt left out when her siblings took riding lessons: she had her music. But riding was also an activity that challenged her small stature, being barely five feet tall. The size of the animal intimidated—how she could walk right under the animal's neck without bumping her hat or had to look up so far to even see the saddle horn. She swallowed when the instructor had her face Daisy, to see the horse's nose hairs move. Her palms turned sweaty. Animals were unpredictable; pianos were not. Maybe riding a horse could wait.

The horse licked its lips, blinked its eyes, moved its ears forward. "She's checking you out, miss. She's calm. No need to fear. She's gentle as a lamb, she is."

Natalie breathed faster. *Where's the old Natalie? Bring that strong note into this pause.*

She exhaled, stepped forward, then reached up to touch the velvet nose of the mare. She looked up into the brown eyes, such long lashes. A snort caught Natalie off guard, and she startled, stepping back, then laughed at her embarrassment.

"She's happy," the instructor said. "See her ears forward? And the snort, well, that says she's looking forward to something. You're a calming person."

"Am I? That isn't something I'd have said about myself." *Intense, driven. Sad.* But never calm. She wanted to do this well, since George said they'd be riding often. She listened to the instructor, holding herself as quiet as a mouse with a cat nearby, as he spoke about hands and posture and cues the horse might give her. This was a large animal and she was so small and it was all new and she was taking too long to acquaint herself with Daisy. She should be able to do this more quickly.

"Here's the correct way to mount," he told her then.

She listened as though her life depended on it, and maybe it did. The instructor led the horse to a platform where Natalie could step up as she followed his directions.

"First, take the reins in your left hand." She did. "Grab a good bunch of her mane in the same hand. It won't hurt her. Don't be easy." Natalie complied. "Now, with your right hand, I want you to pull the stirrup so you're standing facing her hindquarters and put your left foot in it." This was awkward and she barely heard him say, "You don't want *your* hindquarters where her back leg could come up and kick you in the keister. Oh, sorry. Kick you where she shouldn't."

"She might kick?"

"Daisy won't, but you never know with a new horse, so good to build the proper practice. There, with your foot in the stirrup, you can turn yourself to face the saddle. Your foot secure?" Natalie nodded. "Alright. Use that handful of mane to hold yourself, then with your right hand on the saddle horn, pull yourself into standing one-legged in the stirrup. Now with your left hand holding the reins, put that hand on the saddle horn too. Stand there on one leg, the other hanging loose."

It all felt so complicated, but she managed. "Now, after you stand, you'll swing your right leg straight over the back of the cantle and sit as straight as you can, no leaning forward. Hook your right foot into that stirrup and sit tight." The patient instructor seemed to speed up his last words as though he was late for his dinner. "Miss. Are you ready? Will you ride the mare today or come back tomorrow?"

It was so much to coordinate. But taking a deep breath, she pulled herself up, left hand on the horn, straight as a violin bow, feeling vulnerable. Her right leg hung loose. Then she swung that leg over the cantle. She heard her mother gasp at the movement of her limb so open to the sky. Mimsey later described the act as vexing. This was likely why women had always been encouraged to ride sidesaddle to avoid that "vexing" display of leg over saddle.

Natalie caught the stirrup on the far side with her high-topped boot toes and lowered herself onto the leather. She felt a lifting of her chest, corset free. Opening her split skirt to reach her leg into the air and set herself firmly on the horse's back was but one more act of independence. She smiled. She felt secure sitting astride. Her sisters told her riding sidesaddle made them feel vulnerable. Natalie didn't need to feel any more of that.

"Good girl," the instructor said. "Now keep holding the reins but let Daisy get calm, know you're settled and in control."

Natalie sat still. Up high, on an equal plane as anyone else who rode, she could look eye to eye instead of having to look up. She'd acquired height. *Grand.*

"Yes, see, Daisy's licking her lips, lowered her head once. When you're ready, you squeeze your knees and lean a little forward and she'll start walking."

Natalie pressed the reins she held in her left hand against the side of Daisy's neck that she wanted the mare to turn toward. She squeezed her knees, felt the gentle rhythm of the horse's gait, her tempo. She adjusted her hat and waved at her mother, a small action so as not to startle the horse. Out West, she'd have to find an animal like Daisy, one she could have a friendship with. They were becoming a team.

"Squeeze your knees," the instructor shouted. "Lean a little farther forward and she'll move a little faster."

And so she did.

As they circled the corral, Natalie wondered what her mother thought of such an intimate command issued so openly as the "squeeze your knees." The pressure against the mare's withers felt firm, like she sent a message. *You're safe with me. You're safe with me.* Despite not meaning to, she heard a rhythm in her head. A smile made its way across her face and then a soaring joy lifted from her soul. *Why didn't I do this before?* The horse was a companion she wished she'd found earlier. Not a musical one, but certainly one with rhythm.

"Will I have to find a stump or something to mount and dismount? I'm going to the desert Southwest. I'm not sure there are stumps there."

"Rocks maybe. But next time we'll practice without the stand. You're such a slip of a thing."

"But strong. You'll see."

Her mother approached and the instructor turned to Mimsey. "Next week then?"

Natalie overlooked his deference to her mother to confirm the appointment. Instead, she let herself feel the exuberance of the ride as she swung her leg over Daisy's rump, reversing her mounting, left foot still stirruped. Natalie paused for a second, straight as that violin bow, then kicked her left foot from the stirrup and hopped down, her hands still holding the reins.

"You maintained control the whole time, miss. That's very good for the first time."

"She does have a corner on control," Mimsey said.

Natalie felt her face grow warm but decided not to defend a quality that had served her well: command over her skill. Until it hadn't. On this day she'd done something grand: landed solid, with both feet. She was learning to weave a parachute for safe landings from the shards of broken songs.

5

The Consequence of Gifts

he stage. The New York Philharmonic Orchestra, eyes on her. Violinists, their bows readied. French horns flashing in the stage lights. Flautists, silver poised in their hands, waiting. Waiting for her. Walter motions her forward. No, he isn't supposed to be conducting. It's Seidl who has invited her, but there stands Walter. Has Seidl changed his mind? Natalie can advance Walter's status; promote her career, all she ever wanted. No, not all. Discordant sounds. Tuning of the oboes, trombones, trumpets. "Yes." Walter motions her forward toward the stage. His wife sits at the piano. Why is she there? No wife can perform a solo with the Philharmonic. It can't be done. Once betrothed she cannot play for money. Walter admires her talent. Everyone admires her gift, her dedication, skill, a lifelong commitment. Natalie is breathing hard. Her father's eyes full of disappointment. Her siblings, hovering backstage, always backstage of her passion, her piano playing. George waves his western hat like a lasso. "Yes," Walter calls out to her. Her mother, beckoning,

points to her wedding ring. Walter urges her forward. "Now"
he says. "Now." It is an order she can't comply with. Her legs
are heavy, she can't lift them. Can't move. Her heart is pound-
ing, her breath short, gasping, her fingers frozen. She looks at
them. They are old crone's fingers, bent and worn. "Now! Your
future depends upon it. Yes!" Walter has the conductor's wand.
It is magic. Seidl pushes him from the conductor's stand, taps
the orchestra to attention. Silence. "Now." Walter says the word
like honey. She shakes her head, she can't breathe. Spots of light
dance before her. She's failing him. "No!" she moans and then
shouts. "No! No! No!"

"Natalie, wake up. Now. Shush, shush. You're alright. You're here." Mimsey's words comforted, though filled with worry.

Natalie took in great gulps of air. Her heart hurt, it was pounding so hard.

"It was a dream," her mother told her. She stroked Natalie's arm. "Do you remember it?"

Natalie shook her head, still gasping for air. She did remember it, the confusion, the terrible exhausted choice of where her life had been, where music had taken her and her girlhood fantasy of Walter Damrosch. She sat up straighter, smoothed the coverlet of the twists of her dream-thrashing. "Adonis," she called Damrosch in her diary. Warm, engaging eyes. He adored her. Her talent. All she hoped to be that he would help her to become. And yet, he must have known before she did that her choices were limited as a woman hoping to be a professional pianist. Choose orchestral touring for life or meet demands of family and one day marry. Leave her music behind—or herself.

Her breathing steadied. "I'm sorry. I didn't mean to wake you."

"You were shouting 'No, no,'" Mimsey told her, stroking her shoulder.

"It was like . . . that night, Mama. When I couldn't perform." She started to cry. "Will it ever leave me?"

Her mother held her, rocked her as a child, and for a moment she was again safe, not torn by choices, not ravaged by humiliation, disappointing those she admired, loved.

"Shhh. It's alright." She let the pause comfort her. "Dr. Mason does hypnotherapy, you know. Maybe we should ask him to assist—"

"No. I . . ."

"Dr. Mason told me once that when we dream, all the elements in it are a part of us, and it can sometimes help to give a voice to each item or person in the dream." Mimsey continued to stroke Natalie's hair. "You might do that. Write it in your diary." She looked into Natalie's eyes. "Write a song for them, perhaps."

A song for the piano? For Walter? For my paralyzed self? The wedding ring. Give it voice?

The ring symbolized commitment, didn't it? Was she married to her music? Had she been? But now, she was divorced from all she'd known, the commitment gone. Walter was married to his music, but he was allowed a wife. A man could be a professional performer and a spouse. Not a woman. *What am I committed to now?*

"Yes, maybe I'll write some things down. It's not the first time I've had this dream, but it's been a while." She looked at her mother's worrying eyes. "Maybe when one embarks on a new adventure, old trepidations won't visit in dreams. I can hope."

Natalie lay her head back down on the pillow. Her mother tucked her in, kept her hand on Natalie's heart.

"You don't have to keep going through this. Maybe the trip with George is triggering old things and you should reconsider."

"Perhaps," Natalie conceded. "But if I don't go through it, I might always be trying to overcome it. Which will be worse? I can't undo what I did. No, I'm joining George and I'll take the broken pieces with me."

"We all do," her mother said. "We all do."

Three days later Natalie and George walked the red-carpet entrance to the mighty 20th Century Limited. Once in Chicago, they'd take a less elegant car, but Mimsey and Bogey had insisted they leave home on the newly launched, most modern train of the New York Central line.

The goodbyes had been painful, surprising to Natalie. She hadn't expected to see tears in her siblings' eyes, not after the years of her pesky piano playing, at times so annoying hour after hour that her parents had insisted that she use a techniphone keyboard that sounded like pencil taps instead of musical notes. Her gift, her passion in pursuing it, had consumed much of the Curtis household patterns, and her brothers and sisters had been indulgent, sat in the shadow of Natalie's sunlight more often than not. "One can take no credit," her mother had told the family one evening at the dining table when Natalie was eight years old, "for talent we've been given. We must serve what has come to us, nurture it, be faithful to it. And it is up to all of us to ensure that Natalie's musical gift is made available to the world, that she may receive wholeness and the world be enriched." She remembered those words. They had given her purpose and direction—until they became a weight.

As she grew older, trips to Europe were organized around Natalie's musical needs. A sibling preference for a baseball game or a riding event might be set aside so that Natalie and at least one of her parents could attend an important concert at Natalie's instructor's recommendation. Had there been sibling resentment, it had never been allowed to fester. Natalie's musical world was safe and supported. She understood she had a God-given gift and to ignore it would be an act of heresy. That awareness burdened her, even as her siblings bundled up against the December morning at the train station.

"We'll miss you, Nat," her brother Bridgham told her. He raised his voice against the background noise of trains and steam and the rolling of luggage carts across the marble floors at the Grand Central Terminal. "But we'll enjoy listening on the Victrola to something besides a Wagner opera." He smiled at her, bent to kiss her cheek.

"Enrico Caruso is available on the Red Seal label," Natalie shouted back. "You might enjoy his music."

Bridgham nodded. "I'll look for him. Anything but Wagner's *Valkyries*."

Natalie had taken the teasing in good spirits, especially when they'd all come to the station while freshly opened Christmas presents waited beneath the tree. She heard the swish of leather soles on marble, passengers rushing, her own shoes carrying her away. Her family huddled together until the train pulled like a slow snake in wet grass out of the station. Mimsey lifted her hands to the windows, and Natalie kept running through the cars toward the back until she could no longer see anyone still waving, only the black tracks against the December snow.

"You've done it, Nat." George removed his hat, set it on the seat beside him, crown down, while he faced Natalie settled in her cabin. He ran his fingers through his thinning hair. They'd been on their way long enough for the conductor to stamp their tickets and for Natalie to move into the space she'd occupy until Chicago. George's berth was next door.

"Was it exhausting the first time you left?"

"I was anxious for the new adventure," George said. He ran his hand through his hair again, a habit. His blue eyes sparkled. "It's thrilling to see you here, to have at least one other Curtis experience the West that I've come to love. To have my old travel companion with me for maybe six months? Or longer if this landscape steals your heart."

"Mimsey says two months." A tingle of anticipation rushed warmth to her face. "It's almost like the trip we took to Germany that summer, you remember?"

"Yes. But it got cut short. I don't want this one to end the same way."

"A person only has one appendix," Natalie said.

George laughed. "Disaster is what I hope to avoid."

"Your employer. They'll be alright with my joining you?"

"The Bar X? I may have to go back in between our travels." He looked wistful. "It's a good place to spend time at, Nat. But it has some memories." He didn't expand. "We'll play it by ear." He smiled. "There's a phrase for you, isn't it? Did you ever play by ear? Or was it always read notes?"

He had changed the subject from the Bar X for a reason, but rather than press him on what lay ahead, she let herself talk music with him, the click of wheels on the tracks a metronome of sound beneath their chatter. Maybe his heading west had been more than about his asthma. Maybe something—or someone—had kept him there. There was time to discover in the days ahead.

"It's kind of you to disrupt your life for mine." She picked at a seam in the seat. Everything was so new she could smell the spotless leather. "All our siblings and our parents seem to have done that through the years."

"We chose to do that, Nat. You mustn't carry the weight of our decisions."

She nodded agreement, but inwardly she took issue. As children, once her talent, her prodigy, her gift, had been discovered and her parents' decision to support it had framed all their days, her brothers' and sisters' lives had never been the same. *That might even be why George left the first time. I'll have to ask. One day.* Maybe he left to sever himself from the weight of her musical demands that crashed that day in 1897, after which no one could help her—had not been able to help her since. Maybe he hadn't left for his health at all. She looked across at him.

"And did you go 'to the desert' for your asthma, really? Or did seeing my . . . trouble become too much for you?"

He leaned his elbows on his thighs, clasped his hands. "I did what I could, you know that, Nat. We all did." He patted her hand, sat straight. "But I left because I needed a change from the library and a . . ." He paused. Natalie wondered what he had wanted to put in that grace rest. He went from thoughtful to chirpy. "I wanted to explore, and it didn't help to have you see me lamenting that there was nothing I could do to make your life better."

She nodded.

"But that's behind us now. You have taken a step toward something new and different, and what lies ahead will be grand."

"Yes. Grand." She smiled and prayed it would be.

6

The Discovery of Difference

*T*he terrain from New York to the LaSalle Street Station in Chicago wasn't unlike the landscapes of Europe. Small towns. Wheat fields lying fallow, covered with snow like powdered sugar over Cook's forked cookies. Sheets and underthings hung stiff in the cold, crisscrossed by telegraph and telephone lines strung like spiderwebs. Along the tracks, she began to notice what George called semaphore signals, posts on either side with upright arms that fell silently like outstretched hands as soon as they passed through. "Signaling where we are," he said.

"We're not where we've been and not where we'll be, just where we are," she said. "Maybe that's why I feel a little discombobulated. Nothing is familiar."

"Pretty much everything will be unfamiliar from now on, Nat."

She set aside the uncertainty, but exhaustion still played havoc with her heart.

She slept often, read. As the days of travel continued, she took notice of other passengers, looked outward more than inward. She chatted with children, asked for permission to teach them card games that brought out laughter. Her old ease of speaking to strangers seeped back like water through a grassy spring. Listening, that's what she liked to do, hearing their stories without having to share any of her own. Just being where she was. So long as she didn't let herself plunge too deeply into fantasy about them, she could find enrichment in the presence of another. No expectations. No music to play. No conductors to fall in love with.

"That passenger thought we were a couple," Natalie told George after she returned from speaking to a couple in the dining car. "Until she said she decided we didn't argue enough."

He put his book down. "Our parents rarely did."

"But Mimsey keeps her own ways, don't you think? I mean she didn't defer to Papa particularly. She has her meetings, women's things, charities." Natalie smoothed her long skirt across her knees. "But family comes first."

"Can be overbearing, though."

"Sometimes." Natalie thought of her mother's tenderness with her nightmare a few days before George had returned. "Mimsey never wanted more than to have a family, be a good wife. Why can't I aspire to that?"

"You have prodigy bones in your body."

"And where did it get me? Years of practice, performances, and then, the night before my biggest debut, the New York Philharmonic Orchestra . . ." She let the sentence languish in the sad memory.

"When you want to talk, I'll listen," George said.

"I know. Thank you." She picked up her novel. *Typhoon* by Joseph Conrad.

"That one was serialized early last year," George said.

"Was it? You've read it?"

George nodded. "It's quite good." He paused, then, "I'm thinking about writing a novel."

Natalie closed the book. "Are you? That's wonderful. Do you know what it'll be about?"

"Cowboys, I think. I'm making notes."

"Something else we have in common."

He raised his eyebrows.

"Oh, not writing a novel, I've no intention of that. Just the note-taking. I even took notes at concerts. Somehow, writing things down presses them into my memory better. Later I can even recall the place on the page where I wrote the words. Isn't that strange?"

"The same for me."

They each returned to their books, with Natalie having a new recognition of the comfort of merely reading in a room with a friend. A signal of where they were.

∞

They changed trains in Chicago, the first four days of their excursion behind them. The Atchison, Topeka, and Santa Fe tracks swished through the flat Kansas plains in a landscape that let the engines gain speed. Natalie awoke, feeling the tingling of excitement, not unlike those days in her past when she'd performed, singing or playing a sonata for a crowd. But this time, except for George, no one knew the details of her musical past, not even the woman she had chatted with at the postal car the day before. Natalie could be whoever she wished, pay attention to whatever struck her fancy.

There was much to notice. Granary elevators. Unfamiliar shrubs and trees swishing by so fast it was as though she looked through a rainy window. And sometimes it was raining and spitting snow. But no snowdrifts slowed them down. As the landscape changed, she felt the heaviness of the train pulling over a mountain pass. She heard the whistle blow as they approached the town of Raton, New Mexico, and she watched as the terrain changed to rocks and buttes or mesas, George said they were called. It was breathtaking, the change. In Las Vegas, New Mexico, they dined at an adobe Harvey House serving local, luscious food. They packed lunches to take with them to supplement the dining cars whose fare had changed from the 20th Century Limited's grand offerings.

She read, though the landscape kept drawing her from the words to the newness being spread before her. She pointed with the enthusiasm of a child, exclaimed at the pinnacles, the rainbow of colors, the depth of distance as the sun set behind this strange and glorious terrain.

The sway of the train cradled her to sleep at night. Her dreams lifted her, so different from the nights in New York. White wool blankets with red-and-black stripes that George said were from Hudson's Bay kept her warm, and when she woke, they weren't twisted from a restless night but rather lay unfettered across her body. Could the very idea of the surprises that awaited in the West be the sleeping aid she'd longed for?

She talked with George over breakfast, invited strangers to join their table at lunch, sometimes took her evening meal alone in the cabin where she wrote while she ate, the darkened windows reflecting her gaslight she turned up to illuminate the words. But mostly she felt herself unwind. As the rocks changed colors or formed lumps the size of houses, she felt her body begin to ease into this strange but open space dotted with difference.

They passed through Albuquerque, and George told her the Sky City, as the Acoma Pueblo was known, was west.

"Can we get off at the next station and go back?"

"We'll come later," he told her. "I want us to be in Pasadena at Charles Lummis's home for New Year's." Her lower lip moved into a pout and he hurried on. "He's brought some Navajo Indians there as part of the Rose Parade festivities."

"Has he? You've been holding back on me." She smiled. "I'll get to meet them?"

"Possibly. Of course, with Charles, you never know what might have changed. I wanted it to be a surprise, but your face fell when I said we couldn't stop and find the Acoma Pueblo, and I had to redeem myself."

"You have. And it was rude of me to even suggest I was disappointed. If nothing more happens on this adventure, I've already gained so much, George. This land alone is astonishing. Thank you."

He tipped the brim of an invisible hat in acknowledgment.

She would be meeting actual native people. Would she be able to talk with them? What would she ask? The possibilities reminded her of something from the philosopher Kierkegaard's work she'd read. She pulled her notebook out of her bag and found the page where she'd written it.

"If I were to wish for anything, I should not wish for wealth and power, but for the passionate sense of the potential, for the eye, which ever young and ardent, sees the possible. Pleasure disappoints, possibility, never."

Her spirit lifted as her shoulders eased into relaxation. This was the journey of a lifetime, the possibilities, endless.

7

Belongings

"It's . . . it's splendid." Natalie inhaled the balmy California air, took in the palm trees, the blooming bougainvillea everywhere, as though the region was one huge, tended garden. Hordes of people milled about at the train station, hugging new arrivals, laughter a staccato breaking up the steam release of the engines. For a moment Natalie missed her family, but then the warmth on December 31 was so unlike what they'd be experiencing in New York that she felt a grin fill her face. She was tired, her legs ached from having sat so much, her ankles a bit swollen, but she was here, standing in California. The West.

"Charles sent a cab for us. We're to meet them by the luggage station."

They found the driver, who held a sign that read EL ALISAL. "That's it," George said. "That's what he calls it."

The driver helped Natalie into the carriage, led by two fine horses, she noted. Crowds slowed their movements, but no one seemed annoyed at the delays of people crossing streets anywhere they chose, standing in the roadways talking. "All the Rose festivities," the driver said.

"Charles promised quite the day. People dress up dozens of carriages with the blooms and then there's a rose competition. Last year they added a Tournament East-West football game. Michigan against Stanford, 49 to 0." He threw his head back and laughed. "No game this year, so those Easterners are buried in snow and here we are. It's invigorating, isn't it, Nat?" He looked at her. "We've got to get you some new clothes. That wool . . . good for the mountains but not here. It must be eighty degrees."

She couldn't stop smiling herself and removed her jacket when she saw so many women with light linen dresses and what looked like cotton jackets over lace blouses. And all the skirts were well above the ankles. She even saw women in riding attire: tall, almost knee-high boots; khaki skirts midcalf, nowhere near the ankle; a jacket with sequins of flowers and a rounded hemline. Spanish style it must be. A wide-brim hat with a flat top, a string of small red flowers acting as the band. "Where can I get one of those outfits?" Natalie asked. She nodded toward the woman she'd been watching lead a horse decorated with bands of roses over its rump and around its neck. "And maybe a good horse like that one."

"We'll find out," George said.

When they passed a mercantile showing women's clothing ready-made, the driver nodded. "There, miss." She hoped it wasn't too far from this El Alisal.

They eventually left the hustle of horses and roses and took a dirt road up into the hills covered with low shrubs and then white-trunked trees. "El Alisal in Spanish means 'the place of the sycamores.'" George leaned forward. "It's up ahead there, on the side of that arroyo—the gulch. Heavy Spanish influences in the names here."

When they rounded an outcropping, the massive stone house El Alisal appeared. The odd-looking structure was covered with what looked like river rock as siding while windows on both stories were framed by stained-glass panels. A double wooden door with ornate iron features looked like the entrance. A tower, like that of a German castle, breached out of the stone walls; another shaped like a cone nearly reached the branches of the grove of sycamores. She heard laughter from the back. A bell clanged. "Stunning," she heard herself say. Everything around her stunned.

"Tepees." George pointed to the structures set to the side in another grove of trees. "Traveling hogans. The Navajo are staying there. Charlie built this place himself over the past few years. They say he got the inside timbers and some of the big rocks from the Santa Fe railroad. In between writing books, editing *Out West*, and getting himself into trouble with various causes, he did this." George spread his arms to take in the unique, almost grotesque structure.

Natalie was reminded of the artist Gaudi's work in Spain.

"After the parade, there'll be a 'noise' here tomorrow, that might go on for days. A noise is what he calls his gatherings of artists and writers, musicians, and friends he picks up here and there. I expect that's when we'll meet the Navajo." Natalie stumbled against George, inhaled a deep breath. "We can stay here as long as we want, Nat. Until you feel strong enough to head out into the hinterland of Arizona and New Mexico. The amenities there are, shall we say, significantly less."

"I don't think I'll need long to recuperate from the trip." She coughed then, a long hacking sound and her legs felt weak.

He patted her hand again. "Take it all in and let it bring you strength," he said. "Much of the West engenders meditation, a stillness that the desert commands. Don't let all the commotion during this festival fool you." He looked thoughtful. "The West is a state of mind, where you can find yourself alone in the bigness and let the meaning of what life's about seep into your pores and fill your soul."

"A philosopher you've become," Natalie said.

"With the West as my teacher." George lifted the wooden knocker on the front door. "Here we are."

Charles's wife, a slender woman with a gentle, smile hugged George and greeted Natalie. "George has been here before," Lummis's wife said. "But would you like a tour, Miss Curtis?"

"I would. Thank you, Mrs. Lummis."

"It's Eva," she said.

"Please call me Natalie." She'd already found a friend. Eva led them through what she called the exhibition hall, a massive room in the house furnished with chairs of clean lines, not the swirls nor heavy woods of the East. Her moccasins swished against the cement floor.

George left the tour at the room designated for him, and Natalie continued on with Eva, past smooth adobe walls the color of sand. Natalie's boots clicked as she walked. Eva gave a running account of the story of each room. There were a half-dozen bedrooms, furnished with simple beds and square, wooden chairs crafted with pegs and giving a sturdy straight-line sense. Colorful woven rugs marked the wood floors. "Navajo," Eva said when Natalie commented on their beauty.

Each room had a small alcove with a table and chair set beneath a narrow window, the tabletop displaying a feathered fan or a bowl or a stone implement. "Artifacts," Natalie said out loud. "May I?" She gestured toward the pieces.

"I prefer to call them belongings," Eva said, nodding agreement for Natalie to pick the item up. "Each belonged to someone, were likely cherished by them—at the very least, used by them." Natalie held a stone pipe in her hands. "Charles and his friend Adolph Bandelier took excursions together, digging around in places where those ancient people used to live. They always brought something back." She pursed her lips, said the words as though she didn't approve in some way. "Of course, some were gifts from when he lived among the Isleta Pueblo people for a time. Charles says we honor their history by displaying these, but it seems invasive in a way, doesn't it? You'll see many more in the exhibition hall." She looked wistful. "Sometimes it's like we're living in a museum, which isn't bad, of course. But these belongings . . . they're haunted with memories that none of us truly knows. Are we memorializing or taking advantage?" She shook her head. "Sorry."

"No, don't be. Those are important issues, what with the Indian Code I've read about and what we're allowing native people to keep and what we force them to give up."

Eva stared at Natalie. "Yes. My worries absolutely." Then, "Here we are."

In that room, the "belonging" was unlike any of the others: a wooden horse. Eva picked the carving up. It was nicked and looked like a child's beloved toy. "This was our son Armando's room. This horse was his. He took it everywhere with him." She looked at Natalie, her brown eyes pooling with tears. "I would have buried it with him, but Charles insisted we keep it out where we can see it." She stroked the belonging, as Natalie thought of it now. Natalie recalled the museum pieces she'd looked at, wondered about the gifts George had brought back for their entire family. Her Acoma pot hadn't looked old. It looked like something someone made to sell or trade, but maybe it had been used and had its own history as a part of a family's story. Maybe it had been reluctantly given up or had been kept once as a memorial.

"When did your son, Armando, pass away?"

Eva replaced the horse on the alcove table, continued to stroke it. "Christmas Day, 1900. He had just turned six."

"I'm so sorry. Such a terrible loss."

Eva nodded. "I didn't want Armando's things around, I thought they'd be sad reminders all the time. Charles refuses to use the front door since they took Armando out through it after the pneumonia. It's a constant memory for him. In the end, I find the things Armando held have brought me comfort I didn't know I'd need."

"It brings a contentment to this room," Natalie said. "With the lighting from that window, it highlights his treasured horse." She looked around. "It's a healing place."

"Would you like to stay in this room?" Eva turned, eagerness in her eyes. "I don't usually put a guest here, but I can have your trunk brought in. Only if you'd feel comfortable, of course."

"I would," Natalie said.

Eva smiled and Natalie saw her narrow shoulders soften. "It'll be pleasant to have you here. I hope you'll stay for as long as you like. We love your brother George."

"As do I." Natalie coughed again. *Dry air?*

"You're welcome to rest or join us in the exhibit hall when you feel up to the commotion," Eva said. "I'll introduce you to the others. There are children about. Our daughter—George's daughter with his first wife—is somewhere." Her hands were cool on Natalie's. "She's ten. And there's Charlie, of course. He's looking forward to meeting you—as an adult, he told me. Apparently you met him when you were young?"

Natalie nodded. "He was a friend of my uncle, and they came by one day."

Eva put her arm through Natalie's and the two women finished the tour arm in arm, returning to Armando's room, where Eva left her, and Natalie unpacked the small trunk a white-clad man had brought in. When she closed the door behind him, all the sounds disappeared. Natalie sent a grateful prayer to her brother for luring her to this West of magical structures and wounded people finding their way in the world. There was hope for her. With the door closed, she couldn't hear the chatter on the back patio, no footsteps on the stone steps in front drifted up to her. No bird sounds. It was as quiet as a chapel. Natalie lay down and within minutes was asleep. The mesmerizing West had begun its work.

8

Lost and Found

"Would they like me to sing for them?" Natalie asked the interpreter sitting beside her.

It was New Year's Day, after the "noise" of New Year's Eve, then the parade activity, rose competition, and the football game during which Michigan had routed poor Stanford 49–0. She'd seen the Navajo in their regalia on magnificent horses, waving like local dignitaries riding in decorated carriages. A school band marched to a Sousa tune, but it was the Indians, men and women, who rode astride their horses, that had drawn her attention.

The guests had now returned for another "noise." George chatted with writers and artists who had introduced themselves to her. Natalie had changed and wore, as the other women did, a light linen with a scooped neck to catch the evening breeze that cooled as the sun set. Gathered outside under the sycamore trees, troubadours sang while guests were lavished with desert fare. Prickly pear sangria. Bean chili—Eva called it "Everything You Have Chili"—seasoned with diced green chiles, garlic, and onions perfectly blended, yet each ingredient could be isolated for its unique flavor. For dessert, a mesquite banana cake with whipped cream frosting that dribbled down Natalie's chin. Her taste buds had a festival. *I will never lose this weight.* She felt so nourished, though, that she didn't even finish the cake.

The flamboyant Charles Lummis greeted each attendee like a hummingbird against a bloom, sipping quickly before moving on. He wore a bolero, she decided it was, corduroy pants and boots and a thin cord around his neck with a turquoise stone in the center that slid up and down on black cords. And a beaded belt nearly two inches wide. The Navajo guests and all the others sat in a wide circle around a flame that sent sparks up into the sycamore trees.

"Could you ask that if I sing for them, might they sing for me?"

The interpreter nodded. He was a Navajo not much older than Natalie, she guessed, whose English was quite good.

George leaned toward her. "You're being bold, Nat. That's good."

She nodded, had surprised herself with her offer to sing as a part of her request. "I felt I should give them something when I'm asking for something back."

"They agree," the interpreter said, coming back to bow his head at her.

"Grand. Could you tell them that I will sing about warrior women who also rode horses but in the sky? They are called Valkyries and are part of a great composition written by a man across a giant sea."

"You're going to do Wagner?" George asked. His tone suggested surprise.

"It fits. The Navajo women rode in the parade too," Natalie said. "The Valkyries in Wagner's opera were all women. Big women."

"The Ride of the Valkyries" was the most stirring part of *The Ring of the Nibelung* opera, at least for Natalie. Eight Valkyrie women almost shouted their lament preparing to take their fallen heroes to Valhalla. "Tell them when I saw them riding their fine horses, I thought of this song. I will sing it in honor of them."

The interpreter spoke. The Navajo nodded.

In the pause before she began, Natalie could hear the Navajo horses staked beyond, crunching on corn, a calming sound. The prelude was eight minutes long and Natalie didn't intend to sing the entire section.

But then she did.

Standing, she let her voice ring out into the cooling night, the German coming back to her as though she'd just learned it when it had been years since she'd sung the *Valkyries* chorus. She inhaled huge gasps of air, belting out her vocals as though to reach the other side of the El Alisal. She could see the faces of the Navajo people, listening intently, the flames of the fire dancing before them. Her singing voice cracked from disuse, but she hoped they'd see the emotion she put into the prelude, picturing the stage and the curtain going up on a mountain scene and women dressed in armor, their steeds painted on the backdrop, rising into the theater rafters. It was a rousing number and she hoped it was as exhilarating to them as it was to her when she first heard it. She wanted the gripping music to make way for what she expected to be equally stimulating songs from the Navajo.

When she finished, she was perspiring and breathless. It hadn't been her best performance. She should have practiced, but she hadn't. She took in a deep breath, coughed. Silence followed by polite applause from the guests. The Navajo nodded to each other.

"Superb," George whispered. "I doubt few here have heard such *Valkyries*."

"Was it alright, truly?"

"It was." George patted the chair beside him, urging her to sit. She did.

"I know it wasn't my best. My voice instructors would be covering their ears if they heard it."

"Don't, Nat. It was an offering. Let it rest."

She forced herself to sit up straighter, put the lack of "perfect" behind her, but she was shaking, her hands perspired. "Now will they sing?" The interpreter conveyed the request to the Navajo guests.

One of the men, perhaps the oldest, wearing a velvet shirt and a necklace of turquoise beads, a silver concho belt over white cotton breeches, and a headband, stood and looked at Natalie, said something. The interpreter told her he was thanking her for her gift of song. "And they will sing for you."

The group of six stood. Natalie expected a warrior song, not unlike her *Valkyries*. Instead, they began with a low flute while the singers sang "*Ko-la-ra-ne*" that introduced a gentle chanting, voices soft and clear, silences in between notes, song-words extending into the space, calm as the January night broken only by the *pop* of the wood logs settling in the fire and the mesmerizing chant to a drumbeat. Eyes closed, the Navajo sang in unison, voices as one. The drummer patted the stretched hide of his instrument, set the rhythm like a heartbeat but in the background letting the singers capture the audience with their voices, the flute's notes lifting to the stars.

Natalie felt her face grow warm. What she was hearing was beyond anything she could have imagined. Not a fierce, forceful keen or shout. Nothing wild nor raging. Sweet. Tender.

She had so misinterpreted what she had thought their song would be. It was prayerlike, the singers concentrating as though their very lives depended on being in sync with their fellow singers and the flautist and the drummer. She could listen to them all evening, letting the tones and heartbeat of the drum soothe her. She had no idea how long they had sung, but they ended with the phrase that had begun their singing: "*Ko-la-ra-ne*."

Into the finished silence, Natalie stood. Later she would tell George she felt inadequate. But in that moment, all she could think to do was stand in awe. She bowed to them and then began to clap her hands. She clapped and clapped in a sweeping honor to their music, then wondered if that was the proper protocol. Others stood now and also applauded. The Navajos looked at each other and then nodded their heads in unison, cautious smiles lifting their lips.

"Please tell them they were magnificent." Natalie turned to the interpreter, her hands prayerlike before her face, fingers on her lips.

"It was a Hozhonji song, a blessing," the interpreter told her. "It is like your Psalm of David." The interpreter wore his long black hair tied in a bun at the back of his neck. He reached to adjust it now before adding, "A Hozhonji song ends the day and is a hallowed act."

"What a marvelous evening we've had," Charles said, taking center stage beneath lanterns strung and now lit around the courtyard. "East meets West on the chords of sound. We shall do it again sometime when our Diné friends come back to visit, shall we? And now, are there other musicians we can entice to play? Jacinto, bring your guitar. Eva, let's bring out the refreshments and feed this crowd of noisy people."

People moved, formed small groupings, laughter rose up, but Natalie stood at the edge of the courtyard, arms across her chest, debating. Should she apologize for her assumptions about their music, say she was sorry for her rousing vocals so far removed from the gentleness of the Navajo singers? She couldn't imagine how to explain it through an interpreter. She wasn't sure she could explain it to herself. All she knew was that she wanted to know more, listen more, experience more. And she felt terribly deficient. She had failed her art by not singing well and abused the gift of music by choosing a Wagner piece rather than a lullaby.

"Let's talk in the morning." Charles walked up beside her, offered her a glass of wine, which she refused.

"My intentions were good," she said. "I . . . I had no idea. My Wagner choice. It was wretched, wasn't it."

"You chose what you knew. There's no crime in that. I predict you'll write about this evening one day, maybe for my *Out West* magazine."

She shook her head; couldn't imagine she'd ever want anyone to know of her shame.

"You might like to listen to the recordings I made of some of the Isleta Pueblo songs. They're quite different from what you heard this evening."

"I'd like that. I want to hear more."

"It's like that for me too," Charles said. He hesitated, then added, "I felt the most comforted after Armando's death when I attended a pueblo healing ceremony and stayed the night. One can become lost in music. Lost and found again." He patted her shoulder. "I'll bring out the Edison in the morning and we'll have a good listen."

He sauntered off and Natalie heard guitar music waft from the far side of the fire. But she couldn't get the Navajo song from her head and Charles's words about being lost and found in music. She had known that, hadn't she? Once? Perhaps through these distinctive, haunting sounds, she would discover its truth again.

Interlude #1

The Diné left at dawn, taking with them their horses and their regalia. The interpreter—Many Tongues—rode beside the main singer. He missed the goat's milk of home. The *Belagana*, Lummis, who had spent two plantings with the Pueblo people, treated them all fairly. Their horses were well fed. They were well fed. But so many days in tepees close to the stone house of Lummis, too many questions he had to exchange for answers, one language to another. It tired him. Them. Dawn came and signaled a start of the long journey back to that place they were most familiar with.

As they rode, Many Tongues thought about the small woman with the thunder voice. Her song had been full of thunderclaps and lightning and ended without rainbows or a soothing shower to help the corn grow. The Thunder Voice woman had come to him, wished to take back the bigness of her song, to listen again to the Diné make their music that she said reminded her of a stream tumbling over rocks or the whooshing of wind through pinyon trees. She spoke with words he understood, but he did not wish to hear her talk of taking back her song. She had given her voice-gift. There was no need to compare her song with the People's songs. The evening had not been a competition.

The Diné had come to the parade, rode their horses, sang and moved among the belagana people both to receive money to use in trade and to bless the people who waved at them as their horses shied to the flapping flags lining the streets of Pasadena. Singing also helped them keep their songs from being forgotten in all the turmoil of the coming and the staying of people like Thunder Voice woman. People like her could be small in stature but carry a big stick.

For the Diné, songs were prayers. No need to take them back. Better to spread them. Songs spoke of life and healing. The Thunder Voice woman would learn such things if she spent time with the People and held an open heart. Still, Many Tongues admired her willingness to give away her song. He tried to revisit the rhythm of the *Valkyries*, as she called it, humming as he rode. Every gift should be savored. Many Tongues would let her gift linger as he rode into the red desert toward home.

9

Observation or Intruding

*N*atalie heard the raised voices as soon as she opened the door. She and George had been with the Lummis family for over a week, and most of the New Year's guests had left, including the Navajo party whose traveling tepees and their horses were gone the morning after their performance. The evening before, while stroking one of their horse's manes, inhaling that equine scent, Natalie had approached Many Tongues—as he called himself—about perhaps taking back her song. But she had not asked him to convey an apology. Lummis had said Indians— lumping all tribes into one—weren't "prone" to apologies. What's done is done. "You should give a gift of some kind instead," Lummis told her. By morning, they were gone, and their disappearance would prolong her embarrassment—unless she found some other way to face her imperfections and the malaise that followed.

But as the days passed, Natalie's spirits rose, and on the morning walks in the balmy air, she found herself able to enjoy the sights and sounds, feel the warm sun without the constant push to "do" something, "go" somewhere, "fix" herself. She was purpose-less as she had been back in New York, but here it took on a kind of prelude, as though there would be something to follow if she was patient.

That morning, she continued into the dining room where she heard, "You won't believe what they're doing to them, Charlie. It's appalling, that's what it is. Children, treated like . . . like . . . like vermin." It was a woman's voice, but none that Natalie had heard during the "noise" gatherings of the previous week.

"You've made notations?" Charles asked.

"Of course. I've documented it all. But Burton has exiled us from the reservation. We have to intervene some other way. It's deplorable."

"It was a good plan, Charlie. Gertrude made quite an invalid, I must say, but—" This was a man's voice, and he stopped, turned, as Natalie entered the room.

"Ah, Natalie. Let me introduce you," Charles said. "Natalie Curtis, meet Howard and Gertrude Gates. They were, uh, we were just having coffee. Can we interest you?"

"I'm sorry. I didn't mean to interrupt. I'll take my coffee in my room."

"No, no. You might find this of interest." He guided her to a chair with a pillow cover that matched the Navajo rug. "The Gateses have been among the Hopi. On a reservation at Oraibi where there's a day school—"

"Operated by a despicable sub-agent there," Gertrude Gates added. She smacked her lips in disgust, adjusted her round glasses.

Charles pontificated. "Persuasion by six-shooter, civilizing by scissors, and education with a club." He pretended to write the phrase in the air. "I shall title my editorial with those very words. After I send my letter to the president. He must be made known of these—"

"—atrocities." Gertrude plopped onto a dining chair, held her head in her hands. Then she looked over at Natalie. "Are you interested in Indian affairs, Miss Curtis?"

"Natalie, please. I'm not really sure. I am interested in the Indian music I heard from the Navajo guests Charles had here. And we're going to listen to some of his recordings later."

"Oh, you missed an amazing concert," Charles told the Gates couple. "Natalie sang Wagner."

She winced at his mention of Wagner.

"Music is one of the things they try to stomp out," Gertrude said. "Ceremonies too. Dances." She shook her head. "Agent Burton, Commissioner Jones, others in the hierarchy are destined to erase an entire people, all eighteen hundred Hopi that are left, carrying on that wretched Code like it was the Constitution rather than a mere regulation gone awry. Music, like the land, is a part of who these people are. But our government has decided those things—their music, their art, their dances, even their clothing, and certainly their hair—must be eradicated. It's . . ." She threw up her hands.

"Unjust," her husband said. "It's unjust. And being committed by people who claim to be Christians, wanting to win their souls while destroying their spirits. They are not professing the faith that I was taught."

"I shall file a charge with Burton and ask that witnesses be subpoenaed. You, certainly, Gertrude," Charles said.

"They won't take my word. They claim me as a spy."

"Well, we were," her husband reminded her.

"I didn't lie about needing the air for my health," she said.

"But that was a secondary action." Her husband turned to Natalie. "We worked with Charles's Sequoya League to try to improve conditions at Oraibi. But the agents are wily and they are heads of their fiefdoms. We tried to find evidence that they diverted funds meant for the people to their own staffs, their own puffed-up quarters, while cutting fuel oil, food, all sorts of rations for even the slightest altercation."

"Like refusing to send their child to school because they were ill, for example." Gertrude held her head with both hands again, elbows on the table. "The entire family could end up without food for a week, the father put in the guardhouse and forced to work by day for something the agent wanted done at *his* house. Some new window casing or expanding his garden." Her voice quavered. "It's . . . government-sanctioned slavery, that's what it is."

"And we'll stop it. We must." Charles tapped his pencil on the pad of paper in front of him. "I'll write that letter. You be prepared to testify, when the time comes. And it will, it surely will."

"I did read about the Indian Code," Natalie said into the silence that followed Charles's claim of action. "I thought, since it was passed so long ago, that things would be better. And the president, Charles's old schoolmate and my uncle's as well, he surely wouldn't condone treating people like that."

"He does," Gertrude said. "President Teddy Roosevelt does." She straightened her glasses. "They are all so far removed from what is actually happening to these people that they . . . he . . . has too many other things on his plate, I suppose. It's up to us to do something." She sighed. "Now, we've been exiled."

"Maybe we shouldn't have spoken up," her husband said.

"We couldn't stand by and let them destroy the kiva. That's their place of worship," she told Natalie. "Or allow them to forbid the songs. We couldn't."

"But see where it got us. We're here in Pasadena. They're without anyone to speak for them now."

"The Sequoya League will speak," Charles said.

"Will they let people visit, as tourists?" Natalie asked.

The trio looked at her.

Gertrude got her voice first. "Most agents will. They have to, really. We came as visitors. It's government owned. Well, in a way. The reservations belong to the people, but the schools, the rations, all come through the Bureau of Indian Affairs. Very confusing, our government's relationship to the Hopi and all the others."

"My brother and I hope to go to the Acoma Pueblo."

"That's quite a distance from Oraibi," Mr. Gates said. "But if you're meandering, stopping at Oraibi would be . . . informative."

"You might end up like we did, being ousted," Gertrude said. "You've got to stay for a time with the people, you can't really gain the trust of them just visiting for a day or so. Well, why would they trust an outsider with a white face who does such things to them? The Hopi asked for schools, converted to Christianity, many of them, but they couldn't have imagined their children would be whisked away to faraway boarding institutions." She removed her glasses and rubbed her nose. "Worst of all, government workers in the schools talk about the Bible with them at the same time they abuse them for singing or dancing. How can these peaceful people possibly equate the love of Jesus with the way they're treated by those who profess to be his messengers?"

How indeed. Natalie certainly wasn't one to shed the gospel light on a people newly exposed to the faith. She'd struggled with her own spiritual journey ever since she'd visited the farm where Thoreau spent his time in contemplation and her uncle had found Transcendentalism so intriguing. She believed in the inherent goodness of people and she believed God pervaded all things, was everywhere. And the Judeo-Christian charge to seek justice, love mercy, and walk humbly with God—she accepted that without question as what was required of each human being. It didn't sound like justice and compassion were what the Hopi people were being exposed to, though, from what the Gates couple relayed.

Maybe it was *that* reservation, the Oraibi. Maybe other native peoples were being allowed to live their lives as the independent beings they'd been before they encountered the Spanish and then Americans. The Navajo who had visited Charles seemed to belong to themselves, weren't being treated as slave labor, surely. She admired their capacity to be among people foreign to them and remain true to themselves. Charles said two of the members had gone with him to Washington, DC, a while back, were introduced to legislators to help tell their story of the problems their people faced from neighboring tribes, to deal with land issues. They were adapting in a new world for them, still retaining who they were and what they were about with their music, traditional dress, and, she imagined, their food, their dances, their customs. Or perhaps she romanticized them. Yes, if what the Gates couple said was true, life was not a glorious time for the native people. Perhaps what the Navajo presented in Pasadena was an aberration. Maybe most Indians sang and danced and healed surreptitiously, in violation of laws imposed upon them. Still, she envied the Navajo she'd seen. They knew who they were, where they belonged.

The conversation moved to catching up on mutual friends while breakfast was served. Natalie's mind wandered. Had the Navajo been brought to the Rose Parade and to El Alisal as true guests and friends? Or as performers, entertainment, people for others like her to gawk at? Had she gaped at them, not really seen them as individual people?

She had. She'd failed to even ask their names, though Many Tongues had volunteered his. They were there for her enjoyment, to feed her desire to discover new things, assuage her curiosity and that of all the other guests Charles had invited.

This unsettledness, seeing herself as a gawker of the Indians, bothered her. She was drawn by their music, but was that selfish? One more way the people were being exploited as the Gateses described?

Even if she and George did visit the Hopi village, they couldn't stay long. "Two months," Mimsey had said, and then she'd need to go home. There wouldn't be enough time to gain anyone's trust. Or maybe she could extend her vacation with no real reason to give her mother.

She would talk with George. He always set her straight.

10

The Call of the Creative

*N*atalie poured coffee at the sideboard shaded by the syca-more trees. She handed a cup to George, added cream to her own. Orange groves dotted the distance, their green rows like banners spread across the land. It was hard to imagine it was January. Back home, snow drifted at the window wells and her siblings skated on frozen ponds.

"Is it my own curiosity, or could I actually be helpful by visiting the Oraibi school?" Natalie said, continuing a conversation started on their walk. "I want my effort—whatever that might be—to have a purpose more than just feeding my wonder about native music."

"Write some articles for Charles's *Out West*," George said. "Educate people."

"About my western awakening? I hardly think that merits pub-lication." A dog barked in the distance. George brushed the chairs of the ever-present desert dust as they sat in shade. Natalie heard birds making noises in the leaves. Hummingbirds flitted, then flew to magnificent pots brandishing geraniums all over the courtyard.

Dorothea, the Lummises' ten-year-old daughter, skipped toward them, bearing a lizard she'd captured in her small hands.

"I feed them," Dorothea said. Her dark curls bobbed in her enthusiasm. Natalie oohed and laughed with the child as she set the lizard free. Then Dorothea, too, flitted off to another early rising guest stepping onto the courtyard, a steaming cup of coffee held in his hands. The child engaged him in conversation with a trilling little-girl voice.

Such freedom just to be. It was what she'd once known with her music passion. Now she wished for less of a driving force and more of a creative call.

"John Muir." George nodded toward the coffee-drinking guest chatting with Dorothea. "He tramped across the continent like Charles did, wrote that book about our national parks. People enjoy reading his observations of a world they might never experience. You could do that."

"A woman's perspective on the West? Hasn't it been written? Let's see, Mrs. Stevenson and her anthropologist husband that Mimsey mentioned she gave money to?"

"She should inspire you, not discourage you." George leaned back and crossed his long legs at the ankles, his pants tucked into his tall boots. "I never see another author's work as a competition, but as inspiration. See, that woman wrote as wife. You'd be writing as a strong, single woman. You might even encourage other women to step out, not limit themselves to traditional paths. You always said you didn't see marriage in your future."

"Only because it meant I wouldn't be able to have a career as a professional pianist the way a man would have, even if he married. But . . . I don't know. I feel adrift, I guess that's the word. I have shoes but no path to walk on."

John Muir was joined by Eva, and soon others began milling about the courtyard, and George left Natalie to speak to another writer he'd met. Servers dressed in white, wearing colorful sashes, prepared a long buffet table for breakfast, and Eva motioned all to pick up a plate and indulge in the food. Natalie stood in line next to a tall, slender woman who introduced herself as Alice Klauber. "Look at all the colors on this table. Such beauty." Then "I'm a painter, from San Diego. I'm invigorated by colors."

"I've not an ounce of painting talent," Natalie said.

"I'm not sure I have either, but I do enjoy taking classes with masters, here and in Europe." As Natalie filled her plate with huevos rancheros—Alice called the egg dish—the women chatted about European cities they'd visited, artists' works they both liked. They found open seats at a patio table beneath a shading canopy.

"I spoke with Mr. Muir briefly last night," Natalie said as the two women watched the well-traveled man engage guests. "I envy his clear passion for the wilderness." She sighed. "I find myself envying anyone who knows where they're headed and has the courage to step out and go."

"What brought you here?" Alice wiped her lips of a green pepper, drank water, followed by a glass of freshly squeezed orange juice.

"My brother George. His asthma cleared up in the West and he thought I'd be healthier here too." She hesitated. "I've had some . . . health setbacks. For a time, I required a crutch. Thank goodness I'm past that." She took a bite of tortilla, then, "My brother is working on a book. I've yet to find a purpose."

"You sing beautifully," Alice said. "I heard you New Year's Day."

Natalie winced and changed the subject. "George wants to go to someplace in Arizona called Yuma. Not much there but a cheap hotel and a railroad station, he tells me. And a penitentiary. With a library."

"How exotic." Alice laughed. "Tourists to a penitentiary."

"It's for research. As a writer, he says, he can claim everything he does is fodder for his story."

Alice laughed again. "I can understand that. I'm always assessing lighting, color, the feel of a place for a possible painting."

"And I'm drawn to the rhythms and sounds. Or was." Natalie coughed, then explained as Alice's eyes expressed concern. "I feel stronger than I have in months. Leaving my parents' cook's sweets behind has been a good boon to my bones."

"My issue is keeping weight on," Alice said. "I forget to eat when I'm painting."

"Passion for a subject. I'm missing that. It's been five years."

"Creativity can't stay buried long."

George joined the women's table then, his plate stacked with pancakes, grapefruit slices, and avocado boats spilling over with tomatoes. Chunks of white cheese circled the platter-sized plate.

"My brother George. Meet Alice Klauber," Natalie said, nodding her head toward the two.

George smiled. "A pleasure." Then he reached across the table to add a chunk of cheese to Natalie's coffee cup that a server had just refilled. "It's how the sheepherders sweeten their brew."

"How quaint," Alice said. "Me too, if you have enough. I love new adventures." He complied and she tasted. "Not bad."

"It is good," Natalie said. "I wonder if they discovered it when cheese fell into their cup." The trio laughed. "Alice is a painter," Natalie continued. "She says my creativity will reappear." To Alice she said, "I hope you're right."

"If you don't find it, creativity will find you. If you'll let it." George winked.

My philosopher brother Natalie thought but didn't say.

∞

"I'm not sure how long Mimsey and Bogey will support my recovering," Natalie told her brother later as they walked the orchard. "And I can't ask you to provide for me forever. I have to find some way to support myself if I'm going to stay on out here."

"I told you that the West would steal your heart." A crow called to the sunset. "Write some articles," George said. "They'll sell. Maybe sign on with me at the Bar X."

Natalie laughed. "Whatever would I do on a ranch? I can barely ride a horse, which, I'll have you know, I thoroughly enjoyed a month ago. I hope the skill doesn't vanish with disuse."

"Women on those ranches ride side by side with their men. Some even run their own spreads, unmarried daughters. Widows, wives. You could cook, maybe. Or become a shepherd, take a sheepherder's wagon and spend the entire year, if you wanted."

She decided he was joking. "I'm looking forward to Yuma, even though I can't see what the benefit of that visit might be."

"If you waited to ensure the outcome," George said, "you might never start out."

Her life still felt like a hesitation. At least she retained the discipline of keeping her diary and being a notetaker. And she had her curiosity. That hadn't left her. Surely that was part of being creative again.

Alice Klauber approached as they returned to the compound. She was one of the last guests to leave. She handed Natalie her calling card of creamy stock with a splash of color brushed around her name.

"I . . . I can give you my New York address." Natalie looked at the card. "But I don't know when I'll be back there or how long we'll be in Yuma."

"Mail will follow us," George said as he stood up. "Send it to General Delivery, Yuma, Arizona."

"Footloose," Alice said, smiling. "That can be some of the most creative time there is." Natalie would have to get creative about more than the arts if she was to support herself in the West. She'd see what Yuma might bring.

∞

"You have to care about your person," Eva said. "That's part of healing too."

She'd dragged Natalie to a saddle shop in Pasadena where the proprietor carried ready-made clothing Natalie could try on behind the dusty curtains in the back. She hadn't bought new clothes in months. She hadn't cared how disheveled she might look. Tending herself took too much effort. But Eva was right. She was worthy of caring about herself. Natalie chose a split skirt with a front flap and a pair of high-topped leather boots with pointer toes "to fit the stirrups easier," Eva said. She finished her outfit with a leather jacket. "The nights get cold."

Back at El Alisal, Eva gave her a flat-topped hat. "You won't have ample opportunity to wash your hair, I suspect. This will cover it nicely until you do. And it'll defy that desert sun." She also fitted Natalie with a leather bag that attached over her shoulders with straps.

She'd been reluctant to shop but let herself admire her new attire in the mirror in Armando's room. She'd lost weight. Natalie sorted out her luggage. She had two changes of western clothes, two linen dresses, and with the leather pack, had a way to carry what she might need during the day while keeping her hands free to take notes. She carried the Acoma pot buried in lambskin in the shoulder pack. New boots, too. She was ready.

A week later, Natalie and George left behind the vibrant flowers, the orange trees, the cool adobe-stone comfort of El Alisal and its balmy breeze as they descended toward the train station and then the seven-hour journey east to Yuma.

Natalie felt the drier heat within the hour of leaving Pasadena and it only got more intense as they continued on. Like tiny bugs, cacti broke the surface of the dry, dusty desert that spread like a beige blanket on either side of the railroad tracks. The travelers carried canteens of water with them, along with a basket of sandwiches to tide them over until they reached the Arizona town. The luxury of their trip from New York to Chicago the siblings spoke of fondly, but a spirit of adventure permeated the dusty train car this time.

Gandolfo Hotel on Main Street bore the sign that marked an establishment with fifty rooms, though but a few were occupied. "We should have brought more sandwiches," Natalie said when she saw the menu that evening. It featured rice and cabbage in a variety of dishes.

"We'll get by," George assured her.

Their rooms, simple with clean graying sheets and a single gas lantern, cost them a dollar each. But there was a table for writing and the windows were clean so she could see across the Colorado River. *"It is a stark but stellar landscape,"* she wrote to her mother. *"Full of strange plants, small twittering birds, a brilliant blue sky, and desert sand hot to the touch. But it's cool in the morning when my bare toes dig in while I remind myself that if I was at home, I'd be donning snow boots. The sun washes my face. I am in the best health I've been in for many years. Thank you for letting me go."*

In the morning, she and George toured the Territorial Prison, which featured electricity from a generator and a library with more than two thousand books. "A former superintendent's wife started that," the warden told them. He scrunched his nose often. "We let folks from Yuma borrow titles. Keeps them from being too envious of our amenities. We got electricity here, which the town doesn't have, not to mention the band."

"A band?" Natalie made a note.

He scrunched his nose again. "Music soothes the savage beast, don't you know." The earliest prisoners had to build their own cells out of granite, the Warden shared.

She might write an article about the prison, its history serving hardened criminals as well as Mormons who had violated the polygamy laws of the 1880s.

Notes: Two bathtubs. Real bathrooms indoors, no outhouses. A courtyard with palm trees. Will ask about sewage management and nature of prisoners held now. More Spanish castle than prison.

Before supper, Natalie wrote up a short essay but didn't send it off, thinking it might become part of a larger effort, maybe

Musings of a Wandering Western Woman or some such title. She enjoyed the conversation with her brother and the waiter and another guest at an adjoining table while they consumed their supper of cabbage and rice and flavorful tortillas. The diner lived in the town but took his supper at the hotel. He called himself "Texan" and, at Natalie's invitation, brought his custard to their table. He was thin as an ocotillo stem. "I work at the prison, ma'am." His face turned crimson and his Adam's apple bounced like a jumping jack.

"You're a local." Natalie asked then about the reservation across the Colorado River. "I'd like to visit there."

"Not much to see," Texan told her as he forked his cabbage. "We've done our best to neglect it. But maybe that's what them Yuma prefer."

In the morning, George meandered to the prison library and promised he'd be back by late morning and they could go together to the reservation after their noon meal. "Don't go by yourself." She watched from the balcony as George left. The hotel provided a fan that she waved to move the warm air. It must have been 80 degrees even early in the morning. She read for a time, then walked the board streets and encountered Texan leaving the trading post. He tipped his hat, said, "Can I help you, Miss New York?"

"I'm just wandering around," Natalie said. She liked that he'd given her a nickname. "I've been working on an article about the quite surprising accommodations at the prison. It's hardly a dungeon as I imagined. Mostly Mexicans there, I noticed. And those fierce-looking Indians. Are they Yuma, from across the river?" She nodded toward the reservation.

"Apaches," Texan corrected.

"The warden said they were there for murder. It's good they're behind those bars. Probably a more comfortable place than their own villages."

Texan frowned, his Adam's apple bobbing. "It's complicated, Miss. Many are jailed for crimes defending their homelands. Most of us Anglos don't understand what it means for an Indian to be locked into such a small place. They once roamed the buttes and desert and forests. Their world fell apart when we came here. In there"—he nodded toward the penitentiary—"they die a little bit every day."

"You're quite sympathetic," she said. "Doesn't the prison here mean that law and order are here too?"

"There was order before we came," he said.

Natalie considered not the amenities of the prison then, but the degradation that forced confinement brought to a people accustomed to wandering, to being able to abide by their own laws and life. "You've given me things to think about, Texan," she said. She was glad she hadn't sent the article off. She'd rework it.

Natalie watched Texan ride off back toward the prison and turned her eyes to the activity of the Yuma people, their dogs and burros and horses. Activity there lifted dust across the Colorado River as she watched people tending the strip of green along its banks, beyond a levee. Orchards, maybe peach, spoke of a long-time presence. They were close to the American town, and she wondered how much influence the people on this side of the river had on the native people—or how much they influenced Yuma.

By midafternoon, George hadn't returned, still occupied and heedless of time, as she could often get when in a library. At the hotel dining room, a server wiped the table of a thin layer of dust that settled everywhere. She ate a tortilla filled with a sweet meat of some kind. She'd have to find out. Then she wandered over to the Southern Pacific Railroad station. It was their bridge that stretched across the Colorado, moving freight to and from Mexico. Small boats crossed the water with goods from the Yuma people, preparing for trade. Natalie checked the train times and asked the ticket master if there was an interpreter she might hire.

He grunted, "No time for such as them. And don't be trespassing on our bridge either."

The air had stilled. Snow topped distant rounded hills. As she started up the steps to the hotel, she stopped. A song pulled on her like the Siren's songs calling Ulysses. *I must go there.*

She headed toward the tracks, hoping a little trespassing might not land her in the Territorial Prison. If she could find the voice singing, it would be worth incarceration. *Wouldn't that be a letter to my mother!*

A gray bird twittered happy tunes as she walked, pulled toward the music. She crossed the tracks, stepping carefully, seeing the brown rushing water of the Colorado below her. The woman's song called to her soul. Natalie stopped, listened, then hurried on, fearful she might not find the singer before the song ended. She approached the cluster of hogans—flat-roofed, round-sided structures made of weathered wood spread with canvas, some adobe, others formed of discards of whatever seemed to be at hand.

There was no drum, no flute, the song light, happy, traveling from double time to three-quarter time, back to quarter and on to three-eighths. Complex, darting as a bird, dipping and swooping in sound. She made her way toward the singer, ignoring the looks of those who parted for her, this strange intruder. A fuzzy-bodied puppy sniffed at her high-button boots, leading the rest of the litter to cluster around her, yapping, but she kept moving, lifting the pups aside gently with her feet, avoiding sharp little teeth, captivated by the clarity of voice, the lilt of allure. Something broke inside Natalie at that moment. Tears formed in her eyes, and she found a place of peace she had not known for years through the healing wash of the Indian woman's creative song. She had begun her journey home.

11

At the Intersection of Chiparopai and Song

*N*atalie stood as quiet as stone. She had her notepad with her and she would have loved to capture this rare beat, this almost haunting sound. She couldn't break the spell the song put her under. She wanted to listen for the day, a week. *How long can we stay in Yuma?*

"That's beautiful," Natalie said when the woman finished. Natalie wiped her cheeks with her hand, exaggerated her smile hoping to reach across the language border as she had marched with ease across the river boundary. She stood before an elderly woman, removed her hat and wiped her forehead of the sweat, pushing back her damp blonde hair. She held the brim of her hat with her fingers before her, a sign of respect, she hoped. The hot sun beat down, and she either had to put the hat back on or move into the shade the woman sat in. *Will I be too forward sharing her space?*

The singer, an old woman with wrinkles deep across her cheeks, paused the corn grinding she'd been occupied with, her eyes lifted to Natalie's.

"I didn't mean to stop you," Natalie said, wishing she'd asked others where an interpreter might be. What had she hoped, to trot over here like a burro and barge in? The song had drawn her in a way nothing had for five years. "Your song was just so . . . mesmerizing." *Does the woman even know what I'm saying?* "So light and happy. I can't tell you what your singing means to me." She touched her fingers to her heart.

"Um. *Sí*, it is a happy song. You did not interrupt. It ended." She pointed with her chin at Natalie's hat. "Return it. Um, the sun will bake such Anglo skin."

"Yes! Oh, you're so right." She put her hat back on, dislodging a puff of dust. The shade proved a respite to her eyes that grew large with the realization of the miracle she'd walked into. "You . . . you speak English?"

"Um, and Spanish." The woman began with a hesitating sound. "Um, I can speak with those who never learn first language of our people, Yuma." She cracked a half smile, and Natalie lost her shocked look and grinned back.

"You're right I'm unfamiliar with your language. I'm so grateful you know mine. May I sit? I could help you grind corn if you'd like." She had noticed the woman had crooked fingers and held the grinding stone with difficulty. Helping was the first order of entering another world. Wasn't that something her parents' friends had told her? "Would you tell me about the song you sang?"

"Many questions, Anglo woman. Sit. Help. And sí, Mockingbird song. We say *arowp*. Same bird."

"I love that." Natalie clasped her hands over her heart. "It's about a bird like we have in New York." She sat next to the woman, plopping in the dust before her, within the shade of the plum tree they sat under. Natalie pushed her skirt over her knees she bent in front of her, reaching for the grinding stone. With her hand, the woman waved away the reddish dust Natalie stirred up, then showed her how to hold the grinder.

"Song says to notice what is around in the silent desert. It sings of blue skies, a good place in the world, happy. It spreads joy."

"Yes, it does. Would you sing it again for me?"

The woman hesitated. "Um. It is against the law. You know this?"

"I . . . yes." Natalie paused her grinding—which proved harder than she'd thought. "I have heard that you are not to sing the songs from your childhood. I think it's wrong to silence your voices."

"But if I am caught, you will not be punished."

"That's true. I'm sorry. I shouldn't have asked you." At least she hadn't embarrassed herself by offering to sing the *Valkyries* chorus.

The woman nodded.

Natalie wanted to learn how the music came to be, who composed it, what the lyrics were, how music touched the souls of these people. Was it different or the same as the way Wagner and Liszt and Mozart touched lives? She had dozens of questions. What a gift she'd been given with the presence of this Yuma grandmother who spoke English! She had to sustain the relationship.

"I'm Natalie Curtis. I'm visiting Yuma with my brother. But like you, I am a lover of music. Would you tell me your name?"

"Chiparopai. My name is Chiparopai." It sounded like *hip-a-rope-a* to Natalie. This time the woman did not hesitate before she spoke. "I do not live here," Chiparopai said. "My home is where there are no sounds but those of the desert around me." She waved her arm toward the east. "Um, I visit my daughter's daughter who gives new life soon. And there are wells here. The water is good." She squinted her eyes at Natalie. "You are not well."

"Oh. I, I'm feeling much better now. Merely weak, from a long illness."

Chiparopai nodded her head. "I once sing healing songs. I cannot do for you. No ceremonies. No dances. But before, I would ask three questions of the person bearing illness." She sat straighter.

"The answers tell me how far from health you have fallen. Would you like to know them, Many Questions?"

"Yes. Certainly." *How has this woman seen my sadness, my guilt?* But she'd given Natalie a name and she loved it.

"Um, my questions help a person heal. I begin. When was the last time you sang? When was the last time you danced? When was the last time you told your story?" Chiparopai nodded her head as though putting a period on an important sentence.

"Those are good questions," Natalie said as she pondered her answers. "Do you want to know my answers?"

"It would not be polite unless I could give a healing ceremony. Um, but they tell you what road to take to be well."

By this time, a crowd had gathered: shy children with dirt-smudged faces, men with headbands and arms loose at their sides but looking grim, hair cut jagged below their ears. Women with babies in a board upon their backs, baskets of cornmeal on their hips or heads. Young girls wore their hair in rolls of shiny black buns above each ear. The women avoided her eyes, looked down instead when Natalie smiled at them. A small waif took over Chiparopai's ample lap, eyes staring at Natalie, a dirty thumb in her mouth. Then Chiparopai began to sing, this time a different song. The waif looked at her and smiled as the old woman finished.

"Thank you for that." Natalie said it quietly.

"A grinding song." She grinned. "Nothing as you would say deep, only a working song."

Natalie sensed a defiance in the woman, choosing to sing right after she'd told Natalie it was against the law. The waif had influenced her. *She sang for the child.*

"What other songs do you like? Tell me about your people here. How did you come to learn English and Spanish?"

"Always questions," Chiparopai said, grinning.

Am I being overenthusiastic, as Papa sometimes said I can be?
"I'm interested in music. I don't mean to be rude."

"Anglos hurry much," Chiparopai said, intensifying the deep

lines around her mouth, on her sun-bronzed cheeks. Her hair was parted in the middle and she wore a colorful band of cotton around her forehead, her gray-streaked hair pulled back and secured at her neck. "Always hurry-time."

"Yes, that's often true."

"We are People of the River," Chiparopai said then. "Um, that is what our name means. The river rises, leaving behind ready land we plant and harvest and wait until the next snowmelt from the mountains that feeds our river. Our people."

"It's an oasis in the desert." It was the only green for miles except for cacti and sparse shrubs that Texan had called greasewood. "I mean it is a beautiful green border paying honor to the river."

"Sí. The crops grow. Birds sing. We are happy. No matter that we are poor." Like the child in her lap, she stared directly at Natalie. "Yes, we know you think us poor. But what good is life if we are not happy? Your white people think money is what brings happiness. It does not. Happiness is more than what you claim to own. Happiness is inside." She pressed her hand against her heart. "We Yuma think happiness is more." She lifted her chin as punctuation.

"Oh yes, I couldn't agree—"

Chiparopai rose then, tipping the toddler from her lap. Two of the men moved in quickly to help her to stand as Natalie too scrambled up. "Um, things to do now."

"May I come back?" Natalie asked. "Might I take notes as you tell me about your people, the songs?"

The old woman hesitated, then nodded. "You come back."

"Thank you, yes. Thank you. I'll be back tomorrow. In the morning? Will that be alright?"

Chiparopai nodded. "Um. You come sunrise. Cool then and desert sings with arowp. Day is happy."

Then like the shadow of a hawk over a desert mouse, the tenor of the moment shifted. The old woman stiffened as her companions stood straighter as though soldiers at attention.

"And who are you?" The man's voice startled from behind Natalie. It was harsh, demanding. She turned in the dust to face a large man dressed in western clothes, scowling. She thought of Gertrude Gates and too late wondered who would be punished for the music that had called her.

12

The Consequence of Song

I'm Natalie Curtis. And you are?" She reached out her hand, which the man did not take.

"I'm the agent of this reservation and you do not have permission to be here."

"Oh, I'm so sorry. I . . . I heard the singing and was drawn here." *Oh no! I shouldn't have mentioned the singing!*

He grunted. He wore a blue bandana, one to pull up over his mouth to stop the dust, she imagined. His very size intimidating like immovable rock mesas.

Be bold. "I'm sorry, I didn't get your name," she said.

"Barnes. Agent Barnes, and you will need a pass to come again. It's for the protection of these people. We can't have outside agitators riling them. What are you doing here?"

"My brother and I are visiting Yuma."

"This is not Yuma. These people are not to sing their songs. It prevents them from becoming assimilated. You know what that means? You know what the law is?"

"I do, yes. But surely singing while one works doesn't violate the law. It was the dances, their ceremonies, the medicine men you've curtailed, isn't that right? I've read the Code."

"We curtailed. The United States government. You and me." He leaned forward, pointed at her, then poked his own chest. "For their own good." He pointed at Chiparopai.

"But I don't think the president—"

"The law is the law, Miss Curtis. If you came to simply hear the music, you have heard enough and you shall hear no more. Go. These children are to be in school, not standing here gawking at a white woman."

"Mr. Barnes, please, I—"

"Your visit is over." To Chiparopai he said, "You know better." Then back at Natalie he added, "You come first to the agency on the American side of the river if you ever want to come here again."

"Aren't we in America?"

He frowned. Power had a distictive aura no matter whether a conductor in a concert hall or an agent in a hot desert. "I'll report you as arousing these people who are peaceful, who have had no quarrel with the authorities. Do you want to get them into trouble?"

"No, I—" She turned back to look at Chiparopai, whose eyes studied the dirt.

"I'll walk you back," Agent Barnes said. "You shouldn't be here without a chaperone. Are your parents here?"

She straightened her shoulders. "I'm old enough to be on my own, I can assure you. And my family has a connection with President Roosevelt. I know he wouldn't want to exclude me from visiting the reservation."

"I've had name-droppers threaten me before."

"I didn't want to threaten. I merely—"

"Go." He brushed his hands to get her in front of him as they moved through the parting crowd. She hadn't even had a chance to say goodbye to Chiparopai, to thank her. Agent Barnes kept behind her as they walked the railroad tracks back to the American side of the river, keeping the pace up so she had little time to think of retorts. "I know your do-gooder kind," he mumbled, then louder said, "You do them no good if you get them in trouble singing or sashaying around in their ceremonies. These Yuma are peaceful. They are sending their children to the school. They give us no challenge. Don't get in my way."

At the hotel he tipped his hat as she turned on the boardwalk to face him. Standing on the upper step she was eye to eye with him. "This is a free country, Mr. Barnes. And the reservations are a part of this country. I don't believe I will seek a pass from you to enter."

"Don't oppose me, Miss Curtis. A non-Indian can be asked to leave."

"But only if they're causing trouble. I can assure you, I am not."

"Tell your parents to keep an eye on you."

"My parents are in New York," Natalie snapped. "I'm a twenty-seven-year-old woman perfectly capable of making my own decisions."

"Make better ones. And stay away from my people."

His people. She wondered when the last time was *he* had sung a song, danced, or told his story.

But later in the week, after terse exchanges when he denied her a pass, Natalie cozied up to the agent, a part of her hating that she knew how to sway men in power, annoyed that she had to.

"Good morning, Agent Barnes," she said. "Thank you so much for helping me understand the limits of a visit to the River People. I can see from here that they certainly have grand orchards and gardens. Is that something you've been involved in teaching them?"

"Farming's in their blood. Doing it for years. I've tried to get fencing here for them, to keep the sheep out. And the orchards are old, but we introduce new methods of pest control." He spit tobacco into a cup he lifted from his desk.

"I'm sure you're doing so much good for them," Natalie said. She fluttered her eyelashes. "I wonder if I might be allowed a pass to visit, perhaps more than once if I don't upset them. I realize it takes up your time. Chiparopai's granddaughter is expecting, and I'd love to bring a little gift for the newborn, if that's acceptable, and visit the school. The children seem to like to go."

He stared at her. He had a rash on the side of his neck. *Heat.* "I had a talk with Chiparopai," he told Natalie as he wrote out the pass. "She knows the rules. I told her there'd be consequences." He looked up and smiled. "And this week I imposed them."

"What—what did you do?" Natalie felt her face grow warm.

"I've cut their rations for the next two weeks, to remind her."

Natalie kept her bland expression, even though she wanted to gasp. *Cut their rations over singing?*

"You shouldn't go there alone. You never know what might happen to a young white woman. Those people can be unpredictable."

Those people. She'd experienced nothing but kindness from them. "Oh, my brother said he'd go with me." *Not every time. Is that a lie?*

"Excellent. George Curtis, correct?"

Natalie nodded. He wrote George's name on the pass and handed it to her.

"Obey the laws."

Or others will suffer.

∞

Later that week, she and George attended a dinner prepared at the prison where they'd joined the warden and his wife. The woman, tiny as a swallow, picked at her food while Natalie told stories from across the river where she'd been visiting daily, not asking anyone to sing, just dunking herself in the pool of the Indigenous, helping with corn grinding, weeding in the garden while Chiaropai told her stories, taught her a few words.

"I had no idea," the warden's wife said. "They're such a primitive people."

"With a long history," Natalie said. "For a 'primitive' people, as you say, their music and explanations about their origins, their religion, their traditions are quite complex."

"Their music, as you call it, sounds like wailing most of the time." The warden's wife wiped her mouth on the linen. "I hear the drums at night. Frightening, or it was until Agent Barnes arrived and stopped it. Violent history I'm told."

George lifted an eyebrow, warning her to let the conversation drop. But she couldn't. "They're quite proud that not one of the Yuma people have ever been sent to the prison," Natalie said. "They're law abiding. I haven't heard any stories about warring. They were Yuma, then the Spanish came, then we came. They didn't resist."

"And their corn and melons can't be beaten," the warden said. He scrunched his nose. "Our prison farm produce doesn't compare."

"Yes, well, I wash everything twice that comes from there. Don't you find them . . . unclean?"

"I find them to be kind and generous people," Natalie said, "who adapt quite well to the ever-present dust."

"Well, you don't live near them, do you, so aren't aware of their ways. You're traveling through and they treat you differently. More tea?"

She'd been glad to get out of the warden's quarters, despite the fresh lettuce they'd been served, that from the warden's wife's garden, she had assured them. Apparently, the Yuma traded foodstuffs for pots and pans, clothing and tools. Natalie had thought the kind of prejudice displayed by the warden's wife wouldn't exist here where people had a chance to interact with the natives. But maybe the people on the American side rarely crossed the river, never found reasons to change the point of view they'd arrived with. Natalie had questioned some of her views already in the brief encounters she'd had. Experience and exposure had to precede change, she supposed. She actually felt sorry for the warden's wife for all she was missing. It was much of what Natalie had been missing—until she met the Yuma.

13

Interpretation Trauma

I have a pass now," Natalie told George. They were at the hotel, fanning themselves of the heat. "I find it restful to go there." She paused, then, "And when the agent isn't around, they sometimes sing like Chiparopai did that first day. The cadence and tempos are so unique, unlike anything I've ever heard. I don't ask them to sing, but I make notes when they do. It's engrossing and gratifying."

"You do have an amazing ear for sound," George said. He sat, thoughtful, then warned, "The worst that can happen to you is that you get banned. But they'll be punished. Rations reduced like before. The tins of sardines you gave them hardly made up for their loss."

"I know." She brushed at her khaki skirt. Her mother would be appalled that it wasn't ironed and was smudged with dirt spots.

"What do you do when you're there, Nat?"

"I'm making notes so their children and grandchildren will have the songs when they're grown. I'm doing it for them." *Am I?* "I'll translate the lyrics into English, which the children are learning. But it's the cadence and timing that requires such deep concentration on my part. Their music is so singular." She drank her warm tea. Ice was like gold in Yuma. "I've been thinking. When Rome conquered the Greeks, they learned from them. We should be doing the same, learning from the Indians, not trying to silence them."

"Most folks seem to think they've nothing to offer, which is why they want to wipe out their history."

"Make them white, yes, I know. But it's foolish on our part. Look how long they've been here. The ruins tell us their civilizations probably go back to the Roman era or earlier. Their farming techniques are ancient and wise. They listen to the world around them—our world, too—with an elder's ears. We're missing so much."

The siblings sat in silence until George said, "I've finished my research at the library. It'll be spring roundup on the Bar X and I need to be there. We should leave by the end of the week."

"We can't go now." Her voice raised.

"I can't leave you here alone."

"Yes, you can." She twisted in her chair to face him. "I'm happy here, George. I'm getting stronger, and the Yuma people . . . I learn something new every day. The history, legends, the stories and songs around weaving or sunrise or every occasion—I'm fascinated. My diary is full of insights. I love the children, the pups."

"You sound a little like me when I first hit the Bar X." He smiled. "I had to learn a whole new ranch-hand language."

"See? I haven't had this kind of interest in anything since my years of music training. Besides, I've written to Roosevelt about the consequences of the Code enforcement. He'll reply to me here."

"Oh, Nat. The man is busy. I doubt you'll ever hear from him."

"George of little faith," she said. She sat back to watch the sunset ease from amber to rose. "Roosevelt is the only person who can stop this desecration of their culture. He loves history or he must with the books he's written. Besides, I'm convinced there's

103

some reason a song drew me across the Colorado River to the only Yuma woman fluent in English—who is also a singer."

"I don't know, Nat."

"I know the warden now and his wife. I'm fine at the hotel. And I have friends on the reservation. I'm nearly twenty-eight years old." She patted his hand. "I'll be fine."

"What will I tell Mimsey?"

"Nothing. Tell her nothing about our separation. She's already let March come without a summons home. Maybe she's forgotten her two-month warning." Before the week was out, George was off to the Bar X.

∞

The Yuma people welcomed Natalie. She felt no fear among them and wrote of that to her mother, whose friends had been concerned about the "savages" Natalie encountered. She wrote to her San Diego friend Alice, suggesting she come and paint the light of the Yuma desert. She finished an article she hoped that the *Saturday Evening Post* might use. She didn't want Lummis's largesse to be the reason she got published. She didn't know anyone at the *Post*. It would be the merit of her writing that either spoke for publication or a rejection letter.

As an apology for the rationing she had caused at that first encounter, Natalie had brought tins of sardines, having seen empty cans on her visits. She kept bringing them. Aside from the salty fish which the Yuma seemed to like, the little tins served as containers for small treasures like beads or for the children, river pebbles and feathers.

For the baby soon to be born, Natalie crisscrossed with leather cords a polished stone she'd picked up at the beach in Los Angeles. "To hang on the rim of the board, for the baby to look at," Natalie told the very pregnant soon-to-be mother. "Or for you to wear if you'd like."

The girl had bobbed her head and said "Thank you" in English.

"They teach the school," Chiparopai told her. "When baby comes, we hold a Deer Dance. It will last all night long and begins days of welcoming the child." She paused. "You can come."

"I'd love that! Thank you." She didn't mention the risk they must be planning to take, holding a birthing ceremony. She'd wait for whenever Chiparopai was ready to tell her. "Today I'm going to visit the school," Natalie said. She considered asking Chiparopai to come with her but didn't want to burden the woman. She was old and walking challenged her.

"I will go with you," Chiparopai offered.

"I'd like that very much. You can tell me when I do things that are out of step."

"Um." Chiparopai grinned. "Your little feet can make big dust-ups."

Natalie wished she hadn't been quite so eager to agree that she might need an interpreter—or a broker, as Natalie thought of her—someone to explain not just words but what people didn't say, a certain look, a gesture unique to the Yuma or even to an individual family. She'd learned, for example, that Yuma people too—as Lummis had said of the Navajo—didn't like someone to say they were "sorry" but rather to bring a gift. If it was accepted, then all was forgiven. Her sardine offerings.

The school was in an old building and, like the others, over-looked the Colorado River. Treeless hills could be seen through the dust-dotted windowpanes. The children learned by rote English words the teacher gave them, including "Good morning! Welcome! How are you!" These phrases were shouted out at the teacher's direction as Natalie and Chiparopai entered the classroom. They stood in the back, between rows of wooden benches that the children turned from after their greeting. They all faced a long table in front. It held a cake with candles.

"Is it someone's birthday?" Natalie asked.

The teacher nodded and motioned to a child to come up and

stand behind the cake. The girl wore a smudged dress. (Natalie learned that they played in the uniforms too, as it was often the only cloth dress the girl might have.) The child kept her eyes on the floor, her shoulders dropped like a scolded pup. Then like a hen clucking her chicks, the teacher invited the dozen or so other children dressed in worn, beige clothes, hair chopped, to stand around the table. She was cheerful as she clapped her hands. The children all had that whipped-dog look, casting wary glances at each other. The teacher began to sing the happy birthday song. No one joined her. So, Natalie cleared her throat and sang. It seemed a natural thing to do.

The honored child to whom this song was being sung looked as though she'd been bitten by a snake. Her eyes grew large, her face as pale as desert sand. Long black eyelashes blinked tears onto her cheeks. Then, still staring at Natalie—who had stopped singing—the child slid beneath the table.

"Get up here. This lady is singing to you. We're all singing happy birthday. Aren't you pleased by that?" The teacher started to reach for the girl, to pull her out from under the table, when all the other children—without speaking a word—slid under the table and sat surrounding the traumatized child.

"Go," she told Natalie who with Chiparopai let herself be shooed out of the room. The door slammed behind them.

"What just happened?" Natalie asked.

Chiparopai stayed thoughtful, then, "Um, there was no corn, no dance, no drum, no Yuma song. Only Anglo song. The child is shamed and tries to disappear. The others join to comfort her."

"I think I understand," Natalie wrote to George later. *"We Anglos introduced our ways without regard to how they'd be interpreted by the Yuma. Oh, we had the best of intentions, that teacher and me. But the children understood what their friend needed. If I'm to help save these songs, there has to be permission for them to sing and dance their own ways. People don't change until they're accepted as they are. Until the children can sing their*

songs, believe their ceremonies have merit, they'll never find value in any of our white ways. Who can sing new songs when feeling shame?"

How well she knew the answer.

∞

Natalie visited the Yuma reservation daily, played with the children and pulled twigs from the fur of the pups. She watched the ways baskets were woven for everyday use, beautiful no matter their purpose. Her own fingers twisted fibers too loose to hold water the way Chiparopai's baskets could, but she learned. To laughter, she tried her hand at a flute carved from river cane and another that looked like it was made of an old rifle barrel. She fared better shaking gourd rattles. She sketched the intricacies of a hand drum, round, with stretched hides on both sides, and wrote about what she'd seen and her new beliefs about the importance of saving the Indian ways. She sent pieces off to the *New York Post* and one to Charles Lummis's *Out West* magazine; another to *Craftsman*. Maybe she could raise public awareness, feed resistance to assimilation practices. She found herself at home with these Yuma people, and she wrote from an attitude of humility, of how much she hadn't known about this other world and its richness. And when the River People spontaneously sang their songs at risk of retribution, she made notes. But she did not ask them to sing for her, as it was against the law.

∞

"Go out early," Texan told her. "And don't stay long. The desert is a deceptive lover."

"I'm taking my lunch."

Texan shook his head, talked to the burro he'd acquired for Natalie at her request. "You take care of Miss New York. She's a greenhorn. Don't be dumping her and hauling your"—he stopped himself—"hauling your rump back here without her." The burro brayed, lifted her head up and down, rattling the bridle. Texan patted her neck.

"We'll get along fine," Natalie said. She had decided to discover the desert beyond the reservation, to learn more of what the Yuma had known for generations. Eventually she planned a trip to the Grand Canyon, but she'd begin with the smaller arroyos and gorges close by. So many of the stories and the music Chiparopai spoke of grew from the landscape. The sunrise and sunset inspired the staves, the lines and spaces, on which the drums and flutes and voices found their musical homes. She wondered what images came to them as they sang.

She gripped the burro's roached mane, the wiry hairs sticking straight up. She lifted the reins, stuck her foot into the little stirrup, loosed her grip on the mane, stood, then swung her leg over as she'd been taught.

"At least you know how to mount. Good thing you're so little. She won't mind your weight." Texan pushed his hat back on his forehead. "Though there are ladies here who'd sniff at you riding astride. Here's your bag. Give yourself plenty a-time to get back here before dark."

"You worry like my mother," Natalie said, putting the pack in front of her. "And I love you for it."

Texan's face turned plum red. "Miss," he said and stepped back. She'd have to be careful with Texan. He might easily mistake her flippant words of affection for the real emotion of love. *That can certainly happen, that misinterpretation.*

The sun beat down on her shoulders, but her face was shaded by her hat as she rode out past the prison's graveyard, graves marked by rocks piled over deaths on the vast flat. Bonita's gait was nothing like the horse she'd ridden back in New York. The burro trot-trotted, then walked, and Natalie found the rhythm quickly, "keeping her seat" as her instructor had described when she and the animal were in sync together. Bonita slowed, would tug at sparse growth, allowing Natalie to gaze around her and not pay much attention to the route the burro chose. Occasionally, Natalie turned in the saddle and looked behind her, secure when she could see Yuma's railroad bridge and the town beside it.

Facing forward, she encountered scattered cacti dotting the desert, noted the yellow blooms on some, the wide outstretched limbs of others. George had told her that the first branch of a saguaro comes when the plant is sixty years old. Ancient sentinels of the desert. A white bloom caught her eye. It looked like a rose. She sketched it and would try to find its name in the large botany section at the prison library. And ask Chiparopai for the Yuma name too. They rode around sand dunes, and she wondered if they would be there in a week, the winds shifting much of the desert. The West seemed old and timeless and yet it changed within minutes. The air was still but there were noises: the creak of her leather saddle. The sounds of her own breath. The clank of the burro's reins in their rings.

At a rock outcropping sometime into their trip, Natalie dismounted, staked Bonita with a rock holding her lead rope. She poured some water in the canvas feed bag, then put in a handful of corn and let the burro chew.

She was careful to check the shade where she chose to sit. Texan and George had both said to be wary of snakes. There, in that shady rock, she wrote of how she felt, her growing strength. She composed her own haiku, a Japanese form of poetry she added to her notebook.

> *Heat shimmers from sand.*
> *Cacti catches birdsong, light.*
> *I taste the desert.*

She could imagine this spot in what the warden had called the Chihuahuan desert, could smell the earth and maybe even hear an insect chomping. Music everywhere.

She ate her sandwich, drank from her canteen, and she sketched the sagebrush, tiny plants, the purple rocks in the distance, and even a small bird or two, wrens nesting in a cactus. Bonita stood with one hind leg relaxed, head lowered, her eyes closed, resting in the rock shade. Natalie's lunch filled her. This landscape fed her. She sent a thought to George, thanking him for bringing her to this place, and a prayer to the Creator of this surprisingly rich realm. She leaned against the rock, crossed her booted ankles, clasped her hands over her notebook, dipped her hat over her face, and smelled the straw before she fell asleep.

She did not dream. She'd had no nightmares in the Southwest.

Bonita brayed into cool air. Natalie awoke. She'd missed the sunset. As the sun went down, it sucked the desert heat, leaving a chill that, coupled with Bonita's impatience, sent a note of belated caution to Natalie. She had thought of everything but not a warm jacket or a serape or a shawl nor the cost of sound sleep.

She packed up her belongings and mounted again, the burro cooperative at every step. Her heart beat faster.

"Well, Bonita, I kept Yuma in my sights all the way, turning around all those times to make sure my first venture out wouldn't get me lost. But now I can't see much in the faded light." She gave Bonita her head and let the reins lie loose on the burro's neck. Texan had said every good burro knows her way back to the barn. Bonita did and she hurried toward it.

Talking to the animal helped Natalie keep her own anxieties and self-chastisement tempered. She rubbed her arms, finding it hard to appreciate the change of light and how in shaded desert, the saguaro looked ominous rather than as friendly watchmen. She could see the bridge, couldn't she? The little burro trot-trotted, then slowed into darkness. Natalie squinted into the distance. Yuma was too far away to see lights and the gas lanterns too pale. She could feel her breath getting short. She'd made a mistake. She hadn't planned well. *What was I thinking going out alone?* She could spend the night. If she had to.

She sang to keep herself from thinking too hard about danger. Snakes. Aggressive coyotes. Holes to grab a burro's leg and dump her mistress in the dust. Perhaps the desert darkness was why there'd been no escapes from the Territorial Prison, though she suspected the Apache prisoners would have no trouble making their way in darkness. The thought of an escaped prisoner caused her arm hairs to prickle. Or was it just the cold?

Stars dotted the sky, but the night before her was as black as a piano key.

"What's wrong?" The burro had stopped. "Keep going." And then she heard it too: a man's voice, singing.

"Chiparopai sends me," he said when the man—not a boy—appeared out of the dusk and stood beside her, stroking Bonita's neck. "She says you take too long."

"Yes." She couldn't believe how relieved she was.

"I take you back." He was not much taller than Natalie.

"Thank you. That would be grand. Thank you."

The Yuma had been watching her, looking after her.

There was always something to learn, and one didn't need to experience it all in order to get the lesson, the most important being making friends who noticed and took steps to walk beside. It was what she vowed to do for them.

Interlude #2

Chiparopai shakes her head as she watches the woman enter the village, speak to children, smile in kindness. White women did not always listen well nor did they understand what they heard. She had been among enough Anglos and the Spanish, too, to know that they had a way of pushing into a tent like a burro, whether invited or not. More times than not, the burro eventually won over those inside, but not until the irritation of the intrusion had been put to rest. Natalie Curtis was such a burro. Stubborn. Certain. Reckless. But what woman who survived in this world did not have those qualities? This woman, small as a child, this woman, she liked, despite the danger she carried with her. She understood the importance of the songs.

The woman would not experience the distress that the Yuma people would feel when any of them were caught singing, dancing, telling their stories.

She was right. The songs might well be lost if not written down. But maybe she should wait until a Yuma child could write them? Maybe the stories told were better remembered by a Yuma boy rather than this white woman who has a good target but the arrow might better belong to someone accustomed to it, rather than one just learning how to aim.

Still, if the woman could get the ear of the Washington Chief, Chiparopai would welcome her listening to her sing Yuma healing songs. The woman needed healing too. But then, all people do.

14

Missives of Change

*I*n the Yuma mailbag some weeks later, a letter for Natalie
arrived. It was not from Roosevelt.

"*You and George can be of ultimate service if you will go to
the Hopi village of Oraibi. You'll remember hearing the Gates
spies speak of it. A teacher there has contacted me as well. She
intends to leave, as she finds the conditions so abhorrent. The
Superintendent, a man named Burton, is despicable. Harsher
than any I've heard about. I have written to Roosevelt, asking
for an audience with him and intend to be on the same train
when the President comes west to visit the Grand Canyon this
summer. I want an investigation into Burton. It would be of
utmost importance if the two of you could visit there. Suggest
you say it is for Natalie's health. I have also sent you my Edison
phonograph that you might record conversations that will prove
useful to the investigation. And helpful to your wish to record
music. Eva sends regards. Go forth and do great things. Sincerely,
Charles Lummis.*"

He had added a PS. *"Your piece about asking the Navajo to sing was marvelous. So humble to write of your discomfit over your choice of song and such perception of the musicality of their performance. I'm using it in the Spring edition of* Out West. *I've included payment here."*

The small renumeration made her dance around her hotel room and for a moment forget about Roosevelt's non-response and even that George wasn't around for her to confer with about Charles's request. Her first Southwest work had been published. But Charles certainly took for granted that the Curtis duo would accede to his request. She wasn't sure how she felt about that.

Based on Charles's postscript, there must be a box somewhere with the Edison recording device. As she walked to the train station, her mind was busy planning next steps. Before she left for Oraibi, she'd need to learn how to operate the phonograph and would also have to make plans to store items she'd accumulated since leaving New York. Her belongings.

"You have a box for me?" she asked the stationmaster.

"Yes, miss," he told her.

"Why didn't you deliver it to the hotel?"

The stationmaster didn't answer, instead taking her to the freight storage room. "There," he said. "All of those are addressed to George Curtis." Six boxes the size of a child's casket stacked against the wall. One separate box marked *Edison*.

They would fill her small hotel room. She asked for a crowbar or something to remove the wooden covers. And when she did, Natalie peered inside. The boxes contained the cylinders she would need for the Edison recorder. "Oh," was all she could say.

Back in her room she wrote to George of Lummis's request, sending it to the ranch at Houck, Arizona. *"I will come there and bring with me the freight Charles has sent. I trust you can secure a wagon, because that's what we'll need when I arrive on the train. And a good horse or two. We have our assignments. I hope you're available or I shall go alone. Love, Natalie."*

∽

The man had a Philadelphia accent and crooked teeth, but neither kept him from tipping his hat toward Natalie and flashing a smile as warm and welcome as a campfire on a cool desert night. He dropped his leather bag—one like George carried—on the wooden porch in front of the hotel where Natalie had taken respite on a shaded bench and put out his hand. "Frank Mead."

"Natalie Curtis."

He stepped back and cocked his head. "The Natalie Curtis?" He squinted. "Yes. I heard you sing once. In New York."

Natalie felt her face grow warm. "I hope I was at my finest."

"Oh, definitely, you were. A voice like an angel and then you took over the Steinway and *voilà!*" He kissed his fingers to his lips. "We were carried away. I didn't expect to find someone of your stature here, though the agent said siblings were traveling through." He leaned in. "Or at least he sounded like he hoped you'd be moving on soon."

"Yes, that's what we're doing." She invoked George as though he were still there. One couldn't be too cautious with a stranger. "Though we've found much to interest us here. Do I detect Philadelphia in your history?" She looked up at him beneath her hat.

Frank laughed. "Yes, but it's been a while. I'm an architect and have myself connected to the Mojave-Apache and currently to their irrigation project. I'm going to speak with some of the old Apache at the prison, get a sense of what they thought were their homelands."

"You're fluent?"

"I work at it, but I can make my way pretty well. I was hoping to make some headway with the agent too."

"Don't we all," Natalie said. "You ought to meet Charles Lummis if you haven't already. His Sequoya League and architectural interests might fit you well. He's involved in dismantling the Code of Offenses."

"Good luck with that." He loosened his tie and Natalie handed him a hotel fan. "Lummis. Name sounds familiar. Where's he at?" Frank had taken a seat next to her on the bench. Perhaps a little closer than she liked, but it wasn't a very large bench. He smelled of a rose cologne.

"Pasadena. He holds these 'noises,' he calls them, inviting painters and musicians and architects and writers together. And anthropologists. He hopes to make a truly American design, blending Indian and western American ideas."

"The way Dvorak blended Indian and African-American music in his *New World Symphony*. He tried to capture a unique American sound." Frank tipped his head toward her, his hat touching the side of her face. She moved back. "I heard its New York debut. Exquisite."

A man who knows his music. "I was there too. December 16, 1893. But I didn't recognize the Indian music. I guess because I hadn't yet heard their complex sounds."

He looked surprised. "You had to have been but a child." Then he winked at her.

"I was eighteen." *Is he looking at me less like a child and more like a woman?*

"Ah."

She hadn't paid attention to a man for a very long time.

"Would you be interested in supper together?" Natalie asked. "The menu doesn't vary much, so one looks to the company to keep the meal fresh." It was quite bold of her. He was interested in Indian rights, and he knew music—but not as a conductor, so he was probably safe.

He raised an eyebrow. "I would. I'll check in and perhaps your brother can join us."

"I confess, George has gone to the Bar X Ranch to earn some money."

"Pity," Frank said but didn't appear to mean it.

"While I stay here and write articles for Lummis's *Out West*, and soak in the desert air."

116

"That's where I've heard Lummis's name. Of course. His magazine. And yes, I'd be delighted to take a meal with the famous pianist and singer Natalie Curtis. Five o'clock?" Natalie nodded. Frank continued, "We can take dessert on the porch and watch the sun go down. And perhaps the Yuma will risk cut rations and sing a song to reach us across the desert."

Natalie liked him. His crooked teeth didn't detract at all from his kind face. And for the first time in a long time, when he got up and grabbed his bag to head into the hotel, she looked to see if the man she spoke with wore a wedding ring. He didn't.

∞

Five o'clock came and went without Frank Mead's attendance. At first, Natalie thought she might have misunderstood the time. Then she hoped he wasn't ill. The waiter delivered her dessert flan. She wondered if the eggs came from the prison or the Yuma chickens. She tapped her fingers, impatient; blamed her own daring. She ought not to have invited him to supper. He must not have liked a too-forward woman, once he had time to think about it. But he'd flirted with her with his winking and singing her praises, hadn't he? Had she misread him? *A man can be bold, but a woman can't?*

She'd eaten by herself in the dining room quite often, so no one suspected she'd been stood up. *Stood up.* Yes, she had expected him to stand up to his commitment and he had not. Her Adonis back in New York—He Who Had Failed Her, as she thought of him now—he too had posed as someone ready to keep commitments to advance her career, to soothe her anxieties. He had kissed her forehead, her cheek, and once brushed her lips with his before shooing her out of the practice room as though she'd been the one who invaded his space. She had let those moments grow in power. But the promise he kept was to his wife; the tawdry affair another brick in Natalie's collapsing wall. She'd read too much into those small but urgent moments when she thought he loved her, when she was in love. *He ought to also have remembered that I was an impressionable child entering a whirlwind of uncertainty, who wanted to know what my future held.* She was the victim.

Perhaps in her invitation, Frank Mead saw desperation instead of boldness and chose to remain in his room.

She would carry on. She took her flan outside and watched the red sunset reflect against the river. She heard a mockingbird sing while she savored the sweet custard. She was a great conversationalist and a lovely girl. Woman. Like people who sneak out of concerts during the encore to catch the first cabs, Frank Mead didn't know what he was missing.

⤬

Natalie had bought a wagon and two horses and was well ready to head north, forgoing the train when George arrived in Yuma by stage. "We'll have to go back to Houck," George told her, "before we go to Oraibi. I've another ten days or so back at the Bar X."

"Why didn't you stay? I said I would come there."

"Take the train alone? What would Mimsey say? And that was before I knew about your wagon plan." George tweaked her hat brim. Despite his having left her on her own, George still treated her like his little sister. It was both comforting and annoying.

"I'm perfectly capable of hiring someone to help," Natalie said.

"But would you?"

Natalie pulled her gloves from her hands. "Do you honestly think me that foolish?"

"I have my spies," George said. "You did a night ride in the desert."

"Oh blast," Natalie said. She shouldn't have told Texan. "I got back here fine." They'd been loading the crates of cylinders Lummis had sent onto the wagon. She hadn't recorded with the Edison, but the new Yuma mother had sung a lullaby. She'd heard a new grinding song too. Once she got permission from Roosevelt, she'd come back and record the Butterfly tune. Natalie had a notebook full of musical staffs and black circles masquerading as notes. She would need to play back the songs against those markings to get the tunes scored, available for someone else to read and repeat. "I intended to wait as long as I could, hoping Roosevelt would write."

"Oh, Little Sister. If the president were going to respond, don't you think he would have by now?"

"First, you mock my hope in the president replying. Then, Charles decides that we'll do what he says—and we will. Finally, you ignore my suggestions on how to execute those plans by showing back up here even as it makes more work for you."

"Natalie, crossing this country as a lone woman—"

"I'm stronger now than I ever was." She didn't tell him about her meeting with Frank Mead, or rather her lack of one. She felt a pinch when she remembered her dessert on the porch, alone. And when she casually asked the hotel clerk about Frank, she learned he'd checked out the following morning. She had survived rejection and that was the good news. She hadn't wasted a night of restless sleep nor hours of self-scolding over their brief encounter. He might even have led her to a better understanding of what had happened with her Adonis. She misunderstood. It was apparently part of her nature.

"The desert is an unforgiving landscape." George loaded the last of the boxes onto the wagon. "And you haven't slept out, you haven't endured the challenge of real primitive life. Besides, I wanted to make the trip with you. I enjoy your company."

"Blast," Natalie said, but she shook the dust from her gloves against her thigh and sighed. "I enjoy your company too. I wanted to save us the time and not take you away from the ranch."

"This will work out. Besides, you'll like being part of the roundup. We're going into the timbered areas, a totally different landscape. I'll teach you how to use a pistol."

She sighed. George hadn't been wrong on any of his recommendations for her about the West. But she had done well on her own too. For some reason, his acknowledging that would have been nice. And his mocking her wait for Roosevelt felt like he minimized her hopefulness. *Did it?* No. She would take his joking and not abuse herself with it.

"There is one thing I should mention," George said as he pulled his gloves from his hands. "Mimsey wrote. She wants you home."

"I knew she would. I ignore her directives in my letters. What do you think I should do?"

"It's your life, Nat." He walked to the team, ran his hand over one horse's rump, lifted a hoof to check the shoe. He was keeping her safe. But she could do that for herself, couldn't she?

It *was* her life. She would write and tell Mimsey "not yet."

15

Orders and Instincts

They left early in the morning, the wagon pulled by two strong mules that George had said would be better than the horses Natalie had acquired. A trade was made, but Natalie insisted she keep Bonita the burro, who seemed perfectly happy walking along behind the wagon after Natalie arranged a kind of dust mask to cover the burro's nose. She dabbed water at her eyes each evening, and the animal slept standing beside Natalie's bedroll. At sunrise one morning, the burro had lain so still that Natalie thought Bonita had died. But the burro bounded up when Natalie reached to touch her face, startling her into laughter.

"She was playing possum," Natalie told George, who was already up and preparing their breakfast of bacon and pancakes.

"Our entertainment for the day," he said. "We wore her out yesterday."

"She slept right through your pistol lessons." George always made camp early so the animals had ample time to rest but also so they had daylight for the target shooting with the .32 George had given her.

She liked the feel of the grip in her hand and the challenge of hitting what she aimed at. George seemed pleased with her precision. "Thirty-two shells can be hard to come by, so I'm glad there's no need to waste any."

"I'll take that as a compliment." She put the unloaded pistol in a holster, laid it under the wagon seat.

They headed northeast toward the New Mexico Territory border. As they climbed out of the hot Yuma desert, the terrain changed. George had had a canvas fitted over bows on the wagon so they had some respite from the sun and protection of their goods from sudden thunderstorms. But nothing prevented the wind from broiling around their faces, putting grit in Natalie's hair or seeping sand into their bedrolls, the crates. The water barrels held tight. Natalie hoped the heat and swirling sand wouldn't ruin the cylinders or the Edison machine.

"People traveling the Oregon and Santa Fe trails had to put up with this dust for months," Natalie said. "One wonders how they did it."

"Perseverance," George said. "Deciding what really matters and letting the rest go."

In the slow pace as they rattled across the land, Natalie noticed a rhythm more suited to learning than on the train. Different kinds of cacti flowered, some pink, others yellow. There were areas of rosy rocks piled atop each other like children's toys but reaching into the sky as high as the six-story tenements in Brooklyn. She heard the high-pitched scream of a hawk. The stars at night were like a thousand fireflies blinking and clustering. The crescent moon never looked so near.

The mules strained in places and George said they were climbing in altitude. "Houck is six thousand feet above sea level," he said.

She'd felt herself gasping at times and marveled at George's cure of asthma. "How did you manage to get healthier in this thin air?"

"I think being calm and living outdoors most of the year healed me," he said.

They met a few riders, once a family in a wagon not unlike their own who said they were on their way to the prison to visit a brother and son. Another time, two wary-eyed men—one with a mustache and another with his greasy hair pulled into a knot at the back of his neck—pushed their hats back when George pulled up the wagon to talk. Travelers on the road always stopped to "jaw," George told her. They exchanged information about the trail ahead, but the strangers kept pulling their horses closer to the wagon. Then Greasy Hair expressed wonder that they were out there "unprotected." When Mustache Man reined his mount toward the back of the wagon, Natalie bent over and retrieved her pistol. "We're covered," Natalie said loud enough for Mustache Man to hear. "Your companion here can attest to that." She didn't point the pistol at the man but rather laid it on her lap.

"Good to know you're prepared," Greasy Hair said. "Carrying a heavy cargo."

"Nothing of interest except to such as us," George said. "Recording equipment. For capturing desert sounds. I'll show you." He set the brake, tied the reins and eased off his seat, and walked to the back, jawing amiably. He opened one of the crates. "Just like it's stamped on the box." George moved the crate so Mustache Man could not only see into the box but also spy the rifle lying beside it.

Satisfied they weren't hauling guns or gold, the two men rode on.

George and Natalie dissected the encounter as they proceeded and decided they'd bring the rifle up front and that Natalie should wear the sidearm so she wouldn't have to reach for it in an emergency.

"I acted wrongly?" she asked.

"No, no. You followed your instincts. Those two didn't have ponies or pack animals with them, which makes me think they weren't moving from one ranch to another like they said. They acted more like outlaws."

"That's what I thought."

"You did good, Nat."

She strapped the holster around her waist.

That night George sat up with his rifle across his knees until midnight, when Natalie spelled him until dawn. The two outlaws never circled back, and Natalie found it gratifying that she had trusted her intuition and acted accordingly. *That's part of my new strength too.*

❦

Hours might pass in silence while Natalie and George kept their thoughts to themselves. Natalie wrote in her diary. At one point she said to George, "I guess he had no doubt we'd do it."

"Who? Lummis?" She nodded. "He's so committed to stopping the assault on the Indians that he assumes everyone is."

"Yes. But to send all these crates of cylinders." Natalie worked the string on her hat, tucked it beneath her chin. "What if we'd turned him down?"

"Nothing gets in a powerful man's way."

She didn't want to dwell on a niggling feeling she had that men in her life still made assumptions about her willingness to follow their directions. Not that some expectations weren't true. She was interested in interrupting the bullying—which was how she saw the agent at Yuma behaving. And she warmed to the idea of recording the music and voices of another people, the Hopi, even if she'd be doing it on the sly. But still, asserting her independence required having a man's rim around borders she hoped to expand on her own. They were well intentioned, these men in her life, and she felt ungrateful not to savor their protection. But wasn't it in asserting her autonomy, even if she fell, where she'd finally find who she was?

"I wonder what Mimsey would say about our potentially breaking the law," Natalie said.

"For a good cause, I think our parents would support us. Mimsey marched with the suffragists, remember. Some of them got arrested and she paid their bail."

"Did she? I guess I didn't know that."

"She and Charlotte Mason." He let the harness reins lie loose in his hands. The mules took the lead, following the rough road north.

"They both had the safety of husbands," Natalie said.

"And you've got me to protect you. Just like when we were kids." He punched her arm playfully. "And you've got the pistol."

"I'm determined to take care of myself," Natalie told him. "I am getting stronger." She flexed her biceps. "See here?"

"I have liked seeing the old Natalie around. Enthusiastic, a little brassy." The mules' ears twitched before them as George added, "If you ever want to talk about what brought you down, Little Sister, you know I'll listen."

"I will in time. What better place to work things out than as far from civilization as one can get, with only ocotillo and saguaro to eavesdrop."

"They'll never tell and neither will I." He grinned at her, and in that moment, Natalie was content. She would confess her guilt one day to George. Of all the people in her world, he'd be the most likely to understand and the least likely to judge.

16

Rounding Up the Moment

*T*hey broke their last camp before dawn and arrived at the Houck ranch just after Natalie's birthday on April sixteenth. Early morning noises greeted them: the bustle of cowboys coming in and out of long frame houses, spurs clanking on the wood floors of what Natalie assumed were sleeping quarters. Men with bandanas chattered as they tied packs behind saddles while dogs milled around, and good-natured laughter rose from the circles of dust near the corrals. A couple of cowboys attached chaps to their lanky legs, shouting to others about getting a "leg up." They'd arrived in the middle of something. "Is this the calm you said was so helpful to you, George?" Natalie teased. George's blue eyes shone. "I can see you love the excitement."

"You will too."

The trail boss, Jacobs, introduced himself and Cookie, the wiry camp cook, who nodded as he peered into little boxes on the back of his wagon. Natalie got a whiff of cinnamon, then cumin, from the drawers he pulled open. A few buckaroos in their wide sombreros came over to shake George's hand, welcome him back, then removed their hats to hold over their hearts at Natalie's introduction. She tried to remember all the names while George was updated on the activity.

Natalie led Bonita to the water trough and the burro brayed her appreciation. Four fluffy dogs with blue eyes circled behind the burro until Jacobs called them off.

"Those boys will herd anything they can," he said in explanation. "Come meet the boss. Mary Jo'll be pleased to see you. The hands will tend your mules. Good-looking pair. For sale, are they?"

George shook his head no. "They're our riding mules, me and Nat."

"Not into the brush where we're headed," Jacobs said.

"No, sir. They're our show-off mounts."

Jacobs grunted. "They'll stay put here. You get your old cowpony and string, and we'll give a trained one to your sister. Paddy does a good job with greenhorns." *They talk about me like I'm not even here.* That wasn't only an Eastern behavior between men and women.

They followed Jacobs in his cowboy boots still sporting spurs up the porch steps and into the shade of a wide veranda circling the house. He knocked on the door and, without a pause, ushered them in, Natalie first. The furnishings took Natalie right back to New York, with Chippendale chairs and mahogany tables and sideboards. Even a candelabra on the stone fireplace mantel. Nothing like those clean lines of El Alisal with its own kind of beauty. But Natalie now preferred the less ornate furnishings. Still, both households had woven rugs with designs that reminded her of colored lightning. She recognized them as Navajo. In the far corner sat a Steinway piano that made Natalie's stomach lurch. She hadn't played one since 1897.

"George, it's good to see you." Mary Jo gave him a hug rather than a handshake. More like a long-lost friend's embrace that lingered. *Did something special pass between them?*

"Your brother is the kindest cowboy as ever rode on this spread." Her hostess, Jacob's "boss," stuck out her hand in greeting as George introduced Natalie. "I've heard so much about you. Happy you could join us." She was a lean woman in her forties, Natalie guessed. Her handshake was gentle, almost Indian-like, a passing of flesh rather than a gripping. She wore jeans and a white blouse with the sleeves cut out, revealing muscled arms bronzed by the sun. "My husband's choice for furnishings," Mary Jo said as Natalie gazed around the room, holding her hat, and lifted her mashed-down hair with her fingers. "I'm more of a bunkhouse bride."

"Hardly a bride anymore," Mr. Brigand said. He entered the room from what looked like a library. "We're going on twenty years. Ten of them were the best of my life." He laughed.

"If you weren't such a slow learner, you'd have had at least eighteen to enjoy," his wife told him to his smile. Natalie could imagine them bantering like this as a pattern of their days. "Moving on"—Mary Jo turned to Natalie—"I hear you're going to join us for a time. I hope you're up to a little riding. We all pitch in at roundup."

"Yes, absolutely."

"Good. You two grab the breakfast fixings. Eat up. You can get a warm bath after—the last you'll have for a while—then join us outside and we'll get you saddled and ready to ride." Mary Jo had slipped a light linen shirt over her arms and the scoop-necked blouse. She held a leather vest and jacket in her arms, along with a set of chaps. Natalie noticed that her fingers were crippled, and she struggled to manage the items. "You'll want layers," she said. "Protection from the hot sun, then warmth for the night. There are extra women's clothes in the first bedroom. I put a pair of my chaps in there." She squinted at Natalie. "They'll be a little long on you, but they'll still protect your legs. I'll have the bathwater drawn. George"—she said his name softly—"you know the drill."

"I don't want to hold anyone up," Natalie said. She watched George fill his plate.

"You won't. The boys will start out, we'll follow in an hour or so. Plenty a-time for you to get the dust washed from your ears, Natalie, if I may call you that." Natalie nodded, and with Mary Jo's departure, the siblings gathered food and ate alone.

Natalie decided she would do as she was told, despite not wanting to take the time to bathe. She guessed she'd be doing quite a lot of following orders on this next phase of her journey. Still, for a change, it was gratifying to be around a woman who gave them.

∞

It was the stuff of Western dime novels, Natalie decided. She'd read Owen Wister's story about a Wyoming cowboy who tired of the dirt and dust and headed to Boston. Natalie made the opposite journey, east to west. Everything was new and different, including the bandana she wore around her neck that she'd pull up over her nose when the dust stirred up too high. The chaps she might need help getting attached to, but her persistence prevailed.

Cookie had set up his food wagon, and already there were marvelous mixtures of sauces and scents filling the air. She wasn't sure what was on the menu, but it had to be good. George fit right in, and he was so skilled with his horses. Each cowboy apparently had enough animals that they would ride one for only half a day and then change, the terrain and work being so demanding. She imagined George those years in the library, shushing people if they talked too loudly. This was a very different—and very settled—George.

She noticed, too, that if Jacobs hadn't been introduced as the trail boss, she might never have known of the hierarchy, because everyone seemed to be on an equal plane, knew what they were about without the push and pull of competition. Politics and power had been a common theme in her musical world. Conductors eased out by a new philanthropist who preferred another or the arrival of a younger violinist who challenged the chair held by an aging maestro, pushing them into unwanted retirement. And worst of all, no future for a child prodigy willing to spend her life as the dreaded piano-playing spinster in constant need of a chaperone to make any gains. And certainly, no choice if the prodigy in question wanted both a career and a family.

There was something hopeful about this western way that looked not to people's past or political connections but to what they could bring to the moment. Could they sit a horse through brush? Could they sleep on the cold ground without complaint? Could they find satisfaction where they were without the hours of study and demand taking them to some point in the future?

Still, she wished she was skilled in that other kind of politics, in getting Roosevelt to respond to her concerns.

Paddy, her stable mount, didn't dance or skitter, even to the sounds of riders thumping recalcitrant steers with a rope to their noses to get them into the makeshift corral. But Natalie's musings were interrupted when Paddy darted to head off a steer. Natalie's heart jumped into her throat and her hands gripped the saddle horn by instinct or she'd have been separated from her previously steady seat.

"Good job!" shouted one of the wranglers.

"Give the horse its head," her instructor had told her, and the message had never been better remembered than here. She needed to pay attention. Paddy certainly was.

The plan appeared to be to bring cattle through the cedars and brush toward the arroyo corral, separate new calves to wean from their mamas, and then brand them with a hot iron and clip their ears in a special way that distinguished them as Bar X cattle. George had told her that the ear clips could be more easily seen from a distance than the brand, so the cowboys knew which animals were theirs. The calves bawled a mournful sound with the separations, much more than when the hot iron singed the hair at their hips.

"They don't seem to like being weaned," Natalie said as Mary Jo rode up beside her.

"Forced parting is a trial for them. But they get over it and so do their mamas. Just a fact of ranching life." She sat silent on her horse, then, "We're gathering up stock for branding this trip. When the big herds were driven through here in the nineties—before all the fences—there were thousands of head of cattle. As the cattle drives left our perimeter, we got to ride in and let our horses cut out our steers picked up along the way. It was common courtesy."

"These horses know their stuff today too," Natalie said. "I nearly went left while Paddy went right."

Mary Jo nodded agreement. "You're witnessing something few eastern women ever see: cutting and branding. Who knows how long this legacy will last. It's part of the story of the West, but the West is moving on."

Like the Indians' ways of being, Natalie thought. Indians had lived here long before the Bar X was fenced. Maybe she could make their forced change a little better. At least she was ready to try.

Around the campfire that evening, someone pulled out a harmonica. A grizzly faced poet played a guitar while he sang. Cowboys joined in chorus for raucous songs and tender ones.

George stood then, cleared his throat, and began to recite accompanied by another hand's guitar. The poem reminded Natalie of Irish odes without rhyme but full of pathos, of a former time, of a lost love. *He's never told me about this?* Was it a fiction or was he truly expressing a wound she'd never known about? Chiparopai's questions before healing came to her. She'd have to ask George: When was the last time he sang; when was the last time he danced? Had he just told his story?

∞

After two days, George reported that several of the cowboys would ride on to bring back cattle and would be out for four or five days more. "There's a cabin to bunk in, pretty primitive, so you might not want to come along. Maybe go back to the ranch house and wait for me."

"No. I'll come. If they'll have me. Maybe I can even help."

"Cookie's packed jerky and potatoes for us and carrots for your horse, so meals are light. We'll be herding those cows we find back toward the ranch. He's sending along a vinegar pie."

"Sounds delicious."

The small party of four men, several horses, a dog or two, and Natalie headed out. She'd been given a different mount, one more accustomed to the rough terrain they'd be "breaking brush" in, as the poet cowboy called it. The sorrel gelding had a light mouth, George told her. She wouldn't need to rein him in with much strength. "Give him his head. Let him take you where he wants to go."

"I'm getting used to that," she said.

And thus began one of the fondest memories of her life. They made camps at springs and repaired gates made of logs at arroyo canyons serving as corrals. Cattle and their unmarked calves would be brushed from hidey-holes of brambles that would tear any cloth not covered with leather. Pens with lamb's-quarter springing up for feed held all the cattle—mamas and babies—so there wasn't the bawling of separated calves as there'd been at the branding. One night they did spend at an old log cabin, where Natalie swept out the rat droppings while the men grained the mounts.

The following morning, not feeling well, Natalie stayed behind.

"It's nothing, really," she told George. "My monthlies don't need to become a subject of discussion."

"I'll leave my Colt with you anyway. Just in case someone comes by. And we may be back late, so don't worry. Might not come in till dawn, depending on the circumstances."

"You'll be alright here, ma'am?" The poet cowboy had taken to checking in on Natalie throughout the day.

"I'll be fine, thank you, Henry."

As they rode out, Natalie took a deep breath. She hadn't been alone since her desert ride on Bonita and realized she missed it. She rested, heated a rock on the sheepherder's stove, the only appliance in the cabin, though the structure sported three beds, a table, and four chairs. Wrapping the warm rock in one of her shirts, she placed it on her abdomen to ease the cramps. She lay down outside, looked down the ridge, and fell asleep. And when she awoke, she wrote. Later, she sang. And when the sun set, she fixed a potato and what was left of an onion Cookie had sent with them. She heard the coyotes howl and listened to a song form in her mind. She wrote the notes down in her diary, and in the stillness, aware of how tiny she was in the vastness of this land, she put words to the music in her mind. It was no wonder the cowboy songs spoke of loneliness and distance, of heartache more than hope.

That wasn't going to be her legacy.

Yes, there had been a lost love. It was a childish crush if she was honest with herself. But it had assumed grand proportions and had confused the very future she had so long studied for, worked for, dragged her family through years of practice for. She'd been without a piano and its demanding practice for six years now. The Navajo singing and listening to the Yuma Mockingbird song had been her greatest ventures into music in all that time. She didn't count the composing that had been done more to appease her mother than out of any creative urge. She was always trying to please others. But here, in this quiet cabin, alone, she could hear her own music again.

She sang the Mockingbird song "Arowp," looked back through her notes to get the rhythm right as the Yuma sang it. Would the Hopi songs be similar? Would she even be allowed to hear them, see the smiles in the singer's eyes as she had on Chiparopai's weathered face? The anticipation of what she'd find among the Hopi, how the songs could be preserved so their children might learn them in the quiet, where Anglo agents could not silence them— that was what she wrote about in her diary before she fell into contented, dreamless sleep.

17

What Wisdom, Music

"Again, please." Mary Jo Brigand wiped her tear-filled eyes as Natalie finished the sonata on the Steinway.

"The last one," Natalie said. "It's nearly three in the morning."

"What is time to music?" Mary Jo sighed.

"Rather critical, I'd say. Three-quarter time, half time." The women laughed together. Only the two of them were still awake, Mary Jo's husband and George having already retired. Even the ranch-house cook could be heard snoring in his room behind the big stove that had been brought from Gallup, New Mexico—as had the piano—more than fifty miles away. "I will hate to see you two leave."

"You've been most kind to us," Natalie said.

"We love George. You're both welcome back whenever you wish." She sighed. "They won't have a piano at Third Mesa, not even in the school."

"I imagine not. George has told you where we're headed, to the Hopi village?"

Mary Jo nodded. "One more," she said. Natalie had not played the piano, even in the privacy of her parents' brownstone, since before that fateful night in 1897. But when Mary Jo asked her to play, she had. She chose a lullaby by Chopin, the music flowing from memory, her fingers stiff at first until they remembered what to do.

"I used to play that," Mary Jo had said. "That very one. For Arthur."

Natalie stopped. "I'm sorry, I didn't mean—"

"No, please. Continue. Arthur was comforted by music. I think it lessened the intensity of his fits. Seizures, the doctors called them. They could name them but couldn't tell us how to stop them." Mary Jo looked at her arthritic hands. "He was five when they started, after a fall from one of the horses. I suppose we shouldn't have let him ride, but how can you deprive a child of what he loves?"

"Sometimes the very thing we love can bring us harm."

Mary Jo closed her eyes and leaned back in the big leather chair crinkled with age. "He was seven when he died."

Natalie began playing again and marveled that she would find a sister-pianist in the wilds of Houck. Playing again without an audience reminded her of the pleasure the piano had once given her—before she'd become enslaved to it. Mary Jo had given up her classically trained life, not out of despair and mental collapse as Natalie had, but for love, leaving Chicago with Mr. Brigand to make a life on a cattle ranch. Then, as fate would have it, she had to give up playing at all to the crippling of her hands.

When Natalie finished the last song of the night, Mary Jo said, "That's beautiful. At least my playing was still good when Arthur was with us. I surely do miss the music."

"There are recording machines. In fact"—Natalie perked up—"we have one in the wagon. You'd have to get a player, but George and I could record my playing and leave the cylinder with you. Edison is improving them all the time."

"That would be lovely."

"I don't know why I didn't think of it before. Or you could get a Victrola from Gallup."

"I'd rather have your music. Let's do it now. Wake them up," Mary Jo said.

"No, no. I'm exhausted myself. We'll do it in the morning, I promise."

And so, they had.

The recording process had been good for working out some of the kinks for when Natalie hoped she'd be recording Hopi singers. How far away the machine was from the music; whether the cylinders could pick up smaller sounds like the high notes; would they be able to hear the whistle or a distant flute? She wished she'd talked more with Lummis about the details. They would learn. Assuming they could even stay at a government house in Oraibi.

The Curtis pair spoke their goodbyes to the Brigands, to Henry the cowboy poet, and several others who had graciously accepted Natalie among them. She tied Bonita to the back of the wagon and carried with her now both a .32 and a Colt, not that she expected to use either. Mary Jo hugged her tightly. "You come back, anytime."

"You never know," Natalie said. She was beginning to accept that unexpected things happened in the West. Everywhere, perhaps, but she paid more attention here. Navajos in a courtyard in Pasadena. A grand library in a prison. A Steinway in faraway Arizona Territory.

They made the nearly two-hundred-mile trek in eight days, only one thunderstorm darkening the day. Hail the size of Cookie's biscuits nearly shredded their canvas-covered wagon before the storm roiled and rumbled its way beyond the overhanging rocks they'd hunkered down beneath. Bonita shivered. The mules—Sugar and Spice—remained steady through the deluge. She liked the mules but missed the horses.

Later, they came up behind another wagon. Usually the driver would move over to let whoever was behind them pass. "The code of the road," George called it. He shouted out, but still the wagon didn't pull over. Finally, the road widened so they could come aside, and the mules snorted and pranced and Natalie gasped. "Why, it's a monkey driving it. And George, I do believe that's a bear sitting beside him."

George was having a time managing the mules, who wanted to pull ahead and away from this menagerie that Natalie described, when a man stuck his head over that of the bear's and said, "Howdy. Sorry, I was asleep. My horses keep plodding when these two drive."

Their mules lurched forward as the man shouted, "A traveling show. See you in Gallup?"

"Mimsey will never believe this when I write of it." Natalie pulled out her diary and made notes.

Some Indians they met dropped their eyes and didn't speak as they moved past their wagon. "Zuni, likely," George said. "This is all Indian territory, or what's left for them. We're entering Navajo land now. Hopi villages are surrounded by the Navajo."

They stopped and watered the animals from the wooden barrels they carried in the wagon. Natalie dabbed water on her dust-filled eyes.

"It'll be even hotter here," George said.

They had passed through lands with rocks dressed in rainbow colors, and Natalie tried to imagine growing up with these formations: towers touching the night skies, stone pillars piercing daylight. Vistas of boulders wider than the Hudson. Almost no greenery of any kind except for tiny plants that hugged the desert floor; and yet there was astonishing beauty. She wondered how the snakes and lizards survived.

In the distance she saw what George said must be Third Mesa, one of three flat-topped land formations that rose like giant cakes in the beige batter of the desert. "We'll find Oraibi there."

∽

Charlie Lummis's letter accompanying the crates of cylinders had detailed more of the accusations of the Oraibi teacher who had described the aggressive nature of the Indian superintendent, Charles Burton, and his push to assimilate the Indians as the "law requires." Natalie summarized the script to George, noting Burton's greatest sins, as their mules pulled the wagon forward. "It's the insistence on haircutting and forbidden face paint he claims causes so much blindness among the 'primitives' that Burton says has to be stopped." Natalie broke from the narrative to say, "That's a horrible term to use for a people, don't you think? Primitives?"

George nodded agreement. "And the violence is abhorrent. Especially when the Hopi people call themselves 'Little People of Peace.' Seems excessively harmful to treat them so brutally."

"We'll have to see for ourselves, of course. But apparently the teacher thinks Burton is a zealot, mocking children while he cuts their hair in public, while haranguing the parents for not keeping their children safe. Apparently not keeping them safe from people like himself." *How awful for the parents, how powerless they must feel.* "And here's the part where it says the army invaded in January and force-marched children barefoot through the snow, insisting they attend school. One hundred four children, George." *How can the army be used this way?* "I wonder if Roosevelt is aware of this. How could he possibly condone it?" She made plans right then to send yet another letter to him. Maybe she'd enlist her mother to make an appointment to see the president. She'd head back home for that summons if not for her mother's. "Between personal assaults like how people wear their hair and the offensive against their music and their culture, Burton is on the road to eliminating anything of this tribal culture."

Natalie laid the letter on her lap. "Didn't I see a pamphlet put out by the Santa Fe railroad offering a special fare for people wanting to come to see the Hopi Snake Dance? Yes, I'm sure I did. When

I was rummaging through the material at the library. That's one of the dances that's prohibited by the Code. How does that get allowed? Because a business promotes it and tourists like us show up to see it? These people of peace are being squeezed not only by the government but by people like us, George, coming to gawk. They'll be suspicious of us. Why wouldn't they be?"

"We're doing it for a good cause, Nat. To get information that might influence the government to change its ways."

Natalie had been grateful for George's full commitment to Lummis's request that they spy.

"What I don't understand," Natalie said, "is how the Hopi are punished for practicing their religious customs, and those same songs and dances are advertised to bring people to see them. Burton approves because the railroad wants the business? Those poor people. It's racial suicide."

"Lummis says that?" George asked.

"Not the 'racial suicide' part. That's my term. Allowing others to see what had been sacred dances to 'please' the government while not being allowed to perform them in their own villages— isn't that a way of killing off who you are?"

She wanted to discover more about another culture, descendants of ancient peoples, but people like her and George were the foreigners, invaders once again, weren't they? She hoped to record their songs for them but also because their music was returning Natalie to her own love of music. But at what cost to the "Little People of Peace"?

Lummis had suggested they try to engage the village chief of Old Oraibi, Lololomai, who had gone to Washington, DC, as a young leader in the eighties and upon his return had encouraged the white man's schools. But there was also an opposing faction known as the "Hostiles." Lololomai's group was the "Friendlies." The divisions had grown so wide that a second kiva had been dug, against all Hopi tradition, and Lololomai had even been imprisoned within one by the opposition, freed only by the army.

She hoped the teacher exaggerated. "But Charles says if he is still in power of the 'Friendlies' and we win Lololomai over, he may let us record or at least hear the songs that Burton and the Code forbid."

"What did Lummis say about Burton's movements? Is he there all the time?"

Natalie scanned the several-page letter. "He travels between the mesas, spends days at the fort, where the teacher says he forces Hopi prisoners, those who fail to send their children to school, to tend to the officers' gardens. Burton pretty much has control of Oraibi, and Old Oraibi too." She folded the letter, put it back in her pack. "I think we should bypass the village and go first to Fort Defiance, see if we can win him over on his own turf."

"It's a hundred miles out of our way."

"What's another hundred miles," Natalie said. "The scenery is spectacular." It would mean more nights out under the stars. She smiled at the thought.

"Looks like we have our work cut out for us," George said as he chirped at Sugar and Spice to "move on."

18

The Land of Pretty Soon

*N*atalie spied the officers' gardens, a splash of green in the
desert. Even the saddle blankets on the soldiers' horses
carried the burnt red of the surrounding rocks. A ten-foot adobe
brick wall lined one side of the fort, while it looked like the beginnings of a log stockade formed another. Mostly, the adobe
buildings sat around a rectangular field on a flat plain shadowed
by bare, red-earthed hills. "You'd think since the fort's been here
for fifty years, they'd have a few trees planted," Natalie said.

"Water is scarce. And the fort hasn't been kept consistently. If I
remember right," George said, "there were fights with the Navajo
over the prime grazing land. It was abandoned for a time, brought
back after the Civil War. Now it's more the Indian agency than a
government fort, though they keep soldiers here."

"To harass little children in the middle of the night," Natalie said.

As they came closer, Natalie did notice new tree plantings as
well as a chapel on the far side of the fort. And horses grazed on
a green meadow. They pulled the wagon forward, stopping before
an adobe building with a covered porch and flying a weather-faded

141

flag. It looked to be the most prominent structure, and it turned out to be the fort commander's office. Burton, fortuitously, was there and walked out onto the shaded veranda to greet them.

George introduced them and they were invited into the cooler commander's office while Indian workers took their animals to water, Bonita braying as Natalie moved out of her sight.

"Fine set of mules," Burton said. "Hard to come by here. Interested in selling?"

"Maybe later," George said. "Sugar and Spice are good company for my sister and me. Maybe, when we take the train at Gallup back to New York, if my sister gets well, maybe then we'll sell the mules and wagon to you. You have to take the burro too, though," George said.

"They're a dime a dozen," Burton said. He was a tall man with a black beard that looked like it needed a trim. Dark, darting eyes.

"You're in the area to get well?" The commander spoke for the first time, a man in his early thirties, Natalie guessed.

"Look pretty healthy to me, Miss Curtis." Burton was the one in charge.

"I am much improved. My brother works for the Bar X and my time there was quite restorative. But the air at Oraibi has been touted as being healing."

"You're early for the Snake Dance that brings all the tourists." Burton squinted, the wrinkles at his eyes suggesting he squinted often.

"We don't think of ourselves as tourists," George said. "I'm writing a book. Natalie here is recovering. We'd like to rent one of the government cabins at Oraibi, if that's possible."

"The government is always looking for ways to make a little money," the commander said. Burton frowned at him.

Burton said, "It's good you came here to secure that arrangement and didn't simply arrive there."

A bell clanged and Natalie looked out the window to see children pouring from what must be a school.

"Is that the boarding school the missionaries run?" Natalie asked.

"No, miss," Burton said. "This is a government school. Serves Navajo. We have to keep the Navajo separated from the Hopi. There's bad blood between them, has been for years. And now the Hopi argue among themselves." He grinned, then picked up a pipe from the table they all sat around, chewed on the stem. An Indian boy served them a tepid drink that tasted of something fresh.

"Is this mint?" Natalie was surprised at the familiar taste.

"Found near the spring. Only at five thousand feet or above," the commander said. "Good to wrap fresh food in. Lamb especially. I find—"

Burton interrupted, launching from discussions of food to fights. He described the "feud," he called it, between "Hostiles" and "Friendlies" with Spider Clans arguing with Bear Clans. "I can hardly keep them straight, so many clans and whatnot." He went on to tell them of missionary conversions and how those had added to the divisions. "They even have a derogatory term for those who have become Christians," Burton said. "It means 'not Hopi.' I'm told it's an unusual concept for them to apply to one of their own, that they are no longer of the clan they were born into because they were born into the Christian clan." He appeared gleeful in the telling, reveled in the disputes, in the tearing of the fabric of a community.

Neither George nor Natalie gave any indication that they knew anything of the People of Peace's factions. Only their awareness of the railroad's tourist draw for the Snake Dance and the healing air of Oraibi did they offer to Burton and the commander's conversation.

"We appreciate your allowing us to stay at Oraibi," Natalie said when Burton took a pause. "And we should be making our way there."

"At the foot of the mesa, not the old village on top," Burton said. He spoke to George, as though it was he who had made the statement. "I'd advise you to stay away from the old place. Friendlies and Hostiles are there. You never know when a fight might break out."

"But generally, the Hopi people are peaceful," Natalie said.

"There are resistant people there, not interested in assimilation, which is the best course for them as well as the law of the land. How long are you hoping to stay?"

"Until I'm well," Natalie said.

"A convalescing woman is better than those university people coming out to look at ruins and pick up shards to study. They agitate the Indians, make them think their history is important, while we're trying to wipe it away, encourage them to become good American citizens. You're not planning any of that, are you?"

"Picking up broken pottery? No. Nothing like that."

"Good. Well then, I'd guess you can stay in the third cabin. Older than the others, but it's adobe so not as hot as the tin-roof ones. And you're welcome to fill your water barrels at our spring here. Southwestern hospitality. We Anglos have to stick together." Burton smiled for the very first time.

The young commander lifted his glass of mint as though to make a toast.

∞

As Natalie and George headed southwest, the mesas rose, islands of rock seen through wavy heat. Natalie heard the distant bell before she saw the flock of sheep making its way toward a steep trail leading to the Third Mesa. They had passed by the other two to reach the northernmost butte. As they drove closer, the cornfields spread green around the base, and there they could see houses, some with tin roofs that shimmered in the afternoon heat, and above, villages with stone and adobe two-story homes. A contingent of children greeted them, surrounding the wagon, chattering, and Natalie wore her biggest smile, hoping that universal gesture would bridge the language gap. Their wagon rattled along a dirt path, and George pulled up Sugar and Spice before a building with the number 3 painted in black on its adobe side.

"We're home," George said. He stepped off the wagon and was immediately consumed by children dressed in worn cotton shirts and loose pants. The boys' hair had been cut, with straight bangs across the forehead, cropped above the neckline. "The barbers have been busy," he told Natalie while handing one of the boys a pack as the child eagerly held out his hands to help. George carried another pack, and the two headed toward adobe Number 3.

Natalie dug into her pack and gave out hard candies, something Lummis had told her the children liked. They smiled with white teeth, and she hoped she wasn't ruining them with the sugar. Several children reached to touch her wisps of yellow hair poking out from beneath her hat. A hot wind swirled around them as more warm bodies clustered closer, talking. George towered over them as he eased his way back toward the wagon, hands held high, a grin on his face. Natalie was barely a head taller than most of the children. *Little People of Peace.*

"Give lady room," someone spoke in English. "Give her place."

A girl, Natalie's height, elbowed her way forward. She might have been ten years old, no older. "Burton says you OK to be here? OK, yes?"

"Someone from the East must have taught English here," Natalie said to George. "I haven't heard 'OK' since New York." She realized she was doing what she hated men doing—talking about her rather than to her. "I'm Natalie Curtis. What's your name?"

"Mina. I help you to 3." The girl wore her hair above each ear in whirls that glistened in the afternoon light. They looked like little mounds of shiny black bread loaves.

"Yes, thank you." Natalie wondered what faction Mina belonged to and then decided she wouldn't let it matter. The girl had offered her help, and she would accept it regardless of whether it was the "right" group Burton had said to align with. She hoped to befriend them as one people until individually they defined themselves, just the way she hoped they'd treat her.

As the candy disappeared, so did the children, except for a couple of stalwarts—Mina included—who continued to help them unload, then watched with curiosity as Natalie unpacked boxes and bags. "My auntie, she looks after me, good."

"That's wonderful."

"I come help you."

"Whenever you can."

"Leave now." And with that she was off, the straight part that was white as cottonwood blossoms, dividing her hair. Natalie was already smitten by the girl's enthusiasm.

With a corn-husk broom she found leaning against the adobe, Natalie swept out the cabin that had two rooms, one with two single beds, the other with a fireplace and andirons holding a large black pot. She had never cooked over an open fire. George had, though, and he helped stack the food boxes. They had resupplied at the trader's post at Keams Canyon on the way back from Fort Defiance, bringing flour and salt and jerky with them. Cornmeal they hoped to acquire from the Hopi people.

"It's not much of an abode," George said, looking around. "Cool though."

"Better than the line cabin I stayed in all night alone. This one has windowpanes."

"I am sorry we didn't make it back that night."

"Don't be. I liked being on my own. And I'll like being alone here too if you want to return to the Bar X." George did not reply. "Mina will show me the well so we can draw from it. And we can turn Bonita out with their burros, she tells me."

"The girl is out hobbling the mules, getting them used to being here, she says. Tomorrow we'll put them in with the horses." George ran his hand through his hair. "I'll figure out something for us to eat."

"Isn't it a marvel that we meet up with these English-speaking people just when we need them?"

"Like a gift," George said. "Listen, Natalie. About the Bar X. I've no plans to leave you alone like I did in Yuma."

"I did fine there and I'll do fine here. I can spy for Lummis about the conditions. But I really am here to appreciate their lives, to learn about Hopi ways as I did in Yuma. I want to hear their music, and to do that I need to build their trust. That'll be a task whether you're with me or not. Work on your book but don't stay for my sake. I know the Bar X wants you back whenever you can make it. Or maybe there's some new adventure you're leaning toward."

"This one with my sister was the plan. And there's the Acoma Sky City you wanted to visit. You haven't given up on that, have you?"

"That's true." She did want to visit that pueblo with George. And she liked his company. "Stay, then," she said. "And we'll let the land of poco tiempo set our pace both together and alone."

19

To Sing and Dance with the Grandmothers

*N*atalie heard the song when she stood at the base of one of the ladders leading up to the top of the mesa and Old Oraibi. She had risen with the sun, something she did these days, not wanting to waste a moment. It was also the coolest part of the day, and she had sat outside on a bench leaning against the warm adobe, savoring her daily cup of coffee, watching the colors change in the vastness before her. From this vantage point, she could hear the sounds of the sheep being brought down the steep paths, taken out for the day to grazing plots where springs seeped into soil, turning the desert into patches of green. She had offered to help at the school, but she'd been rejected. So, she did what she could to comfort crying babies while their mothers cooked or took mortar and pestle and ground corn or did what work anyone might let her do. Helping was the best way to come to know a people, she decided. She was learning, too, that accepting help was a gift given, not only a burden shared.

George slept in. He was a night owl, writing by candlelight at the foyer table in a room that served as kitchen, living, and dining room. He'd set aside his writing, pour water into the washbasin, splash, and dry, then make his way quietly onto the spring mattress, sounds that most nights Natalie slept through.

This morning, her coffee finished and the day beckoning, she had put her cup back into the boxes they used as cabinets and started up the ladder when no one was around. It wasn't her first trip to the older village, but it was the first time she was going alone. She and George had met a gentle Mennonite pastor who served those Hopi following the Christian way. He waved at her now as he dug in a garden plot. His expression of faith encouraged Natalie, who hoped things had changed at the school since the teacher had complained. But she and George remained quiet about their interest in interfering with the "Americanization" of Indian people by wanting to preserve rather than eliminate their cultures.

She quickened her pace up the ocotillo ladder, knowing that this one would take her not to someone's home but to the courtyard above. *How many feet have stepped on these rungs? And now mine.* The song grew louder, a woman's voice. The notes entered Natalie's consciousness the way Wagner's music penetrated her mind, her soul. She could almost see the notes on a sheet of music, the way her seeing birds on a branch reminded her of a music score. And she could hear the sounds inside her mind. She hadn't yet allowed herself to make the request of these private, quiet, peaceful people that they let her record their private songs. She had written in her diary that capturing the music was like a painter hoping to preserve the shimmer of the desert: impossible, but many would try. Songs rose up as they ground corn, as they bathed their babies, as they formed pots of clay. There seemed to be some signal telling the Hopi that Burton wasn't nearby or that the new teachers weren't around to hear them. Initially, they would stop their voices when they saw Natalie or George, but Mina's auntie must have assured them that these Anglos were "safe." Men sang as they wove. Children sang bringing the sheep down the rocky crags. The music wasn't meant only for ceremony, or perhaps they saw ceremony in everyday life? *Is it sacred music, not unlike the monks who sing in Ireland, or like those who chant in the stone monasteries outside Barcelona?*

As she topped the ladder and could see the singer, she eased closer and made out the repeated word *puva, puva*—sleep, sleep. Mina had told her the word when she pointed to Natalie's and George's beds the day she helped them move in. It was Natalie's first Hopi word she'd learned.

In this morning sunlight, a young mother had a baby on her back, and she swayed gently, rocking the infant whose soft cries Natalie had heard. She wondered if the baby had kept his mother awake in the night and at sunrise had found his rhythm as she shuffled around the center courtyard, surrounded by homes so old they had likely heard this lullaby a thousand times. The stone houses had been here long before the Spanish ever came to other pueblos, long before the raids. Perhaps they'd been carved by desert winds before the People imagined a village into being.

She observed the items on the baby board—shells and turquoise stones, a silver ring—hung to entertain the child as the breeze whispered across them. The baby stared at her, quiet now, the mother still unaware of Natalie's presence.

Natalie backed away. She would find this mother and this child again, when it was not so private an occasion, when she didn't feel like an intruder.

∽∾

"They aren't getting near enough to eat," Natalie told George over their evening meal of corn mush and fresh mutton that one of the women had brought them. Natalie had visited the school and spoken briefly with the cook, who answered in one-word sentences. "All the staff is wary of me. That teacher's report has apparently gotten back to people here, along with Gates's concerns. The current teachers and cook want no interference from the outside. Or at least they don't want to bring down the wrath of Burton on them by letting me volunteer there."

"How much flour do they get?"

"Less than a pound a week per child. I saw the biscuits. Not even a starved Bonita would have eaten it. And the uniforms. Wasn't the army to supply them with decent clothing and shoes since they have forbidden them to wear moccasins because it isn't 'white' enough?" She heard her voice rise. "When they drove them last February from their homes, making the children march down the mountain in the dark, they were barefoot! In the snow, for heaven's sake. No, not for heaven's sake at all. For Burton's show of power. He apparently had a wagon but didn't let anyone ride in it but him."

"We probably have enough information to affirm Lummis's request to start an investigation of him." George crushed mint leaves into the water glass and drank. "And I've been thinking, Nat. I should go back to the Bar X and earn some money."

Natalie tensed. Her few published articles didn't give them much income, and she didn't know when Mimsey and Bogey might cut off her traveling funds, especially since she'd refused to come home. She was hardly being an independent woman still supported by others.

"Just this morning I heard the most beautiful tune," she said, changing the subject.

George stood at the dishwashing tub, but he turned to listen to her, hands dripping wet.

"I've begun writing it down. Look."

George dried his hands, peered at her notebook, which the trader Keams had ordered in for her at her request. "You are amazing, you know. You hear in the particular while the rest of us listen in the general."

"But that's why I'm here. I fear these songs will be lost, George.

And that would be criminal, more of a crime than them singing their songs in violation of the Code. And certainly, less criminal than the agency depriving them of food when they resist. I wonder if there isn't something we can do to supplement their food."

"Dostoyevsky wrote that in a time of despair, 'Beauty is more important than bread,'" George said. "Maybe saving their beautiful songs is what matters most."

∽

The children had started showing up after school, looking through the window to see if Natalie or George were there, long after all the hard candy was gone and there was nothing to gift them in return for their presence, nothing but Natalie and George themselves. Sometimes Natalie got out a cylinder and played an old recording of Handel's *Israel in Egypt* where sounds like swishing water held the children in rapt attention. The scratches were louder than the orchestral sounds. But the music could still be heard, and the children had stared at the machine, reverent. Mina had come up closest, bent to the player, then tried to pick it up to look underneath.

"It's a . . . memory living inside the machine," Natalie explained. "The musicians aren't here. They are somewhere else and we are hearing them in this time. On this cylinder." Natalie had stopped cranking the handle and let Mina's fingers touch the tiny pricks of metal that held the sounds. Natalie didn't really understand the science of it either, but she accepted the presence of the music as a kind of miracle that didn't need explaining. Mina grinned.

On another occasion, she sang into the recording and let the children hear it played back. There had been "oohs" and "hayehs" followed by a willingness to let themselves be recorded and heard. She didn't ask them to sing or even to speak their own language, but they were exuberant and did it anyway. Hearing their own voice say something in English, hearing their song voices, had the effect Natalie hoped for: they were eager to discover new things.

She took the Edison outside and had children around her while she recorded the burro's bray or the tinkling of the bells when the sheep moved past Number 3 up toward the mesa top. The other rule she broke was getting Mina to teach her the meaning of the Hopi words she heard and recorded while the children laughed at her pronunciations. *Puva*, sleep. *Katzínas*, intermediaries bringing Hopi prayers to the deities. *Tawakwaptiwa*, Sun-Down-Shining. "Also, the name of son of chief's brother," Mina said.

"His nephew."

Mina nodded. "I bring him. He will like to come."

Mina's smile could light the night, and when she flashed it, showing her white teeth, or when she let Natalie put her arm around her as they walked to feed Bonita, she thought one day she might like having a child. Maybe many. This day, she felt like the Pied Piper of Hamelin, though she hoped she led the children toward something good.

∞

Natalie ran the pitcher of cool water over her head and used an aloe gel for a shampoo. The pitcher and bowl sat outside on a crude table while birds chirped as she scrubbed the dust away.

"I'm packed up and ready to go." George sat behind her on a small chair, his long legs crossed at the ankles.

"What? Wait until I'm finished." She towel-dried her hair.

"I've been thinking. If you're preserving Indian music as a kind of ethnographic study, you might interest a benefactor who shares those views."

"A rich old man, you mean?"

"Or woman. Maybe Alice, the painter you met at El Alisal."

She was thoughtful, rubbed the towel at the tips of her hair. "She's a friend. I couldn't ask a friend to invest."

"Maybe Lummis, then. What about that Frank Mead you met, the one working with the Apaches?"

"Yavapai," Natalie corrected. She hoped George wouldn't notice her skipping over Frank's name. "Rufus and Charlotte, maybe," she considered. "They've long been involved in the justice issues and the arts." She sighed. "But without Roosevelt's consent, I can't see anyone supporting work that is illegal. I suppose right now I'm indulging myself, nothing more. You go ahead and go," she said. "My staying here might reassure Burton that I really am here for my health. And maybe my presence will temper his retaliation when he learns of the sounds we hear at night from the kivas. I think they continue with their ceremonies, but they do it after dark when the school staff can't hear them so can't report the activities." She let the heat finish drying her hair, her fingers lifting the wispy strands she'd twist into a bun. "They aren't even allowed to sing in school." Natalie remembered being a featured soloist with the National Conservatory Chorus and what singing had once given to her young life. Removing it by force would have been immoral, surely. "It's as though the gift of voice is to be obliterated, not just the songs. They would make them mutes."

"It would be a huge loss."

"The thing is," Natalie said, "this is happening to all the tribal peoples, not only the Yuma and the Hopi. And as Frank told me, the Yavapai are in worse shape because they're homeless too. I'll bet the Navajo aren't allowed to sing either, except as entertainment for people like us." Shame formed in her stomach for how *she'd* treated them at El Alisal. She had offered to trade her own song—poor choice that it was. But really, there was no hope of the laws changing without congressional action.

"Look," George said. He pulled up the chair and sat with his arms resting on the back. "I'll head to the Bar X and earn some money. You write up what we've found and send it to Charles. If I need to contact you, I'll reach you through Keams Trading Post

154

for pickup," he said. "That way we won't have to worry about Burton intercepting letters, in case he does."

"Oh, he wouldn't do anything illegal like putter with the federal mail system. The horror is that what he is doing to torment the families is perfectly legal. That's what has to stop. And since I can't get Roosevelt's attention, I'll do the next best thing and break the law for a reason. No different than the Bostonians and their tea party."

"A little different," George said, but he smiled.

"I'll preserve important aspects of their way of life myself. When it is legal again, or if it never is, they'll still be able to sing and dance with their grandmothers clandestinely." She lifted her finger as if to make a pronouncement. "I'll put them into a book."

A book. She had a plan. The old Natalie had always felt better with a purpose. That it was formed from brokenness had the hope to make it stronger.

20

The Price of Asking

*N*atalie knew she walked across a rushing stream, hoping she could keep her balance on slick stepping-stones, taking her to places she had never imagined she'd go. Mina led the way.

Lummis had asked them to speak with Lololomai, a Hopi leader and a "Friendly." She thought of Lummis's description of how the government defined a "good Hopi." *They send their children to school; non-Indian visitors are welcomed; Hopi would discard their music, their dances, their language, and pay no attention to tribal medicine men; and finally, enforce the practices of cutting long hair.* The latter carried humiliation as deep as the Grand Canyon, because long hair inspired the rains to fall, rains so desperately needed to water the corn and the meadows where the sheep and horses grazed. Every time a Hopi male had his hair chopped off, it was saying to the world that rain did not matter when it so profoundly did. They lived with the constant shame.

"He will have you come," Mina told her one morning two weeks after George had gone. "The blind boy will lead you."

The school was not in session that day, so Natalie wondered why Mina didn't take her, but she did not question the opportunity. Natalie wore her own uniform of khaki, and she'd donned moccasins she found quite comfortable as her feet had hardened traversing the shards of rock that served as a trail. And she took her notebook, tucked into the large pocket of the skirt.

Blind the boy might be, but he was also sure-footed as they moved up through the narrowing rocks that faded to pink and even green against the red-tinted beige. Atop the mesa the old village buildings belied their ancient history, looking sturdier than the tin-roofed houses the government had built down below. Ladders led past windows to the roofs, and stone staircases rose up to the second stories. At the old village, Natalie turned three-hundred-sixty degrees, feeling the warm wind as she surveyed the stunning, wide vistas. Some would say the land was empty, barren, desolate, and bleak. But she saw boundlessness, and that was how she felt about her life at that moment: anything could happen in this land of poco tiempo.

Lololomai, the man considered the chief of Old Oraibi, sat at his spinning wheel, wool threads held taut in his wrinkled hands. "The boy says you wish to speak," the blind boy translated.

"Yes. Thank you. I . . . I know you visited the white chief's home in Washington."

"Keams the trader takes us there, where there were many clouds and the sun looked like the moon." He wore his hair shortened—chopped crudely—to just above his shoulders. He had a wide nose, prominent in his lined, beardless face, and he mixed English words with Hopi.

"Yes, I suppose the sun does."

He motioned her to sit beside him on the stone roof. The warmth penetrated her thighs, her feet.

Lololomai didn't spin, gave his full attention to her. She had noticed that about the Hopi and the Yuma and the Navajo. They concentrated when someone spoke to them, perhaps deciphering

the language barrier, but maybe because they listened to understand rather than to respond.

"I've come to speak with you about something that concerns
your people here."

"*Ancha-a.*"

'Tis well. She knew that word now. "I want to talk with you
about the children who go to school. They are singing songs there
but not Hopi songs. Some of the children are so young, not past
three corn plantings. I fear they will not know the Hopi songs of
the butterflies and the bean blossoms or the corn song."

"*Ĥao, ĥao,*" which Natalie knew meant "even so, even so" and
that she was to continue.

"But a good thing in the school is books. Books can be Hopi
or English, and then the children can read the Hopi words. But
now you have no written Hopi language to put into books, so it
may pass away like the songs."

"*Ĥao, ĥao.*"

"But if you were to read and write, you could put your song
into a book, Lololomai's Song. And your children's children would
know it was of you even after you are gone."

A look of haunting came across his wide brow. Natalie wished
she could take away the sadness.

"But until that time comes, I would be willing to record your
songs and keep them from disappearing like a wind-blown trail.
I would keep them until you were able to write the songs yourself.
Or your children's children can."

He lifted his eyes to her. "The superintendent will not permit
this. Your people have made a law against such things. There will
be trouble. I have already been to prison for trouble."

"I will seek permission from the white father so that the Hopi
songs will not be lost. If I do this, will you give your consent?"

"Burton would agree?"

"I want no trouble for you. I will seek agreement." Whether
she'd get it was another question.

158

"Why do white men wish to stop our dances? This is what I do not know. Why are there such laws to keep the songs from our hearts?"

"White people . . . we don't understand what the songs and dances mean to you. We are a brutish people sometimes and see only what we wish to see. Most of us don't know even one word of Hopi, let alone the words that mend your hearts, pray for corn to grow. We don't know how wise your people are who have kept the stories since before memory. But I will write them down and give them to you and you will keep them as you do other trusted, precious things."

"*Pas lololomai.*"

The interpreting boy told her *pas lololomai* meant "very good." "Yes, it is very good." *His very name contains goodness.* She sat in the quiet and then that bold spirit rose, asking him to be complicit, not waiting for word from Roosevelt or anyone else who could open the door to what she hoped for. "While we are alone here, would you sing a song that I could write down? One of your own making."

He lifted an eyebrow. Perhaps he was wary of this white woman's suggestion that he break the law. Or maybe she offered him a way to protest the betrayal that had affected his life. Whatever the reason, he at last said, "I sing many songs for different plantings, then let them go and start new ones. Those others are forgotten."

"With books and with my recorder, you could keep those songs."

He beckoned Natalie and the blind boy to come to another sunny corner, farther from the lower village. He laid a blanket down and they both sat. She didn't know his answer. Perhaps singing for her was a way to redeem the lost ways of his people since he had invited schools and white ways to the People of Peace where now factions fought each other, so far from quiet Hopi ways. "I will sing my last song. It is a prayer that the corn will grow. I sang it in the kiva." He nodded to her as she brought out her notepad. "Ĥao, ĥao."

And then he began.

The hot sun put a glare on the paper as Natalie worked to make the marks to define the chant, the monotone as steady as a rushing stream or the whisk of wind through trees. Soothing. Enchanting. Never-ending. And then it did.

"I have sung the song." He motioned toward her notebook. "Why does it take you so long to make the marks of it on your paper?"

"You know that when the Hopi sets a trap for the blackbird, that he might wait a long time for the bird to be captured. Your song is like that for me. It is a wild blackbird and the sun may move far across the sky before I capture it." She shared her markings and he nodded his head, repeating "Very good, very good" in Hopi. She repeated the sounds as best she could. He nodded. "It is a beginning." Lololomai rose and walked toward the setting sun, dropped to his knees, and stayed there. She didn't know if he prayed or if he mourned or even if he was concerned about his having broken the law for this intense white woman.

"I should go," she told the blind boy when it was apparent Lololomai would not be coming back to her. She stood and they began the descent, Natalie following close behind. As she placed her feet upon each rung, the song in her own heart grew. This was what she was called to do, to save these songs and more, to give these good people hope that their way of life would not be lost to distant winds. A small step. She had to get Roosevelt to understand. She had to.

❧

"What is this I hear?" Burton barged into Number 3. "The children have been singing songs for you? Hopi songs?"

Natalie's heart beat faster, her palms grew wet. She kept her voice calm, speaking with confidence as she used to with overbearing orchestral conductors. "Children naturally sing. It's nothing mutinous."

"There is a law, Miss Curtis. They break it when they sing. Are you encouraging them?"

"Do I tell them to not violate the codes? No, I don't. It isn't my job to enforce such despicable laws. And you can hardly do so unless you hear the songs yourself. Have you?" Before he could respond she continued, "Of course you haven't. It's a rumor. They're the voices of angels, those children. They sing of everyday things. Beetles and corn and water. In English." It was a half-truth. They sang in their language too. "What is insidious about that? What in such songs keeps them from assimilating into the white man's ways? Would you force the Appalachia people to give up their fiddles to become more 'American' or the Norwegian immigrants of Michigan to give up their rosemaling artistry? You wouldn't."

"Don't press me, Miss Curtis. I can have you removed."

"For what? Disagreeing with you?"

"For inciting lawlessness." His lip curled up and his eyes glared like a mad dog before an attack.

"Among children. Truly, you would do that? I would make a fuss, I can assure you. I write for magazines. My uncle went to school with the president of the United States." No need to mention that her uncle was dead.

He clamped his jaw shut. Then, "What are those?" Burton pointed toward the cylinders.

"Music," she said. "Let me play one for you. If you have the time, of course." Her hands shook as she chose *Israel in Egypt*. "I have played it for the children. There's no law against that." She hoped he wouldn't ask her to play any of the other cylinders, for they were filled with those beetle, butterfly, and corn songs she'd recorded. Evidence of them violating the Code.

He listened. Then, "I won't expel you. But there must be consequences for what you've done. I will cut all the children's rations and say it is because they shared their songs with the white woman. So they'll know who to blame for their empty bellies."

"No, please. Don't do that."

"For a week. No bread. We'll see how they like spending time with you then. Oh yes, I know they've come here. They've sung for you. I have my spies."

"But they barely get enough to eat now."

"You should have thought of that. You do-gooders." Spittle caught on the side of his mouth. He wiped it with his wrist and bent as he stomped out the door.

Natalie sank into her chair. He was right, she should have known. She had hoped expulsion of *her* would be the worst, or maybe withholding of cooking fuel. But flour? She had to do something. It was one thing for her to suffer, but so wrong that they should.

She paced, waited for the children to come after school. They didn't. An idea came instead, one she put into place in the morning.

George had taken the mules, one to ride and one to pack. All she had was Bonita. She packed light, threw saddlebags over the little burro's neck, and led him down the trail, then climbed on bareback. "We will do this, Bonita."

Before long, she was leading the burro and trying to find pleasure in this unplanned-for journey. Cacti stood like sentinels guarding the rock formations. Stillness, Natalie decided, had its own music. She tried singing one of the Corn Grinding songs. The burro brayed her review. It wasn't a good one.

She arrived at Keams Trading Post midday, made her purchases, then lingered, looking at a silver ring with turquoise stones. Like the Acoma seed pot, it felt good in the palm of her hand, warm on her finger. It fit perfectly. As small as she was, she had long fingers and wide palms, perfect for a pianist. She had never worn a ring before.

"It's very fine workmanship," the trader said. "The number seven is important to the Zuni."

"Is it?"

"Spiritual. Biblical too," the trader said. "It means perfection,

162

completion. And remember how many times we are asked to forgive someone? Seven times seventy. It's a healing number, seven is."

She needed forgiveness for violating the law, getting the Hopi into trouble.

She slipped it onto her right hand and told the burro when she lifted the reins, "It's very light." Yet on the thirty-mile journey back, spending a night out under the waning moon, the ring felt heavy. Had she bought a belonging, a treasured item someone was forced to sell? She remembered George had told her that some items were not belongings, carrying ancient stories. They were products made for sale, so the artist could buy tools and flour from the trader. When she purchased those products, they contributed to the only economy left as Indians were driven onto reservations. But it was a forced economy, nonetheless, dependent on honest traders to pay fair prices and to charge fair prices too. Natalie's purchase was a part of the trading system that in this age kept the People alive. She treasured her ring in that light as back at Number 3, she baked bread. Then with the yeast scent permeating the air, she began the task of delivering—the loaves taken from her hands as though they were gold.

∽

Days later, Natalie made her way in the late afternoon to Lololomai's home. She took in a deep breath and inhaled the vista, memorizing as she could the weeping colors, the warmth of yellow sands dotted with pale green shrubs she didn't know the names of but that spoke "sturdiness" to her, as so much of this landscape did. They walked through the plaza to Lololomai's and she followed Mina, who talked nonstop as they climbed the ladder. *Mina keeps a happy spirit despite her sufferings.* Natalie's own self-inflicted miseries those years past paled before the sorrows imposed by the government, her government, here.

Lololomai sat in a patch of shade on the roof of the first-floor structure that served as the porch for the second-floor adobe house. A sheep's bell tinkled in the background.

"I have returned," Natalie said.

"Ĥao, ĥao." The old man nodded, put out his hand for Natalie to touch. He held her fingers within his, soft. His rheumy eyes made their way to look upon her.

"Yes, even so," Natalie said. "One day, the Hopi children will have learned to read and write and record songs."

"When doing so will not cause empty bellies."

"It's my prayer," she said, guilt washing over her, "that the Code will be broken and Hopi children will sing freely." She had stopped the children from singing for her. But she had come hoping to hear him sing, so she could get the particulars of the rhythm correct. But she would not ask him. Mina sat in the quiet.

After a time, he spoke to Mina, and she translated. "He will sing a song as a thank-offering for when we gathered the corn this year. It is a song of the men of his kiva, praying that the corn will grow tall. He says you may make the scratches."

Natalie concentrated on the black notes on her sun-drenched paper as she listened to the musical soft prayer, not loud enough to be heard beyond the rooftop, the plaza, the mesa. She brushed away tears as she continued to make notations, even after he stopped.

The elder pulled his blanket around his shoulders, walked to the edge of the roof, then knelt and began another chant. Natalie hoped he was giving his blessing to the undertaking that he was a part of. The evening glow took over the rooftop and the village below as the chant concluded. She hoped it wasn't the last song of his she'd hear. She took Mina's hand, and they walked in waning light back home, the notes still ringing in Natalie's ear.

21

Andante—Slowing to Walk

Mother has ordered us home," read George's letter. *"I will come to get you. Rufus Mason has died and Mimsey has promised you will sing at his funeral. It will be good to see you again. I will be there by the 15th. They are holding back the service until we arrive. Your loving brother, George."*

Lololomai's nephew had been at the post and brought her the letter she read in the morning sun outside Number 3. Disappointment drifted with the coffee aroma. She was sad about Rufus Mason's death, but she didn't want to leave. She was making good progress with Lololomai's song. And several Oraibi people still came to Number 3, peeked in the window, then entered when Natalie motioned them forward. But she no longer had them sing for her. She played the cylinder music. She kept busy with her notes and listening to the recordings she had already made, knowing her work was but a drop in the ocean of need. And her mother's summons annoyed. All would be interrupted to go back east when ordered, because that was what a good daughter did. "Ĥao, ĥao,

Even so, even so." She would just have to turn her mother's demand into something good.

It came to her the next morning. "If I must go"—she spoke to the tiny bird that twittered on the towel rack while she washed her face—"I will insist on a meeting with the president." She would play some of the music for him, convince him to let her record openly. It was the only way to save these people and their music and their language too.

She would sing at the funeral and fend off her mother's worries about her weight loss, her tanned skin, her unruly hair managed by her western hat. "I will return," she told the birds, the cacti, the sky.

But not before I have an audience shed-uled with Roosevelt.

∞

"Charlotte is so grateful you returned," Mimsey had told them when she and Bogey met George and Natalie at the train.

"Of course we'd come," Natalie said. "It's a tragic loss."

"Rufus was some years older than she, but still . . ." Mimsey sighed. "No one is ever prepared for the death of someone you love." In her next breath she said, "Now, let me look at you, Natalie. Why, George, you've shrunk your sister."

"She did it to herself." George hung his hat on the coat tree. "I think she looks spiffy."

"She's brown as a bean and as slim," Bogey said. "How's your heart, daughter? Lungs? Good? Let me listen later."

"Oh, Daddy, I'm fine. My heart has never been better, my mind is engaged in important things, and I am enthralled with the Southwest. You really must come visit."

"To George's primitive cattle ranch?" Mimsey said, walking her children, one on either arm, into the drawing room.

"They have a Steinway," Natalie said. "I played Chopin on it."

Mimsey stopped. "Did you? How was that?"

"It was . . . alright. The music came back, my fingers moved over the keys like happy ducks swimming across the pond. And Mrs. Brigand, the co-owner, seemed well pleased. She used to play before arthritis crippled her hands. She said the music was healing. They'd lost a son."

"I thought you first played when we made the recording." George gave her an approving smile.

"You men went off to sleep while Mary Jo and I watched the sunrise."

"I'm glad you made some nice friends," Mimsey said. "You can write to them, of course. But I'm ready for you to be back in New York."

"What time is the funeral?" George asked, saving Natalie from the conversation she needed to have.

"Tomorrow, at 2:00 p.m. At St. Thomas. Would you like something to eat? You must be famished."

Natalie didn't know if Mimsey had forgotten her line of questioning or if she allowed George to change the subject. Either way, she had a reprieve from asking for money.

Her old room felt cluttered with all the Victorian hoopla she once thought necessary. Simplicity had settled into her skin, sent there by the River People, the Little People of Peace, the Diné. She compared the heavy drapes, the tapestries, and stained-glass lampshades from Tiffany's to the interior of El Alisal with its spare but unique furnishings. Number 3 was even more sparse and yet it felt more open, freer from the weight of objects in this room, this house of her childhood. It was hard to describe the difference to her parents without it sounding as though she was ungrateful, dismissing her past. She had found a different landscape to love, and it had seeped into her bones.

∞

"Oh my goodness! I'm to join him at Sagamore Hill on Oyster Bay! The president is giving me an audience." The Curtis clan was at their own cottage at the beach when Natalie received the long-awaited message from the president of the United States.

It was mid-July, and Roosevelt had finally not only replied but went further, offering an invitation. She would devote the entire time to convincing him of the importance to all Americans of the value of preserving Indian art, their music, ceremonies, and song. And that she needed his permission to allow the Hopi and Yuma, at the very least, to sing and dance so that she might record their music before it was lost like ocean sand following a seasonal storm. She would also alert him to the injustices at Oraibi and by Burton, and try to pair her own advocacy to that of the president's passion for seeing things in new ways, especially his own interests in both fairness and the arts. She'd be a wreck until the day of the appointment, rehearsing what she wanted to say, deciding on what recordings to share with him, evidence of her lawbreaking but fuel for a president known to have a voracious appetite for new information and an exploring spirit.

The day arrived. She dressed as a proper New Englander in a summer yellow frock, with matching hat and white gloves. She carried cylinders in a large bag made out of a Navajo weaving she'd purchased.

They were in the library at Roosevelt's summer home, where tea and little cakes had been served to them. A single aide sat in the background, taking notes. Roosevelt glared out at her behind those distinctive eyeglasses, that famous mustache framing his clamped lips. He gave her his total attention.

"I have broken the law by encouraging the Hopi to sing to me, and by my recording them on the Edison," she told the president. *My boldness must serve me here.* "I'll tell you that up front," Natalie continued. "But when you hear this music—and I can sing some of the pieces for you if you'd like—you will hear the distinctive, haunting quality and you will want to preserve it as I do. Not only for the people, the Indian people, but for Americans who have much to learn from their singular art and customs and song."

The president adjusted his glasses, motioned for her to play the cylinder on the Edison the aid brought forward. She played Lololomai's recording. He didn't interrupt her with questions. He listened. Then, "Tell me about that song."

Which Natalie did. And she waxed poetic about the people, their efforts toward living peacefully, how by her observations, the most important thing in their lives was family. Their children. "Lololomai, whose song I played for you, came to Washington some years ago and met with government people and was quite taken with books and with schools, and he wanted Hopi children to learn to read and write. Think of how he must feel he has betrayed his people by bringing in the atrocious policies of the Bureau of Indian Affairs."

Roosevelt never flinched, though she harangued about some of his own policies that, if not originating with him, were now his responsibility.

"No speaking of their native tongue. How are they to communicate with their grandparents? Even so, Lololomai has supported sending the children to school even when they are treated so harshly, given half rations, shamed if they break minor rules such as singing a song in their own language."

"You've seen this firsthand?"

"I have. But also, Burton force-marched them in the snow when parents kept them home because of the weather. I didn't see that, but the Hopi told me of it and truth telling is important to them. Burton yanked flour from them for a week because I let the children sing for me."

"They trust you? The Hopi are known to be quite reticent, I've heard."

"Wouldn't you be with someone like Burton hovering over you like a . . . warden holding you hostage? He doesn't have to be rude and arrogant. I'm sorry. I know he's your employee."

"You sound like Lummis now. The man is killing me in his articles in *Out West*. Wants an investigation of Burton." He leaned back in his highback chair. "Maybe, with your information, I'll do that."

She told him of the double standard, asking tourists to come see the Snake Dance while forbidding it to be performed for their own people. And the haircutting, how it was wrapped up with fertility of the cornfields, without which their families would starve.

"You remind me of your uncle George." The president grinned. "He was passionate and quite intelligent. A fine mind." He gazed out the window at the bay. Natalie held her tongue. Finally, he said, "I can see what you're getting at, Natalie. There is merit in preserving what is unique about each tribe, I suppose. And America does not have our own culture yet, not like China or Italy, around for centuries." He put those intense eyes on her again. "What is it you want, specifically?"

Her heart beat faster. "A letter from you allowing me to do this musical ethnography, which is how I see it, on every reservation I might choose to go to. Granting clemency to any who sing for me and for those who practice their traditions that I'm hoping to record and preserve. No punishment until the Code is amended."

"Now, I don't know about the law changing. We have to have order."

"The Code is unjust, Mr. President. Inhumane. I think you know that. You can't strip a people of their identity. It's . . . morally cruel. Racial . . . extermination. You don't want to be known as the leader who presided over such things. These people are free spirits as we are, you and I. Isn't it the American way to honor tradition, to incorporate all that is rich from a conquered people whose land we took—"

"Fair and square."

"I'm not a military strategist, only a musician." She fluttered her eyelashes, the only time she'd tried feminine wiles with him. "Is not a strong leader one who sees the nation able to withstand another's cultural contribution of music, pottery, dance, even theology, though they might differ from his own?"

"They will do better if they assimilate."

"They will assimilate better if who they are and where they come from is respected. I believe that preserving the Indians' art will be an advancement to all Americans in an arena that is now quite weak."

The president leaned his elbows on the table, now cleared of everything except coffee cups, and stared at her. "Yes, you are like your uncle. Alright, I'll see what I can do." He motioned to the aide, who rose and went to the door. Roosevelt stood and walked her toward it. "I do like the music, Natalie. I thought too when I heard the Sioux in the Dakotas that it was a complex sound, not simply drums and chants. You understand that."

"I hope to. Maybe put it in a book for them to have for teaching their children when the elders are gone. A legacy."

"Do the deed," the president said. "I might make this subject a part of my Presidential Address to Congress. It's conservation at its core. Conserving Indian art as part of education of Indians. And the rest of us. I'll be in touch."

⋆⊘⋆

The letter was dated July 22, 1903, the day of their meeting. It was sent to Hitchcock, the secretary of the Interior, advising him of Roosevelt's desire to support Natalie in preserving the artistic ways of the Indian. He had said he agreed with her that artistry was a weakness in the American scene. *"We ought not throw away anything which will give us a chance to develop artistically."* A copy was sent to Natalie for her to carry with her. The president wrote that he wanted every opportunity to be granted to Miss Natalie Curtis, to *"travel through all Indian reservations, and to fully investigate and report on, to me or any official under me, all matters pertaining to the well-being, the education, the artistic*

171

development and industries of the Indians." That he mentioned "education" meant she could also go into any Indian school. She ran her hands over the embossed presidential seal that rose from the paper like a beloved mesa.

It was a stunning level of support. She had succeeded in getting permission. Now what would she do with it?

22

Picking Up the Tempo

I suspect it's a thank-you for singing at Rufus's funeral," Mimsey said. "It was so wonderful to hear that clear voice of yours again." She patted Natalie's hand as she held the cream-colored envelope on expensive card stock. "The poor woman must be bereft."

Natalie stared at the missive from Charlotte Mason. It was an invitation to a luncheon at her fashionable apartment in the city. Seagulls called through the open windows, catching the bay's breezes where her family spent the summers at Wave Crest. Natalie rarely spent full weeks at the Curtis seaside retreat. As a child, she traveled back and forth to the city for piano and voice lessons. This day, she enjoyed the relaxed time. Her mother seemed more rested here too.

"I wonder what you think of this, Mimsey. I . . . that is, with the president's letter of introduction, I have permission to travel to any reservation or school."

"You aren't considering making a vocation out of such obser-vations, are you? There's no future in such . . . effort, especially for a woman. I hesitate to call it work." Her mother pulled at weeds in the window box overflowing with sea oats and daylilies, survivors of salty soils. Have you found no man who tweaks your interest?"

The last was said as a tease, but Natalie knew her mother wanted for her a happy married life with children and a husband who would support her. "Preserving the Indian arts will have wide-reaching positive effects on Indian policy—at least I hope it will. But it will also individually touch lives of people I've met and those I will meet. Being among the Hopi and the Yuma, it's the most alive I've felt in years." Natalie fanned herself with the invitation. "So yes, I am considering it as a vocation, a way of life for me."

"There are more things that can bring you such fulfillment, Natalie."

Mimsey went into the day porch, removed her hat. Natalie followed her. She swallowed. She had wanted to prepare her exact words, but sometimes fate intervened.

"I'm aware of that, Mama." Natalie kissed her mother's cheek. Her mother liked the idea of improving Indian lives in theory, but she had expressed concerns that her daughter—with Roosevelt's letter—would be spending even more time actually among them. Her life of travel and intervention could be dangerous, if not "hygienically challenging," as Mimsey had said when Natalie described the bathing conditions at Oraibi.

But for Natalie, it was those very challenges that filled her ever-curious mind, that reminded her daily that how she saw the world was not the way everyone saw the world and that she could be schooled by people who had lived for generations in a different way, even as their ways were being systematically eradicated. Time was of the essence. It was no longer a land of "pretty soon." And who was to say that how she'd been raised was somehow "more right" than how Chiparopai raised her daughters and granddaughters or that a Tiffany lamp was somehow more expressive and artistic than Lololomai's weavings? The very idea of being able to explore such questions animated her almost as much as hearing a Wagner opera had all those years before.

But she would need money to sustain the exploration, and unlike Mimsey's hope, Natalie had no intention of waiting to find a husband to enable that to happen.

"Would you and Bogey be able to grant me a loan?" The words burst from her. She knew she was asking her parents to support a project her mother disapproved of.

"A loan implies you intend to pay it back. How would you do that?"

"Through my writing. I've made a little with my articles so far, and with this much wider mandate—and Roosevelt's letter—I'll have more magazines interested. *Outside* has said they'd accept one of my pieces. The *Saturday Evening Post* pays quite well. Maybe I could even write a book the way the archaeologists do after they've excavated ancient sites. If it sold well, I'd be able to repay you and support myself."

"I hear a multitude of 'ifs.' Archaeologists usually have universities sponsor them." Her mother fluffed her hair with her fingers as she paused before a mirror. "How much were you thinking of? We're comfortable but not wealthy people. And we have your brother and sisters to consider."

"None of us seems willing to put matrimony onto our schedules. Should I fix us some iced tea?"

"I'm not at all sure why that is," Mimsey said. "Your siblings rarely even accept invitations to parties or dances. They just stay home and read books." She frowned.

"My jumping into a whole new world as George did should make you happy."

Mimsey sighed. "I'm proud of you, certainly. And yes, iced tea would be good. Mint, if you would."

Natalie started to tell her mother about finding the mint leaves in the desert land but stopped herself, needing to keep the conversation about money flowing.

"And goodness we are so delighted that you had the audience with the president. And his asking you to report to him makes you a special agent or something. It lends legitimacy to your roaming about, I suppose."

"I told him in my thank-you note that, though he diminished his own power, or at least said it was limited, that his 'incisive force, clarity of purpose and promptness of action'—which is how he meets every challenge—'make people like me receive an enormous impetus being championed by him.'" Natalie orated as though she stood before a crowd. "I ended my thank-you by writing that I was 'full of plans.' I hope I've intrigued him with the mention of a book and that he might put the 'Indian Question,' as he called it, higher up on his administration's list of issues needing his powerful focus. I intend to help him all I can."

"And the amount of any loan might be?"

Natalie took a deep breath. "Three thousand should make it possible to carry out my work and include George's expenses when he's able to travel with me." There were the costs of the cylinders, lodging—perhaps she could get a pass from the railroads if she convinced them it might help bring people west. But she really didn't want corporate sponsorships, not when she felt the Acheson, Topeka, and Santa Fe Railroad took advantage of the Hopi by promoting their Snake Dance even while it was illegal.

"That is a goodly sum." Mimsey sat, thoughtful. "Maybe a publisher would advance you money. You could write a proposal."

"That's a possibility, getting an advance."

"Mrs. Doubleday has shown some interest in Indian affairs or at least the Sequoya League. I'll speak to your father, of course. But you might do well to seek out a real benefactor. A patron."

"I really don't want to drain you and Bogey. And a patronage would mean I wouldn't need to repay it except to do the work they're supporting."

"Let's make a list and we'll shed-ule appointments to ply your cause. Beginning with Charlotte's luncheon."

Natalie looked at the invitation lying on the table now, next to the tea. "But is it too soon to speak of such matters with her grieving Rufus's death? And his affairs taking up much of her time?"

"It's the absolute best time and she's already reached out." Mimsey stirred a sugar lump into her tea. "After your sister Julia died, I was inconsolable for months. Such a little child. We were a young couple, and I wondered for a time whether living was worth it."

"You've rarely talked about her. I forget I had another older sister."

"I've never forgotten. The healing has taken a long time."

The words of Chiparopai came to mind. *When was the last time you sang, when was the last time you danced, when was the last time you told your story?* "That must have been . . . terrible." She reached to touch her mother, who fought back tears now. *After years of her comforting me, maybe I can comfort her.*

"She was adorable. The most beautiful blonde curls." Mimsey sighed. "She lived only a few minutes. In time—your father was stellar in this regard—I found I needed a new purpose, something that would fill my life in new ways. I think healing comes with new pursuits. After Julia died, that's when I became involved in my many clubs and social doings on behalf of abused children, raising money for hospital charities, somehow giving back. It saved me, it really did."

"I'm so grateful you let me go with George."

Her mother dabbed at her eyes. "I'm still torn about that, but you do look . . . healthier." She leaned back in her chair, closed her eyes, remembering. "Had I done something during the pregnancy that caused her death? Was I not to bear children? So many unanswered questions. I tried to put my faith in God to help me live with the lack of answers as much as the loss." She looked at Natalie then. "In due time I had Constance and all the rest of you upstanding citizens that I hover over like a mother hen." She chuckled. "Charlotte may be in that very same place, seeking something to coddle. Rufus is gone and has likely left her with more funds than she could know what to do with. And she loves music, remember. You are the perfect ambassador to bring Indians and music interests to her in a new way. Who knows, maybe you'll meet some young benefactor who will cherish your plans and travel with you." Natalie raised her eyebrows. "As your husband, of course."

∽

August wasn't the best time to be in New York City with its sweltering heat, but Natalie was pleased to make the hot trip and move her future forward. But despite the beauty of the Spode china and the peach-colored begonia centerpiece at Charlotte's apartment, the four table settings disappointed. Four settings meant others would be joining. High ceiling fans circulated the warm air around, and the windows were open to street sounds. She'd have to make another date to speak of finances. She couldn't do it in front of strangers. It was probably better anyway to find another time to talk patronage. It would be more direct, less calculating.

"Isn't it just so blistering, this heat?" Charlotte fanned herself. She wore a linen peach-colored dress with a long string of pearls. She was barefoot, but her shoes sat primly beside what Natalie assumed would be her chair at the table.

Natalie wore a new khaki skirt she'd had tailored and a white linen blouse and high-top shoes. It had become her expedition uniform, and she was truly on an expedition, this time to acquire funds.

"I should be at our coastal home," Charlotte continued, "but I had this appointment which I turned into a luncheon, if my other guests will just arrive. I detest lateness, don't you?" She didn't wait for Natalie to respond. "But those westerners say time isn't like it is in the East, though you were certainly prompt."

"It's my music training," Natalie said. "If I was a minute late for my vocals with Seidl, he wouldn't teach me. And one can't enter a concert after it starts."

"Yes, I always liked that about concerts. Start on time. End on time. Oh, can you hear that? What is that?"

The two went to the window where sounds rose from the street. Below, a small crowd had gathered. Charlotte shouted down and the man in the middle looked up and waved his western hat at her. *Frank Mead!* He wore western boots and jeans tucked into them, his vest, and a wide sombrero hat.

"It's about time," Charlotte shouted. "Come on up."

Beside Frank was a dark-faced man carrying a black-and-white basket urn nearly the size of him. He grasped it tightly as Frank tried to move through the crowd toward the door.

What can I say? Should I say? Her heart beat a little faster. She felt warm—but it was a hot day in the city.

"We're on our way. Step aside, folks," Frank shouted to the crowd. "Let him by. Yes, he's an Apache Indian. He won't hurt you."

The doorman stepped out to hold the gawkers back as Frank and his friend disappeared into the entrance below. She and Charlotte waited a few minutes until the elevator operator opened the double doors, where Charlotte greeted the two men.

"Sorry we're late, Char. Good to see you, Miss Curtis. Glad you could make it."

He doesn't sound surprised I'm here. I'm surprised he is.

"Natalie, please."

He leaned to kiss her cheek. "Thank you for the introduction to Charlie Lummis, by the way. We're talking architecture, Indian designs. We share all sorts of arts and crafts interests. Oh, please, let me introduce Pelia. The basket urn is his own artistic piece."

"Lovely to meet you, Pelia," Charlotte said. She put out her hand to shake Pelia's, but the Apache kept a tight hold on his basket urn, then wandered around the room, staring at the chandelier, the pottery on the mantel. A Hopi Katsina doll stood on a table by the window.

"We're starved, Char. I could eat a mule." He winked at Natalie.

"I'll have our luncheon served."

Frank tossed his hat at a silk-upholstered chair next to the door. *He's at home here.*

Charlotte motioned Natalie and Frank to seats next to each other and, with her New York accent, said, "Pelia, please join us. You may set the basket by the fireplace. No one will take it."

Frank translated, but Pelia shook his head. He kept his arms around his belonging basket as he made his way to the table. He sat and finally put his treasure on the floor beside him when Frank motioned for him to set it there.

"He doesn't want to let go of it. It's a present."

"For me?" Charlotte tossed her pearls and dramatized the question, as though knowing it wasn't.

Frank looked at Natalie. "It's for President Roosevelt. If we can get a meeting with him. And pose the question of having old Fort McDowell named as the Mojave-Apache's new reservation."

"Which is why we're all here together," Charlotte said. She smiled at Natalie. "Someone we're acquainted with seems to have a way with the president." She sang the words, and the reality of the meeting dawned on Natalie. There *was* to be a negotiation today—just not for Natalie's future.

23

A Duet Becomes a Chorus

*T*he afternoon turned into twilight. Pelia fell asleep on the floor on a Navajo rug Charlotte laid down for him. He rested early, before the sun had set, his basket close at hand. It sat near his head like a headstone. Natalie thought all the chatter back and forth must have tired him. When she tried to understand the Hopi speakers and translate their words, she was often more fatigued than if she'd been digging weeds in the family garden. When she interviewed tribal members to share their music and stories, she needed to remember how tiring learning new things could be. She'd read some of the ethnologist Frank Boaz's work, and he would describe Indian dances and say things like "I suppose it means" this or that rather than having listened to what the Pueblo or Winnebago members said the action or regalia or legend meant. She wanted to know how those she interviewed saw their traditions and religion, not just "suppose" or impose her own views. That's what Americans needed in order to realize what everyone would be missing if those ceremonies, traditions, songs, and dances disappeared.

"I'll get you that itemization of our expenses," Frank told Charlotte as the maid filled his crystal with iced tea.

"Excellent. Be sure to include projection of costs for the return trip for you and Pelia."

"Absolutely."

Charlotte is his patron.

Natalie would have to approach someone else. Who? She wasn't sure her ideas were formed enough to make a presentation to eminent philanthropists like George Foster Peabody, for example. If only she could arrange some way to pay back a hefty loan from her parents. George would help, she knew that. But he'd also told her of his own dreams, to stay in the Southwest, to buy a ranch in Southern California, to have his own cattle, his own roundup, his own hands. "And maybe one day a wife," he'd told her when they rode the train back to New York for Dr. Mason's funeral.

"Anyone in mind?" she had asked.

"Not yet. But I'm not averse to looking." He picked up the book that he'd been reading, then put it down again. "Don't cut yourself off from that kind of desire either, Nat. Having a partner in your endeavor could make the journey so much better. Marriage wouldn't have to mean you give up your hope to save Indian songs. You might find someone to share the dream with you. A real partner."

"I have a real partner," she said. "You."

"And I'm willing and able to travel with you as I can. But since you're feeling better and stronger, I'm less worried about you being on your own. You'll do fine. But you'd do better with a partner."

"You and Mimsey. Thinking matrimony for me."

"Our parents are happy people. That's a good legacy for us. I hope to find the right girl for me and I hope you find the right man for you."

"Unlike you, I'm not looking." She thought of her brief flirtation with Frank; the tragedy of her Adonis.

"Aha, but the Divine smiles down on us." He grinned. "You

never know when—" The train whistle blew as they approached a signal arm, so she didn't hear what else he might have said about the Divine intervening in her life. And when the noise stopped, he'd returned to his book and Natalie hadn't wanted to extend a discussion of matrimony.

New York City street noises of horse carriages, the horns of automobiles, the music of New York's night life drifted up through Charlotte's windows, bringing Natalie from her reverie about the conversation with George. Was being in this apartment this day some sort of divine plan? She'd come responding to a grieving woman, with a sideline of making a financial arrangement. There was no way she could ask now, aware of her support for Frank. Or perhaps it was a romantic intervention Charlotte had in mind? When Natalie told Roosevelt she was "full of plans," dreamy inclinations were not a part of them.

She enjoyed Frank's insights, and his flamboyant way of talking, his prancing around the room, waving his arms, grinning at her as he told stories, green eyes flashing. But she saw he flirted with both Charlotte and herself, and she decided that was just his way of interacting with women, winking like a distant star. His smile was warm, and though she found him attractive, she realized it was his enthusiasm and passion for the Indians' cause—and his love of music—that had made him appealing. That, and his wish to weave the arts and even architecture into contemporary life so that native contributions would not be lost.

But he had stood her up, the cad.

"That basket." Frank pointed with his chin—the Indian way—to the woven urn that sat nearly three feet tall by Pelia. "That will go to Roosevelt if we get an audience with him." He took a deep breath, stopped in front of Natalie as she sat on the white leather divan, boots off, legs curled up under her, as Charlotte took the seat across from her. "Can you help us with that, Natalie, please?"

This, then, was the heart of her having been invited to lunch: Frank wanted something from her, and Charlotte was there to help him get it. *Why should I help you, who left me eating flan by myself? Oh, I can be petty.*

She shared his cause and hoped that disappointment for not being able to press her own case with Charlotte didn't show. "I can try. You're a fine advocate for Pelia's people. I'll write to the president."

"That would be lovely," Charlotte said. "Rufus and I contributed to his campaign, but we also gave to his opponent. I suppose they have a way of knowing that. You're the perfect intercessor and you already have his permission to 'report' back to him. You can report on the Mojave-Apache's needs."

"Actually, Char," Frank said, his index finger in the air as though to make a point. "That isn't their name. They are the Yavapai people, but we Anglos just brush them in with others. Theirs is a long and terrible history." To Natalie, he said, "I found this band starving in the mountains. They're homeless. We violated an agreement to give them their homeland back thirty years ago. Instead, it's gone to Anglo ranchers. The Yavapai got so discouraged, they left the place they were to return to their homeland, when a blizzard hit. I happened along at the right time. Which is why the Roosevelt meeting." He touched Natalie's hand. "I'd really appreciate your help."

"I'll do my best." She extracted her fingers. "I can contact you through Charlotte?"

Frank nodded.

Natalie said, "I should probably head out or I'll miss the last train."

"Oh, spend the night! Use my telephone and call your mother. We can take Pelia around town tomorrow, show him the sights, and you and Frank can talk about the best wording to approach the president."

"Pelia might even sing for you," Frank said. "Give you a taste of a true folk song, from the earliest American people." He winked again.

Charlotte's voice tended to boom, but she held it back so as not to disturb the sleeping Pelia. "I personally believe there are three strands of truly American folk music that must be preserved. You are focused on one. But there are also African-American and Appalachian songs that give us early beginnings of what might be a truly American folk music and art."

"I might add a fourth," Natalie said. "The American cowboy songs."

"Oh, I agree most heartily," Frank said. "They yodel, like they were in Austria, but they do it in a perfectly American way, harmonicas as background music and sometimes even accordions."

"And the guitar. I enjoy the campfire songs," Natalie said. "Simple and soulful."

"Call your mother and then we can talk more. The phone is in the hallway." Charlotte whispered as she passed her, "I need to make a toilet and we can chat more later."

Natalie did as she was told, grateful for the convenience of Bell's invention. She was tired though and wondered when it might be polite to seek her evening accommodations. She'd gotten used to setting her own pace.

"I hope you don't mind my taking advantage of you like this, Natalie." Frank startled her in the hallway. "Charlotte was so impressed with what you'd accomplished with Roosevelt that I couldn't pass up the opportunity to build on our friendship."

"Passing acquaintance might be the better term," Natalie said. She heard the frost in her voice.

He must have heard it too as he stepped back. "Have I offended you in some way?"

"You never came for supper," she said. "In Yuma."

"I . . . I sent my apologies. I was ill. And the next day busy at the prison and with the agent, and I caught the evening train. I am so sorry. I gave my note to a maid to give to you. Described you. Said you'd be in the dining room. Ah, Natalie, can you forgive me?" He sounded genuinely contrite.

"It does make it easier for me to recommend an audience with you and the president. Not that there's any guarantee, you understand. It took me months."

"I can imagine."

"But I was a little concerned that I'd get you an appointment and you wouldn't show up." She said it sweetly but it held some tartness too.

He hit his head with his palm. "I'm so sorry for that mix-up. How can I make it up to you?"

Charlotte popped out of her room and linked her arms with their elbows, leading them back to the living room, where she plopped them both down on the couch. "You're aware that the Hampton Normal and Agricultural Institute has added Indian students to their roster?" Charlotte poured more wine in Frank's glass. Natalie declined.

"I didn't know that," Natalie said, relieved to have gotten more of Frank's story that she was inclined to believe. The hotel maid might not have found her, as she'd gone outside to eat her flan, and perhaps she didn't have her name so couldn't leave it with the desk clerk either. *A misunderstanding.* Her life was full of them.

"It's an experiment," Charlotte said. "But they allow the Indian children to sing their own songs and they've come from different parts of the country. You must go to Virginia to visit the school. I'll go with you before you head back to the Southwest. You can record them right there, save all the travel to their reservations."

"Oh, well, of course that would be a good entrée." Natalie hesitated. "Hasn't there been some recent controversy from W. E. B. Dubois, about how the Hampton Institute focuses too much on farming and household industries over academics, at least for the African-American students? He suggested in his article I read that the white teachers should help the students aspire to greater than what their parents and grandparents did as slaves. They can become scholars, mathematicians, trained musicians, maybe even physicians and lawyers."

"It's another policy in need of addressing," Frank agreed, "but we should focus our efforts on treatment in the Indian schools, praise Hampton's approach for permitting their Indian students to sing and dance their traditional songs so they aren't lost."

"The instruction will evolve," Charlotte said. "It's not true that we only want the black students to be better 'slaves.' We want them to have pride in their work and their efforts. And in their music, that's your interest. You might want to leave the politics alone, Natalie."

She wasn't certain politics could be left out of the erasing of a race, which was what assimilation policies intended. "It is the music I want to explore."

"Hampton allows the Indian students to bring their songs with them. I'm one of their patrons so I'm privy to that information." Charlotte added, "At least they treat their students with dignity, no recent raids to bring them to the school, no punishments for singing."

"They aren't punished for performing?" Natalie repeated to be certain.

"Not at all. And they can take their traditions back to their reservations, not to have been forgotten. It's a very good thing."

"They'll need other skills if they live and work off the reservations," Natalie said.

"That's years ahead." Charlotte brushed her hand as though sending such a thought away. "They want to go back, to be with their own kind, on their own lands."

Natalie wasn't so certain. To truly assimilate, Indians and African Americans would need to find work and live among Anglos, wouldn't they? Or was the government policy meant to make Indians and black students like white people only at a certain level—teach them agricultural and service trades—while holding them on reservations or returning them to underfunded schools where they lived a separate, dependent, poverty-ridden life? Would helping save their music do anything for them, really? Maybe her Roosevelt letter was just an indulgence.

Frank's advocacy invited real change for their lives. He had educated himself on the needs of the Yavapai and had already learned the language and had literally saved them from starvation and extinction. Frank had also been to San Diego and Pasadena and met with Lummis, had severed his ties with his Philadelphia architectural firm and was fully behind efforts to raise the president's awareness of the land-based issues of the Indians. While in Yuma, it was an Apache irrigation project, and now, it was land for the Yavapai. He made justice happen.

"Allotments or homesteads of one hundred sixty acres are not the way to go for a people accustomed to living in pueblos," Frank said as he turned the subject from Hampton to other Indian issues. Natalie's eyes were fluttering as she tried to stay awake. "The Bureau should create permanent encampments along rivers or where their orchards are, like the Yuma have, don't you agree, Natalie?" She nodded. "Not isolate them with only their families on homesteads they have to farm alone. Indians as a whole are a gathering people, tending elders and children, mindful of one another's business. Some might say meddling, but it's how they take care of each other." Frank paused to catch his breath, then continued. "Stuck out on a homestead, they're lonely. And we white-folk neighbors don't come to their aid like we should, so they have to build their barns by themselves. And elders aren't available to teach the healing arts, how to use witch hazel or season a venison stew. Traditions are lost in that separation from their communities."

Charlotte picked up his enthusiasm. "Congress has put so much into the Homestead Act that giving them whole tracts of land will annoy those non-Indian cattlemen who want the grazing areas for themselves." Charlotte had joined in his indignation and the two had waxed poetic about the land and Indian people's connection to it. Complex—just as their music was, so was Indian politics.

"You'll have to forgive me," Natalie said. Her eyes had been dropping for the past hour, and by the chiming of the clock she could hear it was midnight. It was one of her quirks that she could go at full speed and then suddenly, as though a horse stepped on her foot, her body stopped. Once or twice with George, she'd fallen asleep in the middle of a sentence. She was ready to collapse as soon as her head hit the pillow.

"We've tired you," Charlotte said. "I'm so sorry. Frank and I will stifle our voices, won't we, Frank?" He nodded agreement. "There are toilet items in the third bedroom on the right. Your bed has been turned down."

"You're most kind," Natalie said.

"It's only the beginning." Charlotte took Natalie's hands in hers and helped pull her up from the divan. "I'm so grateful for our shared interests. I remember fondly some of those discussions we had about life and purpose before your . . . incident. It's a marvel to see you back, better than ever." She walked with Natalie down the carpeted hallway, her arm gentled over Natalie's shoulder. "I want my beneficiaries to be happy and healthy."

"Excuse me?"

She stopped then, faced Natalie. "You haven't asked, but I'm certain you'll need funding for this song collection effort, as Frank does for his work."

"Yes. I will. I do." She swallowed. "I had intended to ask you, Charlotte, but when I realized you were supporting Frank and you have other projects, the Hampton school, well, I am humbled by your offer."

"My support for your project is given with great love. Rufus would have approved." She stumbled on his name and Natalie saw grief wash across her eyes.

"I'm so grateful." *What had been a loss is also a gain. Little miracles.*

"We'll discuss details in the morning. You rest now." She patted her shoulder.

"I can't thank you enough. And yes, in the morning. I'm afraid my body is telling me it needs sleep most of all."

"And I have some others I think you should approach. George Peabody, for one."

"I actually thought of him, but I wasn't sure my project would meet his interests."

"Peabody took his investment money and put it toward peaceful efforts to lower the divide between the very wealthy and the very poor. Our project is perfect for him. You must write him immediately and fill him in on our plans."

Our project? Our plans? "In the morning." Along with clarifying just what it meant to have a benefactor and how much control over her vocation Natalie would be turning over to those who held the purse strings.

Both Frank and Charlotte could make things happen. Charlotte had contacts. And she had ideas. Natalie decided as she donned the nightdress laid out for her on the four-poster bed, tied the ribbons at the neck, that it wasn't only strong-willed men who sometimes talked over her. Women could be equally as obtuse. One had to learn each other's rhythms to perform a successful duet, let alone engage a chorus.

24

A Pencil in Their Hands

*P*elia did sing for Natalie after Frank assured him it was alright. Charlotte had an Edison recorder and Natalie made notes. The man seemed to be comforted by his singing, his eyes closed as he chanted and moved around the apartment, performing what Frank said was a "Dance Song." The man had cocked his head at the replaying, then nodded, a grin forming on his face. Then the three of them took the diminutive Pelia on a boat ride on the Hudson, him still holding the black-and-white woven urn that strangers would stop to comment on, forcing Pelia to hold tighter to his treasure. They showed him the elevated train, and later Frank pointed out the Statue of Liberty in the harbor. Natalie wondered what such a thing might mean to Pelia: a stone feature that had been a gift to honor all the immigrants who had come to America's shores—and ultimately taken Indian lands and helped erase their way of life.

After sightseeing, Natalie was fully on board with helping Frank's efforts on behalf of the Yavapai. She liked Frank even more, watching his tenderness with Pelia, but as a colleague only.

Pelia seemed relieved to be back at Charlotte's apartment, where he set the basket down and sighed. What a strain this trip must be on him. What he was willing to set aside—the simplicity of his life in the desert to withstand the bombarding of buildings and noise—just to get that audience with Roosevelt.

"Have you written your letter to Roosevelt, Natalie? Do so now, don't you think?" Charlotte directed. Charlotte's chef had prepared a cucumber salad. Pelia had lifted the cucumber and smelled it as Natalie had done when Chiparopai had given her a fruity-smelling red prickly pear cactus to eat.

Pelia was being asked to take in so much.

"Have you thought of your arguments?" Charlotte persisted. "What you'll say to him to get the audience?"

Natalie supposed the earlier the better for writing, as it would surely take time for Roosevelt to respond. And she didn't want Pelia to have to be away from what he knew best any longer than necessary.

"We should plan to go to my Washington apartment to wait out his response," Charlotte said. "It's always good to be close to the heartbeat of power. We can visit a few senators and win over representatives for the western territories for the land project too, Frank. Besides, it'll be easier to visit Hampton from DC anyway."

"I will draft the letter," Natalie said. "But I want it to come on my stationery, so I'll need to go home for that. But I can join you in Washington later."

"That'll do," Charlotte said. "And you and I need to talk money, such a ghastly subject but essential nonetheless. A good benefactor is attuned to raising funds to match her own investments, so a letter to Peabody is warranted this afternoon as well. We can propose a meeting."

Charlotte's use of "we" would have to be addressed, but Natalie had a rule. The first time something upset her stomach, she made a note of it. The second time, she made a note but also geared herself up to deal with it as a pattern was being formed. The third time, she made an appointment to discuss the matter with the offending person, but she had three stories she could relay to demonstrate her concerns. It had helped her find a new course with difficult teachers and keep them as friends. *Except for Damrosch, my Adonis.* She said nothing about Charlotte joining a proposed meeting with Peabody, and instead she drafted both letters. Frank liked her Roosevelt one; Charlotte approved the Peabody missive.

"Good. I'll take the train back to Wave Crest. Maybe the president is still at Sagamore Hill. If he is, I'll let you know, Frank."

"And we'll proceed to Washington, DC. Let's plan a Hampton visit in two weeks," Charlotte said.

Natalie's stomach clenched. *Episode number two.*

❧

George Peabody answered first, sending her a check for one thousand dollars. Natalie gasped as the check drifted from the letter. It was late August, and she had opened the philanthropist's response on the porch while sitting on the rattan rocking chair. He thought her plan to preserve Indian music and arts was "splendid" and "warranted." He'd read her various articles and suggested that she write a small book immediately about her efforts, that such a book could help raise awareness and funds for her endeavor and, in addition, could be used in government schools to educate the teachers and the students. Like Charlotte, Peabody was a trustee of the Hampton Institute, so his interest in advancing government schools came naturally.

Everyone has an idea for how I should do this.

❧

She was at Wave Crest with cooling beach breezes, there in time to say goodbye to George. They sat in sloping beach chairs, watching seagulls drag their legs across the sky, swoop down to pick something up from the sand, then lift again in their never-ending dance. George had his western hat over his eyes. He was packed up and ready to return to the Bar X and would leave in the morning. She would miss him as she had when he left Yuma and Oraibi. Yet she knew he was always there.

"When you decide on your next steps in the Southwest, get ahold of me," George said. "If I can, I'll join you. Sugar and Spice and our wagon will be fine among the Hopi until you're ready to take them on to the other pueblos. I still want to be with you when you visit Acoma."

"Charlotte wants to return with me. Now that she's sponsoring me, I can hardly say no."

"Yes, you can. And you'll have to if you want this project to be yours. It'll be an issue, Nat, with any benefactors. You'll have to balance their contributions with your own needs to do it the way you want."

"I guess I need to consider that before I cash Peabody's check."

"Set the parameters early on. Be willing to adapt them, but only if doing so takes you closer to your goal."

"I'm going to miss you, George. You're such a huge part of this undertaking. Especially my being healthy enough to pursue it." Natalie reached across the beach grasses between their chairs and held his hand.

"We're a team. Always will be, even if we're not riding in the same wagon. I'll do anything I can to support you."

"And I, you."

They sat companionably, like two good friends. This is what she'd want in a lifelong relationship, absolute trust made up of predictability, honesty, reliability, and harmony—the true music of life.

❧

The invitation came from the White House. The meeting was for her, Frank Mead, and Pelia. Charlotte wasn't included. This wouldn't bode well with her, Natalie was certain. Charlotte ran in those upper-echelon circles, and she would have relished a story that included a meeting at the White House. Natalie took in a deep breath, then called Charlotte on the telephone to give her and Frank the news. "It's August thirtieth."

"That's marvelous. They'll be so pleased. You've done it again, Natalie. Good girl!"

Her heart pounded a little faster. "The invitation is only for the three of us, I'm afraid. I did ask to include you, but—"

"Oh, that's fine. I know how these things work. What's important is that Pelia's people get heard and they get their land."

Natalie couldn't keep the relief from her voice. "Thank you, Charlotte, for understanding."

"Were you worried?"

"Well, yes. I know you would have liked the opportunity."

"I've learned to wear disappointment well. I can be strident, but it's always to push a good cause. You did just what you had to do. Next steps. You'll come stay in DC with us, won't you, before the meeting? We can strategize."

Charlotte did have a heart of gold. "Yes. Of course."

"And you'll tell me all about it. Frank won't cover the details and nuances the way we women can. Rufus and I used to see very different things at our meetings with funders. That's why we made such a good team. Philanthropists need reliable crew members." She went on then to talk about how Pelia's English was coming along and she had new words in Yavapai she could speak. "Frank's a fine instructor. Brilliant mind, so eclectic. He's destined for bigger things with Indian policy. I'm certain the president will concur with his request."

"We can hope. I'll be there within the week. Oh, and I've heard from Mr. Peabody and he will support our efforts."

"Marvelous!"

"He wants me to write a little book for use in government schools."

"And what do you think of that?"

"I'm not sure." *Should I express my reluctance with Charlotte? How do I balance the needs of two benefactors?* Then, she decided: "I don't think a government book is a good idea, not yet. I've written some articles and I'll continue that."

"Hampton has its own magazine. They'd publish a few tidbits."

"Yes. A little book could waylay me for the larger project that is so much more important. I want to preserve the music and the art, and educate non-Indians about their importance, but I want to write an Indians' songbook, and I need their trust for that. And that all takes time."

"You tell Peabody. May as well be clear up front. You'll need to do the same with me. Tell me yes and no as you see fit. Rufus said I could be overbearing. I called it bearing down, but you get my point. By the way, I think I'll do with you what I do with Frank. I'll advance you two thousand dollars, and you keep a running tally of expenses. As you get low, you tell me and I'll refill the pot. How does that sound?"

"That's . . . that's most generous. I . . . thank you. Those words hardly seem enough."

"Let's plan our visit to Hampton before your meeting with Roosevelt. But only if you want."

Natalie laughed. "Yes. I do want to do that. I'll see you in poco tiempo. Pretty soon."

❧

The meeting with Roosevelt was smashing, as Natalie described it to George in her letter to him. She sat at her desk in New York, overlooking the lush green grass, oak trees, blooming geraniums, a different beauty than in Old Oraibi. *"Roosevelt said we had brought 'the desert west with us,'"* Natalie wrote. *"He inhaled like he could smell the dust on our boots, which I can assure you, we did not have, having given 'spit and polish' to them and to ourselves, Pelia included. Roosevelt is so quick. He understands immediately. He not only concurred with Frank's suggestion about using Fort McDowell for the Yavapai reservation, he apologized for the long thirty-year delay in the promise the government had made to the Yavapai. Then he told Secretary Hitchcock, who was also there, to put Frank in charge of the transition and help him negotiate the problems that would arise with the white settlers who were basically squatting on the government's land."*

She stopped, remembering how Pelia had relinquished his beautiful woven urn to the president, gifting it to him as though it were his firstborn child. Tears had pooled in Natalie's eyes as Pelia sang for the president. Roosevelt had been equally dignified, noble almost, in his acceptance. Natalie had witnessed something unique in hearing the song, seeing how the paired artistry of music and craft affected the president. She would never forget it nor the warmth she felt in having played such a small part in it.

Finishing George's letter, she began her thank-you note to the president and praised him for appointing Frank Mead as a special agent. Then she took an additional bold step in suggesting that the president might make a larger role for him, as Frank had such rapport with native people and had the added advantage of caring deeply about the Indian arts. *"Perhaps he could be in charge of all Arizona reservations since you are investigating Burton and there might be an opening there?"* Oh, she was getting daring, as she had when she insisted she be included in the Wagner Festival even though she was late in arriving. She'd been strong then. The Indians had brought that forthrightness back.

"If he were to supervise all of Arizona," Natalie continued, *"Frank Mead could perhaps create a model for other states and territories and even other countries who struggle with colonization, about how to both protect and serve the people within a government's realm. Art, Mr. President, can be used for reforming all of us."* She concluded with an appeal to the president's self-esteem, known to be quite developed. She praised him for his ability to choose the right man—or woman—and support them toward the

purpose Roosevelt chose and to be able to do in minutes what it would take other men years to accomplish.

A summer storm threatened as she looked out the window, dark clouds deepening the garden's green. *Am I spreading the adoration too thick? Or am I learning how to be a proper bene-factress?*

Within a week, Roosevelt wrote back. Natalie held the letter and winced when he said the Burton investigation had found nothing to warrant the man's removal. He described the need for it at all as "comical." Natalie felt her face grow warm. He thought them wasting of his time? Still, he had granted a new role to Mead. Frank would become the "Special Supervisor" for four states and two territories. Agents and superintendents would report to him about the development of "industry" on their reservations. And by industry, Natalie knew that Roosevelt meant not only farming and trade, but in the formal sense of diligence and aptitude, talent and skill poured into the arts where the soul of humankind was nurtured, in story, weavings, pottery, paintings, and song. At least among the Southwest states and territories, perhaps the enforcement of the Code would ease. She would find out for herself once she began her collection in earnest.

⚬

Natalie met with Peabody in his walnut-lined office in New York. The scent of linseed oil from a recent polish of his shiny desk tickled her nose. *No desert dust here.* To his suggestion that she write a book now, she said, "I need time to record the songs and make notes and have the performers gift me with their trust." He nodded for her to continue. "There must be enough time to educate me about the meanings of their music. I fear the consequences of sharing my ideas with too many people before the flame has had its chance to kindle the blaze for which it was struck." That flame had been ignited in Yuma and Oraibi. She had to keep it burning.

Peabody was thoughtful, then, "I defer to your wisdom. Let me know what your needs are."

"Thank you." Enthusiasm returned as she sat at the edge of her chair. "You've made it possible for me to do that which I have daily and nightly asked to do, and to do it as we have dreamed and hoped it might be done." She deliberately used the "we" word, because Peabody knew Charlotte supported her work as well. And she knew that benefactors wanted to be a part of something larger, not just a check waiting to be written. Here was the delicate balance George had referred to. "Let me do my small part as scribe in the still hour before the dawn," she said, "and then let the work speak, and the silent people give at last their message of simplicity and truth."

"Well spoken, indeed," Peabody said.

She liked the metaphor of herself as a scribe. It was an old word that meant an interpreter of documents as well as a copyist—for that was what she wanted to do, not to create any art on her own but to copy what the Indians granted her. But a scribe was also a sharp awl used to mark wood or metal to be cut. She'd seen pictures of petroglyphs, cut into stone. It was a part of Indian art.

She would have to cut and edit, but that was nothing new. She did that for articles written for *Harper's* or *Out West*. But being a scribe would give voice to the people she'd fallen in love with. They were her true partners: Lololomai, Chiparopai, Mina, and the others she'd approach, assuring them safety. Burton wouldn't dare withhold rations, wouldn't even risk complaint to Secretary Hitchcock. She trusted that Roosevelt would keep his promises, even if there were those in the government who might not. She had maneuvered a direct pathway to the "great white father" and she wouldn't squander it. The Indians' book she planned to put together would be *their* book. She would be but a pencil in their hands. Sometimes to write their songs downy, and sometimes to advocate for them as she had for Frank and Pelia, but always listening to their voices and, in the process, discovering her own.

25

A Good Heart

1903–1904

*N*atalie didn't let herself dwell on the stories of how some of the students had arrived at the Indian schools: kidnapped at night, brought terrified to lands far beyond any they had known, fearful that they might never see their families again. Weeks of shivering in fear, suffering. Instead, she marveled as she watched the teachers tell the children they could sing their traditional songs. Reluctant at first, they did sing and then told about the dance they performed or spoke haltingly in English of the last time they'd heard their father's voice ring out across the prairie or the lake. She recorded in her memory—if not on the Edison machine—the sadness in their brown eyes as their tongues formed the Zuni or Pawnee or Wabanaki lyrics. Natalie saw healing in the sway of their bodies, shawl fringes shifting gentle as a butterfly's touch, feathers fluttering, all moving to an ancient rhythm. Few had traditional regalia to wear, but the holding of a gourd or a shawl seemed to take the children home.

The students weren't all young children either, a fact that surprised her. The young adults might have come as four- or five- or ten-year-olds, but now they were in their twenties. Some even older, it appeared. She wondered if they stayed because they continued to learn new skills. Or were they forced to remain, their spirits broken, unable to remember those they left behind? A few she learned, had chosen to travel to a faraway school, to be educated in the Anglo ways.

Natalie began her work with Charlotte, visiting the Hampton School more than once. She took cues from the philanthropist about how to approach the teachers with Roosevelt's letter. They offered wary support at first, and then as they too saw the children thrive in those musical moments, they said they'd build in more opportunities for Natalie to meet the singers and record their performances. Charlotte had insisted that she listen to the African-American students' songs as well, and she did love their music, especially when they sang gospel songs. Hampton's newsletter, *Southern Workman*, published Natalie's essays, sending them to board members, benefactors, and the Bureau of Indian Affairs.

"We'll insist that those newsletters get to other Indian schools," Charlotte told her as she handed Natalie the first *Workman* piece. "Let the government pay the postage and pave the way for us."

It was still *us*, though Natalie planned to travel soon with George, who was a better observer and who was a quiet presence, unlike Charlotte, whose very voice boomed sometimes and made the Passamaquoddy and Penobscot children in the Maine schools they visited hesitate to sing their war and love songs. She'd have to broach the subject of leaving Charlotte behind soon.

Students who became comfortable with their presence often shared their artwork, and Natalie sought permission to photograph both her informants, as she'd begun thinking of them, and their drawings. Charlotte approved of the photographing and bought a camera for them to use, but she didn't agree to all of Natalie's ideas.

"I'm not sure we should actually pay them," Charlotte said one evening in a room at the school where the women stayed in upstate New York. Charlotte had brought a mirror from home and combed her hair in front of it while Natalie made notes. Natalie had earlier in the day given money to a Penobscot boy who sang for her.

"Why not?" Natalie looked up from her notebook. "It honors their contribution."

"Still, money is at a premium."

"But what they offer in their songs and art has value. Does a *Pahana*—the Hopi word for a white person, by the way—have the right to take a song without payment of some sort?" She looked at Charlotte's eyes in the mirror, an item most school bedrooms lacked because of the cost and, for some tribes, mirrors violated religious beliefs about the risk of young children seeing a reflection of themselves before their spirits were fully formed. "I get paid for the articles I write for the *Post*," Natalie continued, "so shouldn't they gain some benefit too?"

"The money isn't endless." Charlotte turned to face Natalie.

"I understand." It had been costly traveling to the Eastern seaboard schools. "It's just that, away from the tribal schools, I want access to a variety of singers and not only those deemed chiefs or medicine men. The average person needs to be heard, too, and a little money helps. I want to do this right, Charlotte. Take no advantage of them. That's been done enough." Natalie's heart beat a little faster disagreeing with her patron, but she was fighting for the Indians.

Charlotte stared, then sighed. "I suppose you're right. But be sure you keep track of who and how much you pay out. Maybe we can use it as evidence for the humane way you're going about this, have something to respond with to the critics."

Critics? "I'm very good at keeping records," Natalie said, her voice light. "And George is a wonderful bookkeeper." *If he'll join me.*

"I do have obligations in New York," Charlotte said. "I'm glad you understand. I've been meaning to discuss my need to stay in the East. I want to focus on the Hampton School, get some of the African-American songs recorded for you to analyze and assess once the Indian project is complete. You'll just have to figure things out without me. But I'll join you on occasion."

"Whenever you can," Natalie said. One worry lessened. But what about those critics?

∽

Back at the Curtis home, Natalie wrote letters—many letters—to scholars and researchers and those who had worked among the Navajo, for example. She solicited consultation on pronunciation of Hopi words from Reverend Voth, the Mennonite pastor at Oraibi who shared her concerns, and asked music questions about the Ghost Dance and Kiowa "word-songs," the correspondence flowing back and forth. There were advantages to civilization with access to libraries and letter carriers. And her mother was content that Natalie "worked" but was doing it from home or with a proper companion as a good daughter should. She only commented once about Natalie's "pushing" herself into fatigue.

George returned at Christmas, with good news for Natalie.

"I've changed your mind?" Natalie's joy lifted her voice in the cold air.

"You have," George said. "You're a good bargainer. Besides, I can't let you roam off alone."

"I couldn't hire a better assistant or guide or however you want to be known. Charlotte takes notes but not as copious as yours when I'm talking with an informant."

"What's a brother for?"

That she had convinced George to work for and with her pleased her greatly. This arrangement had also met the approval of her benefactors and thrilled her parents, who had worried once again about her health and the thought of her returning to the Southwest alone. Mimsey told her more how much she enjoyed having her daughters around, and Natalie herself discovered family interactions that she'd been isolated from during her intense years of practice and performing. Music had made her whole then, but it had separated her as well.

There were parties and introductions her mother forced upon her, but Natalie found she preferred the "noises" of El Alisal. There she'd met bold and interesting people, so different from chatter about fashion or husband-hunting. How she wanted to spend her time in New York was poring over her recordings and her notes with her hopes to do her part to break the wretched Code.

∞

When spring came, Natalie and George were ready to return to the Southwest "before I lose all I gained there," Natalie told him.

In Winslow, Arizona Territory, off the train, they sought two good horses, knowing that in some places Natalie intended to go, the wagon wouldn't work. The mules waiting for them at Oraibi would be good pack animals. Bonita too.

At the stable, Natalie settled herself on the back of the mare, patted the animal's neck, and smelled her hands. She loved the scent of horses and leather. She adjusted her hat string at her chin. A warm wind swirled a dust devil across the paddock. She rode the mare around, talking to her quietly, remembering how to sit, how to press her knees to give the horse signals for what she wanted. The owner had praised Bessie for her sure-footedness. "She likes a female hand to her," he'd said. And Natalie held the reins as lightly as she could. They would be a team; she was certain of it.

George's gelding was a taller horse, but the two animals had been raised by the same owner, so their pecking order was established and George's horse, Giant, was in charge, as his name reinforced. Natalie either rode beside George or brought up the trail behind him, which suited her just fine. Each mile they rode, Natalie felt her strength returning. The shadows of the New York skyscrapers and the bustle of people of DC had taken their toll on her health. She'd been so fatigued before they left that she feared a relapse. She would have to remember the pacing, the tempo with which she pursued her life. Horses would be her mentors.

Once they began the two-day ride through the painted desert, across this panorama that had stolen her heart, she felt exuberant, even with muscles sore from riding. She was going home to the Hopi.

As though they'd known the Curtis duo was on their way, children ran through dust to meet them and traveled beside them the mile or so back to Number 3 at the base of Third Mesa. They sang and danced and sauntered, and Natalie couldn't keep the grin from her face. Mina led Bonita, who brayed when she saw Natalie. She loved the music of the burro's cry and the sounds of the welcoming children. She didn't have to quiet them. They were freed by Roosevelt's letter.

Her first visit was to Lololomai as soon as they unpacked and George tended the horses. She climbed the ladder to his weaving rooftop, where his sister would interpret. Lololomai sat quietly when Natalie read to him the letter from Roosevelt. "It is safe to sing now," she told the chief. "No harm can come to you or your people. You can be Hopi 'good in your hearts' even as you sing again."

"*Ho, Tawimana,*" he said.

Natalie frowned at the unfamiliar word.

"It is the name he gives you," his sister Poníanömsí told her. "It means 'Woman Who Sings Like a Mockingbird' and 'Song Maid.' It has two meanings."

"I am honored," Natalie said. "In the future, when I speak with the great white chief, I will tell him the name the Hopi have given me and wear it with pride."

Lololomai grunted. Then, as he handed her back the Roosevelt letter, his brown face darkened by the summer sun lit up. "I sing for you." He told her it was a song he had just composed, a chant, and that it would be taught to his grandchildren to remember him by. Natalie took her recorder out and her notebook and spent the remainder of the day there, until candles were lit and there were stars in the sky when she walked down the trail, past the cobbled horses, crunching on corn. Her Southwest work had begun.

Natalie had the Roosevelt letter safe at hand and had no fear of her being able to do the work she felt called to. Burton could still sabotage her efforts indirectly, though. Getting evidence if he did wouldn't be easy and would take precious time away from what she wanted to do: preserve Indian songs.

"It's certainly clear," Burton told her, handing the Roosevelt letter back to her. She met with him the morning after listening to Lololomai sing. "I'll do what I can to stay out of your way. And if I can help . . ."

"Allowing the children to sing their songs at the school would be wonderful. And you can see, the president approves. I was allowed to do so at Hampton School and others. When they return home, if they tell their elders they are now allowed to sing, it might ease their grandparents into sharing the old songs with them. And eventually, with me."

"I will tell the teachers. Will you mostly be recording at the school, then?"

"Some. But I want to get original music down before those tunes are lost. George and I will travel to the remote areas. Any word you can pass along to the elders about the safety in their sharing that music, and their art, will be welcomed."

"Whatever the president wishes, we'll support."

His solicitousness made her wary.

❧

They'd carried the Edison to the school the next day, showing the teacher the letter. Then she played the cylinder with Lololomai's song on it. The children clustered around, recognizing their chief's voice. When the song was over, she asked if any of them would like to sing. She spent the day and told those she hadn't gotten to that she'd be back tomorrow.

The evening offered no respite. Before they could eat a supper of corn bread and sheep cheese, a Hopi man came to their cabin and asked if he could sing for her.

"Yes. Of course. Let me get my recorder set up." Natalie sang as she worked.

Dusk bristled with heat, but a breeze carried the promise of cooling. He sang his song and told her what it meant. She got his name, made notes, gave him a small coin, and he left. Very soon after, an older Hopi woman appeared, along with Mina, who translated her words.

"Did he sing his song? The man who left before us," Mina said.

"Yes. I recorded it."

"She wishes to hear it."

Natalie played the recording.

"Ho. It is not the right way to sing that song. She will sing it for you."

"Wonderful," Natalie said.

"You put on the machine."

"Yes, of course."

The woman sang, and Natalie made notes while George handled the Edison. When the woman finished, Natalie played it back for her. "Ho. That is the correct way." Then she told Natalie what the words meant, that it was a Katsina song, to help the corn and beans grow. It spoke of how butterflies of different colors kissed the flowers to bring the harvest. "Koianimptiwa makes this song?"

"He said he composed it," Natalie said.

"She composes," Mina told her. "It is her song too. Same song but different. You use hers."

Natalie offered the coin, which the woman refused, curling up her lip. Natalie blinked her surprise.

"No pay for song you keep for our grandchildren," Mina relayed.

The woman bustled out while two more elderly women waited to enter, willing to sing their versions of the song the first man had said he composed. Natalie lit candles and wrote all their names and listened to all, concentrating as she made notes, worrying later how she would include all these versions in her book, or if she could. She would give attribution to them. George recorded the coins given. Only two singers had accepted payment.

"Which will you use?" George asked after they'd all left and the moon rose like a perfect ceramic pot.

"All of them, if I can. How could I not? Each will have a song to give to their children and grandchildren, some who may never hear it sung by their elders."

"I confess. They sounded the same to me," George said.

"They were all slightly different. That's why I'm glad I have the recordings to go over." She tucked the cylinders away after labeling them and attaching the same label to her pages in the notebook. "But I have to say, I hadn't expected the politics of it. I guess that's what I'd call it."

"The competition between singers?"

Natalie nodded. "But it makes sense. Songs are precious. At Hampton, when I spoke with a Hoopa girl, she said that her people believe that each child is born with their own song, and that if an infant is allowed to cry as a baby without being picked up and comforted, the song could be lost. They have sung these songs in

210

their hearts, if not out loud because of the laws. Songs are a part of them like the shape of their eyebrows or the length of their fingers. Unique. And one might start to compare about whose song is better. A very human thing, I think, comparison—even if it is a waste of energy. I want to include them all."

"It's going to be a very fat book, Nat," George warned.

"I hope so," Natalie said. "And I'll have to figure out the money thing. Some seem to see it as a transaction and others almost as an insult." She was thoughtful then, sighed a happy sigh. "Oh, the complexities." It was invigorating to think of untangling these foreign threads so that other Anglos might gain lessons as she had, lessons that had healed.

∽∾

After several days of recording at Oraibi proper, George and Natalie set out on horseback, their start delayed by a gaggle of children wanting to sing for her as she washed her face at the outside box that held her washbowl. George shaved at a bowl beside hers. Natalie grinned as she listened, then sent them on their way, laughing. The Roosevelt letter was doing its work, allowing the songs to be freely sung.

It would not be an easy journey to the outer reaches of the mesa where hogans of sticks and canvas rose up like small bumps erupted in the desert skin. The structures were seldom permanent, could be moved if the flocks of sheep needed to find new grazing. Each was different, while the same in providing the simplest of shelter for the families inside. She had memorized in Hopi a few sentences about wishing to hear the songs of the elders or the mothers and fathers. The recorder was left behind. In each home, using her limited Hopi language, dropping Lololomai and his sister Ponianömsí's names and her few memorized sentences, she would begin to sing a song, then urge the occupant of the hogan to sing one back while she made notes.

Natalie and George would share their mutton and whatever else they had and humbly accept the prickly pear juice offered or the corn bread the Indians baked for the Anglos, a treasure from their stone ovens. Once they joined a family heading to the forested areas and helped knock down piñon nuts onto blankets laid on the ground. People sang while they worked, and she and George were invited to remain for the roasting, the pungent scent rising from the fire, making Natalie's mouth water. There seemed to be a song for every occasion, and it didn't take long to realize that music was as much a part of who they were as a people, a family, a sister or brother, as the stories and memories they held in their hearts. Songs were living things for them. Natalie was Anglo, separate; would always be kept at a distance. But she could still be a part of their stories, especially as she hoped to uphold their history, even as her very presence threatened to change it.

The siblings might spend a day or two at one place, camping out, sleeping on the ground near a spring so the horses could be watered and tear at the grasses close by. Then they'd saddle up again and cross rocky slopes, ravines, clamber through narrow rock walls, hear the coyotes howl at night, wash their hair with wild mint picked up at the trader's. Hopi songs on the other mesas found their way to black notes in Natalie's books. She wrote and even gathered up music sung for them while the herders watched their flocks, sometimes accompanied by a flute. Natalie never felt tired. She'd forgotten that once she had walked with a crutch.

In the evenings, the two talked like the old friends they were. "So how did you break that tooth, Brother of mine?" They were both so tired that night that they had not prepared a big meal, deciding instead to fix a large breakfast in the morning. They talked while the fire flickered low and the full moon rose up over the pinnacles in the distance. Natalie gasped at the bigness of it, the grandeur of it all.

"It was a cowboy mistake," George said. He lay on his back, a blanket across his body, his hands behind his head. "Had to try a buckin' bronc, just once, you understand. It's a sort of initiation. My head went down while the bronc's went up, and voilà, I had a broken tooth courtesy of that horse's very hard head. Not a very interesting story, is it?"

"It speaks to your bravery."

"Ha. Stupidity, more like it. There are boys with riding buckin' broncs in their blood, but this boy is not one of them. I never wanted off an animal as much in my life. When you're a greenhorn, there is no eight-second limit like at the rodeo competitions. You ride until the horse decides it's time to separate itself from you." He chuckled. "I have enjoyed this life so much. Did I tell you that when this foray is finished, Bridgham and I are taking an apartment in Washington where I'll finish my book and try to get it published before returning west? It might be a good place for you to do your editing work when we get back."

"It well might be. Charlotte has also offered me her apartment there."

"Ah, that'd be better. Fewer brother interruptions."

She hadn't thought that far ahead, immersed as she had become in landscape and song. She'd focused on the work of gathering music like harvesting piñon nuts before they were turned into butter. But butter churning lay ahead, along with the anxieties of putting together a book that mattered away from the desert's music. For this night, though, she was full of gratitude for months spent falling asleep on the desert floor to the songs of distant coyotes.

26

Things Left Behind

ang on!" George shouted to her as Bessie slid on a talus slope of loose rocks they'd had to traverse.

"I am!" Natalie's heart pounded and she felt herself slipping, grabbed the saddle horn and refound her feet in the stirrups. She was more worried about the horse than herself, and when Bessie went down, Natalie leapt off but still held the reins. "Easy, easy," she told the snorting mare, who was as frightened as Natalie was.

George dismounted, tried to give the reins of his horse to Natalie.

"No, no. I'll talk to her." She spoke to the animal in the tone of a healer—soft and reassuring, hopeful. Bessie's breathing eased and with gentle strokes on her neck, Natalie's mount sat up, then stood up and limped onto a desert patch away from the slope.

"Here." George had Natalie rub a salve on the mare's leg where she'd sustained a cut. It wasn't deep. "We'll camp here, let Bessie recover."

"And me," she said.

"You did great."

She paused. "I did, didn't I?" It was evening, the sun having splashed into a pool of yellows, oranges, and reds. Their cooking fire lapsed into tepid warmth. She'd write one day about how she'd changed through the aroma of risk. After their supper of jerky, Natalie asked, "That poem you recited at the Bar X last year, was it fiction, part of your novel? Or . . . ?"

"What do you think?"

She hesitated. "It was part of your story. I felt that. Is that why you left New York?"

Moonlight revealed his facial features. "I'd come here to heal my asthma. And a broken heart." The firelight reflected a sadness in his eyes. "Sounds like a dime novel, doesn't it?"

"Rather Curtis-like, really. Touching."

"The climate healed my asthma. And a good woman healed my heart—before it got broken once again." He scoffed into the firelight. "That's the way of life. We break. We mend and rise again to love."

"And like the Acoma pot, we're stronger for it."

"I hope so. Something good coming from the bad or at least the painful." He put his arms under his head, elbows out. "She was a good woman, a grieving one. Maybe that's why we were attracted to each other, two wounded souls. But it wasn't meant to be. She's married and a faithful woman who let me hold her through the night as she held me." He faced Natalie. "I'd call us Emersonian friends," George said. "The kind you can pick up with no matter how long the separation and carry on the friendship, no explanations needed. But the poem is about that first love that could never be."

She wondered if it was Mary Jo of the Bar X, if that was what she saw pass between them with that lingering embrace. But it was George's story to tell. He didn't need questions from her. "A blend of fact and fiction then."

"Like any good poem," George said. "And the truth of it is that I left New York in part because I'd tired of watching you disappear and me not being able to stop it. I felt like I had to get out, maybe find a route to bring you back to health but get myself well first."

"I'm sorry you felt you had to leave," Natalie said.

"Now, don't add that guilt to your load, Nat. I left of my own accord, and because I did, I got to come back better and tend to you." A grace rest came between them before George said, "And what about you, Nat? What really brought about your . . . ?"

"Folding like a battered tent?"

"Not sure I would have described it like that."

Natalie chuckled. "I wouldn't either before our desert trek. But even battered tents can get put back up again, with a little stitching, new posts, and companions. I know you've wondered." *Am I ready to tell my story?* She was glad it was night. She wouldn't have to see if George's eyes judged her.

"Only if you want to," George said.

"Walter Damrosch was my downfall."

"The conductor? I thought you loved his instruction."

"The same. My Adonis," Natalie said. "So handsome. My friend and I swooned of course, as did most of the females in the audience. But I thought there was something special between us. I had these fantasies, that he . . . loved me. The way he touched my hands on the piano keys, how close he leaned over my shoulder to point at something on the sheet music. He said things . . ." Shame crept up her neck, heated her face. "I thought he'd leave his wife," she whispered. "That I could have my music and a marriage, that we'd travel together, our lives rich with rhythm and applause."

Her pause was long enough that George said, "Are you still awake?"

"I saw him flirting with a clarinetist, heard him say the same things he said to me, and when I boldly asked him about *our* relationship, he laughed. 'You're my student, Natalie. A lovely student.' He patted me on the head. And though I was twenty-one years old, certainly old enough to know better, I was devastated.

Of course, I couldn't tell anyone about my perceived loss, my humiliation."

"I'm sorry, Nat. I didn't know."

"It came at the same time as Anton Seidl invited me to perform with the Philharmonic. It was the culmination of a lifetime of study and practice. But I doubted myself. I'd made such a terrible error in Damrosch, was I ready to perform on such a stage? I felt paralyzed."

Natalie was now up on one elbow.

"You've no idea what it's like for a woman, George, not really. Marriage is expected, but if a woman fails to find a mate, doesn't want to marry, doesn't want to 'settle,' then what is she to do?"

"But you were a trained pianist, a singer. You could have toured."

"It would have meant giving up on marriage and sailing on that channel of life forever. Men can have both. I'd devoted— and that is the word—I'd devoted myself to music, to the hours of practice, to the sounds that came into my head day and night. The Philharmonic invitation meant that would then be my direction. How many performances would I be allowed as a spinster woman, playing at the behest of male conductors? Added to that was my naïveté. I was living in two worlds, George. The world of the concert pianist who could live independently and perhaps earn a living at it if I had been a man; and the expectation that I should also marry. Yet if I married, I would only be allowed to teach music." She didn't want to return to that painful place, but maybe it was time. "The night before the performance, confused and doubting, I blamed the music." She felt the heaving grief rise up from her stomach. "I couldn't face it."

"I'm sorry. I keep saying that."

George rose from his bedroll to hand her a red bandana. She blew her nose. Took a deep breath. "And then there was the guilt, the terrible guilt that I'd let Mimsey and Bogey—all of you really— down. I had no romantic interests and I had just blown up my musical career. On top of that, my body decided it had also had enough. I developed that back pain. And used a crutch for a while, remember?"

"You pounded it to the music at concerts, I remember that," George said.

She blew her nose again, sat up and handed George the bandana. He spread it over a greasewood shrub to dry out.

"Breathlessness swept over me like an East Coast blizzard, freezing me out of all motivation, joy," Natalie sighed. "Guilt sang in my head as loud as *Valkyries*."

"I think you might be carrying weight you don't need to." George's voice was soft, barely breaking into Natalie's remembered sorrow.

She leaned back against the saddle she used as a pillow on the trail. "Maybe. 'Make a personal change,' the doctor told me when I spoke of guilt. But I couldn't think of what to do and I was so tired." She wiped her eyes. "Then you came back from the West all bronzed and well. And you invited me to join you. I'll never forget you for that, George."

"Like I said, this has been a grand time for me, traveling with you."

The sound of the horses staked a few feet away broke into the night silence. Natalie said, "I sometimes think what has happened to the Indians, what we've done to them—conquering, breaking agreements, ignoring what they bring to us—I think they walk in two worlds. Trying to honor a way of life that is disappearing. And in a way, that's me and all my years of practice. They've had to move on to something totally foreign, learn new ways, navigate laws and landscapes they've had no choice in. My suffering, though, is self-imposed, isn't it? I think that's one of the lessons of this journey. Their suffering comes from the outside and is so much more damaging, affecting generations. But we are both trying to find ways to be independent and at the same time be 'good in our hearts.'" She felt the desert chill and pulled her blanket up to her throat. "But I at least don't have to face judgment because of my race. The Southwest has taught me that. I'm not paralyzed. And I'm learning from how the Indian people carry on. I admire their resiliency. I think it flows through their music and their arts. Their songs and ceremonies have brought me back. I'm now a part of the larger universe of hope."

"You're starting to sound like Uncle George and Walden Pond, all that," George said.

"Am I? I do share his belief that there is a God that is good who gives life to all beings and that divine laws of justice govern the universe. As I come to understand better how the different tribes view the world, Creator God is certainly a big part of that."

George stoked their campfire and, after a time, said, "You've certainly carried out the doctor's orders."

"How? Oh, getting well, you mean?"

"Making that personal change. Doing what you can to transform the guilt. Did you ever imagine you'd have an occupation as an ethnomusicologist?"

"No, I never did, but you're right. I have taken steps to change. That doctor also said that guilt can help make global changes if we turn it outward instead of inward."

"You're doing both," George said.

"I am." She took a deep, refreshing breath. "And with each song I record, I put a little more of the shame away to make room for something better. Hopefully, not just for myself but for the Indians."

⚭

George and Natalie headed south from there into Navajo lands and then Apache. Natalie had decided she wanted a recording from Geronimo, to share a side of him that wasn't Buffalo Bill–tinged with all the stories of his fierceness. If they could find him.

But they rode first to the Hopi village of Hano, where they were taken by the exquisite pottery of the woman named Nampeyo.

219

Natalie had read about her work and seen examples of the orange and black and yellow dyes painted onto the surface of the smooth pots. Keams sold her work at his trading post ten miles east. It was a way Nampeyo helped support her family, the selling of her pots.

Like Natalie, the potter was small, barely five feet tall, and gentle. She knew some English, as there had been excavations of old Anastasi sites by anthropologists and archaeologists and the other "gists" seeking specimens for their museums, and some had taken meals with Nampeyo and her family through the years.

Natalie and George were invited to such a meal. Natalie didn't ask to make recordings of the Corn Grinding songs she heard. Nampeyo was of the Corn Clan, they'd been told. Instead of making notes, Natalie marveled at the pottery. They'd been told it would not be offensive if they offered to trade dollars for a bowl. She selected a small pot, held in the palm of her hand, one that would fit in her saddlebag beside the Acoma pot. "Spider," Nampeyo said, nodding toward the design in black and white. "White spaces as valued as the painted."

"As in music, the pauses are important. Even on the written page, the eyes need the white space." It was two artists, chatting.

Purely decorative, beautifully designed, it spoke of a talent gleaned from ancestors whose stories and songs still hovered over the ruins those "gists" came to explore.

The potter invited them to watch her work, and she sang while her hands shaped the clay, and for Natalie there was something spiritual in the movements. She asked to make notes of the song, but instead, Nampeyo motioned for her to sit beside her, and Natalie did. The potter placed clay into Natalie's hands, put her own palms over Natalie's as though the two were one. Natalie coiled the clay, then smoothed away the separating lines, pressing with her knuckles, while Nampeyo sang and painted orange on another pot. The clay held no grit, was smooth with the water wash. Natalie's fingers pressed inside and out. She dipped her hands in water, felt the viscosity.

"It's of the earth," she told George later. "I felt a part of it." She held one of Nampeyo's purchased pots up to the twilight. Then, "Oh no! My Zuni ring, with the seven turquoise stones." She held the ring up so he could see. "I've lost a stone. It . . . it must be inside the pot I worked on. I pushed my knuckles like Nampeyo did. It must have been loose."

"Do you want to go back and see?" They'd ridden a few miles from Hano.

"No, no." Contentment overcame her. "I like knowing I've left a part of something that mattered to me there. It feels right. It's part of a healing."

They made their night camp, and Natalie mused on yet another insight. "Nampeyo's pottery incorporates designs on shards found in those ancient ruins, and she brought them back after excavations. It's quite unique. But she blends them with her own artistry of today. It's a philosophy that fits in with the songs. Somehow, in my Indians' book, I need to incorporate the unique designs of pottery, weavings, sand paintings, prayer sticks, musical instruments. Music most of all, but the rest must be remembered as well."

"As I said before, it's going to be a fat book."

∞

They traveled through Navajo country, where Natalie made notes of Songs of the Horse, mountain songs, Song of the Rain Chant, and even a Dance Song of the Night Chant. A certain hunting song intrigued her with its accompanying movements. The Earth song made her heart sing. She watched sand paintings being made and was told their stories, marveling that within hours, the intricate designs would be wiped away as was the custom. Fleeting beauty; memory sustained. She and George attended ceremonies in the kiva, where she heard once again through an interpreter about Hozhonji songs, the holy works that the Navajo singers had told her about at El Alisal.

"*Industrious, independent, fearless,*" Natalie wrote in her notes one night on the trail, firelight flickering. "*Faces are pastoral yet majestic. True son of the silence,*" she concluded, "*the awe, the grandeur of the desert.*" She knew she was fortunate. The songs gave her ease, washing away thoughts that she was taking advantage of the people, finding pleasure in the midst of the tragedy of assimilation.

"I have more Navajo recordings than any other tribe, at least so far," she told George. "And I like so much the Mountain Song for Healing. I wrote it down as *Dsichl Biyin*. I can't pronounce it, but the interpreter said it was a song calling people home when they are very ill, crossing rainbows from mountain to mountain." She paused to look at her notes again.

George stirred a chunk of goat cheese into his coffee, the spoon clinking against the tin cup.

"It's all very structured," Natalie continued. "I mean each section—there are six, he said—must be sung four times, for the four mountains—East, South, West, and North. And every word must be sung perfectly in sequence, nary a word missed. The refrain for the first one is 'Yea, swift and far I journey,' and each song has a different response, each about a person going 'home.' They describe it as a kind of heaven where the person becomes part of the mountains."

"Ashes to ashes, dust to dust," George said.

"Something like that. There are incredible parallels between the Judeo-Christian beliefs if only the missionaries would see that, give them time instead of forcing them into the only way to see the world."

"They gave up trying to convert the adults and focus on the children, the Code hoping to wipe out all that they came from," George said.

"Hence, all the Indian schools." She perused her notes. "The sand paintings of the mountain songs are exquisite, aren't they? I feel so honored that they let me copy them. I wonder if those

222

also are kept from the children so that if they do see them, the experience is cloaked in guilt, like their own history is forbidden. And how would they be able to make a 'personal change' to rid themselves of the weight?"

It was a question that had haunted her. Natalie said, "What man meant for evil, God meant for good. Isn't there some Scripture like that?"

"Genesis 50:20, 'Ye meant evil against me; but God meant it for good.'"

Natalie raised her eyebrows.

"What?" George defended. "I didn't spend years in the New York library reading only fiction. And it's a helpful thought when things seem to spin in another direction than what one hoped for."

"How do we turn the tables on the Burtons of the world who would take the good of Indian history and use it maliciously, make dances and hair length evil? Are children only singing when we are there? Maybe I will write a short pamphlet like Peabody suggested, for government schools, to allow traditional music even if I'm not there to record those songs. Maybe that will ease both fear and unwarranted guilt." She wasn't just an observer, she was an agent of change.

⁂

They found Geronimo in a faraway hogan. He was still stately in his seventies or eighties, Natalie guessed. He was an Apache, one of the last tribes subdued, conquered, or defeated by the military. For the book, she had decided she would write brief introductions for each tribe for which she had recorded music. She hoped she'd be able to do their histories justice in a short paragraph.

"I will sing for your book," Geronimo said. He had experience with Anglos, many in a warring status, but over time his enemies had gained a begrudging respect for his strategy in evading the military for so long. George said his cruelty and cunning couldn't be dismissed, though. But now his dark eyes held surrender. Not a full yielding to Anglo demands, Natalie guessed. She made the request that he sing, and he had agreed when she told him why and that his old adversary and now friend, Roosevelt, had approved.

"It is good to remember the songs," he said. "This one is old. My grandfather taught it." He went on to say it was a medicine song and that when he sang it, "It takes me to a holy place above the mountains and into the sky, changing me to a spirit as I sing." He drew symbols in Natalie's notebook to show his transformation.

"I'll include those drawings," Natalie said, "if you approve."

Geronimo nodded agreement, a sly smile on his face. "My name will be written?" *He likes the notoriety.* He accepted the payment Natalie offered, though he shook his hand asking for more after she laid the first bills in his palm. The curl of his lip when he finally folded the money brought back Natalie's worry that the Indians' book was but another taking from the Indian people, that she was yet another usurper of Indigenous ways. She vowed again to do everything to make the book about them and not about how their music was changing her.

Interlude #3

Nampeyo the potter breathes in the music of the wind that blows across the stone house. It is where she goes to receive what comes to her that she paints onto the pots. From the rooftop, she can see wide spaces and the old stories of Spider Woman, or witness *Kee-sa*, Sparrow Hawk, visiting a cactus. She takes them in and makes them part of the red and black and white of her designs. Migration stories. Prayer-sticks designs. Eagles. Others. They become what she creates in concert with the earth and can trade them to feed her family.

A part of Nampeyo wants to bring the woman, Natalie, to this place, away from Hano; but she wants more time to see if the white woman can hold the stories close, let the music of the desert be the flute she hears at night without wrapping her Anglo music around the Hopi ways.

The woman, Natalie, moved her hands across the clay, helped make the fire, then let the water and the stub of color spread so she could paint it with the horsehair brush. She is a beginner. Will she take instruction? She sees the pot the woman, Natalie, made. There is a bump. With her nail Nampeyo scratches at it. A turquoise stone. She will let the stone stand out on the inside, and if she sees the woman again, she will give her the pot marked by something she left behind.

This day, Nampeyo carries small pots, the size of an infant's palm, with her to the wider desert. She drops them to the earth, fired but unpainted, as she walks along. They are gifts of gratitude for the wind, the clay, the water and fire. If the woman, Natalie, returns, Nampeyo will speak of these small treasures, hopes the woman will understand the importance of not only taking but of leaving small things behind.

27

Of Art, Ethics, and Money

1904

*Y*ou have to go to St. Louis," Charlotte had written. They'd picked the letter up at the Navajo Agency, its having taken weeks to find them. *"I'll meet you there."*

"Well, there's a surprise," Natalie said, waving the letter at George.

"What's in St. Louis?"

"The Louisiana Purchase Exposition. She says there'll be a modern Indian schoolhouse, exhibits from around the world. She thinks we can add to the displays." She tapped her finger on her lip in thought. "I could put something together from the latest songs."

George remained quiet as they walked toward their quarters at the agency. Puffs of dust rose before their boots. They'd encountered a Kwakiutl singer at the Sherman school when they'd made a trek to California to see Charles and Eva and the painter Alice, and to record more songs. Traveling to Yuma afterward, Natalie had captured new pieces listening to Chiparopai.

"Maybe we don't need to go to St. Louis," George said. "You already have several new informants."

"I want to take full advantage of Roosevelt's letter that keeps people singing. Besides, I can't deny my chief benefactress." She stopped, turned to him. "You're not getting bored, are you, dear Brother?"

"No. I'm up for the journey. But I'm starting to wonder how much work arranging all the music and art will be for you."

"The work just leads me onward, carrying me almost. We have to go. Who knows what doors will open in St. Louis."

Arriving a month before the exposition opened, Charlotte had arranged for rooms for them all, and she called upon acquaintances in the city who could help Natalie make presentations, give a few paid speeches extolling the work she'd already accomplished. Her claim to a Roosevelt connection kept opening doors.

"There's interest in your articles," Charlotte said. "*Harper's* would print one a month if you sent them."

"I don't want to exploit them for the price of an article."

Charlotte sighed. "Sometimes, Natalie, you are too ethical."

"There's no such thing," Natalie said and smiled.

"You're an expert now." Charlotte shook her finger at her like a mother to a child. "You have to take advantage of that."

"An expert? Less than two years ago I knew little of Native American life."

"With your articles and your travel and Roosevelt behind you—by the way, he's coming to St. Louis—you have much to offer. Don't hesitate to express your views. Use that on behalf of the Indians."

It was true. Natalie had made an incredible transformation. She had immersed herself in something compelling, doing good for others. But she was also "doing good" for herself. "Let's take a look at what the committee on Native Americans has proposed. Maybe I can add something."

"I should hope," Charlotte said as she fingered the pearls at her neck. She wore silver earrings she said she'd acquired at the Smithsonian. "Zuni," she told Natalie. "Like your ring."

"I left a stone at Hano, in a pot." Natalie showed her the Zuni ring, its missing stone now a symbol of her healing, leaving something of herself behind.

Natalie's task would be to observe how thousands of people would "read" the Indians' story in these St. Louis exhibits. What she had to offer was doing what she could to keep their stories authentic.

They walked through the many buildings, seeking out the anthropology exhibits. Hammering could be heard. The fair took up over a thousand acres, with buildings that looked like they belonged in Europe. A photographer on top a high ladder got a bird's-eye view of the main thoroughfare. *A woman.* Her presence surprised Natalie but delighted her as well. She'd try to speak with her later, but meanwhile the Underwood exhibit stopped her. "A new typewriter," she said out loud as she and Charlotte maneuvered around the workmen putting up the extensive exhibit.

"I'll see what I can do."

"Oh, I didn't mean for you to—"

"They might be happy to advertise that one of their machines is being used by the notable music ethnologist Natalie Curtis." Charlotte squeezed her arm, then headed off to seek a donation.

The "seeking donation" part of Natalie's effort still bothered her, asking for money or favors. What might they ask of her in return? Still, she had no trouble inviting the Indians to sing. Charlotte was wrong. She wasn't too ethical; there were just many moral considerations to weigh in this undertaking.

∽

She'd have to be diplomatic. People had worked for years on this event, and here approached a Johnny-come-lately like Natalie.

The World's Fair, as people informally called the Exposition, would open at the end of April, and the Curtis clan had come on board only early in the month. The Olympics would be run as part of the events. And then there was the gigantic Ferris wheel to entertain fairgoers coming by train from around the country and around the world to see dozens of new buildings, pools, and gardens celebrating industry and agriculture. Progress. The Indian exhibits were meant to show how far the Indigenous people had progressed toward assimilation. But Natalie wanted people to see them for the riches they brought with them, the treasures she hoped to preserve, not how much they'd been forced to change.

Natalie walked softly. Mostly, she commented on the photographic displays. "If it were me," she said, "I would scrub out the background with the metal buckets behind that Navajo man, the cluttered area around his hogan. Let the sky be his background, the land and desert that are the base of who he is. Wipe out that which puts him into our world. Let viewers see him as he once was, and still is in his native land."

"We're hoping to show the assimilation," one of the coordinators said. "It's about progress."

"I can see that. But in my view, merely a suggestion, better to let visitors see what we might be losing if we take away too much, make them too much like us at the expense of who they are. As a nation, we don't want to assimilate to the point of . . . extinction. At the very least, I'd like to see an image, not of the 'savage Indian' the press and the military describe them as, but as a people connected to the land, the music, their religion and their arts."

"To be taken under consideration," the photographic manager said in a way that told Natalie she needed to work on her ambassadorial skills.

"We have an Alaskan group who will be living at the exhibit. People can see how they spend their days." This from an enthusiastic volunteer. "That shows them as they are."

Does it? An artificial village with people wearing regalia they'd never put on except for a ceremonial dance? How does that show them as they are?

It made her think about her book, how she would share the songs but must also include stories, legends, and practices. It would be a delicate balance of preserving and honoring without making the Indians into caricatures, romantic warriors. They were men and women and children, that's what she wanted the world to know about, their uniqueness as a people, their splendidness as artists. *Isn't that how we all want to be seen?*

She wasn't swayed, though, from asking some of the Indians brought to St. Louis to sing for her, after hours. She met Crow and Kiowa Dakota students who sang, San Juan and Pima. Charlotte identified important contacts for her, possible donors. The anthropologist Frank Boaz had taken an interest and made a donation to Charlotte for Natalie's work. Natalie expanded her musical collection without having to travel to far-off reservations. But she missed the desert heat, the wide vistas, the quiet horseback rides beside George.

"Oh, look, George. There's Geronimo." The old warrior sat behind a table, selling and signing photographs of himself.

"He makes a little money," George said.

Natalie was glad for that, though it saddened her to see his once fierce visage reduced to scrawling his name across his photo. But she bought one and he signed it to "Song Maid," handing it to her with sad eyes above that cunning grin.

The Roosevelts arrived to much fuss. Natalie had no chance to sit down with the president, but he acknowledged her with a tip of his tall hat at the mechanical and engineering exhibit.

Music was everywhere at the fair, and Natalie attended concerts by Chinese, Japanese, and Philippine participants. But as she wrote in a *New York Times* article, she favored the Native American music and found their work to be the most artistic. She made sure to write down the names of any of her informants, a part of her believing that she was witnessing not only the humus of an American folk music garden but of individuals who would one day become celebrated artists, anthropologists, lawyers, and the like in addition to everyday musicians and potters and painters. With her Indian songbook, she hoped both the median and the much celebrated would move into the white world without having erased the roots of where they'd first been planted.

28

Of Beadwork and Barrettes

*I*nstead of hurrying back to New York, she and George and
Charlotte—who had made the arrangements—reached Wisconsin in the prime of autumn's leafy color show. Beadwork barrettes the size of a child's palm and worn at the back of a woman's
head were the first crafts or "industries" Natalie held in her hands
at the Winnebago Agency.

It was a smallish bureau in the northern Wisconsin woods, and
she soon learned that when the Winnebago had been removed
from the lush lakes and river oxbows of their ancestors in the late
1800s to the flatlands of the Dakotas, dozens of Winnebago people
had resisted. They'd been so discouraged at the barren landscape
they'd been moved to, they risked their lives by paddling down the
Missouri River at night where the Pawnee accepted them. But a
few had returned to their Wisconsin homelands, and that was the
agency Natalie visited that fall.

A porcupine quill belt, three inches wide, caught Natalie's eye
where the trader had it in a glass display next to tobacco and

colorful barrettes. "Part of the old work," he said. "Tiny trade beads and quills in a pattern meant to represent the lakes they love. They use different beads today."

"It's beautiful," Charlotte said. "Definitely an art form. They can work on such things now that they're stuck on reservations. Before, when they had to do so much just to survive, who had time for beadwork?"

Natalie purchased one of the belts that tied with leather strings at the front. She'd lost sufficient weight that the belt fit perfectly around her slender waist. "It must have been made for a young girl," Natalie said. The quills were smooth as silk and slightly stained. It had been worn. *This was a belonging for someone.*

Once he saw Roosevelt's letter, the agent suggested informants for them to visit and introduced them to a young interpreter. They met him at the school where Natalie recorded several songs, the children delighted to be allowed to sing and dance. She sang first, hoping to assure them that she had learned Hopi and Navajo and Yuma songs, and that hearing them, they might trust her to share their own.

"I try to be an Indian with them," Natalie told the day school superintendent, a Catholic priest.

He scoffed. "That can't be. You're absolving yourself of the guilt timid Anglos feel for what they think we've done to these people. I say, all's fair in love and war. They fought against us. They were conquered. We convert them, save their souls. That's that."

"Surely faith demands compassion and justice."

"Don't interfere, Miss Curtis." He leaned over her. "It takes a special person to live in this godforsaken place."

"I was under the impression that there is no place God's forsaken," Natalie told him. She wanted to say more but could see his throat press against his priest's collar ready to rail against her. "Thank you for allowing us to record." She turned then to the students. "Let's sing," she said, hoping to rescue them from any act of outrage.

∞

"You can't be an Indian, Natalie." George spoke in the sparsely furnished room at the agency they'd been given to work on notes and cylinders.

"What brought that on?" Natalie turned to him.

"You'll be mocked trying to 'be them' rather than 'with them,'" George said. "I'm just concerned about you trying to be too much native."

"I'm not. I just want them to trust me."

"I think Natalie's right," Charlotte said. "To be as much of an Indian as she can makes it possible for trust to build, so she can preserve their songs." Charlotte sat on the single cot covered with a white Hudson's Bay blanket and its red-and-black stripes. She wore a pair of beaded earrings that reached her neckline.

"But that diminishes who they are. It dilutes their uniqueness as a race." George handed Natalie another cylinder. "You can't be an Indian any more than I can be a burro."

"Oh, I know I can't *be* an Indian," Natalie said. "But trying to relate, from a soulful level, for the children's sake, eases their fears if they see me as more one of them than not."

"Maybe." George wore a wool sweater and rubbed his hands for warmth by the woodstove. "It's just that there is no absolving of guilt for the catastrophe of assimilation."

"Assimilation isn't a good thing, even done humanely," Charlotte agreed.

"I want to put them at ease," Natalie said. She envied the Quaker trader Louisa Wetherill, whom the Navajo called One of Them, claimed her as a descendant. But Louisa lived among the Diné, gave her life to them. Natalie came in and out, was a unique observer, not a family member—though she loved Mina like a daughter, Lololomai as a beloved grandfather, Chiparopai as a wise auntie. She hesitated. "One of the Winnebago children asked if the interpreter and I were brother and sister. I thought that was sweet. I said

I wished I was." The Hopi had given her a name, welcomed her, danced for her. But the truth was, she was not of them. She supported from the outside. George was right. She would never *be* an Indian. But she could empathize, and hoped to be something more than a mere "do-gooder," that class of people that superintendents like Burton and that Catholic priest so despised.

∞

They put Charlotte on the train back to New York during a light snowfall. Then George, Natalie, and the interpreter went to an old part of the Winnebago Agency to a tepee the interpreter had suggested. A wisp of smoke drifted up through the crisscrossed poles at the top. They were invited inside as a bald eagle screeched across the treetops in this thick pine forest. They recorded a love song, so Natalie was told. The toothless woman who sang it got tears in her eyes remembering, Natalie supposed, when she was young and her lover played his flute with soft tremors and dreamy streams of sound luring her to see him. But she didn't want to assume and so asked the interpreter if the woman would share the song's story.

"The maiden tells her mother she wishes to see her auntie," the interpreter said as the woman spoke. "But she joins her lover instead. She is drawn to the flute."

The story was told in present tense, Natalie noted, as though it just happened, wasn't something from the past. *Stories in contemporary time.* She made a note.

Afterward, the woman handed the flute to Natalie, and she played it as the Winnebago woman nodded her head. "Her husband made the instrument," the interpreter said.

The woman picked up a bird whistle then and blew through it.

"A duet," Natalie said when they finished. "My first for Indian music."

She asked the woman to repeat the song while she captured the cadence, filled in the score in her notebook, setting black notes to help her remember the tune. She thanked the woman with the wrinkled face, who offered them an herbal tea in the smoky tepee, so warm and comfortable. She showed them a headband she'd made of porcupine quills. "The designs are handed down, given as gifts when an old one dies," the interpreter said. "Only that family member is allowed to repeat the design until it is given away at their death."

"Their arts are as important as their songs," Natalie said.

"She wishes you to take the flute," the interpreter said.

"Oh, I couldn't." Natalie put her hands to her heart, declining with respect. She felt her hands move to her throat, not wanting to offend, being humbled by the offer. "Her husband made it for her, I don't deserve . . ."

The interpreter shrugged. "To accept a gift honors the giver. To refuse a gift . . ."

"I see. Yes. Of course." She reached out her hands. "With respect." She bowed her head, held the flute before her, nodded, and asked for the Winnebago words that meant "good" and "thank you."

Natalie and George had been invited inside so many homes, strangers welcomed as friends, the people sharing the work of their hands and the songs of their hearts. Natalie owed each contributor to her book so much.

I owe them for the richness that is my life now.

On the way back, Natalie's horse shied at something on the trail, and she felt herself slipping but recentered herself on top of the mare.

"Dead porcupine," the interpreter said. He dismounted and with his leather gloves began pulling the quills. "For my grandmother."

"How did it die?" Natalie asked, expecting a narrative of some violent fight, a predator, a battle lost.

"Old age."

"Ah," Natalie said, embarrassed that she could fictionalize so

236

quickly a story. She would have to be careful not to let her imagination discolor the stories she heard or warp their meanings; not behave as an Anglo, romanticizing.

The interpreter bundled up some of the quills. "For you. Maybe you will make a belt."

She accepted the gift. "If not, I'll give them to a Winnebago child at school, for them to practice when a design is handed down."

The interpreter grunted his approval.

In the following days, they visited other round-roofed homes—wigwams, their interpreter called them—and tepees. Once, riding through a clearing in a wooded area, they passed by mounds of earth made in shapes of bears and turtles with colored leaves matting the ground.

"Burial sites," the agent told them when Natalie asked. "Winnebagos—well, they call themselves Ho-Chunk people, some do. Anyway, they are mound people. Bury their dead in the ground and build earth animals over them to mark the graves."

She hadn't even touched on the burial practices of the different Peoples. The book would be so long.

At the agent's office, Natalie noticed a painting hung above worn chairs, papers, and an old desk. It was the only thing of beauty in the room. It appeared that this agent put most of his resources into the people and not his office nor the simple house he lived in with his family. It was an oil painting of a young boy in buckskins with beaded moccasins and his arm thrown across his eyes as though in grief. He sat on a train-station bench, and a uniformed conductor—who might have been an Indian but in Anglo clothes—bent a knee beside him, offering comfort. It was a striking painting. Natalie read the artist's name at the bottom. "Angel De Cora." Natalie had seen the woman's work at Hampton, where she'd gone to school.

"She's Winnebago but not born here. Born in Nebraska," the agent told her.

"Maybe we'll meet her when we go there."

George pulled his fur coat tighter. "It has to be warmer there."

"I can't believe you're cold," Natalie teased. "You sleep out on the ground in Arizona."

"Winds off the lake here are ruthless," the agent said. Then added, "Miss De Cora teaches at Carlisle Indian Industrial School in Pennsylvania. She is well respected and fights for her people."

"She'd be a perfect illustrator."

"If you can afford her," George said.

"We have to. I'll write another article to pay for her services." Natalie imprinted the painting in her mind. "If she'll do it."

From St. Louis to this Ho-Chunk place, to Hopi land and El Alisal, there was always the subject of money mixed in with art and promoting it, preserving it, respecting the artists who made it. Doing that with integrity would be another tributary they'd have to navigate to get the Indians' book out. But maybe Angel De Cora would see value in being a part of this book, advancing a shared cause. It would be a village effort, more and more, not Natalie's alone.

∽

"I guess I thought I'd see him again, be able to bring him the book." Natalie read the telegram from Frank Mead that had found them at the Wisconsin Agency. Lololomai, chief of the Hopi, the *Maqui* as they called themselves, had died. He had taken Natalie under his wing, legitimized her efforts, supported sending children to school. He'd even invited missionaries to teach and live at Third Mesa, to help his people stave off the violence of the Anglos and help them to become citizens. It seemed ironic to Natalie that the first people in this land should be the last to be affirmed as citizens and like women, without a right to vote, and only then after they gave up their music, their religion, their language.

"You'll honor him with the book," George said. "End it with one of his songs," he said. "Nat, maybe we have enough."

"Oh, no. I haven't touched the Plains Indians, the Cheyenne, the Omaha."

"We better hope someone else comes along to open doors for you, or we'll be doddering old siblings looking at notes you took that we no longer understand. Or can even see squinting with old eyes." He paused. "You're not putting off ending the research, are you? A book does have to be written."

"Creativity can't be rushed," she said. "I feel like time is running out for them, so I have to listen." She looked a little closer at the Winnebago love song score, making sure she hadn't forgotten anything important. She wrote the date and *"Learned of Lololomai's death. May God bless his soul and give him everlasting peace."*

She would know when she had enough, wouldn't she? But once finished, what would her story be?

29

The Canyon of Custom
and Time

1904–1905

*T*hey left Wisconsin, spent some time in Iowa where that tribe had been split but were served by a single small agency where she recorded again in a school void of any pictures on the wall except of the president. Then on to the Dakotas, Rosebud and Pine Ridge, but informants there were reticent to sing for Natalie. "Wounded Knee is too recent," the agent told them. "It's only fourteen years past. Too many bad memories to trust white faces who say they only want to save songs, nothing more." Natalie would have liked to have heard their voices, but she knew that wounds took time to heal.

They debated about where to head next when they received an invitation from Frank Mead to join him and the Yavapai people for Christmas, and so they boarded the train south to Phoenix, Arizona Territory, and then by horseback rode out to Fort McDowell, the new Yavapai reservation Frank had managed to secure. The red rocks, hot sun, and time on a horse fed Natalie's spirit.

"It's the least I could do," Frank told them when they arrived, giving a big bear hug to Natalie and handshakes for George. "I owe you, Natalie. Roosevelt has kept his word and given me free rein to negotiate with ranchers and get these people back their land."

Pelia bobbed his head toward Natalie, a grin of greeting saying he remembered those days in New York.

They exchanged gifts on Christmas Day, and Frank told the story to the gathered Yavapai people of a baby who came to save the world and them. He spoke in their language with large hand gestures, acting out the shepherds and the gift giving of the Magi, so even without language, Natalie could follow a story she knew from childhood. Later, she recorded singers. Then both she and George were invited to their ceremonies, including the Ghost Dance. Frank said she was likely the first white woman to see it, listen to the music. She left the recorder and her notebook at their hogan, would make only mental notes.

She entered the kiva by stepping down the rungs of a wooden ladder. With reverence, she descended to the holy place, a large open room in the ground. Frank wore buckskins and moccasins, his New York look abandoned for native clothes. Natalie too had donned a cotton dress with wide sleeves, wore a necklace of turquoise and red coral and the beaded Ho-Chunk belt. She wrapped a wool shawl around her shoulders, its tied yarn as the fringe around the edge. George kept his western clothes and his silence as they sat in the kiva, waiting for the ceremony to begin. Drums of readiness beat in the background.

She didn't understand this religion, but she understood what it meant to these people, and that was enough for her to sit quietly, observe the fluid movements of the dancers and their looks of ecstasy shadowed by flickering candlelight. Later, she'd have to spend hours making notes from memory of chants and drums and voice. Music might be her religion, she thought, a place of refuge. Perhaps that

241

was as close as she could come to truly understanding the sacred of each tribe who allowed her in to witness their ancestral ways.

"Be careful what you do with what you see," Frank said as they made their way back to their accommodations. A light snow sprinkled Natalie's eyelashes. She pulled her shawl tighter around her. Natalie wasn't sure if Roosevelt's letter would be enough to protect them all, should authorities hear that the Ghost Dance was still being performed. It had been specifically prohibited following the tragedy at Wounded Knee.

"It's a dance meant to bring spirits back to relieve the crying children," Frank said. "All dancers in it are crying children. And for the spirits to join them and sweep us white folk back across the 'big water.' But I don't fear the spirits rising nor do I think the Yavapai want me gone."

Natalie understood the need for native people to hold the dances dear, even as they might convert to the Presbyterian teachers' or the Catholic priests' religions and practice some of those traditions too. The very nature of religion for most of the tribal people she'd met was infused within their everyday lives. It wasn't something they *did*; it was who they *were*. Asking them to give up those ceremonies and traditions was asking them to wash away their very skin. She recalled the Hopi word for those who converted to Christianity—it was translated as "not-Hopi," almost a profanity, certainly a violent appellation for the peaceful Hopi people. What could be clearer about the impact of conversion on these people than a name that said they were not what they'd once been? Though she supposed that was the very feature of a conversion, to become something new. She was being converted by the Indian songs, discovering new dimensions to her gift that now infused her life with insights she hoped would serve others. She did believe in a spirit world, and being in service was a way to express it.

Frank told them of an off-reservation school near Phoenix. "Maybe you have enough songs, Nat," George said as the three finished morning coffee.

"Never enough." Natalie grinned.

After the New Year, she and George mounted up on horses and pack animals and went to that remote school, snowflakes melting on the saddle leather. There, she encountered Pima, Apache, Navajo, and Hopi students, the boys dressed in white shirts and black pants, the girls in plain gray dresses. Gone were the hair whirls that might distinguish a clan or tribe. All the boys' hair was chopped across the forehead and below the ears. Seeing the uniformity and the same defeated look in their brown eyes heightened Natalie's need to finish the book, to get it published, to tell Roosevelt that assimilation wasn't the answer. Each of the songs she recorded were singular, none she'd heard before.

But that night, after listening to the children, thinking of Frank and other Indian activists like herself hoping to do good but bringing Anglo ways that intervened, that changed them, Natalie cried. Silent, so George wouldn't hear her. She thought of Wounded Knee and the many deaths there. The rigid dress codes at the schools. The rubbing away of history, with children growing up far from grandfathers and grandmothers. *How will they know how to parent their children when that time comes?* So easily the futility could overtake her if she let down her guard while grieving what had once been—for those children and for herself. She prayed then, that she would be able to bridge a canyon of custom and time. And that the Indians' book would serve the people, bring goodness to better their lives.

∞

Natalie saw him on the first day out on the train headed away from Phoenix. They would visit the off-reservation school in Chilocco, Oklahoma, next, twenty miles north of Ponca City. He was tall, wearing a three-piece suit, his hair in two black braids resting on a stately chest. His shoulders were straight and as sturdy as the rock pyramid she could see outside the train window.

She couldn't take her eyes from the stalwart man, and she wondered what tribe he came from. He had walked past her seat, not making any eye contact, staring straight ahead, and Natalie had watched as he moved to the last car. She imagined that was where the Indians were asked to sit, as she saw no others in their car. After debating with herself, she followed him, found him staring out the window in the very last seat.

"Excuse me. I'm Natalie Curtis." She put out her hand to shake his. He did not offer up his own, but looked up at her. "I've been living in Oraibi for a few months and traveling in the Southwest. I wonder, what tribe are you from?"

"You are a bold white woman." He turned away.

"Yes. I am. I didn't mean to be so. I'm sorry." She started back to her seat, chastened, but then turned around. "Well, yes, I did mean to be bold. It's the only way I know how to be. But I meant no disrespect. Quite the contrary."

He stared at her while her face grew warm as she waited. Then, "So. What did you do among the Hopi?"

She let out her breath. "I listened to people sing. Recorded their songs. For them. For their children." She motioned for permission to sit beside him and he concurred. "I'm putting the songs in a book that will preserve them so people's children will be allowed to hear them even after their grandmothers are gone."

"This singing of our songs violates the Code of Offenses. You will get them into trouble."

"No, no. I have a letter from President Roosevelt. It allows me to do this, to go to any reservation or school. He understands the value of preserving Indian music and art."

"So. I would like to see this letter."

"You would? Oh, grand. Just give me a moment."

She fairly floated her way back to her seat and took out the bag from beneath it with her notebooks and the president's precious letter.

"Where are you headed?" George had woken up.

"There's a man. An Indian. He's aware of the Code and asked to see the letter. I hope he might tell me which tribe he's from. Maybe we can visit it. Maybe he'll sing for me."

"You might want to decide how many more singers you can contain in that book." George yawned, stretched. "I already see it as needing a burro to carry just one."

"Music opens doors, crosses canyons of time," she sang out to George, grabbing seat backs to stay upright as the train rocked its rhythm of the tracks. "Come join me," she shouted over her shoulder, and George did.

"I am Hiamovi, a high chief of the Cheyenne and the Dakotas." He handed the Roosevelt letter back to her after reading it carefully. "I am also an Indian policeman, so this is why I know of the Code."

He took her hand then, a soft holding of her fingers in an honoring way. Natalie preferred Indian handshakes rather than the crunching of the businessmen she encountered when they dared to take her palm instead of lifting their fingers to their hat brims in acknowledgment.

And then as though they'd known each other for eons rather than for moments, the three began to talk. George and Natalie moved their things to the back car, and there, with a few other Indians on the train, they heard Hiamovi's story, Natalie already considering how she would add it in the book.

Interlude #4

So. Hiamovi hoped Natalie's book would replace the stories white people told of massacres that, among his people, were often responses to injustices, protection, fatal efforts to halt change coming like a steam engine to all Indian people.

Yes, violence lived among many tribes. Brutality brewed inside clan feuds. Bloodshed happened. But few spoke now to others of what their time had been before white people arrived. Few sought to understand how traders, trappers, men across the ocean made the cruel paths his people sometimes took, even against their own mixed-blood brothers and sisters.

He knew there would be people who would tell him he should not help the woman, Natalie. Those same people who told him he should not be a police officer, either, especially not after what happened at Wounded Knee Creek. He had not been one of the Indian policemen sent to make the arrest of Sitting Bull—but he had an ancestor who was. That relative died when the soldiers fired. Six Indian police died at Wounded Knee. The Dakota fired back at soldiers, police; soldiers killed women and children, old people falling in the snow, dying in their moans. He had heard the story. It was not that long ago.

So. Many said he betrayed his people by being Indian police. The government, Roosevelt, had forbidden help to the survivors of that massacre, the elders starving, the babies crying beside their dead mothers. But Roosevelt made sure the families of the Indian police received assistance. As a grandson, payments came his way. Did he betray his people by eating the

meat the government gave his grieving family? Did he betray them by helping this woman, hoping to tell a different story than the one white people
carry with them?

He had chosen this path to walk, to help the white man as a way to help
his own people. So. It could be arranged to make Natalie's book better. She
was Natalie to him, already a friend. He had decided when he met her on
the train that he did not let down his people by trying to teach *her* people
of how complicated Indians were—and not only their music.

30

It Can Be Arranged

Cylinders, players, notebooks, and their undaunted spirit left the train with them at the Oklahoma Agency of the Pawnee. Hiamovi would be their introduction to these Plains tribes. He would take them to the Dakotas too, he said, his wife granting consent for him to travel. He was of both Cheyenne and Dakota. He had people there.

"Weren't we once going to winter in New York so you could put the book together?" George said as they disembarked the train. A cold wind blew across the prairie, and even the hotel's welcome sign didn't quell George's chattering lips.

"You aren't getting sick, are you?"

"No. But I'm just hopeful we can stay a few nights here before we head out to collect more songs. I've been away from the cold cowboy nights out in Arizona, gotten soft in my old age."

"I will get you hot water. Mint tea," Hiamovi told George. "And sing a healing song for your shivering body."

"That my sister will record," George said. But he smiled.

"Music opens doors," Natalie said. "We walk through them wherever and whenever we can."

Once again, Natalie recorded schoolchildren. Hiamovi introduced her to straight-backed Pawnee, round-faced Ho-Chunk, stately Arapaho girls, stern-faced Cheyenne boys—especially the Cheyenne, his own people. Hiamovi carried a wealth of information and he shared it with Natalie and George. At night, Natalie smiled to herself and thanked the Creator for the chance to meet Hiamovi, sheltered deep gratitude for his willingness to share what he knew, the stories, the legends. She could not have engineered his presence and was reminded of Goethe's words that once one made a commitment to something, then "Providence moves, and things begin to happen one can't otherwise imagine."

As with Frank when she had first met him, she felt a kinship to Hiamovi. He was thoughtful, walked well on the two roads of his history and his present.

"You don't see a problem with me making presentations to educators, to congressmen and others, possible donors?" she asked Hiamovi as they ate steak at the hotel. "Talking about Indian customs and so on?"

"So. White people prefer to hear white people," he said.

"I don't," Natalie told him. "I'd rather hear you talk about your life and the songs and where they came from."

"It is a show when we do it for Anglos. At home, when we sing or tell the stories, it is a gift. Our spirits are happy then."

"In the book, though, you won't be 'at home.' Your words and music will be spread far and wide."

He often kept a grace pause before he spoke. "So. It is what will be in this new trail we are asked to walk."

She would have to rethink how to involve the Indians in "their book" if making presentations might be seen as that same awkward gawking of a Buffalo Bill show or the more refined exhibits at St. Louis but still a "show."

"You'll help me in the final editing, won't you?"

249

The pause, then, "Editing. What is editing?"

"You would read what I write and correct things I've said that are wrong or are misinterpretations. Make improvements. For example, should I, or rather may I, include the Ghost Dance songs?"

Hiamovi sat still, then, "If Short Bull sings it for you, you may include it. He is a Dakota Holy Man. I can only correct what comes from my people. I know nothing of the Hopi ways."

"I understand. I'll ask Hopi people to look over their sections. And I have interpreters I can consult with. Some of the more friendly pastors at the schools, a few of the language experts like Boaz. But I might generalize in sections, say something about all Indians that might not be true. I want you to correct me on that."

"As we say when we tell stories of Anglos, 'they all do this, they all do that.'" He smiled. "When it is only one Anglo we once saw do this or that." His teeth were as white as aloe blossoms.

"Putting people into a category. Something like that." Natalie sat back in her chair, dabbed her mouth with the white linen napkin. It felt awkward after the days of squatting as she made notes or sitting cross-legged in the kiva, listening. Here was a high-back chair that made her fidget in its rigidness. "You understand my purpose, to have this be the Indians' book, not mine so much, and as unique to each tribe as I can make it. But I want it to tell a story of the Indians' part in the American story, not as a colonized people but as a contributing race." Her voice rose with enthusiasm. "I want the People to be seen as gifted with something to offer Anglos like me, something that could be lost if the intent of the Code is reinforced over the intent of the Indians' book. I want to prove the value in lessening the assimilation policies and educate Americans about the depth of your history and your gifts."

Hiamovi nodded.

"I'm thinking I will introduce each section," Natalie continued. "Write stories of how I encountered some of the songs. There could be trouble in what I compose, despite my best intentions.

I'd still take responsibility for whatever I write, but I would love your . . . eyes upon what I've written, for you to tell me what you see."

Hiamovi's grace pause was longer than usual. George and Natalie exchanged looks.

"This can be arranged," he said at last.

"You could come to New York?" Natalie let out her held breath. "To assist with editing?"

"This can be arranged."

"It won't be for another year or more. It'll take me that long to pull everything together. Charlotte—you don't know her—she has a publisher interested."

"So. You can tell your stories to New York people, while you write the music down. This will be a way for you to make money?"

Natalie nodded.

"This is good. You can finish the Indians' book."

The Indians' Book. She'd keep that title.

"Yes! Oh, thank you. You don't know how much this means to me, your approval and your willingness to travel east when the time comes." She leaned back as the waiter took their plates. "Let's continue with the Cheyenne, then on to the Dakotas, and I hope you'll be one of my informants too. Maybe singing that healing song for George."

"This can be arranged."

∽

On horseback, they found the tepees of Hiamovi's relatives, the Southern Cheyenne known among themselves as "our people."

"So. Our people," Hiamovi told Natalie and George, "once lived in Minnesota but we took different roads. Some to the Dakotas, some joined with the Arapaho, in Oklahoma. North and south bands will have different songs and stories, but all loved the buffalo and horses." Natalie saw how when Hiamovi told his relatives or other Indians about her book, that they believed him when he said her book would be a good thing. She would give him great credit, as he had opened so many doors. These old women with wrinkles for skin or old men bent over leaning on a stick would sing for her, let her take their photographs. They trusted her because they trusted Hiamovi.

"I would start with the Sun Dance song," Hiamovi told her in an evening when they talked about the arrangement of the book. "Because it is a prayer. We call it 'The Offering.' It is you Anglos who gave it the name Sun Dance song. It praises the Creator who also heals. After it, the Buffalo Dance song should appear because only chiefs can sing that one."

"Will there be objections to including the truly ancient songs and stories?" Natalie asked. "I mean, will you receive scorn for sharing them?"

"So. This book is happening because this is true: As there are birds of many colors—red, blue, green, yellow—and there is corn of many colors—red, blue, green, yellow—so it is with men—red, brown, yellow, white. Where once there was only Indian, there are now men of many colors."

His eyes held Natalie's and she felt the intensity of his caring for his people and their stories and the responsibility for what she had undertaken.

"That this should come to pass—the men of many colors are on the same land—was in the heart of the Great Mystery, he who created us. It is right thus. And everywhere there shall be peace."

"Do you think so?" Natalie held the dream of the value of her book. Hiamovi seemed to share it.

"So, there are old stories of men coming to this land, their animals eating our grass, building their houses with our rocks and trees, coming hungry, and we fed them."

The three "explorers," as Natalie had started to think of George, Hiamovi, and herself, were camped in an old buffalo wallow, the high bank keeping wind from pushing out their fire. Even identifying the best camping sites varied with each tribe, handed down through ancient wisdom.

"Your book will tell of these stories before all our children are like the white man and they will forget the good that was."

Their horses were hobbled before a blazing orange sunset, and their presence motivated Hiamovi to reminisce about before "our people" had horses. "We loaded big shaggy dogs to haul our goods." He said "we" even though it was ages before, emphasizing for Natalie the sturdy rope tying past to present. He spoke of how they made bows and arrows, hunted buffalo, how a man in a "faraway place" now called Texas, but then Apache land, saw the horse and tamed it and brought it back. Others caught lost horses and then, in time, they had a herd. "My mother, who is over one hundred years, tells me this when all we had was given us by the Father or we made it ourselves."

Hiamovi had a melodious, low voice and seemed satisfied at each completion of his narrative. Natalie realized he had been waiting to tell these stories to outsiders who listened, perhaps all his life.

At an outlying village, Hiamovi arranged for Natalie and George to witness more dances, and once again Natalie took notes. But she also found herself mesmerized by the drumbeat and the eagle's-wing whistle that sounded together during the song. She put the notebook away, closed her eyes, and let the music bring her peace. As she had with Wagner or Liszt or Chopin, she could give herself to the music and her soul felt deepened, enriched. Her hope was that such would happen when people read her book.

But in the light of day she would wonder—could they, really?

"Talking about the Indian music might be easier than reading about it," she told Hiamovi. He had risen early and invited Natalie along with Wolf-Robe, another chief, to join him as they walked toward a high point on the reservation. The air felt cool. They gathered at the vista as the sun rose and Wolf-Robe sang the Morning song.

"It is one of our oldest songs," Hiamovi told her. "It is always sung at dawn by old men. I will tell you white men's words. *He, our Father, he hath shown his mercy unto me. In peace I walk the straight road.*"

The words washed over Natalie like a healing balm.

At breakfast later, with George joining, Natalie told her brother, "It was a prayer song that any of us could sing."

Hiamovi nodded and sang one verse for George. Wolf-Robe joined in.

"I have thought of what you say," Hiamovi said.

He had a way of answering something she'd asked hours earlier and it took her a few minutes to arrive at the place in the road where he was. "It might be easier for your people to read about the songs than to try to play them from the notes on your page. Maybe you will sing them for them. But both should be there, the words below the notes. Perhaps sounds will carry in their minds that way, or in their hearts."

"It also means I must introduce each tribe with something celebrating their other arts besides music. *The Indians' Book* must be about everything." She turned to George. "We've got to go to more reservations and schools because each tribe is unique. I can't generalize without diminishing a particular tribe."

"I think you like the gathering of material too much," George said.

She looked surprised. "Are you tired?"

"Not in the least. But I do think there will come an end. If nothing else, Charlotte and your other sponsors will suggest you have enough material."

"Not until I've heard the Pueblo songs and seen the Acoma pottery. And conferred about the illustrations and—"

"There's an ending to everything, Nat. You know that."

Something in the way he said it made her stomach tense. *I avoid finishing.*

"It will be arranged," she said and Hiamovi nodded. "It's just going to be a very large book."

Interlude #5

The child was asked to sing. He had not been allowed to bring his voice from home for many months, years maybe. He was the only Kwakiutl in this Cherokee Nation school. Friends, Quaker people they said, ran the school. They were kind, but no one was allowed to sing the old songs, the leaders careful to honor the Code. The child had been sent to this school because the food was steady here. Heat was steady. He would have given those up to remain at home where cedar bark in the beds kept bugs away. There was no cedar bark here and all the children scratched. But his mother had sent him to learn the white man's ways.

Miss Curtis, she called herself, said it was safe for him to sing the songs of the whales, the music of Vancouver Island, the music his grandfather had taught him in the boats the People made to move between the canyons and the sea. So, he sang. She made notes on the paper, and when she asked, he told her stories his grandmother had told him about men who shed their animal skins to dance and how a mouse—who was really a woman—and their chief—who was really a beaver—had not been able to dance and how chief Wakiash rescued them and helped create the first totem pole. The people made a song for the totem pole. He could not remember all of the song but sang some of it.

Miss Curtis wrote everything down, but the boy, the Kwakiutl boy, felt heavy in his heart. It was only him, just a boy, but he knew he was speaking and singing for an entire nation. He told Miss Curtis she should go to his home in the north where tall trees stayed green through all seasons, where fog hovered and then lifted to allow the men to approach the whales. She should go to listen to the songs there, songs to include in the book the Friends told him about. She said she would like to do this and would if she could.

He drew a picture of a rattle with a raven's head and beak. Wakiash, the chief of the river, rode on the raven's back. He drew a grizzly and a whale. He gave the drawings to Miss Curtis, whose mouth turned up. Her eyes smiled. The boy hoped he had not done wrong by sharing what belonged to his people. He did not sleep well in the bed without cedar bark after she left. He missed home. But when he sang the song again and no one punished him, the next night, he slept. He dreamed of when his time in this place ended and he would paddle the boat where he'd slip through the fog with his grandfather to hunt the mighty whale.

31

The Beginning of the End

They took the train west toward the pueblos, heading into New Mexico Territory, arriving first in Santa Fe. Natalie found herself struggling for breath.

"We are over a mile high here," George told her. "But if we stayed awhile, I think we'd adapt."

"Drink water. Walk slowly," Hiamovi told her. The High Chief had agreed to travel with them to the Acoma Pueblo west of Albuquerque and was with them in this old capital city of Santa Fe as well. He had left them to wander on their own while he arranged for their rooms at the hotel on the plaza.

Despite the difficulty breathing, Natalie fell in love with this old town at the foot of the Sangre de Cristo Mountains. "Nampeyo, the potter, has family who helped settle this place," Natalie reminded George. "I wonder if there are potters here who know her. Tewa people. I should try to find—"

"Natalie. You can't spend a month here."

"I know, dear Brother. It's just that each new place we visit in the Southwest takes me over. I want to be there, live there." George nodded. "The truth is"—she stopped him as they stood in the plaza—"I want to stay. Not now. But I love these adobe buildings, the square with the market. The air . . . the light. People could paint here. Or they should. It's a place that could celebrate the artistry and crafts of the Indians."

"You'd have to figure out a way to make a living to stay here," George said.

"Yes." They had moved to an adobe bench in a cottonwood grove beside the seasonable trickle of the usually flowing Santa Fe River.

"You remember that after you return to New York to put the book together, I'll be looking for a ranch somewhere. Probably near San Diego or south of there. That's my future. A little farm. Oranges. Some bees."

"I guess I thought you'd travel with me to promote the book once it comes out."

"I'll help. But after that, you can come visit me. It'll be a place for respite for you, Sister. Frank Mead was telling me about a couple of areas. I want to build the house myself, the way Lummis built his. And finish my novel."

"Of course. That makes sense." This whole trip had been her project, her healing. George had deferred his hopes for hers. She didn't want her disappointment to pierce his dream. But she felt a hole opening in her heart, a goodbye she hadn't expected would happen here, now. It was silly, really. George was alive and well and he would be there for her. She looked at him fondly, admired his strong profile highlighted against Santa Fe's stunning blue sky. Charlotte would help; her other sponsors, yes, but the publication of this book would mark the end of something precious with her brother. George would tell her it was also the beginning of something new.

They didn't stay long in Santa Fe but long enough for Natalie to decide that she'd return one day. She was as certain as when she'd known her life would change with the call of the Yuma song. The town's yellow adobe walls, smoke trees etched beside them, the clarity of sunlight all made her want to paint, a talent she knew she did not have. She said so out loud and Hiamovi told her an artist twenty years before had offered classes here.

"I'm not the only one who sees paints and palettes then in this desert light," Natalie told Hiamovi.

The trio took the stage and then acquired a wagon and horses and drove across the desert to Laguna Pueblo, where the Edison came out while children swarmed around her, using her Hopi name, Tawimana, her reputation having come before her. As they headed away from the pueblo, they encountered a man who said his name was Tuari or Young Eagle. "I will sing you my own song I sing to my wife. Back in Laguna."

"But we're miles from your village. How can you sing it to her?"

Young Eagle stared at Natalie as though she had grown a second head. Then he quietly informed her—through Hiamovi's translations—that they sang to each other regardless of the distance. "My song tells her I am here, working for her. She is to take care of herself, take care of the horses and the sheep and the fields. I do this without words, only music. And she sings back to me." He sang then, but Natalie didn't try to write down the young Laguna's song. She imagined the words flowing across the desert, picking up the wind currents like an eagle, and settling into the village where his wife received them as a gift. Everywhere she went, music thrived.

Zuni songs followed in that pueblo a few miles distant. They heard it on the flat plain near the Little Colorado River as they approached. "They will sing for you, while they grind corn in their stone metates," their interpreter told them. "But those women will not speak their own names. It is forbidden for them to be individual as they sing a sacred song."

Natalie wanted to know why, but Hiamovi shook his head. He lowered the red bandana he kept at his neck to lift up over his nose when the wind whipped up the sand. "It is part of their story. Not all such stories know their beginnings."

All around sat pots colored with intricate designs of circles, squares, lightning bolts, and clouds, the symbols of their religion, their daily lives, their hopes and dreams and gratitude, painted with the colors of their land.

∞

A desert storm cracked its presence with thunderbolts and lightning. There was no place to take cover. All three donned slickers and rain hats; held the horses, talking through the thunder. Natalie eased her own fears while calming her mount with a lullaby. The storm passed and washed the dust into submission, scenting the air with sage. At last they reached the Acoma Pueblo, rising up four hundred feet out of the yellow desert. They found an interpreter, and Natalie followed a blind boy up the footholds that had been used for nearly a thousand years. *So many blind children*. Natalie had noticed this anomaly but had found no good answer. Burton had said it was face paint that caused the blindness, but Natalie wondered if that was just another excuse to limit the dances where face paints were used. Perhaps something happened at birth? Could the cause have been brought to the people by the Spanish or Anglos? Something hereditary? Diet? It bothered her answer-seeking mind not to know. Maybe when the book was finished, she could explore such problems. Or perhaps as Hiamovi said, not all stories can be known.

In the afternoon sun, the windows in the three-storied adobe homes glowed a copper gold from mica schist. "The Spanish thought they found a city of gold but only poor window coverings of my people," the interpreter said. An old adobe church dominated the mesa. In the distance rose Mount Taylor where the interpreter told them the logs for the beams inside the mission church had been hand-carried nearly one hundred miles to please the Franciscans, who three hundred years ago envisioned the massive structure.

"So old." Natalie thought about the ruins at Canyon de Chelly and other Southwest sites that spoke to people living in this desert hundreds of years before. "These people are the link from past to present. There's so much to save."

Water pooled in rock depressions as they meandered around the large square. "Already tourists come here," Hiamovi interpreted for Natalie and George, who had removed his hat to wipe perspiration from his forehead. "People move their work to places where bowls or weavings can be purchased by curious white people."

"I want to be more than just a curious white person," Natalie said. *But am I?*

She watched young girls walking to the north end of the mesa. On their heads they carried large bowls with orange-and-black designs, set above cloaks that reached their ankles.

"Water," the interpreter said when Natalie asked where they were going. "*Tz'itz*, water. There are cisterns that collect the rain."

"Lummis wrote we should see the stone reservoir at sunrise." Natalie remembered from his book.

The interpreter continued. "Once we had a big cistern in the center, and we brought horses and burros here and let them share it. But they did not share well. Women must walk farther to bring back our tz'itz now."

"Can you tell him that we are looking for a specific potter?" Natalie took out the seed pot George had brought back that had begun this trek to capture music and to heal her broken heart. With Natalie's pot in hand, they asked a woman grinding corn if she might know of the maker.

The woman looked at the pot, saw a mark on the bottom, then nodded with her chin toward a home with a small pile of cooking wood stacked neatly next to the door Natalie now knocked on.

No one came. Eventually, a woman approached and told them the person they looked for had gone away. "To the trader."

"When might she be back?" Natalie assumed it was a woman. The informer shook her head.

Disappointed, Natalie looked around. At least she could see what the potter saw while she worked, on top of a mesa more than a thousand miles from New York.

"She is the youngest daughter of two elders," Hiamovi translated from what the neighbor had told him. "The youngest child takes care of her elders. But she also receives all they have when they die. This grandmother gave her the way to make her pottery."

And then the door opened and an old woman came out. "Please tell her that my brother purchased her granddaughter's pot at the trader's." Natalie nodded with her chin toward George, having learned that pointing with fingers was considered impolite among most Indian people. "I like it very much."

"She says she will tell her."

Natalie was sorry she had missed the girl. It had been a part of her vision of the book to include the story of her meeting the Acoma potter. Without any idea of when she might return, it didn't make sense for them to wait.

As they were leaving, the girls who had gone for water returned, and each lowered the pot from her head and offered the guests fresh tz'itz. Behind Natalie, the woman who was grinding corn began to sing. Natalie held her breath. Maybe Hiamovi's presence made the woman feel safe. To the rhythm of the corn song, they drank the precious water. Natalie did not want to break the spell by asking if she could take notes or even a photograph. Instead, she let the music soothe to the beat of the grinding stone crushing white corn onto rock.

Hiamovi broke the spell by speaking to the woman. She stopped, responded to him. "She says you may take your notes about the Corn Grinding song. Maybe the girl who makes the pot you like will return while you listen."

"Really? That's grand." She opened her pack she carried on her back and began the process of recording. It would give them a reason to come back, to bring a copy of the book when it was finished. And because the song was long and the day waned, the travelers accepted the invitation to spend the night. George and Hiamovi took the road to collect the horses and bring them up to the mesa top while Natalie scratched black notes on her paper and hoped her potter would return.

In the morning, Natalie rose before sunrise, the air cool, and walked with her shawl tight around her shoulders toward the reservoir. She watched as the Creator painted a masterpiece over the world, saw it reflected in the water. Lummis had been right. Like most treasured moments in life, the sunrise over the reservoir was worthy of the journey and the wait.

32

Farewell

1905

O ne more trip," she told George. Hiamovi had gotten back on the train to return to Oklahoma, their gratitude to him greater than a sad farewell, knowing they'd be seeing him again in New York. She and George had one more journey to take. It was to be a goodbye to Mina and the Hopi village.

"You're certain," George said.

"I am. The money for travel has about run out, and it's time to start compiling all these notes and recordings into that 'very fat book,' as you keep calling it."

They acquired horses and began the ride out to Oraibi, spending a night with their tent set beneath peach-tree shade near Hubbell's trading post. They'd get fresh water there, food, and walk on wood floors covered with Navajo rugs. It was a reintroduction into a taste of civilization, the trading post family welcoming tourists like them.

"Tourists come," the trader told her.

And possibly more after my book comes out.

Maybe it wasn't the right thing to do, open these private, ancient worlds to thirsty Americans "discovering America first." Charlie Lummis had advocated that approach in his *poco tiempo* book. But she was doing it to preserve the ancient arts, songs, and dances, not to destroy them by bringing tourists. One didn't always have control over the outcome of pursuing a purpose. The publication and promotion would be a balancing act.

Once again, the bells on the sheep spoke the music of her return to Oraibi. At the sound of Natalie's voice, Bonita—her burro—came hee-hawing from wherever she had been and fast-trotted toward Natalie, nuzzling with her big head, pushing beneath Natalie's arm.

"She remembers me! I can't believe it."

"You're quite memorable," George told her, "though I'm told burros have a long memory and can live to be much older than you are."

Natalie scratched the shaggy ears as the burro pushed at her pockets. She smelled of equine and dust.

"Ah, she remembers something else too." Natalie pulled out the carrot she'd gotten from the Hubbell's garden and fed the burro. And soon they were surrounded by children. Mina led them. She would let the superintendent know she was back for a brief visit, but first, she had a gift to share.

❧

Natalie and Mina walked up to Lololomai's home, the girl chattering like an eastern squirrel. She had a happy life here despite the restrictions. Natalie wished she'd been able to see the old man before he died and ask if he still felt his decision to be "friendly" to Pahana people had been worth it. When she knocked on the door of the first-floor apartment, Tawakwaptiwa, his nephew who had sung for her, was there along with Ponianömsí, Lololomai's sister, and a few Hopi friends. And Lololomai's brother. Mina would translate this day.

"I brought a gift I neglected to give your brother when I was here before." She did not say the deceased's name, as with some tribes, Hiamovi had told her, this was not allowed, and she didn't know what the Hopi practice was. She took out the jar of sand she'd carried with her from Long Island. "I brought this sand from the ocean where I return to. The sand beneath the water there is silver where your desert sand is gold." She poured some of the sand into Poníanömsí's hands, who fingered it, then passed it on to the others by the fireside. "If you stand on this sand and look over the water, you cannot see land on the other side."

Mina spread her arms out to show the wide water.

"You return there?" Poníanömsí said.

Natalie nodded. "I will put the Indians' book together there."

"But you will come back to see us, many times," Mina said, not translating, Natalie decided, but asking for herself.

"I cannot come often. It is many days by train."

"How many days must a Hopi run before he finds your land?" asked Lololomai's brother.

"The train rushes four days and four nights, and it runs in one hour what a Hopi runs in one day." Murmuring accompanied the passing of sand between hands. "It's a very different land," Natalie told them. "The mountains there are covered with green trees, not rocks of many colors that you can see here—mostly gray, without the spires, the throats that reach toward the sky. No mesas. It rains often there, sometimes days at a time, not the fast storms that quench the thirst of your corn."

Poníanömsí rose and left. Natalie hoped she hadn't offended her in some way. She'd have to ask Mina later. But the sister returned, carrying a winnowing basket filled with colored corn.

"Blue, black, the spotted," she said. "Pink, the red, the yellow, the lilac, and the white." Poníanömsí was a big woman with heavy arms that moved as she spoke. "I bring one of each kind to remember us by." She paused for Mina's English words. The description reminded Natalie of Hiamovi's use of corn as the story to tell how they were all alike but made of different colors. "You take the corn and the basket. Remember us."

She felt her throat grow thick with held-back tears.

"I will remember you. Will you remember me?" Ponianömsí's words, and Mina's translation of them, were as soft as the lamb's wool Natalie sat on.

Only the firelight flickered in the stone room, the eating room, the kitchen. "Always," Natalie said. "So long as the desert sand covers the ground, that's how long I will remember you."

"We will pray for you, our friend." Ponianömsí handed her the basket, then put her hands over Natalie's, holding the woven bowl. "And when you are in your faraway land by the great waters that cover the silver sand, will you pray for Hopi, that they may have rain?"

"Yes. That they will have rain and be good in their hearts," Natalie said. Tears wet her cheeks.

"It is a good thing to cry tears of remembering," Ponianömsí said.

By the fire, Lololomai's brother stood, the light reflecting on his solemn face. Soon the time would come when the Hopi would plant their *bahos*—prayer sticks. The Hopi would weave prayers into the feathered ends of the sticks. If people were absent, bahos were made for them. She wanted to ask, but for a *Pahana*, an Anglo, to make the request George would say was too forward. But she had gotten nowhere in her life when she delayed asking for what she wished for. *He can always say no.* "Will you make a baho for me?"

The uncle jerked his head toward her and she felt her heart leap. *I've intruded and offended.* But he said, "We are spinning in the kivas. When we make the bahos, I will make one for you and pray for you."

"Pray that all your songs will stay forever in your hearts. And that I will be good in my heart." She stood on tiptoes to kiss Ponianömsí's cheek.

Then she and Mina and the nephew left together. "When the baho is finished," Natalie asked the nephew as they walked, "what will he do with it?"

"He will give it to Poníanömsí. The women take the bahos, and when they put the seed corn in the ground, as the yellow line comes over the mountains, they will plant them."

"Yellow line? Dawn," Natalie clarified. The nephew nodded. "Why do you plant at the yellow line?" she asked.

"The prayers are lifted by the sun up, up to the Power that made the sun, that makes all things, and lives behind the sun."

"So, you do not worship the Katsinas." In this moonlight walk down the path, she was discovering more than she had ever understood before.

He shook his head. "Katsinas carry the prayers only."

Natalie couldn't help herself. More questions. "Does the Power that lives behind the sun look like a man or a Spider Woman or anything the Hopi have seen?"

The nephew stopped the horse he was leading, and Natalie could see his eyes shining as he stared at her. *I am too bold.* "No," he said at last. "It is not a man or anything we recognize. It just is."

The great I Am.

"My father prays for our crops, corn, and melons, and for good health," the nephew continued. "For Hopi, but for all persons. All animals. Every living thing. For the whole world."

"I will think of him at the yellow line, remember all Hopi," Natalie said.

And for the rest of her life, if she was awake at dawn, the Hopi would be the first on her mind.

∞

"Do you have another song, Mina? It's safe for you to sing, along with anyone else who wishes."

"The white chief says it is grand?" *Grand.* Natalie smiled. She had brought more of her eastern experience with her than she realized. She must say that word often.

"Grand. Yes." As was her entire time here, despite the rationing, despite missing Lololomai and not being able to say goodbye. "We'll record from Number 3 and later we can go to outer villages and camps. Will you travel with us?" Mina nodded. "I'd like to take your photograph too. Is that alright?"

"Grand," Mina said.

Natalie added to her book, soaked in the sunshine and the yellow line sunrise, tried not to hear the ticking clock that was George's voice telling her she had to finish and say goodbye.

∞

As Natalie, Mina, and George rode to outlying places for just one more Hopi song, Mina told them of the trouble. "Friendlies have fought with Hostiles," Mina told them. The old friction burst to flame. "Two kivas, not allowed. Burton does nothing to help."

"They couldn't pray about it and use the music to resolve the issue without violence?" Natalie said.

"It does not happen. There are fires in hearts. It is good I spend time with you, where I cannot see the flames."

∞

The siblings did their work. Too much work, George told her after she'd sat up nearly all night transcribing a poet's song he titled "Korosta Katsina Tawi" that combined a corn-planting theme with butterflies being colored with pollen. She'd play the cylinder, look at her notes, sing the song, repeat the cylinder, write on the lines in her notebook. "You can't keep working like this," George said. "You'll do to yourself what you did before. Get yourself sick." He stood in his undershorts, having tried to go to sleep. "It's like

269

when we had to get you to use the techniphone to stop your piano scales up and down, all day, all night."

She looked up at him. "I want to do it well."

"Or perfect?"

She put her notebook away.

"You have to stop gathering music to give yourself time to prepare what you want for production. Once you sign the contract, there'll be deadlines."

"I know. I'm sorry to keep you awake."

"What is it, Nat? Are you worried about what will happen when it's finished and you've sent it to all the people, that you won't know what to do with yourself?"

"I'm not sending. I'll hand deliver to all the singers."

"Then you do have a plan for at least a few months after the book comes out."

"That's as far as it goes."

Maybe she was doing to herself what she'd done before, strained her heart and soul, performed "musical slush," as Bogey called her intensity with practice: piano and song. She could escape inside the music, find refuge there. But if she was going to serve the Indian people, she did have to finish the book and get it to the schools and agents and legislators, if the Code was truly to be broken. Maybe she couldn't stop the haircutting for the boys or those dreadful uniforms at the schools, but if the book advanced singing and dancing and speaking their native tongue, she would have accomplished more than if she'd managed her Philharmonic debut.

∽◯∽

Natalie wondered if any tinkling bell would bring her back to Oraibi and the sheep.

"You can read English, Mina. I'll write and you can write too. Maybe, when you're not in school—"

"My auntie will need me to plant or tend sheep."

"Perhaps for a short time you can come to visit me in New York. But after the book is finished, I'm going to come back west."

"To Oraibi?"

"To visit, yes. But to live. I am going to a town called Santa Fe. It's much closer to you than the ocean in the East. It won't be as long a ride on the train."

Mina's eyes grew wide. "I will ride a train?"

"Yes, if your auntie will allow it." Natalie hugged the girl to her, then brushed black strands behind her ears. "And you'll have many more adventures. We will be like sisters."

"Youngest sister gets everything," she said, smiling. "But has to take care of elders."

"I thought that was only for the Acoma people."

"You tell me this. I like it. I take care of you. When you die, I receive your song cylinders."

Natalie caught her breath. What a lovely thought to be some-how connected to this child for life. "I have to go now. Look after Bonita for me. I'll be back to give you a book with your song inside. I'll also carry it in my heart."

"I carry you in my heart song too," Mina said with tears in her eyes.

Natalie cried as she and George mounted up. She would work out the format for a grieving song first when they got back to New York.

33

The Front Matter

*B*ogey and Mimsey met them at the station as the discordant sounds of traffic mixed with trains bombarded her and George. She was still grieving her life in the West and was grateful George hadn't decided to remain there but to return to help her with the book if he could. "I thought the train travel would be my slow easing back into New York," she said, "but no, it's a full-blown baptism into city life." She looked around. "Is Charlotte here?"

"She's coming to the house," Mimsey said. "I hope you don't mind but I've planned a little gathering for you. Some of the other volunteers from the settlement house and the suffrage brigade. I'm so proud that you've come home at last." Weary as she was, she could hardly say no to her mother, though there would be a reckoning once Natalie moved to Santa Fe.

While they unpacked, an invitation to lunch at the White House arrived. This time, Charlotte was included. Natalie called her sponsor, who gushed at her chance to voice her concerns to the president.

"We'll corner him and tell him a few things about that boarding school," Charlotte said. "Atrocious! And the constant robbing of children, ripping them from their parents and putting them into those faraway schools. Dispiriting it is, if the truth were known."

Natalie, too, was disquieted by the lack of change in policy despite her reports and her letters to the president. "Let's see what the president has to say, Charlotte. I want to secure his support for the book, which I think will have the greatest impact on the condition in the schools in the end. Perhaps it speaks of his continued interest that he's invited us to lunch," Natalie said.

"Does it say who else will be there?"

It did not. But the invitation read "Come at once."

"I'll take copious notes," Natalie assured the sneezing Charlotte two days later. "It's so unfair."

Charlotte spoke into the phone with her stuffy-nose-sore-throat voice. "Life isn't fair, Natalie. Surely you've learned that on your travels. We make of it what we're given. I'll be fine." She coughed. "Right afterward, you must call me."

A part of Natalie was relieved that Charlotte couldn't attend. She couldn't control what her enthusiastic benefactress might say. George was right about his sister: *I like to be in control*.

And so she tried to control her racing heart at the White House on the appointed day. Before her sat senators, congressmen, cabinet secretaries, all staring. Twelve men. The room felt cavernous after so many meetings at firelit adobe hearths, and she felt small, wished she had asked for George to replace the sick Charlotte.

"Miss Curtis will sing for us an Indian grace."

The president's voice boomed out and she could have heard a feather slip to the floor as she walked forward toward the podium where the president himself had just stepped down and bowed at his waist, sweeping his arm as he directed her to the platform.

She had not been prepared to sing. But she imagined herself standing at Oraibi at "the yellow line," singing a prayer of thanksgiving, while the men in their vests and suits leaned forward at the table less to indicate their interest in Natalie's song, she supposed, and more in how to please the president.

No applause—which was fitting for a table grace—and Natalie thought perhaps they had been taken over by the prayer just as she always was, sending praise and gratitude to Creator God from whom Chiparopai said she'd received the song.

Then while servers brought their lamb chops with mint and later baked apples for dessert, the president spoke. He said they were gathered to talk about Indians. He proceeded to do much of the talking, but it included descriptions of Natalie's work, her recordings, her passion for gathering up the essentials of other cultures that Americans might learn from them. "Indians, it turns out, have much to contribute to us non-Indians, or what's the Hopi word for Anglos, Natalie?"

"Pahana."

"Yes, that's right. Miss Curtis is preparing a book to help us all know more about these Indigenous people. It will help us make better Indian policy. Miss Curtis has identified the losses we face by eliminating their music, dances, languages, religions. Something for us to work on, gentlemen."

The meal finished, the president led Natalie and the gray-haired congressmen and cabinet officials into a ballroom where, beside a grand piano, he invited Natalie to sing several more songs. Desert poetry, he called them. She told a few stories as preambles to each piece, jested that she had no need of the piano, though she began a Corn Planting song by tapping the piano like a drum. No one acted as though they had other things to do, a rarity, she suspected, in this government town. Even the luncheon servers had drifted into the room, stood quiet against the walls, as enthralled as the cabinet secretaries.

Can music change policies? If so, she must finish the book.

"It was the healing music itself that touched them," Natalie told Charlotte later. "I must never forget that it's the songs that bypass our critical sides and move directly to our hearts."

"And souls." Charlotte blew her nose. "I wish I'd been there, but I would have infected Congress with my cold while you have infected them with the value of the book, before it's even published."

"Before it's even put together, which is what I must do now."

"You can't spend all your time cooped up with your cylinders. I've some people for you to meet, and we have to return to Hampton so you can begin doing work for Negro songs as you have for the Indians. It'll be a good diversion when you over-obsess about the Indians' songs."

Natalie blinked. "I . . . I can't even think that far ahead. I have to do the very best job for the Indians."

"Oh, you can do more than one thing at a time. Which songs did you sing for the senators? You'll have to write about it. Here's a title: 'To Sing for the Senators.' It has a nice ring, don't you think?"

Natalie knew that she worked best focused on a singular issue, a particular goal that did not become diluted with dozens of other worthy efforts. Charlotte was just being Charlotte. For Natalie, the luncheon had also raised two possibilities: her presentations about her "harvesting songs," as the president had called her work, could open yet more doors for public-speaking events. She could speak and sing at non-Indian schools, provide an education component to American history. She could participate in activist activities of Lummis and Frank Mead, speak on Indian art, work for justice on the Indians' behalf. In fact, the book promotion might require it. Reading of the songs lacked the captivation that hearing them had. A few cylinders played back could be a part of the presentations, but her speaking and singing would add greatly to the Indians' story.

It might also be a way for her to make a living, to be that independent woman without parental support, nor even needing the sponsorship of Charlotte and others. Another gift the Indian songs gave. The book and the music would allow her to make her own way, be free like Alice. And at the same time work to preserve the ancient ways so preciously revealed to her.

∾

Natalie gazed out the window of Charlotte's Washington residence, hot coffee in her hand. She was alone. Her parents had hated to see her go, but they understood it as temporary and were grateful that George remained with them. He would stay often, he told them, in the Curtis family's New York apartment.

Natalie needed space to compile, to work the long hours she preferred, rising early, taking short breaks for meals, her mind spinning and categorizing and blocking out imaginary pages intermixed with notes on score sheets, text of poetry, her own essays of experiences, some of which she'd already had published in *Harper's*, *Outlook*, the *Saturday Evening Post*. She had photographs of people and places, and she did find herself lingering over them, recalling where she'd been when she'd taken the shot. Evening often found her pondering the pictures, hoping to ease the heartache of her having left the Southwest landscape. She lost all track of time.

The book consumed her. She couldn't sleep. Her mind wouldn't stay still. Her heart skipped beats, she thought her breathing became strained. She sat up from her bed at 2:00 a.m. and almost sleep-walked toward Charlotte's piano. She sat on the bench and began playing Chopin. "Why didn't I think of this before?" she asked herself out loud.

An hour of playing and she felt calm, like she did resting beneath the Arizona stars. The Southwest offered her a bigness with its skies and storms one could watch approach from across the mesas, clouds rolling and thundering like a percussion section gone wild. *But Liszt and Chopin are big too.* When she finished playing, there was a new spirit moving within her.

276

She looked at the manuscript and liked how she'd organized it with geographic sections. Eighteen tribes were represented. Each tribal story began with a brief history of the people, comments about their customs, religious beliefs, artistry, and sometimes, as with the Hopi, comments about individual people who had helped her. Her own handwritten notes would bring the music with the Indian and sometimes English words beneath them. *It's good. It'll be good* was the melody she told herself. And when she faltered, she went riding for a few hours or played Beethoven and Bach, their bigness reminding her of the desert and the native people who told its story best.

The Underwood typewriter Charlotte had acquired for her fairly smoked through the days as she worked. She awoke one morning to the realization that something was missing: illustrations. And a solution sent her to the Carlisle Indian school when she remembered what the Winnebago agent had told her. Natalie bundled herself up and headed to Pennsylvania in the wintery month of February. She didn't let Charlotte nor George know that she was going.

"I am not certain of your book." The artist—Angel De Cora—stood in her classroom; winter snowdrifts pushed against the windows of the brick buildings on the campus of the boarding school. Natalie had taken a seat in one of the double desks, looking up at Miss De Cora after her class had been dismissed.

"That's understandable. Here I am, a Pahana—as the Hopi call an Anglo—hoping to preserve important parts of another's culture. But the Hopi also call me Tawimana. That means 'Song Maid' or 'Woman Who Sings Like a Mockingbird.' They have allowed me to record their songs, to view their dances, to sit with them at their fires. And to sing their songs for them and for others. President Roosevelt has allowed it."

Angel wiped the blackboard, her back to Natalie.

"You could use your own artistry while hopefully incorporating unique features of the tribes. Certain bird feathers, pottery shapes, parfleche designs. Animals that might have meaning."

Am I being too direct?

"You've painted book covers. I've seen them. They're beautiful." She knew she was talking too much, wasn't reaching the artist's concerns. "I'll be quiet now."

A long silence followed. Natalie had learned not to enter into it.

"People say I should not do work for Anglos," Angel said at last. "I painted my people in white men's clothes for a book cover." She put down the rag she'd been cleaning the blackboard with. She was tall, her shoulders bent.

"But your art was true to the characters in the story, wasn't it?" Natalie had read *Yellow Star*, the book that had Indian characters, one in Anglo dress, on the cover. "I would only ask that you be true to the songs and traditions in this book."

The artist turned then sat behind the teacher's desk. "When I was six, a white man came to our reservation and asked me and several friends if we would like to ride in a steam car. What child would not like to do such a thing? He assured us it was safe." She shook her head, remembering. "At the end of the ride, we were not returned home but taken to Hampton School in Virginia, far from our Nebraska home. I was there three years. My parents did not know if I was dead or alive."

"I . . . those are the very practices I abhor, that I hope the book will change."

"They wanted the girls to learn white men's ways so we could be good wives and one day help our men become white without argument."

"They used you. I understand."

"You cannot understand." Her jaw clenched.

278

"No. You're right. I'm sure I don't," Natalie said. "I know a little of what it's like to be a woman asked to serve others rather than allowed to be her own person. But it's nothing like what you have endured. What I want, though, is for this book to help educate us Anglos, for us to see what we will be eliminating if we don't honor the past of Indian people. At the same time, I want to work with my Indian friends to preserve their music. I'm calling this *The Indians' Book*. I'm just the pencil. They've written it. I recorded it."

Angel shook her head. "You hold the pencil, so you write what you decide."

Natalie considered, then said, "About how the songs are composed on the paper, yes, I do control that. But not the words, not the rhythms, not the stories I've been told. And not the artist's work that celebrates each tribe, each section." Natalie reached into her large bag and pulled out the Pawnee pages. "See. A Pawnee girl has painted a tepee decorated with a buffalo, the eagle, the sun, a ceremonial pipe. She chose what she wanted."

Angel looked at the page. "You have not named her."

"She asked not to have her name used but for me to call her a 'Pawnee girl.' But what I would like is where I can find no tribal artist, that at least the lettering in each section carries with it the thread of all Indian people. That's what I'd like you to do."

Angel looked at the drawing. "I would make a symbol for the tepee and hang it from a belt, then draw the words 'Pawnee' and 'Indians' down on either side with her tepee at the bottom of the page. In the center."

"Yes! I can see that. Excellent. In full color. Would you like to see the others?"

Angel nodded and the two women bent their heads to the sections while Angel sketched. "Show me the Ho-Chunk and Winnebago pages," she said. "Hmm. This is a big section."

"It is, yes. So many love songs, and I had many informers telling me of the stories of the foolish one," Natalie said.

"Show me." Angel read the sections, looked at the history Natalie had compiled, and nodded. Natalie could see her tapping her fingers to the tunes Natalie had included along with the name of the informant. "Oh, you talked with Chasĥ-chûnk-a. Peter Sampson. Wave, he calls himself in English."

"Yes. We met Wave in Nebraska. He speaks poetry," Natalie said, then recited, "'Throughout the world / Who is there like little me! / Who is like me! / I can touch the sky, I touch the sky indeed.'" Natalie looked at Angel. "I love this sentiment. Who is there like any of us? We are all unique. It's what I want to convey in this book. I hope you'll help me."

"You will use Hinook Mahiwi Kilinaka, my name, as well as my artist's name?"

"On the back of every section page you design."

She looked at Natalie, a wistful smile on her pretty face. "An aunt named me Angel. She opened the Bible and found the word and liked it. But I would want both names."

"It's fitting that your artwork is the opening of each section, proclaiming the Pawnee, the Kiowa, the Navajo." Natalie moved her hands through the air as though writing a marquee atop a concert hall. "Angel means 'messenger' or 'one that announces,'" Natalie said.

"I did not know this."

"It's from Latin but also French. *Angele*, a softer form."

"My father was French." Angel turned more pages. "Beadwork," she said, folding her hands over the pages on the desk in front of her. "It is what I will use to announce the Ho-Chuck Winnebago Indians front matter page."

"Excellent."

"Leave the front matter for the others." Angel knew the publishing term for those sections that came first, that housed short quotations or special designs. Her having worked with another author would be invaluable. "I will make the lettering for you. For all of them."

Natalie clapped her hands. Her exuberance must have been catching, as Angel smiled, showing straight, even teeth. They negotiated a price for Angel's work, scheduled a timeline. Natalie provided a list of all eighteen tribes and the subsections. She gave Angel a copy of the proposed table of contents, which took up four pages, front and back.

"It will be a very fluffy book," Angel said. Natalie looked confused. "Fat. We use 'fluffy' for *fat* as a term of what you Anglos call endearment."

"I like it better than fat, which is what my brother keeps telling me. I'm honored you are willing to be a part of my fluffy book."

Before Natalie left, the two women spoke of others Natalie had recorded or talked with from the Winnebago people, elders and offspring Angel knew of. They chattered like old friends catching up and realized their paths had crossed at St. Louis at the exposition but they had not met. Natalie showed Angel her Roosevelt letter and explained how much she wanted to change the Indian schools, to allow children to sing their songs and dance the dances of their grandmothers.

"It is not easy," Angel said. "But maybe it will help write a different page for all our people." She reached out to hold Natalie's fingers in that soft Indian handshake, but Natalie pulled her into an embrace. She felt Angel's shoulders sink and the two held each other for a moment.

The woman humbled Natalie. Angel had found a way to forgive her captors for tearing her from her parents, for indoctrinating her with white ways with no honor to her own, yet held no revenge in her heart. Instead, she sought justice through education. Could Natalie do as much?

Interlude #6

To Song Maid. Help us. We solved our problem, then they punished us. Friendlies and Hostiles, as they divide our people, we formed a peaceful plan. A line is drawn in the sand and each picked their strongest clansman. Then we got behind our strong man and pushed. Each clan pushed and pushed and the first to get their man across the sand line, that group won. Friendlies won. Three hundred Hostiles packed their burros and drove their sheep to a distant place on the mesa. We cried to see our friends leave. But it was without bloodshed. A Hopi way to solve a problem. Peaceful. No one is hurt, more than the pain of separation. We slept that night, restless, but tension eased.

Then police came, arrested the Hostiles' leader! Then they came and arrested our Friendlies leader. They drag Lololomai's nephew, Tawakwaptiwa, and forty of our people away to Sherman Institute. Oraibi people, gone. No one to guide those left, sing the songs, remember the dances. Gone! None allowed at school. We help the white people and they do this to us. We do not understand.

We sing only death songs, for they are dead to us so far away. It is days of grieving. The moon is high and we are filled with restless sleep, crying still for our people, for Tawakwaptiwa. I am awake and walking by the reservoir, trying to understand how there can be people like Song Maid, and people like the soldiers who arrested our chief.

I look out across the mesa and then I see them. Men on horses riding hard. Toward our mesa, toward Old Oraibi. Dust rises—even in the

282

moonlight I can see it. Dogs bark. My hands are cold. I rush to wake my auntie, climb the ladders. "Rise! Rise! Soldiers come!" Who is left for them to take? We mill around like sticks in swirling water, nowhere to go, our hearts pounding, our mothers wailing, fathers chanting. And then they are upon us, shouting, "Line up! Children of Oraibi, line up!" We know this command "line up." It means to lower our heads, stand shoulder to shoulder, do not look upon the soldiers' faces. The superintendent of Keams school is with them, with horses pushing us together. Eighty of us, together.

I do not lower my eyes and he strikes me with his whip. Once. Twice. My auntie cries. I will not look away. It is not right, Song Maid. I march with my head high even after he strikes my shoulders again. Then I sing. We all sing. They whip us harder as we sing and march. We march long miles to Keams Canyon school. We are there now. They cut the boys' hair. They take away our hair swirls that make you smile. They will not let us sing. You come. Tell them we are Friendlies. You come. You take us home. Mina

34

The Mockingbird Sings

1906

I only have a few chapters to go," George told Natalie. They had arranged to speak at least weekly by phone, keeping each other apprised of progress. George's moved at a snail's pace. "I thought my slow tempo was from spending time encouraging you to finish, but now I see I have writer's resistance."

"I do love where you wrote about your cowboy protagonist trying to convince his eastern love to come west, saying, 'I shall meet you at the train station with a pony and a packhorse.' I love that line. A pony and a packhorse. It has a certain rhythm to it."

"I have a title at least. *The Wooing of a Recluse.*"

"And I have added to my title. It will now be *The Indians' Book: An Offering by the American Indians of Indian Lore, Musical and Narrative, to Form a Record of the Songs and Legends of Their Race.* I'll add 'Edited and Recorded by Natalie Curtis.' Wait until you see some of the artwork Angel has submitted. Harper and Brothers is ecstatic. It's no wonder she became a member of the

American Academy of Design by the time she was thirty-one. Charlotte says I'm lucky to have snared her, but it wasn't a trap at all. We are . . . simpatico," Natalie said. *And Providence moves.*

"She'll definitely add to the book. But the title, Nat. Will there be room on the cover for all that and some sort of artwork too?"

"Angel has painted a parfleche design for the hardcover and a Navajo sand painting for the paper book jackets. But the publisher will have the final say."

"How many pages are you up to?"

"Five hundred and seventy-five."

Silence, then, "Golly, Natalie. I'm amazed you got a publisher." He sounded teasing, but there was truth to his worry. It had taken effort to convince a publisher to include all the material she wanted.

"I can thank Charlotte in part, and Peabody. Roosevelt's agreeing to write something, not an introduction really, but words of support, helped too. He sent an initial letter and it praised me. Too much, I told him. I hated sending it back, but he understood that I wanted the *book* written by the Indians to get his endorsement, not me. I'm hoping to have it by mid-May."

Belatedly, she was concerned about the book's size. With all the songs, production could be costly. But she couldn't find a way to eliminate pieces so reverently shared with her. It was like killing off a special pet to put a song in the wastebasket. She could see each face, recalled listening to each story. *How can I say no?* She had to find a way to not equate the editing out of songs with erasing the experience she'd had in hearing them. Nor that doing so rubbed out the singer's contribution. But she could edit her own introductory words, which she did. Then found that allowed more room for songs. It was as it should be.

❧

Natalie ran her finger over the manuscript, verifying the index against the page numbers. She was close. She needed to turn everything in by December, her publisher had informed her. She had to stop adding, changing.

"There is no such thing as perfect," her editor had told her, "unless you take the literal meaning of the word, which is 'complete.' Finish it, Natalie."

She planned to; she really did. But a part of her resisted, fearing what was next. What would she do with her life once this passionate period of saving Indian music was past? The publication date was June 1907, and once she delivered the books to Hiamovi, Angel, and others, she'd be in that canyon between custom and time. Charlotte had assured her she could do the same work preserving African-American songs, and that intrigued her. But she'd been taken over by the West and wanted to find some reason to stay there. Santa Fe. That's the town that called her name. She supposed she had earned the strength to live with the uncertainty of the "what next?" The years of searching, of not being sure if they'd find a Cheyenne or Kiowa to record, sleeping in the desert, riding through arroyos, had urged her to learn to take one day at a time, that like a desert bloom following the rains, there would be new glories. But she had to keep learning to wait.

The doorbell rang and she answered it, receiving a much-traveled letter in her hand. She opened it, saw tiny script and Mina's signature at the end.

Natalie's hands shook as she read. *How can this be?* The peaceful Hopi people, ravaged like this? How long ago had it happened? Why hadn't she heard of this?

"George." She called him immediately. "Could Charles Lummis know about this? What can I do?"

"Finish the book, get the word out about what truly matters. You don't know how long they've been there. They may have returned already. Complete the book."

"I have to go there."

"Nat." But George's plea was not a song that Natalie could hear.

286

She rushed, packed a small bag, bought her ticket. She might be able to do some work while on the train—yes, she'd take some of the pages with her. She felt rushed, frantic almost. The postmark on Mina's letter was August. The children would be needed for the harvest in September. The boys would work and sing beside their fathers; the girls, grind the corn beside their mothers. Their Hopi world upended, betrayed once again. And the anguish of the children taken, torn. She brushed away tears. Hopeless.

And what good will my book do in the end? I should contact Roosevelt.

She needed to see firsthand. She told George of her plans; didn't tell Charlotte for fear she'd want to come along, and Natalie didn't know what she'd find. But she could not stay in the East when there was heartbreak in her West.

Her bag packed, she called a cab to take her to the station, then opened the door and ran directly into the chest of her brother. "I couldn't let you go alone."

∞

"I guess everyone thought the two factions had settled things well with no injuries, no deaths," George told her. They were on the train headed toward Old Oraibi. "Charles said Commissioner Leupp decided the leader of the Hostiles was dangerous and he had him arrested. Tawakwaptiwa was concerned, even though they'd won, so he asked for federal help. Instead, Leupp had him arrested too."

"They accepted schools and books and education. They found a nonviolent way to solve their own problems and it's all for nothing?" Indignation rode on Natalie's shoulders.

"Leupp arrested the Hostile chief and stripped Tawakwaptiwa of his chief status and then forcibly took him and forty others to the Sherman Institute in California. That's how Lummis knows what happened."

287

"It's the Keams school that worries me. That . . . that . . . wretched place where they withhold food and use the children as workers for the officers' gardens. I can't . . . Oh, George." She felt a wave of grief pour over her. "Angel spoke of the horror of her being taken thirty years ago to a school far away. Now, it happens again."

"You're doing what you can. We'll see firsthand what's happening there. Then go back and get the book out." He patted her hand.

"It isn't enough. Poor Mina."

What was the point of having a book celebrating the old ways and the nurturing practices of a people, while in present time the government continued the violence against them? *Am I writing an obituary rather than a celebratory book?*

∽

George hired two horses from the livery, bought gear, and they began the two-day ride toward Fort Defiance and the Keams Canyon Boarding School. In the midst of her inner turmoil, she was comforted once again by her time on horseback, feeling her knees and thighs against the saddle, the steadiness of the mount beneath her. She must keep horses—and burros—in her life after the publication of the book. She had to return to the West and the landscape of the weeping rainbow-colored rocks, the vibrancy of the sunsets or, as Charles Lummis called it, the "Land of Pretty Soon." Pretty soon she would find her way. Pretty soon, she hoped, she would intrude in a good way for Mina and the other children whisked away to a Navajo school far from their Hopi homes.

"There they are. Hoeing. Honestly, George, they use them as slaves." They rode into the fort's perimeter. Not much had changed from when they'd been there two years before. Natalie squinted to see if she recognized Mina among the girls. But in their government uniforms, they all looked so similar, she couldn't tell. She and George dismounted, and two young soldiers took their horses to a trough to drink. Natalie patted the rump of hers as the mare was led away, then brushed the dust from her skirt. The September sun beat down on her as her boots clicked on the wooden steps to the commander's office. She adjusted her eyes to the darkness. It was slightly less hot inside the adobe.

"I don't know if you remember me," Natalie said to the commander. "Natalie Curtis."

"Oh yes, Roosevelt's girl," he said. "I mean, because of the letter."

She didn't like the designation, but since he made the association, she'd use it. "Yes, and my brother George Curtis." George tapped his hand to his hat. "I'd like to see some of the students. I understand there are new ones here, from Old Oraibi."

"Yes, ma'am. They're here and so is Burton. I'll ask my assistant to tell him what you're asking for."

"We'll make our way to the school first. I am allowed, you remember."

"Yes, ma'am. I remember."

Natalie whispered to George as they walked toward the gardens, "At least he's not challenging my right to be here."

They opened the heavy wooden door and heard a teacher speaking. She stopped as soon as she saw Natalie and George. "May I help you?"

All the heads turned toward them, and before Natalie could answer, Mina leapt from her wooden desk and raced to Natalie, grabbing her around her middle, crushing herself to Natalie's heart. "You come. You come. You save us. You save songs."

"Yes, I came," Natalie said, stroking the girl's shoulder, seeing black hair, so short, her neck exposed. "I came. I did." But she wasn't sure she could save anything.

"Mina!" The teacher stomped toward them. "Sit down."

"It's alright. I'm Natalie Curtis. I have permission from President Roosevelt to visit Indian schools. I want to see Mina. She's like a daughter to me."

289

The teacher stopped, stepped back. "Oh. I . . . have heard of you. Of course, welcome. No one told me you'd be visiting. We'd have been better prepared."

Soon other Hopi children had clustered around her. She recognized them: singers, dancers. Natalie looked around. The room was clean. There were pictures on the walls that children had made—colorful—of horses, burros, bowls, and corn. The children all wore uniforms, but they were clean. She was grateful that at least they didn't look mistreated here—though injured in the separation, by the separation, and being here at all, especially when there was a day school at the pueblo. Natalie touched the backs and shoulders of as many children as she could—never the heads, as that part of the body was considered sacred.

"I wonder," Natalie said, releasing herself from all except Mina, who pressed into Natalie's side. "If I might take Mina with me, to Agent Burton's office."

"Of course, yes. You know which building is the agency?"

"Unless they've changed it, yes."

The three of them, George, Mina, and Natalie, walked across the desert courtyard, and Natalie took a deep breath before she knocked on the superintendent's door.

"What do you have in mind, Nat?" George asked.

"I'm not sure." And she wasn't. But when she composed a piece of music, there was always a pause before the first piano or orchestral note. Not exactly a grace pause, but close. So, when she knocked on the door, the world was uncertain. But she would step into it anyway.

❧

"Superintendent Burton. I'm so glad you're here."

He squinted. "I remember you," Burton said. "I thought you'd gone off to pester some other poor agent or superintendent."

"I imagine I have been a bit of a thorn to you," Natalie said, her voice as smooth as a tanned hide. "But I see you've gotten a good teacher. The children look healthy. I imagine there have been some trials, what with blending Hopi and Navajo children. That doesn't always work."

He blinked, not expecting praise or even understanding.

"It wasn't my idea. The commissioner's," Burton defended. "As punishment for Tawakwaptiwa settling differences, splitting the tribe like they did. Created havoc here, I can tell you."

"I wonder if I might make a suggestion."

"What might that be?" Wariness crept into his words.

"I wouldn't want to have to write about the depravations at Old Oraibi—we'll be riding there, of course—because the children to help with harvest are here instead of with their families. It would be a shame for you to have a bad mark on your record when it was the commissioner's recommendation. Why not let them go home to help with harvest?"

He stood, quiet. Then, "Might help out with the rations here. Of course, we'd have to make sure there were rations enough there."

"George and I would be happy to take a wagon of supplemental supplies and the children, with soldier escort of course, perhaps even add to the flour supply at Keams. Our contribution as a thank-you for letting us assist." She didn't look at George. She'd convince her sponsors of the value of the expense.

"And what afterward, after they've harvested and whatnot?"

"The thought occurred to me that since Tawakwaptiwa is at the Sherman Institute in Riverside, perhaps you would consider letting Mina and the other children join those already there. After harvest and replanting. Meanwhile, they could attend the day school. They've done nothing wrong."

She wasn't sure where the idea had come from, but she played the melody out. "I'd be sure to tell the president of your cooperation. I know you were investigated previously and the president supported you then as he continues to support my efforts. He's writing a letter of endorsement for the book about Indian music that will be published next year."

"Is he?"

"He is."

Mina's fingers pressed into Natalie's side and she heard the girl whisper in English, "Please, Father God, please, Father God." It was a prayer Natalie had said herself during those long years of separation from music and herself.

"Well, why not," Burton said. "It would settle grievances here, that's for sure. Making room for the Hopi children had its repercussions, I can tell you that. Set the budget amiss too. I'll order them back to Oraibi. If you care to spend the night, we can arrange for things to change in the morning."

"And after harvest, if they must leave, they could go to the Sherman school?"

"I'll see what I can do."

She was the pied piper once again. The journey back to Old Oraibi was mixed with singing. Burton provided wagons enough for supplies and to carry children. But mostly they walked beside George and Natalie's horses that the Curtis siblings ended up leading to be closer to the children. They brushed up against them, like hummingbirds flitting to their sides, then rushed back out to chatter to each other and the soldiers. It was almost like a parade, Natalie thought before she stopped herself, realizing what had happened to make this reunion required.

Parents came out to greet them, Mina's auntie crying out in joy. Natalie realized one of the boys had run ahead to take the message of their coming. Natalie shouted to her old friends, and she heard Bonita, her burro, hee-hawing as she trot-trotted toward her, long ears forward, welcoming her home.

"I knew the Song Maid would come, I knew," Mina said. She sat beside her auntie, the woman who had raised her. There had been a meal and the sunset still played with colors across the mesa. "I prayed. You came."

Natalie hadn't thought of herself as an answer to anyone's prayer. "I'm glad you wrote. That was brave of you."

"We will dance the Mockingbird song now," she said. "You join us, Song Maid."

She pulled Natalie into the circle of girls, gave her a shawl with strings hanging from the hem, like all the others. Someone handed Mina another shawl. Apparently, it was a dance for girls, with men singing and drumming. Mina showed Natalie the steps, standing shoulder to shoulder, moving in a circle, the dipping and swirling. Dust covered their moccasins and the toes of Natalie's boots. Soon other girls and women joined the circle, soft-stepping to the beat of the drum, accompanied by the high-pitched tune. Everyone seemed to be singing. It had been a long time since Natalie had danced.

And when the song ended, the drummers and dancers stopped in unison. Even Natalie had anticipated the final note.

"Don't even think about it," George told Natalie when they finished. She knew her face was flushed.

"What?" She folded her shawl as she sat on the wooden bench next to him. People chattered and a wren chirped in a nearby cactus.

"You have more than enough songs for your book," George said.

"You're right. I have to get this book published. But I'll make notes when we camp tonight, for my own memory." *And maybe I can add just one more dancing song to the book.*

35

The Tracks We Leave

1906–1907

*Y*ou arrive with the breath of the West," Natalie told Hiamovi, the high chief of the Cheyenne and the Dakota, when he reached New York. Natalie and George had returned East with the goal to get the book completed. Harper and Brothers had assigned two new editors, one an Episcopal canon with a specialty in Gregorian chants and another a composer. But it was the Indian informers whom Natalie most wanted involved in the final decisions.

"So. The train does not smell much of the West."

"You're here, and right in time. I need you to review what I've written about the tribal histories, descriptions of the dances, the legends. Do I have the stories about a hare or turtle right? Have I described what a rattle was made from correctly? And if I've said something insensitive, well, please tell me."

"It can be arranged." And he set about the slow work of reading each of Natalie's introductions.

She brought him a lunch of a ham and cheese sandwich, left

him alone. He stayed the night with her brothers, returned to study more. Natalie nervously chewed the side of her fingernail, an old habit once given up. Finally, he announced her renderings "good." She sighed relief.

"I read the Roosevelt letter who sings praises." Hiamovi quoted, "'These songs cast a wholly new light on the depth and dignity of Indian thought, the simple beauty and strange charm—the charm of a vanished elder world—of Indian poetry.' His words of elder world, this I like."

"It's a marvelous letter, I agree."

Hiamovi left the table where he'd been working and returned shortly with an artist's canvas. "My wife, White Buffalo, and Hiamovi, we wish to make a painting contribution." He turned the painting around. "We call it 'Things of the Olden Time.'" He showed her seven objects in full color, from a case for a bow and arrow to a parfleche to a pipe. They were all on one page and reflected all the tribes, Natalie thought, with a porcupine-quill-decorated satchel to a buffalo-hide bag for carrying cherries.

"It's grand," Natalie said.

He had included a separate page with short explanations of what each item was and its use. "This will be the first in the front matter," Natalie said. "Before the title page, even. It's so splendid." She knew her editors might fume with the late addition, but it was perfect. She'd convince them so they wouldn't say no.

That afternoon, after Hiamovi's stamp of approval, she and George and Charlotte and Hiamovi carried the tome to Harper and Brothers and handed it over. They had a celebratory lunch at Charlotte's with the two editors. Natalie and Hiamovi sang a grace.

It was finished.

Natalie didn't feel a whit of satisfaction.

In the days that followed, she felt empty. Or maybe it was anxiety. It was different from what she'd felt when she'd stepped back from her debut. That's how she thought of that time of sorrow now, a stepping back rather than a collapse. A pause.

"You fall off a horse, you get right back on," George told her when she confessed her emptiness and worry about how the book would be received and the what-next part of her life. They were at the brothers' apartment in New York.

"I hardly think I fell off a horse," Natalie said. She sipped hot tea. Mint.

"You get my point. When you finish something—or something is taken from you—you grieve it. Remember what Hiamovi told you before he left. 'We will be known forever by the tracks we leave.' You've made tracks. But there are more trails to walk. Take a new breath and get back to work. African-American music awaits, doesn't it? Charlotte has a plan for you."

Natalie smiled. "She always does. You may be right. I'll go to the Hampton School more often." She looked around the apartment George had lived in while he helped her with the book. It was filled with "belongings" from the West. "I'll never be able to thank you for staying away from your beloved West for so long."

"Because of you, I have a chosen landscape so much better than I might have. I'm ready for the next adventure—knowing just where it'll take place. Somewhere east of San Diego."

"And I know too. After the promotion of this book and putting together the African songbook—which will not be five hundred seventy-five pages"—George laughed with her—"I'm heading to Santa Fe. I need creativity in my life—but I also need the West."

∞

She kept a steady correspondence with Agent Burton, and following spring planting, he had moved Mina and the other children to the Sherman school as she'd suggested. She had hoped he'd let them stay home, but she'd pushed her influence as far as she could. And at least they'd be with Tawakwaptiwa, their old chief, once again. Natalie fumed at her impotence in stopping what was happening at other Indian and boarding schools. When the book came out, she would hand deliver it to every superintendent, every Indian boarding school across the country, and she would make sure that the students knew that it was there and that it celebrated who they were, where they'd come from, and the music and stories that would not be forgotten.

∽

"I've received my first copy!" Natalie called George, then Charlotte, then her parents, then Peabody.

"How much does it weigh?" George asked.

"Three pounds. Exactly. How did you know I'd weigh it?"

"You'll break your back carrying them around." But George's voice held joy in it, joy for her.

"Maybe I'll enlist my burro. Actually, that's a good idea," Natalie said. "At least for when we deliver the books to Old Oraibi."

George laughed. "What is this *we* business?"

"You'll come with me, won't you?"

"How could I not?"

Harper and Brothers had sent out dozens of review copies across the East to museums and government officials and musicians, especially musicians. For Natalie, it was about the music, and yet she knew people would be seeing such unusual scores for the first time and she hoped it would meet the exploring minds of composers and performers, their commitment to novelty blended with compositions from great maestros of the past. Secretly, Natalie hoped a composer might pick up the music from her book, see the potential in it, and create an original work to acclaim the melodies of the Hopi or the five tribes of the Wabanakis of the East, those who had first welcomed white people to their shores.

She had begun the book with them. She had ended it with the Hopi contributions. *Family*. It was how she saw the Hopi, the people with the good hearts.

The reviews had been exceptional. Her editors said it was selling like hotcakes. It was feeding an interest in Indians. They weren't seen as warriors only or broken people but as survivors full of art and song and stories. She found herself dancing about in her family's brownstone, following a signing party her mother had arranged. In her old bedroom where she'd cried herself to sleep so many nights, awakened to nightmares during those five years of sadness, she slept contented. It wasn't only the success of the book, but that she had struck out to do something she felt mattered. She'd blended her passion for music—which had nearly destroyed her—and justice, creating something new: a book of Indian music that she hoped would be a healing for the people so abused. She thought of Mina, who wrote that the Sherman school was not so bad. They could sing and dance there with their Hopi chief. *"I will make it grand, Song Maid,"* she wrote. Words of a strong Hopi girl.

∽

Natalie had asked to hand deliver the copy of the book to Walter Damrosch, her old Adonis, and had made an appointment to meet him at his home. His wife would be there. Both Charlotte and George wanted to go with her. Charlotte especially wanted to meet the famous conductor, and George knew of the unrequited love, the guilt of failure, the despair of being lost with concert piano playing no longer in her life.

"I need to go alone," she told them. "Some things must be set aside in a singular way."

"Natalie," Damrosch said, greeting her with a bear hug. He smelled of onions. "It is so good to see you. Ach, you look wonderful." He stood back and gazed at her. *"Wunderbar,"* he repeated in German.

"Margaret?" she asked as he took her cape.

"She's been called away. My wife speaks her regrets."

Natalie had a moment of hesitation being alone with him. She stepped back but then regained her rhythm. She pulled the book out of her carpetbag to hand to him.

"Yes, yes, I hear of this work, how you spent your time these many years. I look forward to reading it. It is a work of love, deep passionate love, yes?"

Natalie's face felt warm with the words *love* and *passionate* coming from his mouth.

Damrosch didn't seem to notice. "You'll have tea here, *ja*?" He rattled on about Natalie's wonderful talent and how she had put it to such good use while he poured the water over the tea leaves. "Not settled to teach urchins," he said. "As so many women must. But to change how people see music, this is good work, Natalie. Commanding, innovative. I will write a review."

"Only if you find it worthy," she said.

"It is worthy, *ja*, I know this without even opening it because you only do magnificent things." He lifted the book, bounced it. "Though it must weigh, what, two pounds? Not bedtime reading." He laughed and she once again latched on to his word "bedtime." *Goodness, it's who he is, a man who talks of love and bedtime.*

"It would break a nose, dropping on one's face if they fell asleep while reading." She laughed. "I simply couldn't leave anything out."

"Full rapture," Damrosch said. *Rapture.* "Ja, that was always you, and I loved you for it. What will you work on now, hmm?" He sipped his tea.

"African-American folk music," she said. "And then I think cowboy songs that remind me so much of Irish ballads. Perhaps Appalachian folk songs, the four unique strains of American music, including Indian music, don't you think?"

"An interesting study, to be sure. America has no unique music like the folk songs of Norway or Germany."

"But it does," Natalie said. "That's what *The Indians' Book* is all about."

He tapped the tome lying on the coffee table between them. "But now, you will tell me your favorite parts of this."

"I . . . they are all my favorites," she said. "Each has a memory written into my life these past five years. I could tell you stories."

"Sing one for me. I will read along the score to see how you arranged it, see if I can hear it from the notes, ja?"

Natalie took the book from his hands and paged toward the back. "It's a lullaby and I've made notations to show how the mother swayed back and forth with the beat." She showed him.

"Ja, ja, I see."

She sang then from memory, her voice clear. She was back in Hopi land.

"Superb," he said when she finished. "May you sing it many times, perhaps to put a child of your own to sleep."

She smiled, drank her tea. *Wouldn't my mother love that.*

"You'll give a copy to Ferruccio Busoni, yes? Your old piano teacher. He adores you."

"Actually, I have. I've also given him a few Edison recordings. I have a hope he might use them to create an original composition."

"Wunderbar," he said. He had an annoying habit of sniffing as though he had a cold. Had he done that before? She saw him in an entirely new light, she no longer a girl with a crush; no longer seeing the Adonis she had once ogled over. Music had taken her heart apart. But now, music put it back together and she carried no thoughts of nightmares in which Walter Damrosch once starred. They were colleagues, nothing more.

∽

The reviewers raved. Her mother's society friends lauded. Musicians marveled and the book sold despite its weight and unique subject. Natalie signed copies at bookstores. She was invited to speak at events where she sang and sold copies of the book "at the back of the room," as George described it. He handled many of the sales.

Then she began the hand delivery to the participants, the Penobscot informants, the Kiowa, Angel at the Carlisle school. The two women shared the joy that so many reviewers commented on the beauty and artistry of Angel's paintings, of how they had made the book so much stronger. The old combining with the new.

Among musicians who had been a part of Natalie's other life, she gained new status, her disappearance from the music scene nearly ten years before, forgotten. She moved among a world of creators and wove within her own mind the possibilities of Indian artists, potters, weavers, not just producing things for everyday use but as works of art, for galleries, to "edify" all humankind. Her friend Alice from San Diego came by a signing and to a gallery opening in New York. It was a heady time when Natalie became known as a music ethnologist, an expert on Indian music, lore, and legend. And most of all, she was recognized as an advocate to move government policy from the belief that Indian people were "primitive" who needed "protection and subjugation until they progressed" and became "like whites." No, they were people with their own rich history, and Natalie saw it as her task to make certain no more of what had been taken from them would be stolen.

She would have to talk again with Roosevelt. He had only two more years in office.

And she would have the conversation with her mother to tell her that when the book promotion ended, she'd be heading west for good.

36

Renewal

*N*atalie coughed. The cold seemed to penetrate her bones, and even the hearth fires and the hot toddies at her parents' home couldn't get her warm. She was at the brownstone with all her siblings and she was exhausted. The promotion of the book had paid off, but there'd been no end to requests, presentations. She was a celebrity, and she thought it odd that years before, she'd experienced some of the same demands as a child prodigy. And it had almost killed her. But she was older, wiser now, and she knew what she wanted and what she needed. "I've got to feel the hot sun and walk the mesa, look for roadrunners." She sneezed. "And sit with my back to adobe and listen to the desert music."

Despite her cold, she'd gone to Charlotte's New York apartment to look at reviews and consider next steps in promotion. If she was honest with herself—and she was doing so much better at that—she had to admit that the desert called her so she could get away from some of the critical comments she'd received about

302

the book. Most came during the question-and-answer sessions at her presentations at conservatories and museums. People were disparaging not the artwork—which had been praised—or the inclusion of music—considered innovative and unique. But rather her essays that introduced the various tribal sections, histories, customs, legends, and lore. Even some from the Indian Rights Association felt that as a white woman she had usurped the Indian stories better left to be told by the Indians themselves. They took exception to her view that she had been a mere pencil in the informants' hands.

"But their stories were being lost, wiped out," Natalie said. "Don't people understand that?"

"You're too sensitive," Charlotte told her. The two women sat on Charlotte's divan. "They're jealous the book is such a smash."

"I see their point, though. Who am I to be the one to tell their stories? Hiamovi could have written his section. Well, he did for the most part." She had asked him to write an introduction to the book, which he had. "But so many of the other informants didn't know English. They're just learning how to write their stories down. With the law forbidding them to share the songs, dances, and histories, how were they to have anything to pass on?" It was what had propelled her toward the project in the first place.

"They've told you," Charlotte said. "They would have written them down themselves, as Hiamovi did—if they knew how. Don't let the naysayers get to you. You were called to this work and you responded brilliantly."

"I was so hopeful that the book would bring about good change."

"Change comes on little steps," Charlotte reminded her. "Your feet are small, but they keep moving."

"The book is evidence of the depth of experience, complexity of culture, and the need to stop assimilation," Natalie said. "Isn't it?" Those were the points she emphasized in her presentations. *But when will that policy change?*

Charlotte stood up to freshen their tea while Natalie remembered her last meeting with the president. It had not gone well. He'd happily talked up the book, given it to members of Congress where he thought a gift coming from him might bear more weight than coming from Natalie. He had wondered if the Indian senator from Kansas, Charles Curtis, was related, but Natalie said, no, he wasn't. Roosevelt signed the senator's book personally. She'd thanked Roosevelt again for his endorsement.

When she raised concerns about the divisive actions of arresting the Hopi, separating the children, he listened. Yet when she expressed her opinion on several bills the Indian commissioner had championed that took land from Indians while supposedly acting in trust for them, Roosevelt dismissed her. "You're spending too much time talking to Lummis and those Indian Rights people. I listen to them, Miss Curtis, I do, but they are wrong in most things while the Commissioner of Indian Affairs, I find, is right. You fight for Indian pots and poems and music, their art. I'm behind you with that. But best you stay out of legislative affairs."

He didn't call me Natalie.

His words stung.

"My influence has waned," she'd told George when her brother came to visit her in New York a day after her meeting.

"Not necessarily. He sees you in the corral of Indian music and art, so any arguments you make against government people have to be roped around those efforts. Argue conditions in the schools or even against the appalling kidnapping of children in the government's name, especially as those acts set their parents against assimilation. But make it about the desire to not lose what the Indian people bring to the American experience. I suspect he'd hear you about that."

"But he didn't. When I told him how the arrests of the Friendlies' and the Hostiles' chiefs affected the children, he said, 'Children are resilient, Miss Curtis. Especially Indian children.'"

"You'll have to build on that, then. Do what you can to enhance that generation so they'll have the songs and art to pass on to their offspring."

∽

"Do you suppose I'll ever see these people from the tribes again once I give them their books?" Natalie put the question to George in October as they rode the train west, taking the same route as they had five years before.

"There might be reason to come back. It's not like they haven't become our friends."

"I do want to know how Chiparopai's great-grandchild is doing and how Hiamovi's family fares. And of course, Tawakwaptiwa and his fate. They interest me beyond an anthropological curiosity. Mina. But I'm not family. They aren't family the way you are."

"Blood being thicker than water, and all that."

"Still, each informer has been a bit of medicine they gave without realizing how broken I was. It's been the adventure of a life-time. I wouldn't have given it up for anything in the world. My breakdown might actually have been worth it."

It's less time that heals than having a purpose. A creative purpose. She would be sure to tell Hiamovi that when she handed him his copy, with gratitude for all he'd given and especially for the preface he'd written beginning with the words, *"To the Great Chief at Washington, and to the Chiefs of Peoples across the Great Water, This is the Indians' Book."* She could never thank him enough for saying it was so, that she was but a pencil in the Indians' hands.

∽

Their arrival at El Alisal was met with joy from Charles and Eva Lummis and guests they'd invited. Frank Mead, who now worked with Lummis on architectural innovations, and Alice Klauber, who had just returned from a painting class in France.

305

Natalie wore her cotton "Indian" dress, as she thought of it, with ease, the Winnebago porcupine-quill belt, a beaded necklace from the Cheyenne with a silver horseshoe from the Navajo hung from the end of the beads. On her hand, she still wore her Zuni ring missing a turquoise stone. Instead of high-button boots, she wore white silk dancing slippers, as close to moccasins as she could find. Alice wore her hair in a bob, easy to maintain, Natalie thought.

"You two are a pair," Lummis said. "Stubborn, persistent, focused, a little irregular—"

"I'm not," Alice said. "And Natalie isn't either. I'll accept wave maker, maybe even eccentric, but there's nothing irregular about us. We've gotten where we are by brute force and awkwardness."

"Haven't we all," Eva said.

Natalie laughed. "I think you've covered it nicely."

"It's a fine work," Lummis said, patting the book. "You do the League proud."

She gave Eva and Charles a copy of the tome and signed it. She'd shipped two cases of *The Indians' Book*, and Frank Mead and Alice received one too. She would be taking books around to Oraibi and the Acoma and back to where it had all begun, the Yuma. The group sat beneath the sycamore grove, listened to the mockingbird and wore the desert heat like a fragrance. Natalie reveled in their kind words that meant more than the published reviews. Whether good or bad, she vowed to read what others said about her work, then toss the words away, not allow them to defeat her nor give her puffed-up bravado. This was not her book.

As she listened to the chatter of these activists and artists, she thought of the conversation with her mother. She hadn't realized until she finished the book how she and George were the black sheep of the family, though her new notoriety had pleased her mother to no end.

"I can't remain in the East," Natalie had told her. "I'm not rejecting you nor my family nor all you gave to support my music all

306

those years. But I have found my métier. I've found myself, Mama. And isn't that what you always wanted for me, in the end?"

"It is." Mimsey dabbed at the tears in her eyes. "But I wanted you to find yourself here. With a husband. Grandchildren."

"I'm still young. That could still happen—the marriage and children part. But not the East for eternity. I'm a westerner now. It's where I feel alive."

They had hugged each other, and her mother's shoulders shook just a little with her tears. She was saying goodbye to something while Natalie was saying hello. She'd give her mother time to cross that bridge to acceptance of what is. After all, it had taken time and music for Natalie to find her way.

37

Tricksters

*I*t was a fifty-mile journey to the Sherman Institute from Pasadena, but Lummis owned an auto, one of fifty-six hundred on the roads of Southern California, he'd bragged. Alice, always one for adventure, asked to come along, making it a foursome with Natalie and George.

At eight miles an hour, the "explorers" might have gone faster with horses. After six hours on dusty roads, passing herds of burros and scattered goats, they arrived in Riverside and would stay at a hotel where Indian students were "trained" as housekeepers and workers on the farm that supported both the hotel and the school.

"They've quite an operation here," George noted. "'Free labor,' they call training."

"I imagine there is some actual skill building, isn't there?" Alice asked. "At the school, I mean."

"They are supposed to teach English, math, and various industries like harness making and nursing, but I've always thought the schools don't think high enough," Natalie said. "They're training servants, not lawyers and doctors. It's as though they think Indian

308

children, and the African children at Hampton, don't aspire to the same things children everywhere do. I'll be writing about this. The curriculum of these schools leaves much to be desired."

They approached the institute, a single-story Spanish-style building surrounded by nine other structures, some boarding-houses, Natalie assumed; others teaching sites. Natalie introduced herself and her entourage to the superintendent and asked to see Tawakwaptiwa.

"Who are you?" the superintendent asked, his brow furrowed.

"Natalie Curtis. Here is my credential. From the president of the United States." She showed him the letter, well-worn.

The superintendent grunted. "He's in section C. Curtis? I know your name," he said. "Yeah. I know you. We'll get the chief." He frowned as he barked the order to a student sweeping the lobby area. He gave them no eye contact as the young Indian quick-stepped out the door.

"Yeah, we call him chief, as though it has some weight, but we all know it doesn't," the superintendent said.

"It ought to," Natalie said. "He is a leader among his people. Has he not been a model student?"

"Oh, they broke the mold after they made him."

Natalie cringed at the sarcasm but stepped over it, fearing—Roosevelt letter or not—she wouldn't be allowed to see him if she lectured the superintendent.

She had last seen Tawakwaptiwa leading his white horse on the way down the steep road from Oraibi, talking about God and the bahos, the prayer sticks. He'd sung a butterfly song for her, and in the book, she had used a photograph of him with his hair free at his neck, his eyes looking up as though he sang a prayer.

When he came into the room, his eyes lit up at seeing her. But she sensed his sadness too. His hair was short, a blunt cut like the government required. His shoulders drooped, no longer tall and proud.

"It is good to see you, Song Maid," he said. He took her hands in his. He was much younger than she was, but he'd seen much more trouble and it had aged him.

"And you. I have held you in my heart as I shared your stories in this book." She bent to lift the tome from the carpetbag she carried it in. "Here is your copy." She showed him his photograph.

"I remember this day," he said. "We talked long and sang many songs."

"We did. You made a great contribution to this work. And your English, it is excellent."

Tawakwaptiwa nodded. "I am able to read and write like you do. Almost like you do." He smiled. "But these two years of white men's ways, these are hard times for the Hopi who stood beside the white father's wishes, did as we were asked, settled an argument without violence, and then were destroyed."

"It was unjust. It is unjust. I will try to find a way to get them to release you."

He nodded.

"Do they . . . do they let you sing?"

"The children sing white men songs. One plays a clarinet, and they learn other instruments. Music lives here. But it is not our music."

"I will insist that the superintendent allow you to sing the songs and dance the dances in this book." She tapped it with her hand. "He will see that the president approves. You may sing here. This book dilutes the Code." They sat at a round table, the book lying before them, the superintendent now behind a closed door. George and Lummis fanned themselves on a side divan. Alice stood in the doorway as though capturing what she saw for a future painting.

Tawakwaptiwa turned the pages, stopping at the color introductory sections. He found the Hopi music, using the table of contents, found the pages with his songs on them. He began to hum, and Natalie tapped a drumbeat with the palm of her hand. The song moved to a quavering high tone that descended until it died away as though a storm had passed, leaving finished silence, the song and the drum stopping concisely, as though one. He had kept his voice low, but the Hopi words had returned to him and Natalie knew the words and rhythm. They looked at each other and smiled at their surreptitious violation of the Code.

"It has been two years since we are brought here, two years since I have sung that song," Tawakwaptiwa said. "This book. It is a present."

"An early Christmas present," she said. "My hearing you sing."

They sat in silence and then Tawakwaptiwa said, "It would be Trickster's plan."

Natalie wasn't sure what he was talking about as he thumbed through many tribal contributions in the book. "Singing and dancing from this book will permit the Kiowa and the Pima and the Hopi children to learn their dances here, at this place so far from what they know and may have forgotten. Instead of forgetting the dances, Trickster would have them sing here, then take them home and share them with their parents." He grinned, the first real expression of joy she had seen.

"Am I the trickster?"

"We are, in this book." He tapped the copy. "Our old music is not what the superintendent wants us to take home. That is not what the Indian schools are for." He laughed openly then. "He wants us to take the English and the white ways back and forget the rest."

"Yes. Tricksters—coyotes, right? Turning things on their heads. I remember hearing about coyote inventiveness." Natalie grinned, liking the image of being a trickster.

"We will be coyote while we are here," he said. "And we will restore what has been taken when we go home."

"You came!" Mina's voice rang out as she pushed past Alice in the doorway and rushed into the room.

Natalie's heart skipped a beat. She was going to ask to see her next, but word of their arrival had gone before she could.

"See, I am here. They bring us here to Sherman. It is not home but it is better. All the taken-Hopi are together. It is because of you, Tawimana. Because you came to capture songs."

The child—a young woman almost—looked healthy, her brown face beaming. It was true she wore the uniform and her Hopi swirls were not allowed. But her eyes were bright and she chattered about how she learned to run the sewing machine and that Bonita her burro was taken care of by her auntie and how she could speak a few other Indian languages, learning from her new friends. "I miss my auntie, but it is better here, Tawimana. Better because of you. When do I come to visit? It will be soon, yes?" Her rush of words swirled like a dust devil. "You write to tell me." And then she was out the door again, saying, "I have another friend I bring to meet you."

A small step toward a happier life, and each had helped the other on the path.

Before they left, Natalie spoke with the superintendent, showing him the songs she'd included, and asked him where the students at his school came from. When he hesitated, she showed him the president's words in the front of the book.

"It is required that they be allowed to sing their traditional songs, play their tribal instruments. Especially if they are complying with your rules about learning English and their hair being cut and following work orders."

"They sure don't like their haircuts."

"I'm sure they don't. But they comply, and as this letter says, I am allowed to come in anytime to see how the school is being conducted and who is allowed to sing and who is not. Why, they might even teach you a hand-game song. Those are quite fun. See, right here on page 161. This one is from the Cheyenne."

Tawakwaptiwa stood off to the side, near George, but well able to listen to the conversation between Natalie and the superintendent.

"I'll leave this copy with you. All the schools are getting them, so you won't be alone in permitting the traditional music and dances while the students are here."

"I suppose it won't hurt 'em. What page is that endorsement from the president on?"

"Right after the list of illustrations, of which there is one of Tawakwaptiwa. And see, it says '*White House, Washington*,' followed by his words and that grand signature."

"And that other letter you showed when you first came in?"

"You received a copy of it in 1903 when I began this journey. It's in your files. I'm certain you'd do everything as required, including keeping such a letter." *Should I raise the issue of sending Tawakwaptiwa home? Diplomacy, not political.* "Meanwhile, I'll be conferring with the president about what is necessary for Tawakwaptiwa to return home and for his status as a Hopi chief to be restored. So be looking for a letter from the president about that."

Her influence might have waned, but Roosevelt's hadn't. She would see what could be done to expand it to touch this rigid superintendent.

She saw Tawakwaptiwa nod his head in agreement. She had brought *The Indians' Book* as a thank-you especially to that family, to Lololomai's descendants. But Tawakwaptiwa had given her the best gift of the book tour, making them kindred spirits, describing them as Tricksters, who take what was meant for evil and convert it to good.

Interlude #7

Tawakwaptiwa waits. Weeks. The Song Maid does not return with a letter from the great chief to allow me and my family and others taken from Oraibi to go home, the children brought from Keams Canyon, to go home. We hoe the gardens, make cabinets in the woodworking shop, do as asked by the Pahana, but no one comes to say that "friendly" behavior toward them sets us free. I am a chief. I descend from a long line of chiefs. I have failed my uncle Lololomai and his father and our Hopi people. I try to keep a good heart, but my heart has been broken. What the white men taught is that the Indian is required to wait, his time is not his own. There would come men like Charles Lummis and women like Song Maid. They come to help the people and they might help. I can read about my people in this book; I can sing the songs now. Trickster has made it possible that the children will carry the songs home, songs they did not know before they found them in the book. But I cannot sing them where I wish, on Third Mesa, on the roof of Uncle's house, where the yellow line appears in the morning under clouds like butter. I am not free here to make the music that sets my soul free.

I do not hold blame in my heart for Song Maid that she cannot set us free; but at night when I cannot see my mesa or hear the sheep bells or feel the desert breeze I know deep sadness. Those times I wonder what has the book accomplished except for me to meet a good woman who sings with a Hopi heart?

The Old Blended
with the New

1908

I hope she hasn't died," Natalie told George. "Lummis hasn't heard anything, has he?" They had taken the train from Pasadena to Yuma, where they were met by Texan.

"Miss," he said tipping his hat. "Can I get your luggage? Unless you've got a dozen crates like the last time."

"Just a couple of boxes. Books!" She removed her hat and wiped her forehead. It was only March, but it was hot already. She and George had stayed at El Alisal through the New Year and then gone to Santa Fe, where Natalie had found a three-room casita she claimed as her own. But she looked forward to seeing Chiparopai. "Do you hear anything about the Yuma people?"

"No more than usual," Texan said. "Though I see more girls working in town. Schools are teaching housekeeping and such."

"I hope to encourage their instructors to consider more complicated jobs, become teachers and doctors and lawyers."

"Not sure we need more lawyers," Texan said.

"If you were an Indian, you might." Natalie shook her finger at him but smiled. "Chiparopai, she's alright?"

"She's still alive, yup, she is. I expect you'll be heading out that way."

"In the morning. We'll walk," Natalie said. She liked the idea of crossing the river with her brother, moving toward the pumpkin fields to the sounds of hawks and the scatter of a roadrunner.

The next morning, she saw children dotting the earth with their baskets, planting corn, singing as they worked.

"At least people make music here," Natalie said. "I hope Chiparopai is not back at her hogan. She told me she preferred to be alone, away from people." But then they saw her in the shade of a peach tree, and Natalie waved her hat, called her name.

"Um, Many Questions. You come back." Chiparopai's wrinkled cheeks highlighted a toothless smile.

"I have. You remember my brother George?"

Chiparopai nodded. "It is good to have family. Are you better now?"

Natalie remembered her first visit when the woman had recognized Natalie's sorrow.

"I am well. I can even answer your three questions. I sang with my Hopi friend Tawakwaptiwa last week. I danced the Butterfly Dance with my friend Mina at Third Mesa, and I have told my story to many who told me their stories back."

Chiparopai nodded. "Um, this is good."

"I've finished the book."

"This is good." She paused, cocked her head, which usually preceded her teasing. "You do not have a husband yet?"

Natalie laughed. "I do not. But never rule it out. It could still happen."

"Our mother would like both of us married off," George said. He squatted in the shade.

Marriage was on her mother's mind, but not hers. She now knew independent, capable single women—like Alice. And while Alice had a trust fund—and Natalie didn't—she could see an independent life that was acceptable to her mother's society friends: giving lectures on Indian music, American and Indian art; finishing work on Charlotte's African-American music project. She could stay in tune with music while living a full and adventurous life in the West. She already had an invitation to speak in France about her book, fine honoraria and expenses included. And she was bound to meet even more people as she undertook the African music collection. George Peabody and Charlotte had already offered to fund those efforts. "I am married to music and art."

Chiparopai squinted, her dark eyes filled with laughter. "Um, I think it will happen one day. I will sing a marriage song for you."

"I'd love that. If and when the time comes. But I'm too busy to worry about it." She had an article for the *Saturday Evening Post* due in a month.

"I sing it. Then the one you wait for will find you more easily. He will travel on the notes the mockingbird sings."

Natalie smiled. "I won't try to record it, but I will enjoy hearing you."

"You come tomorrow and bring your machine. I will sing it again for you." Chiparopai grinned. "It is a song you should remember."

And so the old woman accepted the book Natalie gave her and found where she was mentioned. "I will use it to put my feet on at night when the desert is cold." She smiled. "Books have many uses."

And when Natalie returned the next day, Chiparopai sang a marriage song for Natalie, who recorded it on her Edison. George had teased Natalie about lugging the machine with them, and this was the only time she'd used it on this book-giving trip. It was one last recording made in the shade of a peach tree while the Colorado River flowed by.

Natalie and George arrived back at the hotel, her heart filled with Chiparopai's song and Natalie's hope for her future. She tossed her hat on her bed. "Busoni liked what I sent him. He didn't commit to incorporating Indian music into a composition, but maybe. I had no marriage songs to share. I'll send this cylinder to him. Chiparopai's marriage song might be just the one to speak to him."

✺

It hadn't been on their itinerary, but George suggested they head to the Bar X Ranch before Natalie returned east and George made his way west to find the land that would be his new home.

"But I don't have any songs from there in the book," Natalie said.

"No, but you played the piano at the ranch for the first time in a long time. The Brigands might like a copy of the book that led you there."

"They might," Natalie agreed. "And I know you'd like to see Mary Jo again."

"And her husband. They're friends, Nat. Always will be."

After George proposed it, she found herself looking forward to seeing Mary Jo and hearing a cowboy song or two. Maybe they still had the horse she'd ridden. It could be a lovely time to ride with the cottonwood trees green against the red rock ridges. They telegrammed ahead and Mary Jo herself met them at the station.

"We can't stay long," George said.

"But it seemed a shame not to stop by and make a little noise," Natalie added.

"That we will," Mary Jo said.

Next to the Steinway stood a tall-back player piano with keyboard that utilized cylinders like the one Natalie had made of the lullaby and left for the Brigands. They listened to a few, and then Mary Jo took a seat on the bench, pulled out a piece of sheet music, and played a syncopated tune called "A Ragtime Nightmare." She was sweating when she finished to her audience's applause. "I started playing again after you stayed here," Mary Jo told Natalie. "Haltingly, as you could hear." She held up her crooked fingers.

"But you allowed yourself to try again. And my playing here made you want to try again?" Natalie asked.

"It surely did. I still can't bring myself to try Liszt's lullabies. I play the cylinders for that. But my fingers found their way on the keys, and I think the practice has helped my arthritis. Playing this fast-paced-not-for-dancing ragtime music is good treatment for my fingers and my heart. It takes me to a new place."

"The old with the new, making you stronger."

"Something like that," Mary Jo said.

They spent the next day on a long ride up into the hill-country cedars above the ranch house where they'd ridden for the roundup. Natalie's horse's ears perked forward when Natalie dismounted and talked to her.

"She remembers you," Mary Jo said.

"That's so grand."

Natalie heard music in the creak of saddle leather, creating an equine rhythm. That night, sitting on the wide veranda watching the moon rise, cattle comforting their calves, she heard a cowboy strum his guitar in the bunkhouse. Strains of music like a bouquet of flowers beautified her life. Indian music was a part of a wide circle of creativity she'd had the privilege to step into. Doing so, trusting without knowing where she was going, had helped her find herself. With what Mary Jo had said, sharing her journey helped others find their way as well.

Natalie and George had one more stop to make. They spoke their goodbyes to the Bar X and headed to the Acoma village where they'd deliver the book to the corn-grinding woman. She wouldn't go back to Oraibi this trip, having met Mina at the school. She'd miss not seeing her burro, but there'd be other trips, she knew. For now, Natalie hoped, she'd meet up with her Acoma potter at long last.

This time, they led a burro up the road instead of taking the stone footholds and handholds as they had the first time when they'd followed the blind boy. Natalie heard flute music as they approached the plaza and the massive church. Horsetail clouds washed the blue sky, reflected in the pool where a burro drank his fill. Natalie caught her breath. It was a good climb up in thin air. They had an interpreter with them, but Natalie remembered which two-story terraced home belonged to the corn-grinding woman, and she made her way there. She would give a book to her and she would leave one with the head man for all the Acoma to have. She'd brought an extra with the hope she'd find the potter.

After gifting the corn-grinding singer, Natalie knocked on the potter's door. This time, a small, round-faced girl, of marriage age, Natalie guessed, but still young, invited them in. The grandmother they'd met before leaned on a cane behind her. "I hear you seek me," the girl told Natalie. She spoke English.

It had been nearly two years since they'd been there, looking for the artist who made Natalie's seed pot. It pleased her that she was remembered. Memory was a part of all people's music, Indians and non, wrapped into all artists' works.

"Yes. I wanted to thank you for making such a beautiful piece of art." Natalie brought the seed pot out of its lambskin protector. She had carried it with her all these years.

The girl ran her fingers over the design painted on the pottery. "This is corn. I sing a prayer each time the corn meets the earth, that the earth will honor the seed and grow."

"That's lovely," Natalie said. "I love the story of this treasure you made. And did you use it to plant, before you took it to the trader's?"

The girl nodded. "I needed cloth for my grandmother and a flute for my grandfather."

"Art is often wrapped up in money," Natalie said. "The trader told my brother that the Acoma pots are made of old, fired clay that has been broken and discarded. Then elders found the shards, crushed them, and mixed the old powder with new clay. Is this so?"

The girl nodded. She gave Natalie back her seed pot, then lifted a basket and gestured that Natalie should take a handful of the broken shards nestled in there. "From these, with new clay, I make the pots. Beautiful and strong. That one"—she pointed with her chin to Natalie's pot—"I also give a throat through which the seed passes."

Natalie ran her fingers up the throat, so smooth, so vital to the planting. *The throat*, she thought, *the area of commitment. To speak, to eat, to talk, to sing, to breathe, and here, to plant. All goes through the throat, the channel of life.*

Hiamovi had told her once that when the peace pipe is shared, that the holder draws the smoke toward his throat to show that the discussions are seeped in trust, commitment to the decisions for which the peace pipe is being smoked. Natalie had taken a photograph of him smoking the pipe, his hands in the mist of commitment. He had permitted her to use it in the book.

She felt tears form in her eyes as she saw the rhythms of music, art, the human body, and creation all blending, the old making the new stronger.

The Indian music had made Natalie resilient again, not the fragile woman she'd been. *The Indians' Book* was her hymn to life, to return to living. There would be times ahead when she would question her toughness, but she would remember the combining of the fired clay and the new, and that together they offered both beauty and strength.

They stayed until sunset, listening to the Indians' songs, contented. The brother and sister spoke without talking. And as with George, Natalie knew at last; she had found herself.

Recessional

A light snow fell onto the February night but failed to dampen Natalie's spirit. This was the moment she'd dreamed of. Busoni, her former teacher, would play the piano and Leopold Stokowski would conduct Busoni's symphony for an orchestra he'd titled *Indian Fantasy*. She had attended a rehearsal and was enthralled. Now, this evening, everyone would hear a piece of music that combined American melodies with Native American songs. At the rehearsal, with the first strains of the violins, she'd been transported back to the vistas, the deserts and sunsets, the mountains and mesas. She rode in arroyos and through canyons; watched the yellow lines of sunrise spread across her day. And she heard all the Indian music that had healed her, though only the Marriage song and the Mockingbird song had been incorporated into the composition.

So much had happened in the years since *The Indians' Book* was published. Bogey, her father, had died following a long decline, during which Natalie had raced from Santa Fe to New York to care for him, a time she cherished. She had returned in some small way the love and kindness her father had given her. She'd worked on the African-American songbook, still in the collection phase.

She'd grown even closer to her mother during that time. Alice had joined them for art gallery openings and stayed to visit and, with George, helped convince Mimsey at last to take a trip west.

"You'll enjoy El Alisal and my three-room casita in Santa Fe," Natalie had promised.

"It's adorable," Mimsey agreed upon her first—and only—visit to Natalie's Santa Fe home.

"Made all the better with a few paintings of Alice's on the walls," Natalie said. "There is culture in the West, Mimsey."

George had found his farm east of San Diego and had met the woman he said he'd marry. Natalie had ventured into more art and museum activities, composing her own works—including "Cowboy Song" that had yet to be performed but she was certain would be. She wrote articles, gave lectures, and thought of herself as an Indian activist through efforts of the Sequoya League and an ethnomusicologist through association with museums and universities.

She brought all that history and future with her as she found her seat in the large auditorium, chattering with Alice, who had made the trek from San Diego to share this Philadelphia Philharmonic performance with her. Her siblings—minus George—attended, along with Mimsey and Charlotte. Natalie hoped Angel De Cora and her husband would attend as well. They'd gotten the publisher's permission to use artwork from the book on this evening's program. After all, none of this would have happened without the success of the book, and Angel's artwork had been a huge part of that.

In the years since its publication, Natalie had continued to badger Roosevelt, out of office but still influential, about the needs of Indian people. Just before he left, he had recommended the release of Lololomai's nephew and the Hopi—including Mina—from the Sherman school. It wasn't until 1910 that Tawakwaptiwa was allowed to take his people home. Four years he had remained at the Sherman Institute. She'd actually introduced the two—Roosevelt and Tawakwaptiwa—when she'd given the former president a tour of Oraibi. The president had come there for the Snake Dance in 1913. He was reeling from his defeat as he'd run for president as a third-party candidate and lost. She'd told him the Indian music could help him heal. They had conferred about an article the "Colonel"—as the former president was now known—was writing about Indian policy for *Outlook* magazine. She'd been so pleased that he understood much of her concerns about the schools, about preserving the history and art, about mitigating the bad effects of assimilation. Breaking the Code. Roosevelt had attended the Hopi Flute Ceremony along with her and Alice, a rare offering for two white women to witness. She and Roosevelt had gotten on good terms, and she'd even met his two sons, who had ridden horses across the desert with him. She wished he could have attended this debut, but he was likely off on some new adventure.

"I don't know where he is," Alice said. She stood up at her auditorium seat, looked at her wristwatch. "He said he'd be here."

"Who?" Natalie said.

"Paul Burlin, the artist."

Alice had convinced a young artist—eleven years Natalie's junior—to attend this performance. Natalie had seen his work at the Armory Show in New York, the youngest artist represented. The pieces had been inspired by Santa Fe, the colors and light, though they were modernist canvases. Natalie's mother had commented, "I don't understand it."

"Don't worry," Natalie told Alice. "If he makes it, he makes it. Does he have an interest in music? It's a long way to come for a concert."

"He's doing something in New York." Alice sat back down and whispered in Natalie's ear, "I have an ulterior motive. I introduced your brother to his future bride, and I thought I might just do the same for you."

"Oh, grand." Natalie rolled her eyes. "Just what I need. A complicated relationship. I'm perfectly content with the way things are. I'm too busy to fall in love."

"And that is the perfect time *to* fall in love, my friend. Oh, there he is! He walked right past us." Alice stood, called out, waved her program at the serious-looking young man. He nodded and headed back to the empty seat Alice had left for him next to Natalie. The auditorium was packed. "My good friend, Natalie Curtis, meet my good friend, artist Paul Burlin." He nodded his head toward her, wore a shy smile. But his eyes were like the desert—warm and brown and all-consuming.

The lights lowered and *Indian Fantasy* began.

With the swells of violins and the oboes, she gave herself to the music, the cadence a balm to losses and disappointments while granting hope for what the future held. She was so grateful.

Then a melody brought forth from Busoni's piano an Indian song, and Natalie was back in the Southwest, brushed by desert breezes, awash with sunrise over mesas. Her heart swelled. It caused her to turn and look at Paul Burlin, the artist next to her. He was staring back. He smiled and reached for the fingers of her hand. Her piano-playing fingers. She wore the Zuni ring still missing one turquoise stone. She felt her face grow warm, returned to the crescendo of the orchestra, and remembered the day she'd first heard echoes of that song now coming forth from Busoni's Steinway—the Yuma Marriage song. She could hear Chiparopai singing it on the hot Arizona desert. For some reason, she associated it with the healing questions the Yuma woman had asked her. *When was the last time you sang? When was the last time you danced? When was the last time you told your story?* She would have to tell Paul all about it.

Glossary

El Alisal—panish, "the place of the sycamores"; also, Pasadena home of Charles Lummis

Diné—Navajo word used for themselves, "The People"

Hozhonji—Navajo, "holy song"

Belagana—Navajo, "white man"

Old Oraibi—Hopi town in New Mexico; also another town named Oraibi, at foot of mesa

Moquis—Word Hopi people use to describe themselves, meaning "People of Peace"

Ko-la-ra-ne—Navajo, the opening and closing of a Navajo Hozhonji song

Quechan or **Cochan**—Yuman-speaking people on the reservation near Yuma, AZ

arowp—Yuman for "mockingbird"

Pahana—Hopi for an Anglo, American, or white person

Lololomai—Hopi, "good"; also, the name of a Hopi leader

Pas Lololomai—Hopi, "very good"

Hao, hao—Hopi, "even so, even so"

poco tiempo—Spanish, "pretty soon"; also, title of a book by Charles Lummis

Yavapai—Distinctive Southwest tribe often erroneously referred to as Mojave-Apache

Tawimana—Hopi name for Natalie, "Woman Who Sings Like a Mockingbird" or "Song Maid"

baĥos—Hopi, prayer sticks with feathered ends

Dsichl Biyin—A Hopi song near end of life

Author's Note

I discovered Natalie's story in the book *Ladies of the Canyons: A League of Extraordinary Women and Their Adventures in the American Southwest* by Lesley Poling-Kempes. It won the WILLA Literary Award for Creative Nonfiction in 2011, and I was fortunate enough to read it and hear a presentation by Ms. Poling-Kempes at Ghost Ranch, New Mexico, in landscapes Natalie would have known. Whatever mistakes one finds in my version of Natalie's journey are my responsibility. But if you are encouraged by this remarkable woman, much credit goes to Ms. Poling-Kempes. While her book begins with Natalie, it is woven through with the lives of three other women: Alice Klauber, Carol Bishop Stanley, and Mary Cabot Wheelwright. My novel had to make concessions of how much of Natalie's story and the intersection of the lives of others I could weave—without it becoming a 575-page novel. I made the decision to tell the story of Natalie's musical healing beginning in 1902 when her brother George invites her west, and ending the narrative shortly after the publication of *The Indians' Book* in 1907. The Recessional brings a tad more to the story. I highly recommend reading Ms. Poling-Kempes's lyrical book to learn more about Natalie's life.

I used the word "Indian" to describe Indigenous people because Natalie titled her book with that name. Other terms at the time were "aboriginals" and less often, "Native Americans." And a series of derogatory terms I chose not to use at all. For clarity, I stayed close to the Indigenous tribal names that Natalie used at the time, e.g., Yuma rather than Quechan.

A few words about cultural issues seems important in 2021. Natalie was ahead of her time in many ways as she understood both intellectual property rights—owned by the holder of the music or the story—and the importance of respecting the informants of *The Indians' Book*. She truly believed her book was "written" by the Indians with Natalie as merely "a pencil in their hands." One can argue how successful she was, but she made every attempt to honor individual Indian stories and contributions. Her purpose, I believe, was to crack the Code of Offenses, preserve Indian music and art both for Indian people and non-Indians, and educate Americans about the value of Indian people to form a truly American culture. That she allowed Indian music to heal her was a surprising gift of grace.

Today, many tourists retell or reprint stories told them by Indian people without attribution to the individual or without permission, which can be described as intellectual theft. At the time of Natalie's publication, there is not only evidence that she paid singers and drummers and poets for their contributions, but in the final book, each song or poem or story of a legend or description of a dance is attributed to that teller by name. The illustrations are attributed by name. Natalie's own introduction describes herself as editor rather than the book's author. The book jacket reads: "Recorded and edited by Natalie Curtis." And Hiamovi, a Cheyenne-Dakota high chief, did write the introduction, offering an endorsement, as did then-president Theodore Roosevelt.

In my novelizing Natalie's story, I drew on my own experiences with music. I played the piano from the age of five until twelve when I took up the flute. My older sister and I often sang together at church and for events. When I was a child, music was, as Maya Angelou once wrote, "My refuge. I climbed inside the space between the notes and curled my back to loneliness." Music is still a healing presence in my life. I also drew on my seventeen years working for the Confederated Tribes of Warm Springs in Oregon and visits to pueblos in the company of Indian friends; and as a tourist. I tried to inform myself by reading archival material, books written close to the time of Natalie's work, to see how Indian people were portrayed, as well as contemporary works. I hope I was sensitive to issues of racism, intellectual property, and injustice that existed then, behaviors and attitudes that weren't seen as demeaning then by most Americans. Within the novel, I too have used the names of the singers and poets when referencing a song, dance, or poem. Mentions of legends or practices of different tribes include the informant who told Natalie the story, and I have respectfully not described in detail a Snake Dance or Ghost Dance, but only commented on how Natalie might have felt seeing or participating in ceremonies. Fiction is the realm of feelings, and I drew on my own from the times when I was included in evening medicine sings for healing, wedding celebrations, and dressing ceremonies honoring the deceased.

The seven "interludes" are written in the voice of Indian people, some fictionalized and some drawn from what Natalie recorded about individual lives in her articles or *The Indians' Book*. (For example, thoughts from Mina fully fictionalized as opposed to Natalie's interviews with Tawakwaptiwa, the Hopi leader stripped of his chief status in 1906 and removed to the Sherman Institute in California.) In my years of work on the reservation, I had the privilege of meeting people who were willing to be what I called "cultural brokers." They allowed me to learn, ask questions, be forgiven for faux pas, and be transformed in my own life by the lessons learned. My Lummi Nation friend, Jewell Minnick, who lives on the Warm Springs reservation, has acted as my cultural broker in reviewing this manuscript and I am grateful to her and blessed by our long years of friendship.

An American Indian might well tell Natalie's story—and I hope they do. But stories find their tellers, I believe, and this is a novel about a white woman being transformed by Indian music. I have tried to be faithful to the experiences of people in cultures other than my own while expressing this story of another white woman who worked among the Indians. You, dear readers, will judge how well I did that.

Natalie was born to Augusta (Mimsey) and Edward (Bogey) Curtis, the third surviving child of six in 1876. Bogey did attend to President Lincoln following his assassination and was one of two physicians asked to perform the autopsy. Mimsey was active in various social causes as portrayed and expressed concern about Natalie's choice to spend her life in the West. She was also of the era that believed when a single daughter went away for a "short visit," she was expected to come home when her mother called and be the dutiful daughter until she married.

Natalie studied music in New York and Germany, devoted her life to her gift. She did have the breakdown in 1897 that severed her lifelong connection to performing. She composed a little during those five years until George convinced her to come west, but she did not perform.

Natalie may have learned about the Code of Offenses through the Masons' advocacy and the involvement of her parents and other family members in justice issues. The Code spoke less about crimes and more about the elimination of a culture, outlawing practices such as gift-giving at a time of a marriage, practices of medicine men, ways that people provided for their families already affected by forced movement of tribes onto reservations. Retired law professor Robert N. Clinton refers to the Code as "federal ethnocide" rather than any codifying of what one usually considers a criminal offense. (For more of Clinton's assessment of the Code, see http://robert-clinton.com/?page_id=289.)

While Natalie's permission from President Roosevelt issued July 22, 1903, to visit any schools or reservations, record songs and dances, and report to him directly, was real, the enforcement of the Code wasn't muted until 1920–1921 and not amended until the administration of Franklin Roosevelt and his appointment of John Collier as Commissioner of Indian Affairs in 1933. A contemporary version can be found in 25 C.F.R. Part 11 that does include actual criminal offenses and how they are to be handled. It is also true that the Santa Fe railroad offered special rates for people wanting to view the dances—acts prohibited by the Code.

Roosevelt's promotion of Natalie's activities and *The Indians' Book* reportedly did reduce Code enforcement, and further, it allowed many Indian people to sing and dance again. The meetings she had with Roosevelt are documented. He did invite congressmen to a luncheon to hear Natalie speak about the consequences of the Code and she did sing for the senators. He also did bring up the "Indian question" in his address to Congress the January after he told Natalie he might. While the policy of assimilation was amended, it was followed by other government programs that threatened—and still do—to diminish the lives of Indian culture and practices, including land decisions, resettlement efforts, law enforcement issues, including the search for missing Indigenous women, etc. Ongoing struggles over health care, education, boundaries, voting, and other rights in peril, can be seen as remnants of the Code and the devastating racist Indian policies it engendered. The appointment in 2021 of Laguna Pueblo member Deb Haaland as the first Native American Secretary of the Interior for the United States promises a louder voice for Indigenous people. I believe Natalie would be pleased.

Natalie's brother George was an asthmatic and former New York City librarian who found healing and freedom in the Southwest. He was critical to Natalie's physical and emotional healing. Whether he first left New York in the middle of Natalie's malaise because he felt powerless or due to a lost love in addition to his asthma is unknown. It's also unknown whether he was concerned about her repeating her breakdown due to finishing *The Indians' Book*, but his concern for her seemed plausible. George worked on a ranch in Houck, Arizona, but the Bar X is fictional as are the Brigands. George did marry when he was in his late forties. He built his ranch east of San Diego, where he also dabbled in beekeeping. He finished and published his novel in 1927, *The Wooing of a Recluse*, under the name Gregory Marwood. The book included, among other beautifully written words, the line Natalie quoted about meeting his *amor* "at the train station with a pony and a packhorse."

Natalie wrote of her encounter with the Navajo on New Year's Day, 1903, in an article for the *Saturday Evening Post* titled "Navajo Indians at Pasadena." She did sing Wagner to them and writes of how different her *Valkyries* was from the Navajo gift of music that evening. Eccentric journalist Charles Lummis's El Alisal compound in Pasadena is a historical site that can be visited (https://www.laparks.org/historic/lummis-home-and-gardens). In addition to editing the *Los Angeles Times* and writing poems on birch bark, he spent time with Isleta Pueblo people and recorded some of their music; walked across the continent; had guests like John Muir, Will Rogers, and others stay at his compound; sponsored "noises"; wrote *The Land of Poco Tiempo* that Natalie read (I did too); edited *Out West* magazine; and was an Indian activist and historic preservationist. Lummis was also instrumental in the formation of the Arts and Crafts design movement, was a Harvard classmate of Theodore Roosevelt, and did work with Frank Mead on a variety of cultural and Indian rights issues.

Whether Natalie met Alice Klauber at El Alisal is unknown, but Alice was an artist and her involvement in Natalie's later life is greater than shown in my novel. (See Ms. Poling-Kempes's work for more.)

Natalie also wrote about her compulsion to cross the Colorado River upon hearing a mesmerizing song in Yuma, AZ, that began her journey in Indian music. We don't know for sure why she and George were in Yuma, but I've given them a motive. The Territorial Prison did have a massive library and the other amenities as described. Chiparopai (sometimes written Hiparopai), the Yuma woman, did speak three languages and it was a gift that she should be one of the first Indians Natalie encountered. I don't know if Chiparopai asked the three healing questions, but they are real. Also based on fact are Natalie's encounters in Yuma with Texan; meeting Frank Mead, arranging the meeting with Mead and Pelia, and later recommending Mead to Roosevelt and Lummis; Charlotte Mason and George Peabody as sponsors; Natalie's singing at Rufus Mason's funeral; and Natalie's writing and lecturing. The scenes with many of these real-life people are fictionalized but are based on historical descriptions and documentary evidence—with the exception of the romantic inclination I created with Frank Mead.

The progression of Natalie and George's journey: Lummis did ask them to "spy" at Oraibi and had reports by teachers and the Gates couple who witnessed the severity of treatment there. Natalie did likely violate the Code in recording by pencil and paper and the Edison machine. The conditions at the Keams Canyon and Oraibi schools and Agent Burton's involvement in these and other problems, I gleaned from government reports and a book chronicling men hoping to change the federal government policies (see Hagan). Natalie spent time on George's ranch known to be near Houck, AZ, but Mary Jo and Natalie's playing the Steinway for her are strictly fictional, though many large ranches at the time did furnish their homes with eastern treasures. George and Natalie did travel to St. Louis for the Louisiana Purchase Exposition (also called the World's Fair) and Natalie pressed her ideas about the photographic displays there. The siblings also visited the Winnebago Agencies; the Hampton, Sherman, and Carlisle Indian schools; and with Hiamovi's introductions, the Dakota sites to record and interview songs from eighteen tribes, a remarkable feat given Natalie's earlier physical and emotional limitations.

Natalie and George traveled to outlying hogans and tepees, slept out, and went for days cooking over a campfire or being guests of Indian people. They often drove a wagon. The incident on the trail with the circus participants was inspired by a story told in *No Life for a Lady* by Agnes Morley Cleaveland. Natalie flourished in these conditions and wrote often of her desire to return whenever she had to leave the Southwest. Natalie met up with artist Angel De Cora, whose story of her abduction to the Hampton School is based on fact. She was a celebrated artist. Nampeyo is the well-regarded Hano Hopi potter who innovatively designed pottery from the archaeological ruins by adding her own inventiveness, and Natalie is said to have met with her. The Acoma story of strength and beauty that drove this story in many ways continues to be told to tourists at Sky City, one of four Acoma villages where I first heard it.

Natalie's meeting with Walter Damrosch to give him a book is fictionalized, but her description of him as "Adonis" is documented and her relationship—schoolgirl though it was—carries informed speculation that he played a role in her breakdown. Ferruccio Busoni did request recordings that were included in his composition *Indian Fantasy*, performed in 1915 in Philadelphia. He performed the piano solo at the debut that Natalie attended.

When her father became ill, Natalie returned to New York from her casita in Santa Fe for a few years to care for him. The census records of 1910 say she was in New York with an occupation as a "lecturer." All her siblings except George were still at home in 1915, three years after Bogey's death; but Natalie's family's love and a debt she may have felt to her family for the years of support for her might have added to her reasons for leaving Santa Fe for so long. She considered the New Mexico city her home.

Natalie went on to write numerous articles while in New York and collected African-American songs, published in *Negro Folk Songs*. In 1920, the Musical Art Society of New York featured her "Three Songs of North America," which included "Cowboy Song," bringing back her time with cowpunchers on the Arizona ranch she traveled to with George. Of the cowboy life she wrote, "It was a grim, monotonous existence, but somehow it was especially big," words included in the program of the performance.

Natalie met modernist painter, Paul Burlin, in 1915. My novel ends there, but their story goes on. They married in 1917 in Santa Fe, New Mexico, on July 25. Natalie was 41. She wrote that it was a marriage "based on sound friendship, mutual aims, and absolute intellectual and spiritual rapport." Paul was eleven years younger than Natalie which may have been why there was no large wedding in New York. (For more about their life together, refer to the Poling-Kempes book, as well as the Michelle Wick Patterson book, *Natalie Curtis Burlin: A Life in Native and African American Music*, which includes a bibliography of all of Natalie's publications.)

Early in my writing career, I received a letter from the "First Violin Section/Viola Section, and Various Members of the Los Angeles Philharmonic Orchestra." They thanked me for writing my first novel, *A Sweetness to the Soul*, a story based on another white woman who lived a life close to Indian people. Stacy and Mick Wetzel, both members of the orchestra, wrote of what they called prose that was "elegant, poetic, lyrical (all things so appealing to us musicians!)." They went on with kind words and encouraged me to keep writing. I framed their words (it's on the Philharmonic letterhead, how could I not!) and read it now and then to remind myself how music and story mirror each other and how important both are to our lives. I think Natalie understood this.

Natalie had only a few short years of shared bliss with her husband, Paul. On October 23, 1921, after having given a speech on Indian arts and music at the Sorbonne in France, she stepped off a bus on a rainy night in Paris and was struck by a car driven by a doctor hurrying to an emergency. He had not seen the small person in the dark night. She did not regain consciousness. Natalie is buried in the North Burial Ground in Providence, Rhode Island. On All Saint's Day, October 30, 1921, a funeral was held in Paris. She was eulogized around the world. A scholarship was created at the Hampton Indian School in her name among other accolades. But she might have appreciated most of all a Hopi man's words after he heard of her death, as told to Alice Klauber: "But she cannot die. She is singing now—somewhere with her Hopi friends." That's how I will think of her as well and I hope you might too.

Acknowledgments

Where to begin? First, I must acknowledge the work of Lesley Poling-Kempes and her book *Ladies of the Canyons: A League of Extraordinary Women and Their Adventures in the American Southwest*. Beautifully written, with the landscape and relationships deftly conveyed, this book first introduced me to Natalie. I found a copy of *The Indians' Book*. My version was an edition published in 1987 by Bonanza Books. The title is *The Indians' Book* instead of the original *An Indians' Book*. I didn't know in 2011 if I would write a novel based on Natalie's life, but finding Natalie's book later might well have proved impossible, or I'd have been priced out of the market. I kept it for the ten years it would take me to listen to the calling of this story.

A second source I'm grateful for is *Natalie Curtis Burlin: A Life in Native and African American Music* by Michelle Wick Patterson. Well-marked by me with the astonishing details of Natalie's life and work, including quotes from Natalie's published articles, her diary, her workbook notes and letters. She writes of Natalie's early life in music and her journey to become a renowned ethnomusicologist, Indian activist and lecturer, singer, and classic pianist.

My most valuable source was *The Indians' Book* itself, which did include the names of the Indian informants, whose songs, dances, and stories Natalie gave full attribution to, and whose 575 pages suggested to me that Natalie had a very difficult time leaving anything out. Oh, how I can sympathize. A number of other books proved valuable and I've included a bibliography of them at the end.

And now to my helpers, as Mister Rogers advised us to find in a time of trial. CarolAnne Tsai, my ever-faithful researcher, sent me to websites to read Natalie's other published works. She also provided encouraging words when a planned trip to Oraibi and surroundings had to be cancelled due to COVID-19. I'm so grateful to her and for her prayers. Chaparral Books in Portland, Oregon, located *Daughters of the Desert: Women Anthropologists and the Native American Southwest, 1880–1980: An Illustrated Catalogue* by Barbara A. Babcock and Nancy J. Parezo. In it, I found quotes, photographs, and snapshots of Natalie and forty-four other remarkable women who were Natalie's contemporaries, forging new paths for themselves in the Southwest. Their stories granted me insights into the possible thought processes and motivations of a classically trained pianist and singer finding herself adrift.

I especially thank endorsers Lesley Poling-Kempes, Susan J. Tweit, and Lori Benton, all remarkable writers and lovers of the Southwest. Gratitude to Susan for her poetic works about the desert, loss, and healing, and our conversations over our spouses' journeys through cancer. She will be forever treasured, as is our friendship. Her photographs of the desert bring me to Instagram more than any other posts. Author, teacher, and historian Lesley Poling-Kempes, who spent many hours researching and writing Natalie's story in her book, agreed to read for possible endorsement, and I am humbled that she found my version of Natalie's story a worthy way to keep alive the remarkable life of Natalie Curtis. I have long admired Lori Benton's work, both photographic and fiction—especially her rendering of stories featuring the interactions of Indigenous people and non-Indian. I thank them all.

Thanks to Revell and the team that not only holds me together but adapts and promotes even during a pandemic. Special shout-outs to editors Andrea Doering and Barb Barnes, copyeditor Carrie Krause, marketing guru Michele Misiak, and publicist Karen Steele. A phenomenal team. Equally as significant is my agent of now thirty years, Joyce Hart of Hartline Literary. Her patience, reassurance, and enthusiasm for my work especially during the dark days when I'm sure no one will want to read what I've written, cannot be equaled. I am grateful.

Other contributors of importance is first reader and copyeditor Janet Marenda; Women Writing the West members Heidi Thomas and Nancy Fine, who answered questions from their own experiences living in the Southwest. I thank my friend Marilyn Davis, who was an early reader and who sent me a Raymond Redfeather handcrafted flute, along with many encouraging words. I am also indebted to the Pacific Northwest Booksellers, who have hand-sold my work, encouraged my writing through the years, and who do the significant work of making stories available to readers.

Much gratitude to friends and former colleagues from the Confederated Tribes of Warm Springs—Lorissa Quinn Morales, Jewell Minnick, Julie Quaid, Sue Matters, Shilo Tippett, Carolyn Strong, and others affiliated with the reservation—who have encouraged my work through the years. Thanks to my prayer team of Judy Card, Carol Tedder, Loris Webb, Gabby Sprenger, and Susan Parrish, as well as prayer warriors Mike and Marea Stone, John and Janet Meranda, Jerry and Georgia Brackett, and Dick and Millie Voll, the latter two being our desert pals who brought us to the California desert for our six months a year. Thanks as well to our family at Bend First Presbyterian for prayers and connection. To my friend Kay Krall, for calls and support as our spouses dealt with advanced cancer issues; Sandy Maynard, who is there whenever I might need to talk day or night; cousins Mike and Linda Rutschow; my Bend walking partner Sarah Douglas and neighbor Jess Galbreath; thank you. And to my brother and his wife, Craig and Barb Rutschow, for their support and for, among other things, sending me videos of happy fainting-goats from their Minnesota farm. To my children, Matt and Melissa Kirkpatrick and Kathleen and Joe Larsen; and to my grandchildren, Mariah, Madison, Adam, Josh, and Neil; and to friends and extended family too numerous to mention—thank you all for your encouragement.

And to Jerry, my husband of forty-five years, who said he wanted to go south for the winters and who the week before we left to do that (and for me to start writing this book in 2019) was diagnosed with stage IV melanoma. Thank you for leaving your native Oregon and trying something new (including immunotherapy) at the age of ninety. As of this writing, his cancer is in full remission and we thank many for countless prayers. As Jerry was not able to do his precious maps for me, I invite you, dear readers, to visit the internet or atlas to find Houck, Arizona, and Third Mesa and Yuma where, for Natalie, it all began.

Finally, the three questions were told to me by an Indian healer. I share them often at presentations to remind people of the importance of singing, dancing, and telling our stories. It's a reminder for me to do the same. In addition to my books, my storytelling part is often met through Story Sparks, my monthly newsletter available by signing up at https://www.jkbooks.com, where you'll find more of my story and hopefully words of encouragement.

And last but not least, thank you, dear readers, for making room in your life for my stories—including this one about the healing of Natalie Curtis.

Warmly,
Jane Kirkpatrick

Book Group Questions

The author is grateful for the many book clubs who have chosen her books to read. She is available virtually, by phone and in person—when feasible. Please contact her at her website https://www.jkbooks.com for arrangements. Meanwhile, enjoy these possible discussion questions. Jane thanks you for making room in your lives for her stories.

1. How would you answer Chiparopai's three questions regarding the last time you sang, danced, or told your story? Why are these actions important to all lives including Indigenous people?

2. What role does music play in your life? Are the memories that certain songs or compositions evoke healing for you or do they bring you sadness? Is grief a first part of all healing?

3. Did the author meet her goal of showing how Natalie's obsession with music brought her down and that a renewed passion for Indian music helped heal her?

4. Natalie identified areas of healing in her life: purposefulness, the arts, relationships, forgiveness, learning new things, acceptance, making personal changes, seeing new

possibilities. Are you familiar with any of these? Are there other elements you've experienced in your life that have proven to be healing?

5. Was the relationship between Natalie's informants—Lololomai, Mina, and Chiparopai, among others—authentic? Was there a reciprocity or was Natalie "using" them for her purpose of preserving their work and making a career for herself?

6. What do you think about Chiparopai's words about Natalie's work, that "the songs might well be lost if not written down. But perhaps she should wait until a Yuma child could write them"?

7. Why was George worried about Natalie repeating her physical and emotional collapse while she worked on *The Indians' Book*?

8. Before the Roosevelt letter giving permission to Natalie to record the songs, she broke the law. What do you think about that? Was she justified? Were you surprised that one person could influence the president of the United States as Natalie did? Did the Roosevelt letter help bend the Code if not break it?

9. How would you describe Natalie and George's relationship? Do you have either a biological or nonbiological sibling or cousin or friend of the opposite gender that you would be willing to travel with for four years in less than accommodating circumstances? What qualities of character allowed them to successfully develop a flourishing sibling relationship?

10. Poet William Stafford wrote, "I have woven a parachute out of everything broken." How did Natalie weave her parachute from her time of brokenness? Can you identify a time in your life when you felt broken? What material did you use to weave your parachute?

11. Did Natalie Curtis help the cause of reducing the suffering of Indian people or did she appropriate the Indians'
stories by publishing *The Indians' Book* and then lecturing
about her work with them for years after? What contributed to your responses?

12. Do you wish the author had included more detail about
the individual dances or ceremonies? Why do you think
she didn't?

Suggested Additional Reading

Babcock, Barbara A. and Nancy J. Parezo. *Daughters of the Desert: Women Anthropologists and the Native American Southwest 1880–1980. An Illustrated Catalogue.* Albuquerque: University of New Mexico Press, 1988.

Cleaveland, Agnes Morley. *No Life for a Lady.* Lincoln: University of Nebraska Press, 1969.

Clinton, Robert N. Office of. *Code of Offenses.* http://robert-clinton.com/?page_id=289. 2020.

Curtis, Natalie. *The Indians' Book: Authentic Native American Legends, Lore and Music.* New York: Bonanza Books, 1987.

Gillmor, Frances and Louisa Wade Wetherill. *Traders to the Navajos: The Story of the Wetherills of Kayenta.* Albuquerque: University of New Mexico Press, 1953.

Gillmor, Frances. *Windsinger.* Albuquerque: University of New Mexico Press, 1958.

Hagan, William T. *Theodore Roosevelt and Six Friends of the Indian.* Norman, OK: University of Oklahoma Press, 1997.

James, Harry C. *Pages from Hopi History.* Tucson: University of Arizona Press, 1974.

Lummis, Charles F. *The Land of Poco Tiempo*. Charles Scribner's Sons, 1893, Albuquerque: University of New Mexico Press, 1952.

Niethammer, Carolyn. *Cooking the Wild Southwest: Delicious Recipes for Desert Plants*. Albuquerque: University of Arizona Press, 2011.

Patterson, Michelle Wick. *Natalie Curtis Burlin: A Life in Native and African American Music*. Lincoln: University of Nebraska Press, 2010.

———. "Singing Wagner to Navajos: Natalie Curtis's Journey from Classical Music to Native and African American Folk Songs." *The Journal of the Gilded Age and Progressive Era*, 13:1 (Jan. 2014), 93–108.

Poling-Kempes, Lesley. *Ladies of the Canyon: A League of Extraordinary Women and Their Adventures in the American Southwest*. Tucson: University of Arizona Press, 2015. See also her body of books, including fiction.

Roediger, Virginia More. *Ceremonial Costumes of the Pueblo Indians: Their Evolution, Fabrication, and Significance in the Prayer Drama*. University of California Press, 1941.

Stewart, Irene. *A Voice in Her Tribe: A Navajo Woman's Own Story*. Foreword by Mary Shepardson. Edited by Doris Ostrander Dawdy. Ballena Press, 1980.

Teller, I.M., Secretary to Hon. Hiram Price, Commissioner of Indian Affairs. "Rules Governing the Court of Indian Offenses." Letter to Department of the Interior, Office of Indian Affairs, Washington, March 30, 1883.

Tweit, Susan J. *Barren, Wild, and Worthless: Living in the Chihuahuan Desert*. Albuquerque: University of New Mexico Press, 1995.

———. *Seasons in the Desert: A Naturalist's Notebook*. San Francisco: Chronicle Books, 1998.

Weston, Julie Whitesell, text. Gerry Morrison, photography. *The Magical Universe of the Ancients: A Desert Journal*. Big Wood Books, LLC, 2020.

Zwinger, Ann Haymond. *The Mysterious Lands: A Naturalist Explores the Four Great Deserts of the Southwest*. Dutton. 1989.

Turn the Page for Chapter 1
of Another Powerful Story by
Jane Kirkpatrick

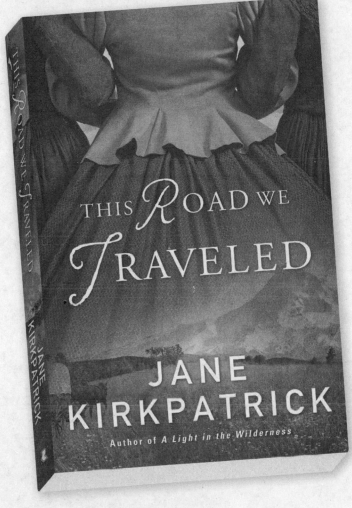

AVAILABLE NOW

Prologue

It was a land of timber, challenge, and trepidation, forcing struggles beyond any she had known, and she'd known many in her sixty-six years. But Tabitha Moffat Brown decided at that moment with wind and snow as companions in this dread that she would not let the last entry in her memoir read *"Cold. Starving. Separated."* Instead she inhaled, patted her horse's neck. The snow was as cold as a Vermont lake and threatening to cover them nearly as deep while she decided. She'd come this far, lived this long, surely this wasn't the end God intended.

Get John back up on his horse. If she couldn't, they'd both perish.

"John!"

The elderly man in his threadbare coat and faded vest sank to his knees. At least he hadn't wandered off when he'd slid from his horse. His white hair lay wet and coiled at his neck beneath a rain-drenched hat. His shoulder bones stuck out like a scarecrow's, sticks from lack of food and lost hope.

"You can't stop, John. Not now. Not yet." Wind whistled through the pines and her teeth chattered. "Captain!" She needed to sound harsh, but she nearly cried, his name stuck in the back of her throat.

This good man, who these many months on the trail had become more than a brother-in-law, he had to live. He couldn't die, not here, not now. "Captain! Get up. Save your ship."

He looked up at her, eyes filled with recognition and resignation. "Go, Tabby. Save yourself."

"Where would I go without you, John Brown? Fiddlesticks. You're the captain. You can't go down with your ship. I won't allow it."

"Ship?" His eyes took on a glaze. "But the barn is so warm. Can't you smell the hay?"

Barn? Hay? Trees as high as heaven marked her view, shrubs thick and slowing as a nightmare clogged their path, and all she smelled was wet forest duff, starving horseflesh, and for the first time in her life that she could remember, fear.

Getting upset with him wouldn't help. She wished she had her walking stick to poke at him. Her hands ached from cold despite her leather gloves. She could still feel the reins. That was good. What a pair they were: he, old and bent and hallucinating; she, old and lame and bordering on defeat. Her steadfast question, *what do I control here*, came upon her like an unspoken prayer. *Love and do good.* She must get him warm or he'd die.

With her skinny knees, she pushed her horse closer to where John slouched, all hope gone from him. Snow collected on his shoulders like moth-eaten epaulets. "John. Listen to me. Grab your cane. Pull yourself up. We'll make camp. Over there, by that tree fall." She pointed. "Come on now. Do it for the children. Do it for me."

"Where are the children?" He stared up at her. "They're here?"

She would have to slide off her horse and lead him to shelter herself. And if she failed, if her feet gave out, if she couldn't bring him back from this tragic place with warmth and water and, yes, love, they'd both die and earn their wings in Oregon country. It was not what Tabitha Moffat Brown had in mind. And what she planned for, she could make happen. She always had . . . until now.

Part One

1

Tabby's Plan

1845
ST. CHARLES, MISSOURI

Tabitha Moffat Brown read the words aloud to Sarelia Lucia to see if she'd captured the rhythm and flow. "Feet or wings: well, feet, of course. As a practical matter we're born with limbs, so they have a decided advantage over the wistfulness of wings. Oh, we'll get our wings one day, but not on this earth, though I've met a few people who I often wondered about their spirit's ability to rise higher than the rest of us in their goodness, your grandfather being one of those, dear Sarelia. Feet hold us up, help us see the world from a vantage point that keeps us from becoming self-centered—one of my many challenges, that self-centered portion. I guess the holding up too. I've had to use a cane or walking stick since I was a girl."

"How did that happen, Gramo?" The nine-year-old child with the distinctive square jaw put the question to her.

"I'll tell you about the occasion that brought that cane into my life and of the biggest challenges of my days . . . but not in this section. I know that walking stick is a part of my feet, it seems, evidence that I was not born with wings." She winked at her granddaughter.

"When will you get to the good parts, where you tell of the greatest challenge of your life, Gramo? That's what I want to hear."

"I think this is a good start, don't you?"

"Well . . ."

"Just you wait."

Tabitha dipped her goose quill pen into the ink, then pierced the air with her weapon while she considered what to write next.

"Write the trouble stories down, Gramo. So I have them to read when I'm growed up."

"When you're *grown* up."

"Yes, then. And I'll write my stories for you." A smile that lifted to her dark eyes followed. "I want to know when trouble found you and how you got out of it. That'll help me when I get into trouble."

"Will it? You won't get into scrapes, will you?" Tabby grinned. "We'll both sit and write for a bit." The child agreed and followed her grandmother's directions for paper and quill.

The writing down of things, the goings-on of affairs in this year of 1845, kept Tabby's mind occupied while she waited for the second half of her life to begin. Tabby's boys deplored studious exploits, which had always bothered her, so she wanted to nurture this grandchild—and all children's interest in writing, reading, and arithmetic. So far, the remembering of days gone by had served another function: a way of organizing what her life was really about. She was of an age for such reflection, or so she'd been told.

Whenever her son Orus Brown returned from Oregon to their conclave in Missouri, she expected real ruminations about them all going west—or not. Perhaps in her pondering she'd discover whether she should go or stay, and more, why she was here on this earth at all, traveling roads from Connecticut southwest to Missouri and maybe all the way to the Pacific. Wasn't wondering what purpose one had walking those roads of living a worthy pursuit? And there it was again: *walking those roads.* For her it always was a question of feet or wings.

Sarelia had gone home long ago, but Tabby had kept writing. Daylight soon washed out the lamplight in her St. Charles, Missouri, home, and she paused to stare across the landscape of scrub oak and butternut. Once they'd lived in the country, but now the former capital of Missouri spread out along the river, and Tabby's home edged both city and country. A fox trip-tripped across the yard. Still, Tabby scratched away, stopping only when she needed to add water to the powder to make more ink. She'd have to replace the pen soon, too, but she had a good supply of those. Orus, her firstborn, saw to that, making her several dozen before he left for Oregon almost two years ago now. He was a good son. She prayed for his welfare and wondered anew at Lavina's stamina managing all their children while they waited. Well, so was Manthano a good son, though he'd let himself be whisked away by that woman he fell in love with and rarely came to visit. Still, he was a week's ride away. Children. She shook her head in wistfulness. Pherne, on the other hand, lived just down a path. And it was Pherne, her one and only daughter, who also urged her to write her autobiography. "Your personal story, Mama. How you and Papa met, where you lived, even the wisdom you garnered."

Wisdom. She relied on memory to tell her story and memory proved a fickle thing. She supposed her daughter wanted her to write so she wouldn't get into her daughter's business. That happened with older folks sometimes when they lacked passions of their own. She wanted her daughter to know how much being with her and the children filled her days. Maybe not to let her know that despite her daughter's stalwart efforts, she was lonely at times, muttering around in her cabin by herself, talking to Beatrice, her pet chicken, who followed her like a shadow. She was committed to not being a burden on her children. Oh, she helped a bit by teaching her grandchildren, but one couldn't teach children all day long. Of course lessons commenced daily long, but the actual sitting on chairs, pens and ink in hand, minds and books open, that was education at its finest but couldn't fill the day. The structure, the weaving of teacher and student so both discovered new things, *that* was the passion of her life, wasn't it?

Still, she was intrigued by the idea of recalling and writing down ordinary events that had helped define her. Could memory bring back the scent of Dear Clark's hair tonic or the feel of the tweed vest he wore, or the sight of his blue eyes that sparkled when he teased and preached? She'd last seen those eyes in life twenty-eight years ago. She had thought she couldn't go on a day without him, but she'd done it nearly thirty years. What had first attracted her to the man? And how did she end up from a life in Stonington, Connecticut, begun in 1780, to a widow in Maryland, looking after her children and her own mother, and then on to Missouri in 1824 and still there in winter 1845? Was this where she'd die?

"'A life that is worth writing at all, is worth writing minutely and truthfully.' Longfellow." She penned it in her memoir. This was a truth, but perhaps a little embellishment now and then wouldn't hurt either. A story should be interesting after all.

■ ■ ■

His beard reached lower than his throat. Orus, Tabby's oldest son, came to her cabin first. At least she assumed he had, as none of his children nor Pherne's had rushed through the trees to tell her that he'd already been to Lavina's or Virgil and Pherne's place. It was midmorning, and her bleeding hearts drooped in the August heat.

"I'm alive, Mother." He removed his hat, and for a moment Tabby saw her deceased husband's face pressed onto this younger version, the same height, nearly six feet tall, and the same dark hair, tender eyes.

"So you are, praise God." She searched his brown eyes for the sparkle she remembered, reached to touch his cheek, saw above his scruffy beard a red-raised scar. "And the worse for wear, I'd say."

"I'll tell of all that later. I'm glad to see you among the living as well."

"Come in. Don't stand there shy."

He laughed and entered, bending through her door. "Shyness is not something usually attached to my name."

"And how did you find Oregon? Let me fix you tea. Have you had breakfast?"

"No time. And remarkable. Lush and verdant. The kind of place to lure a man's soul and keep him bound forever. No to breakfast. I've much to do."

"So we'll be heading west then?"

For an instant his bright eyes flickered and he looked beyond her before he said, "Yes. I expect so." He kissed her on her hair doily then, patted her back, and said he'd help her harness the buggy so she could join him at Lavina's. "I'm anxious to spend time with my wife and children. Gather with us today."

"I can do the harnessing myself. No tea?"

"Had some already. Just wanted the invite to come from me."

"An invite?"

He nodded, put his floppy hat back on. "At our place. I've stories to tell."

"I imagine you do. Off with you, then. I'll tend Beatrice and harness my Joey."

"That chicken hasn't found the stew pot yet?"

"Hush! She'll hear you." She pushed at him. "Take Lavina in your arms and thank her for the amazing job she's done while you gallivanted around new country. I'll say a prayer of thanksgiving that you're back safely."

"See you in a few hours then."

"Oh, I'll arrive before that. What do you take me for, an old woman?" Beatrice clucked. "Keep your opinions to yourself."

Orus laughed, picked his mother up in a bear hug, and set her down. "It's good to see you, Marm. I thought of you often." He held her eyes, started to speak. Instead he sped out the door, mounting his horse in one fluid movement, reminding her of his small-boy behavior of rarely sitting still, always in motion. *Wonder where his pack string is?* She scooped up Beatrice, buried her nose in her neck feathers, inhaling the scent that always brought comfort.

But what was that wariness she'd witnessed in her son's eyes when she suggested that they'd all head west? She guessed she'd find out soon enough.

Jane Kirkpatrick is the *New York Times* and CBA bestselling and award-winning author or contributor to thirty-nine books, including *Something Worth Doing, One More River to Cross, A Name of Her Own, All Together in One Place, A Light in the Wilderness, The Memory Weaver, This Road We Traveled*, and *A Sweetness to the Soul*, which won the prestigious Wrangler Award from the Western Heritage Center. Her works have won the WILLA Literary Award, the Carol Award for Historical Fiction, the 2016 Will Rogers Gold Medallion Award and 2021 Silver award. They have been short-listed for the Christy, Oregon Book Awards, and the Spur Awards. A clinical social worker and former consultant to the Confederated Tribes of Warm Springs Early Childhood programs, Jane now divides her time between Bend, Oregon, and Rancho Mirage, California, with her husband, Jerry, and Cavalier King Charles Spaniel, Caesar. Learn more at www.jkbooks.com.

"Once again, Jane Kirkpatrick creates a bold and inspiring woman out of the dust of history. Jennie's triumph, in the skilled hands of one of the West's most beloved writers, leaves its mark on your heart."

—SANDRA DALLAS, *New York Times* bestselling author

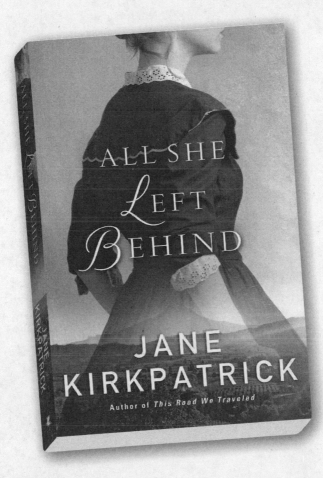

Some Things Are Worth Doing—
EVEN WHEN THE
COST IS GREAT

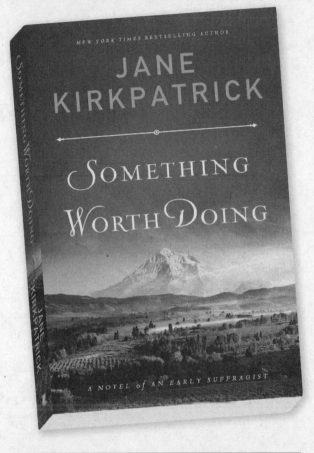

Based on a true story, pioneer Abigail Scott denies herself the joys of a simpler life to achieve her dream of securing rights for women. But running a controversial newspaper and leading suffrage efforts in the Northwest carry a great personal cost. A tender, powerful story of a woman's conflicts— with society and herself.

Revell
a division of Baker Publishing Group
www.RevellBooks.com

Available wherever books and ebooks are sold.

Adversity can squelch the human spirit
... or it can help us discover strength we
NEVER KNEW WE HAD.

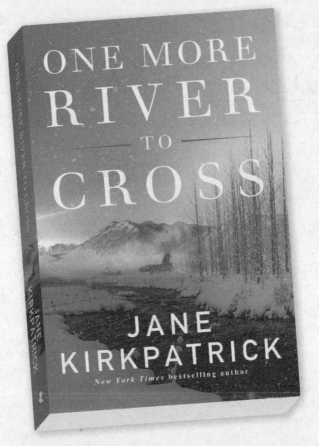

Based on true events, this compelling survival story by award-winning novelist
Jane Kirkpatrick is full of grit and endurance. Beset by storms, bad timing,
and desperate decisions, eight women, seventeen children, and one man
must outlast winter in the middle of the Sierra Nevada in 1844.

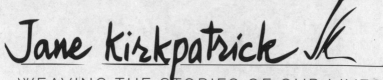

WEAVING THE STORIES OF OUR LIVES

Get to know Jane at

JKBooks.com

Sign up for the *Story Sparks* newsletter
Read the blogs
Learn about upcoming events